PLAIN
DEAD

ALSO BY ANDY MASLEN

Detective Ford:

Shallow Ground
Land Rites

DI Stella Cole:

Hit and Run
Hit Back Harder
Hit and Done
Let the Bones Be Charred
Weep, Willow, Weep
A Beautiful Breed of Evil
Death Wears a Golden Cloak

Gabriel Wolfe Thrillers:

Trigger Point
Reversal of Fortune
Blind Impact
Condor
First Casualty
Fury
Rattlesnake
Minefield
No Further
Torpedo

PLAIN DEAD

A DETECTIVE FORD THRILLER

ANDY MASLEN

THOMAS & MERCER

Published by Thomas & Mercer, Seattle

www.apub.com

Amazon, the Amazon logo, and Thomas & Mercer are trademarks of Amazon.com, Inc., or its affiliates.

ISBN-13: 9781542021067
ISBN-10: 1542021065

Cover design by Dominic Forbes

Printed in the United States of America

For Jo

Me hands they bean't lily white,
Me coat may not be trim,
But you may know, if fightin' comes,
I'll fight as well as him,
Although they pad his shoulders out
To make his waist look slim.

– Marguerite Hall, 'Jealousy'

CHAPTER ONE

Pale rays of early morning September sunlight striped the soldier's face.

She sat with her back to an overturned wooden cart. Bootleg DVDs spilled across the gritty tarmac.

On this particular Sunday, the temperature on the plain hovered at just above freezing.

A burned-out car shredded by an IED lay on its side to the soldier's right. To her left, tacked to the front door of a white-washed two-storey building, a crudely painted sign read 'Baghdad Marriott'.

Bearing a full-colour advert for Al Jazeera, a scrap of newsprint drifted through the mist-shrouded village towards her.

The paper fluttered a few centimetres above the ground, then, caught by a sudden gust of wind, picked up speed. On it sailed for a few more yards before catching on the soldier's left boot.

It rattled on her toecap then detached, snagged momentarily on the knife in her right hand, and blew across her face. For a few seconds, the wind held it fast, moulding it to her features, before snatching it away and sending it swirling up into the air.

A small, iridescent green fly flew up from the pool of blood in which she sat. It crawled across the gently curved surface of her right cornea before flitting to the wound in her throat. There, it began laying its eggs.

Sixteen miles to the south-east of her position, the bells of Salisbury Cathedral chimed six times.

◆ ◆ ◆

Inspector Ford slurped down the last of his breakfast coffee and picked up his guitar. It had been a wedding present from Lou. A '62 Fender Stratocaster in Fiesta Red. Holding it, he allowed himself to remember holding her.

Whenever he took it out to gigs, guys would come up to him in the interval or afterwards, as he and his bandmates were packing up. They'd make small talk, then hit him with the inevitable question.

'It's not for sale, is it?'

And he'd always smile, shake his head, and maybe grip the neck a little tighter.

As the amp's valves warmed up and intensified the hum from the guitar's pickups, he strummed a chord. He had no need to be quiet. Sam was away on a climbing trip, one Ford had agonised over for weeks before finally caving in and giving Sam his blessing.

It had been one of the most difficult decisions he'd ever had to make: whether to let Sam spread his wings, which, at sixteen, he was entitled to demand, or to protect him from the dangers of the mountains. Which, deep down, he knew were worse for the father than the son.

Sam had gone with a bunch of his classmates including his best friend, Josh Pitt. Josh's parents, Miles and Eleanor, lived a few doors along Rainhill Road from Ford. They had helped him through his grief after Lou's death.

'He'll be fine, mate,' Miles had said after dropping the boys off at the coach station and coming round to Ford's for a beer. 'Mr Moyles is a climber himself and the instructors at the centre are absolutely top-notch. I checked out their CVs online.'

Ford had smiled at that. How like Miles to have researched the background not just of the chemistry teacher leading the trip but the guys at the climbing centre.

In a final effort to allay Ford's fears, Sam had installed a new app on both their phones. He'd shown Ford how to share their locations.

'You'll be able to see where I am, Dad.'

Ford tried it the first full day of the trip but experienced such a rush of anxiety when he saw the little pulsing dot in the middle of the mountains, he vowed to leave it alone.

He began playing 'Stormy Weather', then stopped abruptly as the song's minor chords made him well up. An old Delta Blues tune lifted his mood. He stayed in Mississippi for another hour, working out the kinks in his mind by cycling back and forth through others' stories of love and loss.

At eight, he rested the Strat back on its stand, switched off the amp and went for a shower.

The day stretched ahead of him, gloriously free of any responsibility. They'd just closed a case and for once there weren't any others piling up on his desk or anyone else's.

His phone vibrated on the desk beside him. Heart pounding, he snatched up the phone. Saw the name Sam – the rest of the text blurred. Was he OK? In hospital after a fall? Homesick?

In the Jag, Ford could be with him in under three hours if he caned it. But would an E-Type be suitable for bringing a wounded boy home again? Better take the Discovery. He breathed out and berated himself. Read the message, then decide.

climbing is awesome

check this out

Relief surging through him as fast as the adrenaline just a moment earlier, Ford tapped the image attached to the text. Sam in an abseiling harness, a grin splitting his face.

He tapped out a quick reply, in two separate messages, making sure to follow his son's strictures on the 'correct' way to text. *'Punctuation is so formal. It's like you're an old person.'*

You "rock"

Haha

His phone buzzed a second later.

u funnyman

Smiling, Ford shook his head, pleased to have Sam's approval and congratulating himself for having learned that less was definitely more.

Instead of hurtling up the motorway to rescue Sam, he pressed the Jag into service to fetch the Sunday papers. The car had been a wedding present from Lou's father, a wealthy collector. Getting to the Co-op in Downton involved passing two other places that sold newspapers, but included a glorious stretch of sweeping country roads.

Forty minutes later, he was home again with the smell of petrol clinging to his skin and the chatter and clash of the engine's metallic parts ringing in his ears. With a fresh mug of coffee, he settled back in his favourite leather armchair and shook out the paper.

Ford had just reached the music reviews, which he always saved till last, when his phone rang. He reached over to grab it from the table. Maybe it was Sam with something too exciting to be boiled down to a text. He smiled at the thought.

'Sir, it's Control. Got a dead body for you. Out in Imber.'

Ford's reaction clicked over from fatherly indulgence to professional alertness. 'Who's there now?'

'The military police called it in, actually, sir.'

'Right. Get DC Harper out there, please, and everyone in forensics who's on shift today. Dr Fellowes lives near me. I'll call her. If she's at home, I'll pick her up on my way.'

Ford jumped out of the chair, scattering the papers from his lap on to the floor. He called Hannah Fellowes, the deputy chief CSI.

◆ ◆ ◆

Hannah sat by a window overlooking her garden. The rest of her day was to be divided equally between reading, a walk in the countryside following a route she'd entered into a new app on her phone, and preparing dinner.

A long-haired grey and white cat came into the sitting room and levitated into her lap, plucking at her trousers with its claws before completing three circles and settling down for a sleep.

Hannah scratched the cat behind its ears, eliciting a deep purr that reverberated through her thighs.

'Hello, Uta Frith,' she said. 'Did you know you sleep for an average of nineteen and a half hours in every twenty-four? That's seventy-nine point one seven per cent of your day. You could be a lot more productive if you stayed awake longer.'

The cat yawned widely, revealing the corrugated pink roof of its mouth.

Hannah picked up a folder from a side table by her left elbow and turned to the first page. With a frown, and despite having read the document seven times already, she began once more.

Her phone rang. She tutted and glanced at the screen. Seeing the caller ID, she sat straighter. For a moment she allowed herself to imagine Henry was calling to invite her out for a walk, or to have dinner with him. Then she frowned and bit her lip. *Stupid Hannah!*

She took a second to put a smile on her face before answering.

'Henry,' she said. Though of course this was unnecessary. He knew his own name.

'Morning, Wix. We've got a suspicious death on the plain. Are you available?'

She looked down at the stapled sheets of A4 paper.

'I'm at home reading a very interesting article in the *International Journal of Forensic Science*. But it can wait,' she said. 'I'm not on call, but I would like to come. Are you going to collect me?'

'Five minutes.'

Hannah ended the call but kept the phone to her mouth. 'Hey, Siri,' she said. 'Set timer for four minutes and thirty-five seconds.'

She rushed upstairs, dislodging Uta Frith, who mewled once then stalked off to find a quieter spot. Applying make-up in the bathroom, Hannah stared at her reflection. She knew at least seven men had found her attractive since she turned eighteen. But Henry didn't, and she just had to accept it.

◆ ◆ ◆

Ford grabbed his murder bag from the wooden pew by the front door and was swinging the Discovery out of his drive moments later.

Hannah was waiting on the road outside her house. Behind her, the thatched cottage looked incongruously peaceful for the home of someone who was often elbow-deep in other people's blood and body fluids. A few remaining roses, their peach and cream petals browning at the edges, drooped from their wired-in stems above the front door.

Like Ford, she had a holdall – tough black nylon where his was scuffed brown leather. It contained the tools of her trade, from a white Tyvek Noddy suit to fingerprint powders and brushes, alternative light sources and phials of chemical reagent.

She climbed in beside him and fastened her seatbelt. He watched her click it into place then release and refasten it, tugging experimentally on the belt for a couple of seconds before leaning back.

'Good to go?' he asked.

'Sorry, yes. It's not OCD, if that's what you're thinking.'

'I wasn't.'

'Well, anyway, it's not. But my anxiety levels are a little elevated this morning.'

'Any special reason?'

'No, everything's fine. Just fine.'

Hannah was an expert on a range of fields outside her professional specialisation at Bourne Hill. After graduating, she'd moved to the US to complete her PhD before working with the FBI at their headquarters at Quantico.

She'd written scholarly papers on methods for detecting lies in witness testimony, but ironically was a terrible liar herself. Her Asperger's lay behind that, Ford had realised. Knowing the truth made it impossible for her to deny it to another person. He drove on. Clearly something wasn't fine, but now wasn't the time to push it.

He focused on what was to come. Actions he'd want to take, people he'd need to bring in. The last village he drove through was Tilshead, a smallish settlement strung out along the A360 that ended in a petrol station with a convenience store.

'Have you eaten?' Ford asked.

'Yes, thank you. I had porridge with sliced banana and sultanas at nine fifteen.'

Ford nodded, gently amused at Hannah's answer. 'I'm going to stop anyway. I'll get some snacks just in case we're out here for a while. What do you want?'

'Nothing, thank you, Henry.'

He pulled in and hurried into the shop. With a couple of Mars Bars stuffed in his jacket pocket, he climbed back up next to Hannah and pulled out from the forecourt.

'Next stop, Wiltshire's ghost village,' he said.

'I looked it up while I was waiting for you to collect me,' Hannah said. 'The Ministry of Defence evacuated it in 1943 so American troops could practise for the D-Day landings. They never let the inhabitants back in. It's used for urban warfare training now.'

'Most of the surrounding area's military land, too,' he said. 'If you walk up the hill from my house you can see puffs of smoke when they're firing rockets or the really big shells.'

'It's quite sad, though. They found the village blacksmith weeping on his anvil when it was time to leave. Apparently he died of a broken heart a month later.' She paused. 'Although medically, that's not possible.'

Ford followed the road up a hill and on to a piece of high ground. The plain stretched away from them to the horizon on the left, the right and straight ahead.

Copses of deciduous trees cloaked in orange, red and yellow foliage punctuated the gently rolling grassland. Every five hundred yards or so Ford passed a cross-track marked by steel posts topped in yellow, with signs informing the public, 'TANKS CROSSING'.

Hannah pointed one out. 'Do you think the tank drivers have to wait for a green soldier to light up?'

8

Ford smiled. Hannah's sense of humour was off-centre, to put it kindly. But that wasn't a bad one.

'Funny,' he said.

'Was it funny? Really?'

'Yes. Not bad at all.'

'Excellent. I'll make a note later.'

He turned off the A360 on to a smaller B road, then immediately right past a black barn, inside which pieces of agricultural machinery lurked. Red, blue and green, with drooping arms and jointed booms covered in shiny steel prongs or discs. They resembled deactivated robots waiting for a signal to roam forth across the landscape, scarifying, piercing, slicing and cutting through the soft earth.

He drove fast along the single-track road, heading west for a couple of miles. They passed a herd of brown and white cows. Ford caught the eye of a long-horned bull that watched them as they approached, then sped past.

At a triangular gravelled lay-by he swung left, past a tall pole from which a large square red flag flapped, and descended a short shallow hill into Imber.

CHAPTER TWO

Ford followed the winding road down into the centre of the village. On an S-bend, he looked across to a collection of buildings. Their unglazed windows reminded him of a skull's eye sockets. They passed a red-brick house with a steep pitched roof.

'That's Seagram's Farm,' Hannah said. 'I found a chart online marking all the buildings.'

Ford pulled into a gravel lay-by. Three other vehicles occupied the space: Jools's sporty Audi A3 hatchback, a Citroen C3 in blue and yellow 'Battenburg' livery and a gunmetal-grey Vauxhall Corsa. The police vehicle bore the words MILITARY POLICE along its lower flanks in large blue capitals.

'Looks like we're late to the party,' he said as he and Hannah walked up to the centre of the village.

The wind blew from the north, straight down across the plain, its progress unimpeded by anything that might slow it down or relieve it of the freight of icy cold it delivered.

Hannah pointed left. 'St Giles' Church.'

Ford followed her finger and saw a square tower ornamented with carved finials at each corner.

Now they could hear voices. They walked between a handful of the block-built houses: all windowless, all with either brick-red or slime-green tiled roofs. They'd been crudely whitewashed, to approximate the look of an Afghan or Iraqi village, he supposed. Ahead, a burned-out car lay on its back, every shred of non-metallic material incinerated. More set-dressing.

In front of a whirring, snapping cordon of yellow crime-scene tape, two soldiers in red berets, a man and a woman, were talking, heads bowed towards each other. Beyond them, Ford could make out a slumped human form leaning against a wooden object resembling half a pram.

He approached the female soldier. 'Good morning.'

She turned, frowning.

'Can I help you?' she asked officiously, stepping towards Ford and Hannah.

Ford held out his warrant card. 'DI Ford, Wiltshire Police.'

Hannah drew level with him. 'And I'm Dr Hannah Fellowes, deputy chief CSI at Bourne Hill Police Station in Salisbury.'

She stuck her hand out. The woman – a sergeant – ignored it, focusing on Ford.

'Sergeant Carpenter. Are you the duty DI from Salisbury? We were told to expect you by your colleague, DC Harper.'

'In one,' Ford said. 'Where is she?'

'Conducting a recce, sir.'

Ford looked past her. Closer now, he saw that the dead soldier was female. And sitting in what appeared to be a sizeable blood pool. The wooden object was an upturned cart.

'I established a cordon and we've secured the area, sir, but apart from that, we were waiting for you. What do you want to do first?'

'Let's get a look at the deceased.'

Beside him, Hannah was climbing into her Noddy suit. He did the same.

They stepped under the cordon and identified themselves to the loggist, a third MP who couldn't have been much older than Sam, by the look of him.

Hannah pulled out her digital SLR and took pictures. She squatted to capture the body and a reference point, in this case the two-storey building behind her bearing a jokey-looking sign: 'Baghdad Marriott'.

Ford walked closer and knelt by the corpse's left shoulder. He judged the dead woman's age as between late teens and mid-twenties. She was strongly built with a round face and powerful arms and shoulders. The skin on her face was pale, with blue-green veins showing beneath.

Her head was thrown back and her arms lay by her sides, palms uppermost. Blaring its way into his consciousness, a scarlet scream in the subdued colours of the village, was a gaping wound across her throat.

The front of her uniform tunic was soaked in blood, staining the mixture of grey, green and sand a deep red. A name-patch on the left side read PADLEY. They had a name for the victim already.

More blood had pooled beneath her hips; although, as he looked around, he saw no blood spatter. That was interesting. Standing or sitting, if she'd severed her carotid arteries, he'd have expected to see arcs and sprays for six or seven feet in front of her.

He looked at her right hand. The fingers, thick and muscular, were curled lightly around the hilt of a knife. It looked like bone: a ridged cream and chestnut grip. The blade was about six inches long above a compact brass guard. Blood smeared the steel, which was otherwise in good condition, glinting in the sunlight.

Suicide. That's what the scene before him was declaring. But its voice was a little too strident. *Look!* it shrieked. *She's holding a bloody knife! She's come out here to end it all and cut her own throat. What more do you need?*

Ford settled his weight back on his heels. He placed his palms on his thighs. Yes, what more *did* he need? A less brutal method would be a start. By far the most common – for both sexes – was hanging. Followed by self-poisoning.

Using a sharp object was vanishingly rare, but especially for women. On a recent seminar he'd attended, organised by the Samaritans, the figure for women was lower than two per cent.

The way the knife lay inside the just-curled fingers also bothered him. He made a mental note to check something when he got back to the station.

He got to his feet, wincing from the pain in his quads. *Could* it be a suicide? It was a possibility. But his instincts were telling him a different story. The girl had been murdered, then posed to suggest to inexperienced army cops that she'd taken her own life.

He parked the thought. He stared at the road surface, wanting to find drag marks. But the tarmac was keeping its secrets.

Behind him, he could hear Hannah muttering to herself as she took pictures. He stood and asked her to see if she could find a phone on the body, then walked away, back to Sergeant Carpenter.

'Do we know who she is?' he asked. 'Her patch says Padley.'

She nodded. 'One of my lads recognised her. Private Rachel Padley.'

Ford made a note. It was a good start. Or as good as investigating another suspicious death ever could be. More details would follow, he was sure. The army was a lot like the police, reliant on meticulous record-keeping. At least they wouldn't have to waste any time identifying the victim.

'Who found her?'

She turned. 'Kennedy!' she barked.

An MP trotted over and came to attention in front of them. 'Sarge?'

'Tell DI Ford what happened this morning.'

He turned to Ford. 'Me and Private Forrest, that's him over there, sir,' he said, pointing out a black soldier in conversation with one of the other MPs, 'we came out to do a walk-through.

Live-firing exercises all this week and we have to check everything's set out right in the mornings.

'We walked up to the crossroads and that's when we saw her. Rachel – I mean Private Padley – she was just sitting there. I thought she must have come out early or something,' he said. 'I shouted out to her but she never said nothing, so we went closer. That's when I saw she'd cut her throat. I radioed for help and then me and Andy waited for support.'

'What time would this have been?'

'Oh-eight-oh-three, sir. I checked the time.'

'Did you see anyone else around during your walk-through? Anything out of place?'

'Presence of the abnormal, absence of the normal,' he said with an eager nod. 'No, sir. Everything was just like it ought to be. Obviously apart from Private Padley.'

'We'll need to take a formal statement from you later. Thanks for now.'

'Yes, sir. Will there be anything else, Sarge?'

She shook her head. As Kennedy hurried back to his mates, Jools appeared.

'Morning, guv,' she said.

'Morning. Anything interesting?'

'Nothing obvious. Wix and her lot might find something, but I couldn't.'

Sergeant Carpenter pointed to the dead woman. 'Clearly, what we're dealing with is a suicide. She's got the knife in her hand,' she said. 'Technically it's suspicious, but it looks pretty clear to me what happened.'

Ford looked at her. He didn't enjoy pulling rank, but this was the moment to get a few things straight. He'd worked joint investigations with the RMP before and it hadn't always gone smoothly. In fact, after one too many jurisdictional standoffs, his boss, Detective

Superintendent Sandy Monroe, had written the national protocol for cooperation between the civilian and military police.

'Let's not assume anything at this point, Sergeant. All I know is what I can see, which is a dead woman with a knife in her hand.'

'But she's cut her throat, sir. Look!' Carpenter raised a hand and pointed at the body again, as if he might otherwise look in the wrong direction.

'We don't know that. If you want me to be more specific, I'd say we have a dead woman with a knife in her hand who has sustained a massive wound to her throat,' he said. 'But for all we know she might have been shot, stabbed, bludgeoned or poisoned first. Do you take my point?'

'Yes, sir. Sorry. I was just trying to be helpful.'

'I know and I appreciate that. Look, it's a pretty crappy way to start a Sunday. Let's just take it one step at a time, eh?'

She nodded and offered a tight smile. 'Fine by me, sir. Do you need me for the moment? Only I have other duties, and I need to get back to the barracks and start the ball rolling.'

'On what?'

'Informing next of kin, for a start.'

Ford shook his head. 'No. Don't do that. This is going to be a joint investigation between us and the SIB. But we have primacy. That means, in plain English, I'm in charge. I'll do it.'

He'd used the army jargon 'SIB' deliberately. Showing he knew how the RMP worked alongside the Special Investigation Branch would, he hoped, give him a little more credibility in her eyes. It worked. Plus he was sure she'd jump at the chance to be relieved of doing the death knock.

'Very good, sir. Then unless you need me . . .'

'Can you get somebody to secure Rachel's quarters, too, please? We'll get over there tomorrow for a search.'

Once she'd gone, Ford turned to Jools. 'What do you think?'

She wrinkled her nose. 'At first glance it does look like a suicide, guv.'

'Want to add a "but", Jools?'

'What do you mean?'

'I mean does anything about the scene strike you as odd?'

'It would take a lot of determination to do yourself in like that. But successful suicides always do show a lot of determination, don't they? I mean, otherwise they'd be alive, not dead.'

It was a reasonable point. Ford remained unconvinced. He tried again, willing Jools to start thinking his way.

'I think it was staged. I think she was murdered.'

Jools's eyes widened. 'Really? Why?'

'I can't put my finger on it.'

Jools gave him a sceptical glance. 'This isn't your gut talking again, is it, guv?'

'No!' He pointed at the corpse. 'We've both seen suicides, haven't we?'

She nodded. 'Too many.'

'They're messy, aren't they? People lose control of their bodily functions in their last moments. Go into spasm. Have you ever seen a beautiful corpse? Because I haven't.'

Jools sniffed. 'I'd hardly say a bloody great knife wound across your throat is beautiful.'

'No, but apart from that, she looks posed to me. As if she's sat down for a quick nap before the fighting starts.'

'Maybe. But please, guv, let's not go off into the long grass before we've cleared the ground under our feet.'

Ford grimaced at her use of the phrase he employed when teaching younger detectives. 'Meaning?'

'Let's go by the book. It's an apparent suicide. We should start by looking in that direction. If it doesn't pan out, *then* we look at homicide as an explanation.'

Ford offered a noncommittal shrug. If Jools chose to interpret it as agreement, fine. But she had it round the wrong way. You ruled homicide *out*, not in. He walked back to Hannah, who was kneeling by the corpse and peering at the throat wound through a large magnifying glass.

'No phone in her pockets, though I found her car key,' she said, handing a black plastic fob to Ford. 'Could you hand me the tweezers from my evidence collection kit, please, Henry? And a debris pot?'

He fetched the requested items from her bag. 'Here you go, Wix.' He used her nickname – short for Wikipedia, given her encyclopaedic general knowledge – more than he would normally, because he knew how much she liked it. She'd told him once she felt it showed she'd been accepted. 'What have you seen?' he asked.

She didn't respond at once, instead plucking something from the wound and tapping it free into the squat transparent plastic pot. She twisted the lid on, labelled it and dropped it into a clear plastic evidence bag, which she sealed with red tape, initialled and dated.

'I'm not sure. But it isn't flesh.'

Ford nodded. He rubbed his chin, scratching at his Sunday stubble. 'Transferred from the blade?'

'Maybe we'll know when I get it back to the lab and analyse it.'

A white transit van trundled up the road towards them. Marked 'Wiltshire Forensic Service' on its side, it came to a stop thirty yards back from the cordon. Three CSIs climbed out, suited up and rustled over to Hannah. After a quick discussion, they began marking out a grid extending away from the body to the buildings on each side of the road.

Ford turned towards the building with the Baghdad Marriott sign. As he did, his boot skidded on something hard. He looked down. And for the first time he realised that the gritty tarmac was littered with brass shell casings. He shook his head. Good job she hadn't been shot or they'd have had the devil's own job with ballistics.

Georgina Eustace, the pathologist from Salisbury District Hospital, turned up in a metallic turquoise Mercedes SLK sports car. She'd had the roof down, despite the cold. In her oversized sunglasses and black baseball cap, she looked like a glamorous actress going incognito.

Ford smiled at her once she'd arrived. 'Morning, George. Sorry to drag you away from whatever you like to fill your Sunday mornings with.'

She took off her cap and shook out her silver hair, which she wore in a short bob.

'Raking up dead leaves isn't exactly a hobby of mine,' she said, returning his smile. 'Glad to get away from it, tbh.'

Ford raised his eyebrows. 'What's this, we're doing text-speak at SDH now?'

George grinned. 'Come on, Henry, you're not that old.' She offered a look of mock concern. 'Or are you? Should I fetch you a blanket? To keep you warm?' she asked loudly as if speaking to someone hard of hearing. She laid a hand lightly on his left arm.

'I think I'll manage, thanks. Should I bring you a Harry Potter book to read in bed?'

She winked. 'Nice try, H, but my bedtime reading tends to be more sophisticated than boy wizards. Now, what can you tell me about the victim?'

'Her name's Rachel Padley. She was found earlier this morning. And it appears that she's cut her own throat.'

George frowned. 'Appears?'

'Just do your thing. We'll talk about it later.'

Back at the crime scene, Ford watched as George began her preliminary examination. She peered at the wound to the dead girl's throat. But then she leaned closer still and looked round at the back of the head.

'There appears to be some blunt-force trauma here,' she said. 'She could have sustained it falling back against the cart if she was standing to start with. I won't know more until the PM, but it's interesting nonetheless.'

Another post-mortem. Another human being reduced, systematically, to just a set of weights and measures, pieces of tissue. But in a cause. The cause to which he'd dedicated his life. Bringing justice to the dead.

The phrase 'post-mortem' sparked an association. The timing of the head wound was crucial, wasn't it? If it had been sustained *post-mortem*, it could point to suicide, Padley having knocked her head in her death throes. If had been inflicted *ante-mortem*, then it would point to murder.

CHAPTER THREE

Ford returned to the lay-by where he'd parked and looked in through the Corsa's side window. Was this Rachel's car? She couldn't have walked. It was miles from the nearest barracks, at Larkhill. He tried the key. It worked.

The interior was spotless. Nothing that could give so much as a hint as to the owner's identity. No sign of a phone, either. He sniffed. No smell of toiletries. But it was the only vehicle there apart from the MPs', so it was probably hers.

Walking away, he saw other tyre tracks. Army vehicles, probably. After all, if they were in the middle of a live-firing exercise, there'd be all kinds: trucks, armoured personnel carriers, Land Rovers and observers' vehicles.

He already had one crime scene: the body. Here was a second. Her living accommodation and workplace would constitute three and four. And where, exactly, was a soldier's workplace? Ford took advantage of the moment of quiet to collect his thoughts. What did he have? A dead girl who had apparently driven out to Imber to commit suicide. Found with a knife in her hand.

He chose to ignore his gut for a minute and respect Jools's insistent regard for procedure – because he wouldn't get far with Sandy unless he could definitively rule out suicide. Could he assume the knife in Rachel Padley's hand was the same weapon that had inflicted the wound to her neck? No, he could not. Could he even be sure the wound was the fatal one? Again, no.

Even without working alongside George for years, he'd learned that nothing was a truer guide to police work than the old mantra: ABC. Assume nothing. Believe nobody. Challenge everything.

George wouldn't pronounce on manner or cause of death until she'd completed her post-mortem. And despite Sergeant Carpenter's rush to judgement, Jools's doubts and Sandy's desire to avoid unnecessary homicide investigations, he wouldn't either. Because even this early in the case, the peal of alarm bells was growing louder.

They were still too quiet for the MPs to hear, but he wouldn't have expected them to be listening out for them. The red berets were more used to rounding up drunken squaddies after pub brawls in the barracks towns. Even the SIB were more usually faced with lower-level events such as burglaries and assaults on base.

Suspicious deaths always came to the civilian police, and Ford had handled more than his fair share, either working with the SIB or on purely civil cases.

What didn't sit right with Ford he found hard to put into words. Even to himself. He pushed himself. What was it, *exactly*?

Two things stood out for him. There was the method, of course. But that was hardly conclusive. He'd worked cases where people had used unimaginably horrific methods of ending their own lives. One guy, a tree surgeon, had managed to decapitate himself with a chainsaw wedged into a forked branch.

The second was less data-driven and more based on his own experience and intuition about people. Rachel Padley was a young woman in secure employment with her accommodation paid for. At a stroke, that removed two of the major anxieties in young people that might precipitate suicide. Nor would she be socially isolated in an infantry unit where people lived in close proximity and worked and played together.

In his experience, serving soldiers, more than members of the general public, had a sense of purpose and direction to their lives. Of course, it didn't mean they never committed suicide, but the odds were against it. Outside of combat, deaths were more likely to occur as a result of accidents on training exercises or so-called 'beastings', where raw recruits were subjected to brutal initiation rituals. These were so infrequent that when they did occur, they were national news.

On the other hand, there was his own favourite saying, which Jools had used against him earlier: *let's clear the ground under our feet*. Faced with a dead body, his process was always to begin with the most obvious scenarios.

Take murdered children. If there were no signs of sexual abuse, nine times out of ten the killer was a parent or guardian. If there *were* signs, it fell to less than one in ten. A dead wife, you looked at the husband. A dead drug dealer, another dealer.

So, a woman with her throat cut holding a blood-stained knife was, in all probability, exactly what it looked like: a suicide. The bump to the back of her head could have been caused by falling, or her head snapping back.

He didn't know which version he hoped were true. A young professional woman killing herself because she felt she had nothing to live for. Or a young professional woman with everything to live for having her life brutally ended by somebody else.

He shuddered. In the place inside him where he kept the memories of his dead wife and their final moments together lived just such a 'somebody else'. A killer. A person capable of abandoning all the rules governing human decency and causing another's death.

Though consulting this secret part of him caused immense pain, he retreated there now, anxious to feel what a killer felt. Know what a killer knew.

He let his eyes drift out of focus. Became, not a murder detective, but a murderer. He closed his eyes. And he visualised Rachel Padley's last minutes, as he now believed they had passed, through her killer's eyes.

I lure you out here. You come willingly. Eagerly. Curiosity disabling your defences. Because we know each other. We love each other. Who else would you come for? This is the middle of nowhere and it's freezing cold.

I see the sweep of your car headlights as you drive down the curving road into Imber. I know you'll see my car and park next to it. I watch you walk up the road and approach the killing ground. My heart is drumming in my ears and the sound blots out everything else.

You're strongly built and in peak physical condition. An infantry soldier trained in unarmed combat. In short, a formidable opponent. That's why I've planned a surprise attack, from behind. I'm going to knock you cold with a lump of masonry from one of the buildings.

You're looking around for me. Calling my name. My fingertips are tingling, my heart's racing, my breath is coming in quick gasps. I creep up behind you, smash you over the head and watch you collapse. Then I get behind you and slash your throat. Your head's lolling forwards and it contains the arterial spray. The blood – so much blood! – pumps out and down to soak into your tunic.

But I can't just leave you in a heap. You meant something to me when you were alive. I drag you over to the cart and lean you back against it. Give you a few shreds of dignity before I leave. I pose you with the knife, which I wipe down. No prints but yours.

A car horn tooted from behind him, yanking him back to reality. He turned to see a big black BMW waiting for him to move. He'd wandered into the centre of the road and they were indicating to park. He stepped to one side and waited to see who would emerge.

Three of the doors opened simultaneously. A uniformed female officer emerged from the driver's seat and settled a khaki beret on her head. Ford clocked the distinctive pom-pom and scarlet cockade of the Black Watch.

Her front passenger was a man in his early fifties. Iron-grey hair and wearing the same beret, which, Ford recalled, the Black Watch called a Tam O'Shanter. Both wore medal ribbons and had plenty of ornamentation on their uniforms.

From the rear of the car emerged a second woman. She'd tied her blonde hair back in a bun, but wore civilian attire; specifically, a forest-green puffa jacket over a black trouser suit and low black shoes. She'd clearly come to the same decision about work clothes as Ford. Keep it dark and simple, and nothing that looks bad if it gets blood on it.

The man strode forward. 'I'm looking for Inspector Ford.'

His voice surprised Ford. No upper-class accent. Quite the reverse. He sounded like Ford himself, a comprehensive-school boy from somewhere in the south of England. Not a typical officer-class type then. Must have worked his way up. Probably not from an army family, either.

'You've found him. And you are?'

'Lieutenant Colonel Hemmings. I'm CO of the Black Watch. This is my second-in-command,' he said, turning to the female officer.

'Major Fiona Robinson, pleased to meet you.'

Unlike her boss, she offered her hand, which Ford shook. Firm, dry grip. Quick efficient shake.

The woman in civvies stepped forward. She had dark, alert eyes. 'Lieutenant Charlie Daniels, SIB. Pleased to meet you, sir.'

They shook hands.

'Well, now we all know each other, perhaps you could tell me what's going on. I hear one of my men has taken their own life,' Hemmings said.

'It's one of your women, actually,' Ford said. 'The pathologist is up there now. We'll know more once we've done the post-mortem.'

'Fine. You'd better show us. I'll have a better idea of what we're dealing with if I see with my own eyes.'

Ford turned without speaking and led the trio back to the crossroads.

Of the MPs, all but the loggist had disappeared. Hannah and her CSIs were pacing out over the grid they'd marked, heads down. George was closing her bag and straightening up just as they arrived at the cordon.

The colonel looked at the body. He turned back to Ford, hands on hips. 'You're seriously suggesting you have any doubts that's a suicide?'

Ford had taken an instant dislike to the man. He'd climbed the army's greasy pole to the commanding heights of colonel. And because of that, he felt he could throw his weight around.

'Let's just say if I'd bashed you over the head, laid you down and slit *your* throat, I wouldn't expect one of my officers to assume you'd killed yourself. I owe Private Padley the same degree of professionalism.' He met and held Hemmings's eye. Was he getting into what Sandy would no doubt call 'a dick-swinging contest'? Probably. But he couldn't help himself.

Hemmings surprised him by laughing. A short guttural explosion that had about as much mirth in it as a funeral.

'Fine, *Inspector* Ford. Do what you have to,' he said. 'I've got fifty soldiers due up here any time now for our next live-firing exercise, so whatever you decide, I'd appreciate your being quick about it.'

'You're going to have to cancel it, I'm afraid. This is a crime scene. I can't have soldiers trampling all over the place destroying evidence.'

Hemmings's eyebrows ascended towards the band of his Tam. He took a step closer to Ford and dropped his voice to what he must have imagined was a threatening tone. 'I'm not cancelling *anything*. I am charged with defending the realm, which I can't do with half-trained men. So they *are* coming up here, and they *will* be exercising according to plan,' he said, with narrowed eyes.

Ford squared his shoulders. 'Very well. But please be aware we'll probably want to interview some of your men – and women – so I'd appreciation your cooperation.'

Hemmings smirked. 'You'd better get a move on then, Inspector. The Black Watch are flying to Somalia on the twenty-first of next month. If you don't like it, I can give you the number of the Ministry of Defence. I'm sure they'd be delighted to hear your suggestions for redeploying one of Her Majesty's frontline combat units.'

He about-turned and strode off in the direction of the car.

'Can you wait here a moment, please?' Ford said to the two women.

He ran over to Hannah, waving a hand to catch her attention.

'What is it, Henry?'

'You're going to have to move fast, Wix. Any moment now we're going to have a truckload of infantry piling in here shooting live ammunition and scuffing up the ground,' he said. 'Get whatever you can and then we're going to have to stage a strategic retreat.'

She clamped her lips for a second then nodded, twice. 'Leave it to me.'

Ford knew he could trust her. Even the colonel wouldn't authorise live firing when civilians were present. But that wasn't his biggest headache. He had precisely twenty-four days to solve the mystery of the young soldier's death. Then virtually everyone who might be able to shed some light on it would vanish to one of the world's most notorious trouble spots.

With the two female officers again, he offered to accompany them back to the car.

'Steve's just under a lot of pressure,' Major Robinson said. 'I'd suggest you ask Charlie for anything you need. She'll relay it to me, and I'll work in a way that keeps everybody happy.'

Ford nodded. 'Thanks. My first priority is to inform Rachel's next of kin. Suicide or not, I want them hearing it from me, not social media or the regimental grapevine.'

The roar of a stressed diesel engine made them all turn around. An olive drab-painted Land Rover tore up the street, slewing to a halt fifteen feet away from them with a screech of tyres on tarmac. Blue burned-rubber smoke enveloped them.

Charlie looked at the driver, then Ford. 'Too late,' she said.

The man who emerged from the Land Rover was short, no more than five foot six or seven. Compact, muscular build. He wore the uniform and Tam of the Black Watch.

He raced up to them, eyes wild, face pale. 'Where is she? Where's our Rachel?'

The man's name patch bore the same name as the dead woman. This had to be the father.

'Mr Padley, please stop there. You can't go any further. My name is—'

'I don't give a *fook* what your name is!' he yelled in a broad Yorkshire accent. 'Where is she?'

He pushed past Ford and, seeing the scene before him, emitted a strange, croaking cry. Ford put a restraining hand on his right shoulder. Padley swung round, grabbed Ford's wrist, twisting it hard, then punched him in the solar plexus, driving the breath from Ford's lungs. He fell to his hands and knees then keeled over sideways, fighting a wave of panic as he struggled to inhale through the crushing pain in his midsection. He felt as though he'd been stamped on.

He saw the world tilted on its side, Padley rushing over to the crime scene, ripping the snapping tape aside and crouching by his dead daughter's side.

While Hannah, George and the others looked on, Hemmings strode over and stood behind Padley. 'Sergeant Padley, let's have you on your feet,' he said in a loud, clear voice. Not a shout, but the tone of command was there.

Padley glanced over his shoulder, reddened eyes staring. He looked as though he was about to attack the colonel. Then he saw who'd ordered him to stand and visibly restrained himself. He got to his feet, straightened and snapped off a salute.

'Sorry, sir. I lost control. Unprofessional.'

Ford's bruised diaphragm was still refusing to function properly, but he'd managed a sip of air and, with Charlie and Major Robinson's help, had levered himself into a sitting position.

'You've had a shock, Sergeant,' Hemmings said. 'A terrible shock. I want you to return to your vehicle and park in the lay-by next to my car. I'll join you in a second. Yes?'

'Yes, sir. Sorry, sir.'

'On you go, then.'

Padley climbed into the Land Rover, started the engine and drove back towards the parking area.

Hemmings came over to Ford. 'That's Private Padley's father, in case you hadn't worked it out,' he said. 'I'll see he gets back to the guardroom and they make him a mug of tea. I'll leave you to recover and then everything I said before still stands.'

'Fine,' Ford said, pulling on Charlie's arm as he got to his feet.

'Oh, and one last thing, Inspector. I'm going to assume you won't be charging Sergeant Padley with assault or anything silly,' Hemmings said, glancing at Charlie and Major Robinson as if summoning reinforcements. 'The man's obviously grief-stricken. He didn't know you were a police officer.'

Ford grunted his assent; for the first time since that single devastating punch, he'd managed to fill his lungs. 'Don't worry, Colonel. I've had worse. Goes with the territory.'

Hemmings nodded curtly. 'Major?'

Then he turned and marched back to the lay-by.

'Are you all right?' Charlie asked, her green eyes wide with concern.

Ford realised he'd been massaging his stomach. He grimaced. 'Yeah, I'm fine.'

'David Padley's a Provost Sergeant. That's the regimental police,' she said.

Ford nodded, not ready for conversation just yet. He knew who the Provos were. They weren't MPs. Just regular soldiers tasked with maintaining discipline on base. Some saw them as the MPs' muscle, but the truth was simpler than that. Whereas the military police were attached to the barracks, the RPs were part of the regiment itself. They reported to the regimental sergeant major and their remit was more about stopping squaddies crossing the parade ground or having their Tams on askew than solving crime.

'I want to speak to the mother,' he said.

'Records will have their address. Let me just get the colonel squared away.'

'We'll take my car,' Ford said. 'One more thing.'

'Yes,' the two army officers said in unison, which disconcerted Ford for a moment.

'Whatever the *manner* of Rachel's death, suicide or otherwise, I am treating it as suspicious. That means it's a joint investigation between my team and the SIB and I am the lead investigator.'

The major looked to Charlie to answer.

She smiled. 'Don't worry, Inspector. I've read the protocol. I'm not interested in starting a turf war. I'll leave that to the colonel.'

Then, so briefly, he thought he might have misread the signal, she winked at him.

They arrived back at the lay-by. The colonel was standing off to one side, smoking a cigarette and speaking into his phone. Major Robinson went over to talk to him; Ford caught a number of glances thrown his way.

Finally, the colonel shrugged and climbed back into the BMW's passenger seat. They pulled away, executed a neat three-point turn and drove back the way they'd come.

Charlie came over. 'Sergeant Padley got the news through the MPs. He said his wife doesn't know. He said he's happy for you to tell her. Basically, I think he's gone into shock. He's just talking about maintaining barracks discipline and an inspection he's got later.'

Ford pointed to the Discovery. 'Let's take mine,' he said.

'Head for Larkhill,' Charlie said. 'I'll phone Records on the way.'

She made a call and gave Ford the address.

CHAPTER FOUR

Larkhill, where Rachel's parents lived, was a small garrison town ten miles north of Salisbury. Ford turned off The Packway into Lightfoot Road. It was the last street on the patch of army housing before open countryside. Silver birches grew up through a thorny hedge to their left.

After parking, he reached into the glovebox and pulled out a ready-knotted black tie, which he slipped over his head and tightened.

He turned to Charlie. 'How do I look?'

'Hold on,' she said. 'Your collar's all over the place.'

She reached out and tugged his shirt collar around before fastening the top button. He remembered Lou performing the same casually intimate action and fought down a sudden urge to pull away.

'Better,' she said.

They got out together and walked up the concrete path to the front door. The front garden was immaculate, with a neatly mown patch of grass and a couple of shrubs bearing tiny yellow flowers.

Ford readied himself. Delivering the death knock never got any easier. Murder or suicide, it made no difference. You still had to burst into a family's life and swing a wrecking ball at them. And even though David Padley already knew, that still left Rachel's mother.

He stretched out a finger and rang the doorbell.

The woman who opened the door could have been anywhere from thirty-five to fifty, but she was the mother of a young woman, so had to be at least late thirties. A printed red and blue bandana covered her hair, which was straight and dark. No make-up. Very thin.

'Yes?'

'Mrs Padley? Mrs Helen Padley?' Ford asked.

The woman nodded. Her eyes flicked between Ford and Charlie as if unsure whom to focus on.

'What is it?' she asked in a softer version of her husband's Yorkshire accent.

Ford introduced himself and Charlie, showing Helen his warrant card. 'Could we come in, please?'

She looked down, then up at Ford. She nodded and they followed her inside. The tiny sitting room felt too small to contain three adults and the grief that was about to assail one of them. A large grey velour sofa took up a third of it. The room smelled strongly of lemons; some kind of furniture polish. Ford sneezed.

'Bless you,' Helen Padley said.

Two armchairs in matching fabric were squashed into the facing corners. A low table bearing a TV and the usual assortment of black and silver boxes somehow found room between them. Family photos clustered together on a shelf and more hung on the walls. A large picture of Jesus holding a lamb in his arms dwarfed them all.

The bandana, the painting: Ford wondered if Helen Padley belonged to the Plymouth Brethren. There were a few small groups of the strict Christian sect's adherents in Salisbury.

When they were all seated, Helen Padley on the sofa, Ford and Charlie in the armchairs, Ford cleared his throat.

'Mrs Padley, I'm afraid I have some very bad news. This morning, at about eight o'clock, two military police found your daughter Rachel dead in the centre of Imber,' he said. 'We're treating her death as suspicious, although we believe there may be a chance she committed suicide. I am so very sorry for your loss.'

He stopped then. Once the words were out, it was best to give the next of kin a moment to collect themselves. Some officers seemed unable to stop talking, perhaps hoping that by doing so they could prevent the tidal wave of grief from engulfing them along with the relatives. Ford preferred to wait, though it left him with nothing to do but try to avoid thinking of his own fractured family.

Helen Padley just looked at the carpet, her hands clasped in her lap, tight enough to make her knuckles stand out as white knobs. She began muttering, and Ford realised she was praying.

'How?' she whispered after a couple of minutes.

Ford wracked his brain for a way to soften the dreadful facts.

'She suffered a large, incised wound to her neck,' he said, immediately cursing himself for falling back on quasi-medical jargon.

Helen's brow furrowed. 'You mean she cut her own throat, is that what you're saying?'

Taken aback by her bluntness, he didn't correct her. But then people reacted in strange ways. He'd even seen people burst out laughing. Laughing that turned violently into hysteria when he didn't grin and offer a 'gotcha' wink.

'That's what it looks like. We'll take Rachel to Salisbury District Hospital,' Ford said quietly. 'There'll be a post-mortem, at which point I will be able to tell you how she died.'

'What about her body?' Helen said. 'When can we have our Rachel back? She needs a Christian burial.'

'That will be up to the coroner,' Ford said. 'I promise I'll be in touch as soon as I know more. We'll see ourselves out.'

'No, I'll show you.'

Ford followed her to the front door. He pointed to an ornate key rack carved from what he thought might be rosewood.

'That's pretty,' he said, for want of a neat closing line.

'My husband made it for me last year. A birthday present. He has a gift for woodwork. Like our Lord.'

◆　◆　◆

Ford and Charlie drove straight over to the guardroom at the barracks. They found David Padley sitting on a hard chair, a half-full mug of tea by his elbow. He'd removed his Tam, revealing a shaved head disfigured by a couple of ugly scars. With the luxury of time to form an impression, Ford took in a broken nose and a cauliflower ear. Had Padley been a boxer at one time? His punch would suggest it, he noted wryly.

David looked up when Ford and Charlie entered the cramped space.

'I'm sorry for hitting you earlier,' he said gruffly. 'I weren't thinking straight. What wi' seeing Rachel like that.'

Ford waved away the apology. 'I'm sorry for your loss, Sergeant Padley. But I must ask you some questions.' He turned to the other men in the room. 'Could you give us a minute, please?'

Alone with David, Ford pulled a second chair over so they were sitting almost knee to knee. Charlie stood back, in a shadowy corner. A move he appreciated.

David Padley was old school. Very old school. Ford could see that. And his old-fashioned ideas about masculinity were probably behind his clamped-down emotional reaction. The scene at Imber had been an aberration, Ford realised. David was embarrassed at having been seen letting his emotions get the better of him. Especially by his CO.

Ford had seen it before. Men trying to cope with the sudden death of a loved one. There'd be tears, all right. But later. In private. When nobody could see you, nose running, eyes puffy, distraught with grief, calling her name out and not caring if you woke Sam. He forced himself to return to the present.

He thought David would appreciate plain speaking, so he asked his first question as straightforwardly as he could manage. The question they always asked. The question they hoped would unlock a case before it became a runner.

'Did Rachel have any enemies?'

David snorted. 'Only the bloody Taliban.'

'She hadn't confided in you about anyone she'd, I don't know, got on the wrong side of?'

'Confided? She were a grown woman, Ford, not a child. You'd do better asking Helen.'

'And we will. I just thought Rachel might have talked to you because you were both in uniform.'

'It weren't enemies that did for her,' David said, looking straight at Ford. 'The poor lass couldn't cope with the stress.'

'What do you mean?'

'She'd only just qualified as an infantry soldier, hadn't she? They let girls do any job now, right up to combat. Fools!' he said. 'Anyone could tell them the front line's no place for a lass. Now my Rachel's gone and killed herself because of their stupid policy.'

Ford had imagined he'd be proud of his daughter making it in a man's world. Especially as she'd followed him into the Black Watch.

'Do you not think they should allow women into the army, then?'

David rubbed his bristly scalp. 'Not for me to say, is it?'

'But you must've been proud that Rachel followed you into the Black Watch?'

'Must I?' David glared at him. 'If I were, a fat lot of good it did me. It's like Helen's always saying, "Pride goeth before a fall." An' it certainly did for our Rachel, didn't it?'

The proverb set off an association with the Padleys' house. Ford could feel the perilous path he was treading narrowing further. On

35

one side, information, on the other, a thousand-foot drop towards a complaint from a bereaved father.

He took another tentative step. 'That's a Biblical proverb, isn't it? About pride?'

'Aye. You may have noticed, Helen's a fully paid-up member of the God Squad.'

'You don't share her views?'

'Oh, don't get me wrong. I'm a God-fearing Yorkshireman and proud of it. Let's just say when that glorious day comes around and we're all marchin' through the pearly gates, Helen'll be right at the front wi' a bloody big banner like a miners' gala. I'm more in what you might call a support role.'

Ford realised he didn't know why he'd asked the question. He glanced at Charlie. She was looking puzzled. Time to wind it up.

'Do you have any other children? I didn't ask Helen because she was too upset for more questions.'

'Aye. Jason. He's a mechanic. Works over in Tidworth. Raj's Bodyshop.'

'Do you have his contact details?'

'Helen keeps them. I don't do addresses, emails, all that.' He tapped the side of his head. 'One too many KOs buggered my memory.'

After saying goodbye to David and dropping Charlie off at the SIB office, Ford called the coroner at home to report a suspicious death. He and Raymond Webb went back a few years. They'd achieved a good working relationship, discovering mutual respect and a shared interest in old-time American music.

'If you're telling me it's suspicious, that's good enough for me, Henry. I'll get an email over to George straight away requesting a post-mortem,' Webb said. 'First thing in the morning, I'll get my clerk started on opening an inquest.'

'Thanks, Ray. I'll keep you informed.'

Ford drove straight back to see Helen Padley to ask for her son's contact details, just in case he wasn't at work. She invited him in and offered tea, which he declined.

Helen led him into the sitting room. She was not alone. A man got to his feet as Ford entered. Aged around thirty, he wore a shiny grey suit over a shirt and tie. He was bald but for a fringe of sandy hair reaching from ear to ear around the back of his head. It gave him the look of a monk from a child's illustrated history book.

His sallow complexion spoke of days spent indoors, away from the spreading miles of countryside surrounding the town of Larkhill. Yet he was far from the popular image of a meek country parson, mousy of demeanour and weedy of frame. He had an athletic build only partially disguised by this baggy suit jacket and was the same height as Ford.

Ford introduced himself.

The man smiled. 'I am Pastor Simeon,' he said, placing his palms together at his sternum. 'I minister to the Padley family and am here offering Helen such succour as God allows. "Blessed are those who mourn, for they will be comforted." Matthew, five, four.'

Ford took an immediate dislike to the pastor. Something about his sanctimonious little speech and pitying facial expression. But then he didn't warm to the priestly caste in general. They'd been worse than useless when his parents' marriage had collapsed as a result of his father's increasingly unreasonable and violent behaviour.

Their vicar had offered what he'd been pleased to call 'non-judgemental counsel', in the course of which he'd more or less pleaded with Ford's mother to stay in the marriage 'for the sake of your son'. Even though the woman facing him had a black eye that wouldn't have shamed a back-street brawler.

Ford made an effort. After all, this young man had nothing to do with his own troubled family.

'I need to have a chat with Jason,' Ford said, speaking to Helen. 'Your husband said you had his contact details.'

She nodded. 'My address book's in the kitchen. I won't be a minute.'

Left alone with the pastor, Ford offered a tight smile but nothing more.

In exchange, the pastor bestowed upon Ford a soulful expression. It came off as false, as if he'd spent the intervening moments conjuring up a memory of a dead family pet.

'What despair must Rachel have been facing? To take her own life like that,' the pastor said. 'A sin, of course, though not an unforgivable one.'

'I'm not entirely sure she did kill herself,' Ford said. 'And as for sin, if it exists, I'd say it applies more to murder than suicide.'

The pastor's eyebrows lifted a fraction. '"If it exists," Inspector? Do I take it you're not a believer?'

Ford knew that if Sandy were sitting beside him, she'd be willing him not to rise to the pastor's needling. But she wasn't. 'I believe in the law.'

'But not in God?'

'Sorry.'

'"Whoever believes and is baptized will be saved, but whoever does not believe will be condemned." Mark, sixteen, sixteen.'

Ford looked down at his clenched fist. Made a conscious effort to relax his fingers, but not to prevent his response. 'The only person who's going to be condemned is Rachel Padley's murderer. Ford, one, one.'

As the pastor opened his mouth to reply, Helen returned clutching a fat caramel-coloured leather book. She sat down and ran the nail of her index finger down the thumb-tabs. Finding the correct letter, she opened the book and turned it around so Ford could see.

He copied down Jason Padley's details. He had a flat in the centre of Tidworth, another nearby barracks town, and worked at a local bodyshop half a mile from his home.

'Have you called him yet?' he asked.

She looked at him as if he'd asked her to solve a difficult scientific problem. 'Called who?'

'Jason.'

'Oh. No. Do you think I should?'

Ford felt a flood of pity for the woman sitting blank-eyed before him on the grey sofa. Shock. He'd seen it many times before. It had rendered her incapable of movement, of even the most basic ability to answer questions.

'Would you like me to go and see him? I could ask him to come round.'

She nodded. 'Yes, please.'

He got up to leave and then turned. An old trick, and one he felt bad for using, but if Rachel Padley *had* been murdered, he couldn't afford to hang around.

'Just one other thing,' he said. 'Do you know if Rachel had fallen out with anyone recently? A boyfriend, someone in the regiment, someone she met?'

Helen's lips compressed for a second as if she were unwilling even to consider the possibility that her dead daughter had been anything less than a saint.

She shook her head. 'No. No enemies. Not our Rachel.'

Ford looked at the pastor. 'Someone at your church, perhaps?'

The pastor gaped.

But Helen forestalled whatever answer he was preparing. 'Rachel didn't come to church.'

◆ ◆ ◆

Raj's Bodyshop was closed. Thinking somebody might be putting in some weekend overtime, Ford rang the bell at the double-wide doors leading to the workshop. The Indian guy who came to greet him shook his head when Ford asked if Jason was working.

'He usually plays football on Sunday afternoons. The Tidworth Oval.' He pointed back the way they'd come.

'Yeah, I drove past it,' Ford said. 'Thanks.'

Five minutes later, he was making his way across some muddy grass towards a small group of spectators. Mostly men and boys, they huddled near a stand emblazoned with the leisure complex's name in white capitals on a blue background.

'Are you waiting for the football match to start?' he asked the nearest man.

He nodded. 'They should be out in ten minutes,' he said, lifting his chin in the direction of a low brick structure Ford supposed was the clubhouse.

Ford walked round the edge of the pitch to the building and entered. He spotted a sign for the changing rooms and crossed the large space crowded with round tables and metal framed chairs of the type that could be stacked when not in use.

'Sorry, love,' said a plump woman with dyed blonde hair showing an inch of dark roots. 'Players only back there. Cafe's this way.'

Ford turned and held out his ID. 'I'm looking for Jason Padley. I don't suppose you'd know if he's back there?'

She nodded, but her mouth tightened. 'He is, love. He's not in trouble, is he?'

Ford shook his head.

Even without the helpful signs at eye level, Ford could have found the changing rooms by smell alone. A pungent mixture of sweat, deodorant and liniment led him straight to the door. He pushed through, into the middle of a team meeting.

A group of men ranging in age from late teens to mid-thirties were gathered round an older man dressed in a blue padded jacket, black tracksuit bottoms that bore the classic three stripes of Adidas and lime-green trainers.

'Now, Bulford are dirty bastards, so be careful in the—' The coach, or manager, turned at the sound of the door opening. 'What the bloody hell do you want?'

Ford held out his warrant card for the second time since arriving at the club. 'I'd like a word with Jason Padley, if that's OK?' he asked, scanning the faces now turned in his direction.

A young man with short dark hair razored at the sides and back raised his eyebrows. 'That's me. What's this about?'

The coach looked outraged. 'Are you mad? We've kick-off in' – he consulted his watch, a chunky plastic number covered in subdials and buttons that reminded Ford of Hannah's – 'fifteen minutes. And the lads have to be out on pitch in ten. Can't it wait?'

'I'm afraid not.' He caught Jason's eye. 'Jason? Five minutes.'

Jason shouldered his way through his teammates, muttering a 'Sorry, Lee' to the coach and joined Ford.

'Not here,' he murmured.

He walked out of the changing room. Ford followed him. Outside, Jason turned left and walked to the end of the corridor. He pushed through a fire door, wedging it open with an empty drinks can lying on the ground on the far side.

'What's this all about?' he asked.

Ford explained, keep his sentences short and avoiding any flowery euphemisms. Telling the whole story, stopping short of his growing conviction that this was a murder.

'I'm sorry for your loss, Jason. But I need to ask you a couple of questions about Rachel.'

Jason dragged a hand down over his mouth. 'I can't believe she's dead.'

'I know, and I'm so sorry to be the one to tell you. I just came from seeing your mum. I think she'd like to see you as soon as you can get yourself over there.'

Jason nodded. 'I'll have to tell Lee.'

'It looks as though Rachel committed suicide,' Ford said, feeling sure in that moment he was lying to Jason, 'but I still have to treat her death as suspicious. Do you understand?'

Jason nodded. 'I've seen how it works on the telly.'

'Can you think of anyone who might have wanted to hurt Rachel? Maybe she'd had words or rubbed someone up the wrong way? Got into any aggro in one of the local pubs or anything like that?'

'She only mixed wi' army people, and she never shared none of that wi' us,' Jason said. He had the same flat vowels and Yorkshire accent as his parents.

'How would you describe your relationship?'

'What, me and 'er?'

'Yes. Were you close?'

Jason shrugged his shoulders, which were broad and clearly muscled beneath his thin nylon shirt. 'Not really. We 'ad nowt in common,' he said. 'Never did. Then she joined up couple of years back and, you know, that were that, really.'

'The two of you hadn't had a falling-out or anything?'

'Nowt to fall out over, were there?'

Ford felt he had to give it one more try. 'Can you think of anyone, or anything, that might have been a reason for her to be murdered?'

'No! I keep tellin' you. Anyway, I'm surprised anyone could've managed it,' he said. 'I mean, she were in the bloody infantry, weren't she! They're the ones go round doin' all the killin' an' that. And our Rachel, well, she were hardly Kylie Minogue, were she? Must've been a bloody big bloke, that's all I can say.'

42

◆ ◆ ◆

Ford was at his desk when Hannah called later that afternoon. Her team had managed to complete their investigations before being ushered away by armed soldiers anxious to begin their exercises. She'd labelled and filed everything in the evidence locker.

He put his phone aside and returned to the American homicide textbook he'd been studying. Among the gruesome crime-scene photographs, he'd found the one he'd been looking for. Captioned 'Cadaveric Spasm (CS)', it depicted a man's hand in close-up, tightly gripping a pistol with which he had shot himself. The author, a retired homicide detective, described how those who killed themselves by violent methods could often be found with CS as the hand locked closed around the weapon.

Those who staged suicide scenes to cover up murder often placed the weapon inside the victim's hand. In these cases, the absence of CS wasn't definitive, but 'the investigating officer would do well to direct his or her attention to other possible interpretations of the crime scene'.

At home that evening, Ford took a mug of coffee to the back door and stood looking out over the garden to the fields beyond. Rain and wind lashed the trees into a manic dance. Never mind cadaveric spasm – if Rachel had committed suicide, there ought to be a suicide note. He didn't think they'd find one. Because he didn't think it was suicide at all.

However long he spent turning it over and over in his head, trying to come up with different explanations for her death, he always arrived at the same conclusion. Rachel Padley had been murdered. The real question was, who would want to make her murder look like suicide? The answer to that lay folded into another question. Who was Rachel Padley?

CHAPTER FIVE

Monday dawned grey and cold.

As soon as he got into work, Ford stuck his head round Sandy's door. The Python, as she was known, was at her desk. His boss had acquired the nickname, some said, for the dramatic hugs she bestowed on officers she felt deserved especial praise. Others claimed it stemmed from her days as a top-quality, Tier 3 interviewer and her ability to squeeze the truth out of recalcitrant villains.

Ford knew the truth. He'd been Sandy's bagman shortly after he transferred from Derbyshire to Wiltshire. They'd been working alongside Avon and Somerset Police on a series of break-ins at Longleat Safari Park. In an effort to catch the criminals in the act, they'd staked out the offices, hiding in what was supposed to be a specially cleared glassed-in enclosure in the nearby reptile house.

At 2.15 a.m. on the first night of the op, it became obvious that the keepers had been less than rigorous, and had left a sliding wooden door unfastened.

A seven-foot-long Burmese Python decided that the two interlopers had no business in its territory and stealthily re-entered its enclosure. It climbed a dead tree in sinuous silence, until, a foot above the crouching DI's head, it – she, they were later told, christened Dolores by her keeper – lowered itself down on to her shoulders.

Sandy's scream shattered the quiet, almost giving DS Ford a heart attack. But in an act that combined quick thinking and astonishing physical bravery, Sandy flung it into a corner, yelling, 'Who let a fucking python into my stakeout?'

Thankfully the snake was unharmed, bar minor shock, but Sandy was from that point on saddled with her moniker.

'Got a minute, boss?' he asked her, smiling at the memory. He held up the mug of coffee in his left hand.

'Is that from CID's secret stash?'

'Fairtrade Costa Rica, medium roast.'

She grinned and held out a hand.

'What's up?' she asked, before blowing on the coffee and taking a careful sip. 'Mm. That's good.'

'Suspicious death up at Imber yesterday. A young soldier. White female.'

'OK. What are the circumstances? And why are you wearing your "Henry's Hunch" face?'

Ford summarised the way they'd found Rachel and the aspects of the scene that had set his copper's instincts pinging. 'Post-mortem's in half an hour,' he finished.

Sandy dragged her fingers through her ash-blonde hair. 'I get that you've got a thing for bringing justice to victims. Stronger than most. It's why we get into this job in the first place,' she said. 'But when George does the PM and says suicide, don't go looking for dirty work where she sees a sad but unexplainable death.'

'I won't. But it's not a suicide, boss, I can feel it, and that means I'm going to need you to give me some cover. The Black Watch CO has already put me on notice. They're all deploying to Somalia on the twenty-first of October. I need to move fast.'

'I've got your back, H, you know that. But, like I said, not every suspicious death is a homicide, OK?'

Ford frowned. This wasn't like Sandy at all. Other bosses he'd worked under were far more safety-first, let's-keep-the-numbers-down types. Sandy was more of a 'follow the evidence wherever it takes you' kind of a cop.

'What this all about, boss?'

She puffed out her cheeks. 'Sorry. It's just, every new homicide investigation is putting a crick in my neck and a pain in my arse,' she said. 'The crick is Assistant Chief Constable Starkey and the pain is our dear Police and Crime Commissioner Martin-bloody-Peterson. It's all, "How much is all this going to cost?" from Starkey and "How does this affect the Salisbury brand?" from Peterson.'

That explained it. Assistant Chief Constable Geoff Starkey was a man with a mission: the mission in question being to ascend the greasy pole as far as his bandy legs would carry him. Being an astute financial manager with a reputation for running what he always referred to as 'a tight ship' came second only to his desire to cosy up with the chief con himself. And their political masters higher up the chain, all the way to the Home Office.

As for Peterson, Ford agreed absolutely with Sandy's pithy estimate of his value to Major Crimes. Ford's team would fight harder to save the tea-room kettle than the PCC.

'If George comes back with a report in which she states, unequivocally, that Rachel Padley took her own life, I'll think extremely carefully before I do anything further,' Ford said.

'Which, from what you've told me, seems extremely unlikely.'

Ford shrugged. 'On my first day working for you, you told me to follow the evidence. When you promoted me to DI, you said, "Go and catch the bad guys," or words to that effect. I've never stopped obeying you, Sandy.'

She offered him a wry smile. 'Bugger! I hate being kept honest by my own quotes. Fine, do what you always do. But if it does turn into a homicide investigation, will you please try, for me, not to stick a red-hot poker up Colonel Hemmings's bum?'

Ford held up three fingers. 'I'll do my best. Scout's honour.'

Her eyes widened. 'I didn't know you were in the Scouts.'

He reached the door before answering. 'I wasn't.'

He left for Major Crimes with a ripe expression of Sandy's ringing in his ears. It made him grin all the same. Scout or not, Ford intended to do whatever it took to get to the truth about Rachel Padley's death.

Ford called Charlie and asked to meet Rachel's squad leader, or section commander, or whatever the correct army lingo was. Plus the other soldiers in her unit. And he wanted to have a look at her living quarters. If he was going to find her phone, her room seemed the likeliest place.

Charlie promised she'd set up the necessary permissions for the interviews. 'But it probably won't be until tomorrow.'

'That's OK. I've got a post-mortem to attend first.'

Before leaving for the hospital, Ford gathered his team around him and in a few terse sentences, explained that within a few hours he expected to be launching a homicide investigation. And when that happened, they'd have less than three weeks to clear it.

On the way out, he stopped by Jan's desk. 'I want you to search Rachel's quarters. I'm assuming it'll be a single room in one of the blocks. Talk to Charlie Daniels about getting into the base and any other permissions.'

She nodded. 'Anything in particular you want me to look for?'

He dropped his voice. 'Officially? We're looking at reasons for her to have taken her own life. A suicide note would be helpful.'

She took her reading glasses off and gave him a searching look. 'And when you say "officially" . . .'

'I don't think you're going to find a note. I want you to look for anything that might indicate why someone would want Rachel Padley dead.'

47

Ford's next stop was Forensics. He crossed the hushed space to Hannah's desk.

'Hello, Henry,' she said. 'What can I do for you?'

'I want you to start work on the physical evidence from the Imber crime scene. I'll have the clothing couriered over as soon as George cuts it off the body.'

She frowned. 'But Sandy's just been in and told me not to. To leave it until you're sure it wasn't suicide. She said you're still eliminating that angle.'

'For now, the official line is we're keeping an open mind, but I'm sure, Wix,' he said, hoping he could trust his gut and it wasn't about to bring Sandy's considerable wrath down upon his head.

'Then I'll make a start,' she said with a smile that popped two curved dimples into her cheeks. 'Off the books,' she added in a stage whisper.

Ford drove up to Salisbury District Hospital and made his way to the forensic post-mortem suite. He inhaled the scent mixture that permeated the clinically clean space. Pine disinfectant. The sharp, sappy, snapped-branch odour of formalin. And the sweetish, bad-meat smell coming from the body lying on the stainless steel gurney at the centre of the group.

He smeared George's home-made mixture of camphor, thymol and menthol on to his top lip. But it did little, merely adding a minty, herbal tang of its own. For really bad cases, he used his patented 'stinkbusters' – roll-your-own cigarette filters drenched in menthol and shoved up his nose. This didn't come close.

Garbed as usual in visor and mask, scrubs, rubberised apron, white rubber boots and two pairs of gloves, George stood at the corpse's head.

As there was no conclusive evidence of foul play – yet – Ford had come alone this time. Every member of his team had a heavy caseload. He saw no need to drag any of them away from their work for what might turn out to be nothing more than confirmation of a suicide.

He nodded at George and smiled. Her eyes crinkled at their outer corners.

Standing beside George was Pete, her regular mortician. He was also the drummer in Ford's band, Blues and Twos, when they had time to rehearse or play live. Which, Ford reflected ruefully, was hardly ever these days.

Along with more money and responsibility, and his own office, his promotion to inspector a year or so earlier had also brought more in paperwork. Plus such essential CID functions as staff appraisals, completing performance spreadsheets and attending management meetings.

A photographer was priming her camera, checking the battery and adjusting various dials and switches, ready to document the proceedings as George reduced a recognisable human being to an anatomical demonstration. Ray Webb's deputy, a short, rotund man with a salt and pepper moustache, completed the quintet of living people.

George drew back the dark-green sheet covering the body and handed it to Pete. Using trauma shears, she cut away the clothing, handing each item to Pete to be bagged and tagged. Beneath the camouflage uniform, Rachel had been wearing a khaki T-shirt and plain white cotton bra and knickers. They'd all be couriered to Bourne Hill for Hannah.

Ford saw a young woman with impressively developed muscles. Not the ridged and bulging physique of a bodybuilder, but clearly possessed of great strength when she was alive. The blood had soaked through her clothes, staining the skin of her torso. George would provide exact measurements, but Ford estimated her height at five-nine or ten.

'Help me turn her over, would you, Pete?' George said.

Together, on George's count of three, they rolled the body over and resettled it on to the steel surface of the gurney.

Livor mortis, the process of blood-pooling when the heart stops pumping, had resulted in darkened blackish-purple patches on Rachel's shoulder blades, buttocks, thighs and calves.

George pointed to the depressed area on the back of the head. The impact had torn away part of the scalp, revealing sharp-angled bone fragments smeared with blood. She turned to the photographer.

'Get a few of the head wound, please.'

She stood back while the photographer took half a dozen shots, the flash emitting a mosquito whine as it recharged.

'We've got a severe depressed fracture,' George said. 'It's torn the dura mater and exposed the brain. So she hit, or was hit with, something heavy and hard.'

'Enough to cause death?' Ford asked.

'It's possible. But from the amount of blood at the scene, it doesn't look like it was the fatal injury. More likely that she hit her head falling.'

'Do you think she could have sustained that level of head injury just from falling back against a wooden cart? It looks pretty messy.'

'Again, it's possible. And it's also only about five minutes into this post-mortem.'

It could have sounded like a reproach. Ford was sure that if Olly, an ambitious university-educated DC in his team, had been the recipient, that's exactly how he would have taken it.

But Ford and George were friends. Sometimes he caught a look and wondered if there could be more. There'd been a couple of times during the ten years they'd known each other when an unexpected flicker of desire had ignited in the pit of his stomach. So he took it in good part and kept pushing.

'But if she killed herself, you're saying she would have cut her throat standing, then lost consciousness and fallen back?'

'That's your department rather than mine, but yes. If she killed herself, that's the only sequence that makes any sense.'

Ford heard the whole sentence, but louder by far than all the other words was the smallest, echoing his own. *If.* 'You don't think she did?'

'Come on, H, I've only just started. Let's do a bit more work first before we start speculating, shall we?'

Ford watched as George bent her head close to the dead girl's throat and examined the wound, gently opening it wider with her fingertips. The skin above and below it bore none of the wounds known as hesitation or practice cuts – short, shallow incisions created when a person attempting suicide lost their nerve, either completely or momentarily, and stayed their hand in the act of cutting.

He pointed it out to George, who nodded. 'It'll all be in my report, along with photos, but that's a good spot.'

Overnight, Ford had formulated a hypothesis that would point either towards or away from suicide as the manner of death. Another tick in the column labelled 'homicide' and one that didn't rely on his intuition. It rested instead on the direction of the incision.

Rachel had been found with the knife in her right hand. If she'd inflicted the wound herself, then the natural movement would have been to draw the blade across her throat from left to right. If, however, the blade had gone from right to left, then suicide, while not ruled out altogether, moved from being the probable to an unlikely manner of death.

Direction of travel wasn't conclusive. It was perfectly feasible to cut one's own throat right to left, even with the right hand. Clumsier it might be, but not impossible. But it didn't *feel* right.

'Can you tell the direction of travel of the blade?' he asked.

'Both carotid arteries have incised wounds. The right is completely severed. The left is damaged but the posterior wall is intact. I'll take some detailed measurements and include them in my report. I can't say more now.'

'Please, George. What's your gut feeling? A deeper cut on the right than the left. What does that suggest to you?'

She put her hands on her hips, smearing blood across her apron. '*Gut feeling*? I'm a doctor, H. I don't do guts. Not unless I'm examining them.'

Ford opened his mouth to try again.

She cut him off. 'However, from a cursory visual inspection and what I know from previous PMs of suicides, I'd say there's at least a fifty-fifty chance that the cut went right-left, not left-right.'

'Thanks, George. I won't ask again.'

She nodded, though he felt sure he could see her eyes twinkling with a smile beyond the visor and her own glasses.

She picked up the right hand and rotated it outwards. 'If you want something to get your teeth into, have a look at this.'

Ford rounded the table to stand beside George. He caught a whiff of her perfume. She gently straightened the dead girl's fingers, exposing the palm. The colouring and blood distribution were even.

'No imprint of the knife hilt in her palm or the insides of her fingers. Absence of cadaveric spasm,' Ford said.

He cast his mind back to the scene when he'd first seen Rachel. Her fingers had only been half-closed around the handle of the knife. It was all wrong. If she'd killed herself, then she'd either have died gripping it fast or dropped it as she died. Yet there it lay, as if placed inside her unresponsive fingers by a conscientious set-dresser in a TV show called *A Soldier's Suicide*.

'The lack of CS isn't conclusive: death by exsanguination is slower. But the way the knife was positioned relative to her fingers at the crime scene *may'* – she stared at Ford – 'point to a different narrative than suicide.'

Ford nodded again. He'd seen three separate artefacts on the body that, for him, pointed towards murder.

First, the BFT to the back of the head, which might have come from the wooden cart, though he doubted it. He thought the cart would just have shifted, robbing the impact of most of its force. Then there was the direction of the incision. Why would someone about to take their own life adopt such a clumsy and unnatural action? Finally, he had the lack of CS.

Then there was the absence of an artefact that he *had* seen before in cases of female suicide: self-harm scars. Their location varied, with the tops of the thighs and the insides of the forearms being the most common locations. But those ladders and webs of criss-crossed white lines and ridges told their own miserable story.

Taken individually, each artefact could be explained away. Taken together, they were telling Ford that his hunch was correct: he'd be leading a homicide investigation. He excused himself and left for the car park. He had work to do. And his first task was to go back to see the Padleys and let them know he suspected their daughter had been murdered.

CHAPTER SIX

Hannah spread the evidence out on an inspection table. The clothing, just arrived by bike from SDH. The knife. And the fragment she'd tweezed from the neck wound.

Lit by overhead halogen spotlights, every crease and wrinkle in the young woman's uniform threw a sharp-edged shadow across the fabric. The blue-white light made Hannah edgy, but there was nothing she could do about it. She frowned and concentrated, trying to block out the anxiety caused by the harsh lighting. Breathing slowly and humming to herself, she began.

The front of the tunic was soaked in blood. She moistened a swab with distilled water and rolled the cotton tip across the surface, then stuck it in a capped evidence tube.

She repeated the process with the blade. Now she had two blood samples from the crime scene. She asked one of the other CSIs to run them through the blood analyser. It would give blood groups for each in a handful of minutes. She returned to the clothing.

The pockets in the tunic were all empty. Hannah moved on to the trousers. The right hip pocket was empty. So was the left. Or was it? Had her fingers grazed something right at the very bottom, pushed hard into the seam?

She tried again. She pushed her hand in a little deeper, closed her index finger and thumb around the object and gently eased it clear.

The tightly rolled piece of paper she brought out was curved where it had been squeezed against Rachel's hip. Hannah opened it out until she had a flat, creased sheet in her hands. It was A5 in size, but one long edge was rough. It must have been torn from an A4 sheet.

In a standard sans serif font she identified as 11-point Arial, it read:

> Rachel.
>
> I've got something important to tell you. TOP SECRET!
>
> Meet me at the Baghdad Marriott in Imber at 00:00 tonight.
>
> Don't call me! I'm worried the MPs are monitoring my phone and we can't risk the concequences of getting caught.
>
> Love you lots.
>
> J xx.
>
> PS I can't wait to see you.

Tutting at the spelling error, Hannah was still pleased. She nodded with satisfaction. Rachel Padley had been lured to Imber. And murdered. Henry was right. Of course he was! He was a very competent detective.

The note was printed on what was almost certainly generic printer paper. She picked it up and flapped it in the air a couple of times: 80 gsm. Available from every stationery shop, office supply store and website in the world. If it had any evidential value it lay not in the paper, nor the toner, but the words.

She dusted it for prints, but the few she found were partials and so degraded by rolling or contact with the fabric of Rachel's trousers that there was no point even trying to lift them.

The rest of the garments yielded nothing useful either. The knickers and bra were clean, undamaged and bore no signs of semen. The grit on the soles of her boots matched a sample Hannah had taken from the road at Imber.

She moved on to the knife. 'Are you a murder weapon?' she murmured. It appeared to be old. The handle was bone, the natural off-white surface stained the yellowish-brown of nicotined fingers. Rudimentary grooves ran in the same direction as the axis of the knife.

The single-sided blade measured 15 centimetres from the point to the guard. She knew that was the only detail Ford would need but she found the temptation to examine and name the other parts irresistible. She spoke them aloud to herself, delighting in their arcane sounds yet entirely specific meanings.

'That small notch between the edge and the ricasso is known as the choil. It allows the full length of the edge to be sharpened,' she said, as if lecturing FBI agents-in-training. 'The ricasso is the part of the tang protruding from the handle. The thick, unsharpened side of the blade is called the spine. And the curved portion of the edge nearest the point is called the belly.'

Not really expecting anything, she dusted the handle for fingerprints. Revealed in the black powder was a single, perfect set of four. Using the lab's digital SLR she photographed them at 1:1 ratio and moved to her own workstation, where she called up the prints she'd taken from Rachel's hands at the crime scene.

After downloading the prints from the camera and launching a comparison program, she hit the green start button. As the software did its careful, point-by-point analysis, she performed her own equally meticulous visual inspection. The two sets were clearly a match, confirmed a few seconds later by the computer.

She held the magnifying glass above the tiny piece of material she had retrieved from the neck wound. It was shaped like a long, narrow arrowhead.

Against a transparent plastic ruler, she read off the measurements: one millimetre by three.

'How did you get into the wound?' she whispered. 'Were you caught on the choil and transferred when the killer struck? Are you part of the sheath? That's Henry's department, not mine.'

Next, she placed the fragment on a thin, fragile glass slide and slipped it on to the stage of the microscope beside her desk. Under the greater magnification, and despite the blood-staining, she saw that it was a piece of wood.

Hannah could see nothing that would help her identify the species of tree. Especially, as she reluctantly admitted to herself, botanical analysis was one of the forensic science areas in which she had neither specialist expertise nor even that of a passionate amateur.

But she knew someone who might be able to help. Her name was Dr Merilyn Goldstein and she was a professor of botany at the University of Reading. Merilyn's specialist field was dendrology, the scientific study of woody plants including trees, shrubs and lianas. They'd met when Hannah had been investigating a case for the FBI in Hawaii. A young man had been strangled with a juvenile monkey ladder vine.

Ellen came over with the slips of paper from the blood group analyser. They matched. Both were AB-negative. Only a DNA test would confirm they were both Rachel's, but for now, Hannah didn't think she needed that level of confidence. She also didn't have the time or the budget.

On the other hand, if Henry launched an official homicide investigation, which now seemed likely, she'd re-examine the knife in greater detail, looking for traces of the perpetrator's blood. It wasn't unknown for inexperienced killers to injure themselves with their own murder weapons.

She created a new document on her PC.

Padley_Homicide_Preliminary Findings_HF

CHAPTER SEVEN

Ford needed to assign a family liaison officer to the grieving Padley family. Who was capable? Who was reliable? And, most importantly, who was available? He offered the role to a DC from General CID who'd shown promise in her first couple of assignments, Kate Chisholm.

He and Kate drove out to the barracks in Ford's Discovery. On the way out, he reminded her that the FLO's role was, as he put it, 'Big I, little s.' Meaning, put the emphasis on investigation, not support.

Ford had seen FLOs undergo a transformation akin to Stockholm syndrome, where kidnap victims started to identify with their captors. The officer would adopt not a detective's but the family's mindset. Not fatal to an investigation, but a hindrance given how often the murderer turned out to be a family member.

He parked outside the Padleys' house and rang the doorbell. Helen Padley answered. As soon as she saw Ford, she looked down at the floor and wouldn't raise her gaze again.

He tried to overcome her shyness. 'Hello again, Mrs Padley. This is Detective Constable Chisholm. May we come in, please?'

Silently, Helen stood aside and let them into her home. She offered to make tea, but Kate forestalled her. After asking for directions to the kitchen, she disappeared, leaving Ford alone with Helen.

'How are you coping?' he asked.

Helen nodded, raising her head briefly to offer a small smile. 'With God's help, we're managing,' she said, then looked at Ford expectantly.

Ford leaned forward and clasped his hands between his knees. 'Is your husband home?'

She shook her head. 'He's on duty.'

It wasn't ideal. Ford would have preferred to deliver the news to both parents at the same time. But it couldn't be helped.

'I have some news about Rachel, and I'm afraid I don't know whether you'll find it comforting or simply more distressing.' He paused, and swallowed. 'I now believe Rachel didn't commit suicide at all. I think she was murdered.'

He'd thought she might display some sign of surprise, or horror. Having a child take their own life was a terrible experience, one he couldn't imagine coping with. But then to learn that they hadn't been suicidal at all; that they were in fact happy and content with their life, but had had it cut short cruelly by somebody else . . . It would break him, he was sure.

Instead, her head seemed to pull back into her shoulders. She nodded a second time. 'What does that mean?' she whispered, tears creeping over her downy cheeks.

'Well, first of all, it means I have launched an investigation so we can try to discover who killed her,' he said, grateful now to be on firmer ground. 'We'll be talking to people on the base, people in Rachel's life. We need to build up a picture of who she was.'

Kate reappeared with three mugs of tea. She set them down on the coffee table. 'Here you are,' she said. 'I couldn't find any sugar . . .'

Helen shook her head. 'I ran out. I haven't been to the shops yet. I'm sorry.'

Kate smiled as she handed a mug to Ford. 'That's OK. We don't take sugar, do we, Inspector?'

'That's right,' he said.

Kate was impressing him with her calm approach to a woman who was clearly suffering from shock.

'Has Inspector Ford told you what my role is?' Kate asked.

Helen shook her head again.

'My official title is family liaison officer. We shorten it to FLO. I'll be your point of contact with the investigation team in Salisbury,' Kate said. 'If there's anything you want to ask, or if you think of anything you want us to know about Rachel or the people she mixed with, you can call me or email me at any time of the day or night. Here's my card,' she added.

Helen took the proffered card and placed it on the coffee table, face down.

'Mrs Padley,' Ford said, deciding in the moment to continue using her formal title. 'At some point in the next day or so, I'll be holding a press conference where I'll ask the public for help in finding Rachel's killer. I would very much like to show a picture of Rachel. Perhaps one of her smiling. Do you have a recent photograph we could borrow? I promise to take good care of it and Kate can bring it back to you.'

Helen looked up at him then. Her eyes were glistening. 'No. No photos. Rachel . . . she didn't want them. She hated being photographed. The army has one, I think.'

Ford left Kate with Helen Padley, asking her to make sure David Padley heard the news as soon as possible.

◆ ◆ ◆

Ford looked up from a desk covered in paper to see Hannah navigating Major Crimes, using her habitual route that kept her equidistant from each other person. She reached his office and entered without knocking.

She sat and passed an A4 evidence bag across the desk to him. 'I found that in Rachel Padley's hip pocket. I agree with you, Henry. I think she was murdered.'

He read the note, which sparkled with a few stray grains of fingerprint powder. Yet more confirmation that this was a homicide. It tied in with the PM evidence, too. Maybe the spelling error would be revealing when they had somebody in custody.

'It reads like she was in a relationship with the letter-writer, doesn't it?' Hannah asked.

'It does. Or the letter-writer knew about their relationship and faked the note.' He made a note in his policy book. 'J' had just become a person of interest, if not his prime suspect.

'Do you think Rachel could have had a jealous ex who tricked her into going out to Imber and then murdered her in cold blood?' Hannah asked.

'It's a possibility,' Ford agreed, smiling at Hannah's use of language that wouldn't have looked amiss on the cover of a true-crime magazine.

'I found a wood fragment in the neck wound.'

'Could it have come from the cart?'

'I don't know. I'd need to examine it again to see if it's been recently damaged. And take a sample from the cart for comparison.'

Ford had a vision of high-calibre rounds slamming into the cart on that day's live-firing exercise. 'Not sure we'll manage that. I'll see what I can do.'

'Thank you, Henry. What are you going to do now?'

'One, start tracking down "J". Two, go back out to Imber and have a look around some of those buildings. I think she was clobbered indoors and then dragged out to the crossroads. Can you be ready for a team briefing in an hour?'

'Of course. I can update everybody on what we've come up with. There was one more thing. I want to send the wood fragment to an external expert for analysis. Is that OK?'

'Absolutely. It sounds like you have someone in mind?'

'I do. She's based at the University of Reading.'

'Fine. Leave it here and I'll sort it out. You'd better give me her details.'

Hannah reached for a scrap of paper and wrote out, in a careful hand, the academic's name and address.

She looked up. 'How is Sam enjoying the climbing trip?'

Ford experienced a flash of anxiety. Pictured his son's broken body lying at the foot of a crag. He swallowed it down and smiled. Earlier that year, Hannah had conspired with Sam to persuade Ford to let Sam go on the school trip.

'He's loving it. I want to thank you for helping him persuade me.'

'Really?' she asked, her forehead crinkling in puzzlement. 'You gave me quite a telling-off about it at the time.'

'I know. It's because I was afraid for him. But he's growing up. I have to let him have his head from time to time,' Ford said. 'And better on a supervised school trip than deciding he's going to go off and do something stupid on his own.'

Hannah nodded. 'That's a very rational point of view. It accords with all the statistics on deaths among young men. In fact, for boys under eighteen—'

'Actually, Wix, could you spare me the details? I'm not sure I want to hear about that.'

'Oh. Of course. I have to go anyway. More work to do.'

She got up from her chair and left, shooting him a brief smile over her shoulder on the way out.

Ford called Charlie Daniels and invited her to attend the briefing. She promised to be there. He took the lift down to Traffic and found a couple of motorcycle cops chatting by their bikes, sturdy white mugs of tea in hand.

'Either of you fancy a trip to Reading?' he asked as he reached them.

'I'm about to go out,' the taller of the two men said, 'but you could do it, couldn't you, Paul?'

'What've you got, sir?' the other cop asked.

Ford handed him a padded envelope containing the serial-numbered evidence bag. 'I need you to take this up to a Dr Merilyn Goldstein at the University of Reading. Full address on the label. Keep the chain of evidence nice and tight.'

'Do I need to brief her, too, sir? Labelling and all that?'

Ford shook his head. 'Forensics've used her before so she'll know the score.'

'Better safe than sorry, though, sir, eh?'

'You're right. Just run her through the protocol and then you can come back. She might want to hold on to it in case we get as far as a defence brief wanting it examining again.'

Leaving Paul to fire up his BMW, Ford made his way up to Sandy's office. He wanted to talk to her about holding a press conference. Like a lot of coppers, Ford had decidedly mixed feelings about the media. On a good day they were an invaluable conduit for information; on a bad day, prying vultures whose desire for a scoop or a sensational titbit muddied the waters and even scared off potential witnesses.

But for Rachel's murder, and locating the mysterious J, he felt it would be an option he couldn't ignore. J was either a suspect if the note was genuine, or a witness, if someone else had used their initial to lure Rachel out to Imber. Either way, he wanted to speak to him.

Sandy's reply to his request stunned him.

'Sorry, Henry, I can't allow that. Not at this stage. It's too public.'

'Of course it's bloody public! That's the idea!'

'I mean, it's not just the *general* public who'll see it. It'll bring ACC Starkey down on my neck even harder than usual. Have you totally exhausted the possibility it's a suicide?'

Ford hesitated. Fatal.

'Right,' Sandy said. 'Well, until you can look me in the eye and say yes without thinking about it, no media.'

◆ ◆ ◆

Ford marched out of Sandy's office, all manner of barbed retorts swirling in his brain, but thankfully not leaving his mouth. Back at Major Crimes, he called Jools into his office.

'Guv?'

'I'm launching a murder investigation into Rachel Padley's killing.'

'Right,' she said. 'What do you want me to do?'

'I want you to start poking around at Larkhill. Can you liaise with Charlie Daniels in SIB, please? And ask her to get a list of all the personnel and civilians at Larkhill whose first name begins with J.'

She rose from her chair. 'On it.'

Alone in his office again, Ford leaned back and looked at the ceiling, searching for patterns in the speckled, greyish-white tiles. According to the statistics, Rachel's killer would most likely be a man. Probably her spouse, or current or former boyfriend.

Ford didn't particularly like statistics. All they did was tell you about crimes from the past, and only the solved ones at that. They weren't useless. Not at all. But they were only a part of a good detective's arsenal. He thought the ability to connect two seemingly unrelated events or pieces of evidence using a mixture of gut feel, doggedness and determined questioning was worth a thousand 'data points', as Olly would call them.

He righted himself and stared out of the window, which was smeared with bird shit. He could just see the cross on the top of the cathedral's spire above the nearest roofs.

Somewhere beyond the glass, a murderer was walking around free. And Ford had less than three weeks to find him.

CHAPTER EIGHT

Jools was already foreseeing problems tracking down J.

'How many people are there on a typical army base?' she asked Charlie as they walked together across the barracks at Larkhill. They were heading towards a football pitch where a group of soldiers were engaged in a game of five-a-side.

'It varies. Battalion strength is just under one thousand. But by the time you've added in families and civilian staff you could double that.'

'Given how popular names like Jack, Jamie and Jo are, we could be looking at hundreds of people,' Jools said. 'Not to mention the brother's called Jason.'

'Plus there's you and Jan in Major Crimes,' Charlie said with a grin.

'Funny.'

In a voice that cut right across the hundred yards that separated her and Jools from the players, Charlie shouted out a name. 'Private Willis! Over here, please.'

The game faltered as the ten men turned to see who'd just bellowed the command. One broke away from the group and trotted over to the sideline.

He looked to Jools to be about twenty. Short reddish-blond hair above a scarlet face beaded with sweat.

'Ma'am?'

'This is Detective Sergeant Harper from Wiltshire Police. She wants to ask you a few questions about Rachel Padley.'

His eyes fell, then he looked at Jools. 'It's a real shame she topped herself. She were a great soldier. One of the guys, really.'

'Did she ever show any signs of being unhappy?' Jools asked.

Willis shook his head violently, sending droplets of sweat flying left and right. 'No, ma'am. I mean, she were pissed off if we didn't do well in the exercises or whatever. But she was positive, you know? A real team player. Everyone loved her.'

'No problems because she was a woman?'

Willis's eyes, a pale blue with dark outer rings to the irises, widened in what looked like genuine surprise. 'You're joking, right? Listen, I know the army has its problems, but not in the Black Watch,' he said. 'If a lass makes it through selection, she's as good as the guys. Maybe better 'cause she's had to work twice as hard. In the unit, we've got each other's backs. You have to.'

Jools nodded, smiling. 'Of course. I didn't mean to suggest any of you were giving her grief. But was anyone else making life difficult for her?'

Willis glanced up for a second, then back at Jools. 'No. Well, if they were, it weren't anyone on base. I'd have known. We were tight, me and Rachel. I still can't believe she's gone, to be honest.'

'All right, thank you.'

Willis turned to Charlie. 'Can I go now, ma'am?'

She nodded. 'Thank you, Private.'

He came to attention then turned and sprinted back to the game, shouting for the ball, his right hand high in the air.

Back at the visitor car park, Charlie promised to start the process of getting the list of Js at Larkhill.

'Don't hold your breath,' she called, as Jools unlocked her car. 'I've seen glaciers move faster than army records.'

◆ ◆ ◆

Ford slept badly that night. He dreamt he was back at Imber. Dismembered corpses were strewn across the gritty streets as if a giant had toyed with them, pulling them apart like dolls.

Waking for the third or fourth time, he checked his alarm clock and sighed. Why did people always wake at three? Was it some inbuilt mechanism to ensure the fears of the night held maximum power? A safety device in the primitive part of the brain to prevent them leaving their caves and confronting the real terrors that lurked just beyond the circle of the fire?

The case held no fears for him. Homicide or no, it was a straightforward operation, very much in the intelligence-gathering phase. Was it Sam, then? He'd been gone for three days, with four to go. Since he'd dropped Sam off at the coach station at 5.30 a.m. on Saturday, Ford had striven not to check his phone every ten minutes for a text or WhatsApp message. But it was hard.

He had visions of Sam lying at the foot of a rock face, his limbs broken and twisted at unnatural angles; or dangling hundreds of feet above rock daggers waiting to impale him on their points if his gear should fail.

He'd worked logically through his fears, telling himself that the instructors would have double- and triple-checked every rope, carabiner and belay device. But the fears refused to quieten.

Climbing had claimed his wife. He prayed it wouldn't take his son, too. Because then what would he do? Drink himself into an early grave? A caricature alcoholic cop with nothing to live for outside of the Job? Kill himself like Rachel Padley was supposed to have done?

He thought back to that fateful day on his and Lou's last climb. And out of the dark, as he lay on his back, listening to the wind outside the bedroom window, her voice drifted through his mind. 'Don't go!'

His heart started racing and he felt a wave of panic break over him. He got out of bed and crossed the room to the window, opening the curtains and throwing the window wide.

A storm was lashing the tall trees at the bottom of the garden, their slender branches whipping this way and that, silvery-grey in the moonlight.

No, that wasn't right. She'd been screaming at him to leave her. They couldn't both die or Sam would be orphaned. He reran the memory, listening more carefully this time. 'Go,' she'd screamed at him. 'For Sam's sake, go.'

He drank some water in the bathroom straight from the tap and went back to bed. He feared sleep would elude him and he'd have a disastrously tired day, plagued by the dreams and his own failure to save Lou. But instead, it overcame him almost as soon as his head hit the pillow.

He awoke at seven, ready to work. A text informed him that Charlie had arranged for him to meet Rachel's squad leader, a Corporal Wren, at 10.30 a.m.

Arriving at Bourne Hill a little after eight, he headed for his office and opened the first of many documents he'd have to read that day. Jan knocked and entered. Without a word, she set a plate down on which rested a Chelsea bun, its spiral top browned and twinkling with sugar grains.

As breakfasts went, he wasn't sure his doctor would approve. He consoled himself with the thought that it contained dried fruit, which counted as one of his five a day.

'Thanks, Jan.'

'You're welcome. I was just finishing the report on my search yesterday.'

'Did you find a suicide note?'

'No. There might be one on her laptop, which I have downstairs. But it's passworded.'

70

'But suicides usually leave their notes where loved ones can find them, don't they? Otherwise what's the point?'

Jan nodded. 'I couldn't find a phone either, and there wasn't one on the body. Odd?'

'Maybe she dumped it somewhere. Was Charlie helpful?'

'Nice girl. No side to her, is there? She got me in no problem. The army brass seem keen to help us clear it up.'

Probably because they could move past a young woman's suicide easier than her murder, Ford thought.

'Anything apart from the laptop?'

Jan shook her head. 'Clothes, make-up bag, toiletries, a few books. Some weights, a bit of cash. She lived a pretty spartan life for a young girl, to be honest.'

Ford nodded. It was probably much the same for all the young soldiers at Larkhill. He didn't imagine they had much room for more than the essentials in any case. 'Did you happen to make a note of the book titles?' he asked, more for completeness than anything else.

'There were only three. *Black Watch*. That's a history of the regiment. No surprises there. An American book called *Women in Combat*. I checked the price on Amazon. Thirty-eight quid. Not cheap. And a tatty old paperback. *The Price of Salt* by someone called Claire Morgan.'

'Was there anything in her room at all that suggested she was depressed or considering suicide,' he asked, 'or even self-harm?'

'No. From the look of it, you'd say she was a normal, well-adjusted young girl.'

Ford nodded. 'Thanks, Jan.'

The internal drumbeat was louder now. *Murder. Murder. MURDER!*

71

Half an hour later, Ford and Charlie were sitting in her office in the SIB building together with Corporal Wren. The office was a functional affair, with thinly padded chairs upholstered in a hard-wearing royal-blue cloth surrounding a small round conference table.

Wren was sitting with a straight back. His keen, narrow-set eyes stared at Ford from a pale face pocked with acne scars. He was well over six foot and proportionately broad. His size gave the table the appearance of having been designed for a smaller race of beings.

Ford had just asked Wren if he'd noticed any changes in Rachel's behaviour in the days or weeks preceding her death.

Wren shook his head. 'Nope.'

'Can you elaborate?'

Wren sighed. 'Rachel was fine, sir. She was totally jacked by the thought of the live-firing exercise.' His accent placed him in Glasgow, maybe one of the tougher districts.

'Did she ever mention, even in what may have looked like a jokey way, wanting to harm herself?'

Wren shook his head a second time. 'Nope.'

He folded his arms. It could be a defensive posture. Ford knew some detectives set great store by interpreting such gestures. But he reminded himself it could just as easily be that the man habitually sat like that. Or that he was cautious in the presence of the civilian police.

Sensing that asking direct questions would lead to more monosyllabic answers, he tried a more roundabout approach.

'Tell me about Rachel.'

'What about her?'

OK, not a perfect response, but it was a start. Ford smiled. 'Give me an idea of what she was like. As a soldier.'

Wren shifted his weight in his seat. 'Disciplined. Tough. Performed her duties capably.'

'Just capably?'

Wren's eyes flicked from Ford to Charlie, then the window, then back to Ford. 'Aye. She was a solid member of my section, you know?'

Ford shook his head. 'No, I don't know. That's the trouble. I went out to Imber yesterday and I saw a young woman with everything to live for who had apparently committed suicide,' he said, maintaining a level and quiet tone. 'So I am trying – and this is why I want you to help me – to understand what, if anything, drove her to it. You see, Corporal, so far, I *haven't* found a reason, and that leads my copper's brain in a completely different direction. A direction that leads to a murder trial.'

Wren spread his massive hands. 'I don't know what else I can tell you, sir.'

A thought occurred to Ford. 'Had Rachel ever seen action?'

'No, sir.'

'Have you?'

Wren shrugged and offered a half-smile. 'I might've seen the odd scrap or two.'

'They've only just opened combat roles to women, haven't they?'

'Don't know about *only*, sir. It was 2018.'

'What's your opinion on that?'

'On what, sir?'

'Women on the front line. Would you have been happy to serve alongside Rachel Padley? For her to have your back in a firefight?'

The pause stretched out to several seconds. Wren's gaze was as restless as one of the autumn leaves currently swirling past the office window.

'Corporal?' Charlie prompted.

'I'd have to be, wouldn't I, sir? Ma'am,' he said, finally. 'That's the way it is now.'

'But you have your doubts,' Ford said.

Wren grimaced, as though his guts were griping. Ford saw it. Understood. He was facing a traditionally minded man from a tough area of a tough city. Brought up with a view of women that was fine with their working. Fine, even, with their serving in the armed forces – but in support roles. Out of danger. Nowhere near the men when things got kinetic. Had he killed Rachel because he couldn't trust her when the enemy was real and not just empty buildings in a ghost village?

'Listen, sir. I don't know if you've ever served. I know a lot of coppers have. But things can get really fuckin' hairy—' He blushed. 'Sorry, ma'am,' he said to Charlie.

She waved it away. 'Please speak freely, Corporal.'

'Thank you, ma'am. Well, there's a big difference between popping off live rounds up at Imber and facing the enemy close up. I mean,' he said, warming to his theme, 'kill or be killed, right? That's bad enough. And if I'm told girls can do that, OK, have at it.'

'But you don't think they're up to it,' Ford said.

Wren frowned, his brows drawing together, shading his eyes. 'This isn't some sexist thing, OK? But the Taliban? Al Qaeda? Daesh? They're right bastards,' he said, showing small even teeth. 'And they don't go in much for the Geneva Convention, you know? They capture a woman, they don't put her in a nice little cell and bring her three squares every day and the latest *Cosmo*. They rape, they torture: all that. It's bad for morale for the guys knowing that's what's going on.'

'Listen,' Ford said, 'you're a combat veteran. You can look at a dead body and probably tell quite a lot about how someone met their end. Well, I'm a murder detective and I can, too. And right now, my experience tells me Rachel Padley was murdered and her killer wanted it to look like suicide. My question to you, Corporal, is did Private Padley have any enemies?' A beat. 'You, for example?'

Wren frowned again. 'I thought she was found with the knife in her hand.'

'She was. But on its own that proves nothing.'

Charlie leaned forward. 'Inspector Ford asked you a question. Answer it, please, Corporal.'

Wren let his head fall back on his neck, revealing thick ropes of muscle. He stayed like that for ten seconds. He righted himself and looked at Ford.

'Honestly, sir? No, she didn't have any enemies and especially not me. Whatever she experienced, it was no better or worse than any of the lads got. Maybe some teasing or mucking around, hiding kit, silly pranks.'

'Any bullying? Initiation rituals that got out of hand?'

'Hand on heart?' He made the gesture. 'No. No bullying, which I totally would not stand for, by the way.'

Ford nodded. 'Thank you, Corporal. I don't have any more questions. Lieutenant?' he asked, turning to Charlie.

'Just one question, Corporal, then you're free to go. Was Rachel in a relationship?'

'Not as far as I'm aware, ma'am.'

'Thank you. Dismissed.'

Ford waited for Wren to close the door behind him. 'I imagine there's quite a lot of that in the infantry.'

Charlie smiled. 'Not wanting girls on the front line, you mean? You can't really blame the guys. It's a big change.'

'But one you're in favour of, I assume?'

'Not sure a senior detective should be assuming anything,' she said, her smile widening into a grin.

'My bad. So, are you?'

She frowned. 'I don't know. It's tricky. On the one hand, yes, I believe women can do anything men can,' she said. 'And, right up to the point the fighting goes from shooting to hand-to-hand, why not? So much of modern warfare is technological. Drones, artillery, cyber, even sniper rifles: women can handle all of those things as well as, or better than, men.'

'But when the bullets run out and you have to pull a knife . . .'

'Yes, or fix bayonets, or carry a wounded comrade to safety over five hundred yards of rough terrain, I don't know. Maybe?'

'But they have to pass the same tests as the blokes, don't they? So if a woman has the physical strength, the endurance, the right attitude or whatever the requirements are, then surely she'd be as good as a man in a combat situation.'

Charlie huffed out a breath. 'You're probably right. I'm just trying to be honest with you.'

'Sorry, of course. I didn't mean to start an argument. Tell me, what's *your* take on it? You know this world better than I do. Am I off the mark pursuing a murder investigation?'

Charlie spun a biro lying on the table. She watched it rattle around in an erratic spiral. When it came to rest, she spoke. 'No. You're not. I didn't know Rachel particularly well, but I knew *of* her. She always seemed very happy. Very motivated. Can I ask, though, why you were so sure, so quickly, that it wasn't suicide? I'm not doubting you,' she added hurriedly. 'I just want to understand. I can learn from you.'

Ford nodded. 'One, I'm looking for reasons, but I'm not finding any. Two, look at the primary crime scene. I've dealt with suicides before. Too many. People usually do it somewhere private,' he said. 'Their own home, usually. A garage or a shed. Maybe the bedroom if they've taken pills. If it's outside, they tend to choose somewhere secluded like a spot in the woods.'

'Or they jump off a bridge or throw themselves in front of a train. That's pretty public, isn't it?'

'Yes, but that's because the location is also the method.'

'Anything else?'

'I attended the post-mortem yesterday. The neck wound's all wrong. And the bash she took to the back of her head? No way was that made by a wooden cart.'

'You're saying it was staged.'

'That's what it looks like, yes.'

Ford spent the rest of the day in court on an unrelated case. But at four, when he walked out of the lift and into Major Crimes, it was to find a note on his desk in Jools's handwriting. *Sandy's looking for you.*

Ford called his boss.

'How did it go today?' she asked.

'The defence barrister tried to shaft me on PACE but I'd say it was honours even when the judge called a recess.'

'Good. Because I've got some news for you.'

'Go on,' he said cautiously, detecting a hint of resignation in Sandy's voice.

'We've got a meeting with Geoff Starkey in an hour.'

'Oh, great. What is it this time – budget overruns? Burglary statistics? A new alphabetical filing system for homicide reports?'

'He wouldn't tell me. Also, Martin Peterson is going to be there.'

Ford caught a hint of anxiety in Sandy's voice, which worried him. He grabbed a tie hanging on the back of his door and headed over to her office, knotting it as he went.

He found Sandy looking sharp in a tailored plum-red jacket and black leather skirt. As he entered her office, she was misting her throat with her favourite perfume: Chanel No5.

She paused to look him up and down.

'Is that your best black suit?'

'That bad, eh?'

She grimaced. 'It's fine. Compared to that peacock Peterson, you could wear a handmade number from Savile Row and he'd still probably look down his beak at you. Come on, let's go.'

CHAPTER NINE

Sandy pulled out of the car park, hitting the accelerator hard enough to draw a squeal of protest from the rear tyres.

'So, why the sudden interest in what, publicly at least, is a suicide?' Ford asked her as she piloted her shiny black Mercedes E-Class up to the ring road before heading north-west towards the headquarters of Wiltshire Police.

'Publicly?'

'She was murdered, Sandy. I'm sure of it. All the evidence points to that conclusion.'

'What about the evidence you haven't seen?'

'Well, as I haven't seen it yet, that's a hard question to answer.' He thought how Hannah would probably answer it. 'What you might call an unknown unknown.'

She tossed her head back. 'Fair enough, and I'm not in the mood for philosophy, anyway,' she said.

They reached police headquarters fifty minutes later. After undergoing the usual security checks and formalities, they found themselves being ushered into ACC Starkey's palatial office.

Ford preferred brass that came with a decent proportion of high-quality copper. Officers so good at the job that their superiors had reluctantly promoted them out of operational roles and into senior management, where they could inspire and manage a new generation.

The alternative was a cheaper alloy, light on copper, heavy on the worst kind of substitute: politics. Kicked upstairs where they could do less harm to active investigations, though now able to wreak havoc of a more subtle kind. ACC Starkey was a fully paid-up member.

His office bore witness to his ascent. A neatly arranged grid of black-framed photographs filled the wall behind his wide, highly polished cherrywood desk. Starkey was the constant presence: he beamed out, shaking hands with various civic dignitaries, senior officers, local aristocrats and even a minor member of the royal family.

Ford had only met the ACC a couple of times and thought it fair to say they hadn't hit it off. Starkey, short, stocky, with bushy ginger hair and a hair-trigger temper, had always seemed more interested in numbers than criminals – or victims for that matter.

Peterson wore yet another expensive suit, plus a mauve silk tie paired with a matching pocket square. He must have visited the barber that morning: short hairs speckled the collar of his lilac shirt.

With refreshments procured, Starkey got straight down to business.

'I hear you've had a nasty suicide over at Imber.'

Since suicides and homicides were both counted as suspicious, Ford opted to tell Starkey part of the truth. 'I'm investigating a suspicious death, yes, sir. A young female soldier. Private Rachel Padley. Black Watch Battalion, 3 SCOTS.'

'Exactly. And no need for all that "sir" business. We're all friends here, I hope. Geoff's fine by me. And I'll call you—?' He left the question mark hanging in the air between them.

'I'm happy with Ford.'

Starkey cleared his throat and Ford caught a flash of irritation cross Peterson's face. That the man resented the way he refused to play the 'all-mates-together' role gave Ford a small measure of satisfaction. He knew it was juvenile, but he couldn't help it. Antagonising Peterson had become a form of light relief from the pressures of the job.

'Yes, well, from what I hear it's pretty clear the young girl took her own life,' Starkey said. 'Tragic and all that, but I really hope we won't see you launching some sort of crusade to prove she was murdered. No need for you to open a homicide investigation.'

Ford frowned, glad now that he hadn't told Starkey that was exactly what he'd done. 'Crusade, Geoff? I'm sorry, I'm not sure I understand.'

He caught a small movement beside him, below the level of the table where neither Starkey nor Peterson could see it. Sandy patting the air. He knew what she meant. Cool it. He resolved to try.

'Look, Ford,' Starkey said with a smile that didn't reach his eyes, 'everyone here knows you're a top-notch homicide detective. Your clear-up rate's in the top three in the south of England. But there's no need to go looking for trouble where there isn't any.'

Ford nodded, preparing himself to show Sandy he was at least willing to appear compliant with the top brass. 'Absolutely, Geoff. I totally agree. If there's no smoke, you can rely on me not to go looking for a fire.' He thought the use of the cliché would please both men, Peterson probably more than Starkey.

'Good, good.'

'Can I ask, you said it was "pretty clear" Rachel committed suicide,' he said. 'I'm just wondering how you managed to form that impression? Only the pathologist hasn't released her PM report yet and our investigations are still ongoing.'

Starkey leaned forward, making the table creak. 'Don't get smart with me, Ford. You might be a top homicide investigator but you're still just a DI.' He tapped the silver embroidered wreaths and tipstaffs on his shoulder boards. 'I'll thank you to remember that these insignia on my shoulders do, actually, mean something.'

Sandy interrupted. 'Sir, I don't think DI Ford meant any disrespect.' She turned and glared at Ford. 'Did you?'

Ford met her gaze. Her eyes were narrowed and shooting out a signal so plain he was amazed there weren't actual little red daggers beaming out across the two feet that separated them.

'No, sir. I didn't. Sorry.'

Starkey harrumphed. He leaned back and stretched his neck inside the stiff white collar of his uniform shirt.

'Very well. Apology accepted,' he said. Peterson smirked. 'If you must know, I had a call from Colonel Hemmings this morning. He's got his own people looking at it. They all seem perfectly happy that it's no more and no less than what it appears to be. I mean' – he spread his hands in exasperation – 'isn't it obvious, even to you, Ford? The girl had the knife in her hand. She's sitting out there all alone with her throat cut. What other conclusion could any rational person possibly come to?'

Ford opened his mouth to offer the ACC half a dozen different conclusions anyone with half an interest in human nature could have come to, but heard Peterson's voice instead of his own.

'What Geoff's trying to say, Ford, is that there's no need to try to boost your clear-up figures by creating imaginary murders that you can proceed to solve.'

Now it was Ford's turn to feel the grip of anger. 'Unlike you, Martin, I would *never* use other people's misery as a springboard for my career, and I resent the insinuation. Take it back or I'm leaving right now.'

Peterson reddened. 'I have never, this is outrageous, I mean—' he blustered.

'That's enough!' Starkey snapped. 'From both of you. Ford, listen to me. Like the police, our colleagues in camouflage have to be mindful of the prevailing winds in society. They – and we – must reflect the people they serve and protect. Now, if this young woman couldn't cope with the pressures of the job and killed herself, well, it's obviously a tragedy for her family, but let's not rush into anything we'll regret later.'

'Sorry, sir, I don't understand.' Ford understood all too well, but he wanted Starkey to say it out loud. That he wanted the whole thing hushed up for political reasons.

Starkey's eyes widened and he ran a hand over his gleaming scalp. 'Jesus, man! Do I have to spell it out for you? What if it's a sexist thing? Because she was a woman in a man's world? The fallout would be appalling.'

'But if it is a sexist thing then it would be my sworn duty to investigate – as a hate crime. As it would be whatever the motive.'

Starkey screwed his mouth up and winced. 'Well, yes. Obviously. But we don't want the media crawling all over the place, printing lurid headlines suggesting the army – or Wiltshire, for that matter – is a hotbed of misogyny. I mean, the army is actually very keen on diversity nowadays.'

Peterson's lips parted. Ford had a horrible feeling he knew what was about to emerge.

'Geoff's right. The optics would be terrible for the army's brand.'

Ford took a deep breath. He looked at Sandy and tried to signal an apology for what he was about to do. Then he smiled at Peterson and spoke calmly, despite the thudding in his chest. 'I don't, actually, give a fuck about the army's *brand*, Martin. And quite frankly, I find it offensive that you would even hint that you'd weigh adverse publicity on the same scales as a young woman's murder.'

'I didn't mean to suggest—'

'I haven't finished,' Ford snapped. 'I *am* a detective. A homicide detective. I'm not a crusader,' he said, eyeballing Starkey, 'nor a glory hunter.' Back to Peterson again. 'Let me make you a really simple promise. I'll run *this* investigation the way I run *all* my investigations. Without fear or favour.'

'Which is all we're asking—' Peterson began.

'—but as I have *already* determined that Rachel Padley did *not* commit suicide, I am launching a homicide investigation, and I will follow the evidence wherever that leads me. If that's a problem for you, sir, then you can take me off the case.'

Starkey's face was puce. That he'd had a triple heart bypass the previous year was common knowledge in the canteens across the county. Ford half-hoped he'd triggered something that would see the ACC back in hospital.

With evident effort, Starkey spoke. 'No need for that, Ford. We shan't be turning you into a burning martyr just yet. You carry on with your' – he paused to catch his breath, the high colour leaching from his cheeks – 'excellent . . . work over at Salisbury. You say it's murder, not suicide, I can't stop you. But be aware it's your neck on the block and there's a bloody big axe dangling right above it. That'll be all.'

◆ ◆ ◆

'Well, that was fun,' Sandy said as they drove back to Salisbury.

'Why do you think Starkey was so keen to push the suicide narrative?'

'He mentioned Hemmings. Men like them meet more often than you'd think,' she said.

Sandy was right. In Salisbury, the army, the cathedral and the landowners comprised the nexus of the city's power base. They liked to stay in touch with each other. Keep things ticking over nice and smoothly.

'You haven't answered my question.'

She blew out her cheeks and took a hand off the steering wheel to ruffle the hair at the side of her head. 'I don't know! I can imagine Hemmings not wanting you crawling all over his outfit looking for a murderer.'

'That's his problem.'

'Yes, but it might become mine.'

'Not you, too, boss. Please don't say you're worried about the PR angle.'

'Of course not!'

'Look. We're getting ahead of ourselves. Let's deal with one thing at a time. PM report first. Maybe I'm wrong. Maybe George'll put the whole thing to bed and that'll be that.'

He knew it wouldn't be, but this seemed to placate Sandy. She nodded, glanced down and turned on the radio. The volume faded up on the seven o'clock news.

'. . . the tragic suicide at the weekend of a member of the Black Watch. Private Rachel Padley was taking part in a live-firing exercise on Salisbury Plain. Police believe that poor mental health led to the young woman's decision to take her own life. In other news—'

Ford stabbed out a finger to turn off the radio. He felt a cold fury surging through him like the wind on the plain that had chilled him on Sunday morning.

'What the hell was that?' he demanded.

Sandy slowed for a roundabout, swung the Merc on and off, before answering him.

'I have no bloody idea.'

'Someone's trying to railroad me and I don't like it. It's either Peterson, Starkey or that prick Hemmings. I'm going to put out a press statement first thing tomorrow.'

'No! Don't do that.'

'Why not? Give me one good reason.'

'Because,' Sandy said with a sigh, 'it'll look like we don't know what we're doing.'

'But someone's just released disinformation to the media. Don't you think that warrants a correction?'

'I do. But not like that. What if it *was* a suicide? We'll look stupid going yes it was, no it wasn't, oh, wait, yes it was after all.'

'I don't care about looking stupid.'

'No? Well, I do!'

Ford bit down on a response that would lose him his only ally if it came to a standoff with HQ. 'Then you'd better hope George is a hundred per cent for suicide,' he grunted, then folded his arms and stared straight ahead. Neither spoke for the rest of the trip.

CHAPTER TEN

Frustrated by the slow pace of the investigation, Ford spent the following day reading everything the team had amassed so far on the victim. He'd requested her military records, but the army were dragging their feet, insisting he use forms that so far as Ford could tell didn't exist.

The looming deadline, when the Black Watch would fly thousands of miles away from his investigation, was making it impossible to concentrate. At 6.00 p.m., finding he'd read an entire page without taking a single word in, he slapped the file shut and leaned back in his chair.

Unexcited by the prospect of another night at home, during which he'd probably end up working, he wandered out into the main office. Olly and Charlie were the only ones there. Olly had his phone clamped to his ear and was taking notes. Ford wandered over to Charlie. They'd agreed that for the duration of the investigation it made sense for her to work from Bourne Hill so she and Ford didn't have to waste time travelling to each other's offices.

'Don't suppose I can tempt you away from your desk for a drink?'

She looked up at him and smiled, her eyes crinkling at the corners.

'Sounds great!' She closed her laptop and stood. 'I haven't eaten since breakfast either. Maybe we could get some food as well. The Bricklayer's Arms has a new chef apparently. Shall we try there?'

◆ ◆ ◆

Charlie beat Ford to the bar and bought the drinks: a pint of Wadworth 6X for him and a large glass of Chardonnay for herself. He followed her to a table in a quiet corner, half-hidden by a dark wooden bookcase. Its shelves were piled with old hunting, fishing and shooting manuals that had long ago lost their dust jackets. The effect was of a neglected library in a country house.

Ford sank into the embrace of a deep-red leather sofa, its buttoned arms worn to a sand colour by a great many elbows. He took a pull on his beer and looked around at the other drinkers. No cops. No police staff or CSIs, either. The Bourne Hill crowd mostly drank in the closest pub to the station, the Wyndham Arms on Estcourt Road.

Beside him, Charlie half-turned to him and tucked one leg under herself. Ford smiled. Why did women do that? Lou had done it and he'd seen others assume the same posture automatically as they sat in anything more comfortable than a side chair.

'What?' Charlie asked, smiling.

'Just the way you're sitting. I was asking myself why women do that?'

She looked at her leg then back at him. Her eyes twinkled with humour. 'I'd never really thought about it before. It's comfortable, I suppose.' She sipped her wine. 'So, tell me, what does DI Ford do to relax when he's not solving murders?'

'I play guitar. Listen to music.'

'I had a boyfriend who was a musician,' she said, taking another sip of her Chardonnay and looking at him over the rim. 'A pianist. He had these incredibly long fingers.'

Ford couldn't think of a suitable response and covered by taking another pull on his beer.

'Does that go for guitarists as well?' she asked.

'Not in my case.'

'Show me,' she said.

He held out his hands and she took his left in hers, turning it this way and that as if it were a piece of evidence. Her fingers were cool to the touch: from the wine glass, he thought. This close, he could smell her perfume. It hadn't been obvious at the station. Maybe she'd sprayed a little on when she excused herself to visit the ladies.

'Your fingertips are calloused,' she said.

'It's from the strings.'

'I suppose it hurts if they're too soft.'

Ford nodded. Were they just talking about guitarists' callouses or was something else going on? He found his lack of certainty disquieting.

She released his hand and asked him a question about the case. It broke the tension he'd been feeling and they began chatting about how far they'd progressed.

After ten minutes he gestured at her empty glass. 'Another?'

'Please.'

When Ford returned with their drinks, Charlie smiled at him and clinked glasses. 'I like Hannah, by the way. My God, she's smart. You're lucky to have her working with you.'

'Yeah, she's got a brain the size of a planet. She puts the rest of us to shame.'

'But she's less sure of herself in social situations,' Charlie said.

Ford wondered whether he should say something about Hannah's Asperger's. It wasn't his place. And Hannah was more than capable of letting people she trusted know about her diagnosis.

Charlie saved him the trouble. 'I've a cousin on the spectrum,' she said. 'But unlike Hannah, Clare tries to hide it. Women are much better than men at doing that. It's called masking.' She paused. 'She quite likes you, you know.'

Ford felt himself growing hot. He gulped down some beer.

'I don't blame her,' Charlie added.

Somewhere along the line, Ford ordered a third round of drinks, then Charlie a fourth. He was feeling pleasantly drunk. Beside him, Charlie raised a new glass of Chardonnay to her lips. She'd just got back from the ladies' after, as she put it, popping in 'to freshen my lippy'.

At the station he hadn't really noticed her make-up. Now her lips were a glossy scarlet. He noticed she had a fleck of red on one of her canine teeth.

He put his pint down. 'You've got some on your tooth,' he said.

As he raised his finger and tried to indicate which side, his balance wobbled and he lurched towards her. Instead of rearing back to avoid a collision, she leaned into him, catching his face between her palms. She kissed him full on the mouth.

Her lips felt sticky against his. He could taste her wine and he could smell her perfume stronger than before. He closed his eyes and let the sensations wash over him.

She put her hand around the back of his head. He felt her fingertips caressing his neck. Liked it. He was dimly aware of drinkers at the other tables in the little room off the bar but found he didn't care.

CHAPTER ELEVEN

Jools thanked the barman and turned with the bottle of wine and two glasses to join Hannah at their table. They'd arranged to get something to eat together after work. 'The Bricklayer's Arms has got a new chef,' Jools had said. 'It was in the paper. I thought we could go and check it out.'

'There you go,' she said, putting the bottle in its aluminium cooler between them. 'Let's get a couple of glasses poured and we can choose what we're going to – Hannah? What is it?'

Hannah's face was immobile. It was as if she'd been hit with a tranquilliser dart. Jools followed Hannah's gaze. And she understood.

Through a perfect one-person-wide gap in the crowd she could see into the snug. And there, half-hidden by a bookcase, but not hidden enough, Ford and Charlie Daniels were engaged in a passionate embrace.

'Oh, Jesus!' she said under her breath. She turned back to Hannah and sat down, pouring two big glasses and spilling some wine on to the polished tabletop. 'Hannah, I'm so sorry.'

Hannah smiled. But the expression didn't reach her eyes. She took the glass Jools had placed in front of her and swigged half of it. 'Thank you. That's lovely. Right,' she said, pulling a menu from the wooden stand beside the wine cooler, 'I'm starving. Let's order.'

'Do you want to go somewhere else?'

'Why? Because I saw Henry kissing Lieutenant Daniels?'

'Well, yes.'

Hannah shook her head. 'Just after I started working at Bourne Hill, we went out for a drink together. I told him I fancied him and I asked him if he felt the same way about me.'

'What did he say?'

'He was very clever. He didn't say no, but he didn't say yes. He said it was too soon after Lou's death,' she said. 'I can see now that it isn't too soon any more.'

Jools was at a loss. She hadn't picked up any signs that Ford fancied Charlie, or thought of her as anything more than a member of his team. Yet here they were, acting like a couple of drunken teenagers at a party, snogging away as if their lives depended on it.

Maybe that was it. Alcohol was a powerful disinhibitor. Half the calls on Friday and Saturday nights had their origins in booze. For some, it led to thrown punches or swung saucepans, for others, risk-taking. Sexual and otherwise.

'And you're OK with that?' she asked.

'Of course! Why wouldn't I be? Now I know where I stand in relation to Henry, it means I can look elsewhere for a sexual partner.'

'And that's all it was to you?' Jools asked, frantically trying to recalibrate the way she thought about her friend's interest in Ford.

'What do you mean?'

'What do I *mean*?' Jools gulped some wine. 'I mean, I thought you—'

'You thought I what?'

'I thought you, you know, because you told him how you felt about him, you wanted a relationship with him,' she said finally, realising as the words left her lips how utterly lame they sounded.

Frowning, Hannah toyed with her wine glass. 'I suppose having sex with someone would *lead* to a relationship. I hadn't really thought it through that far.'

Jools laughed. 'Oh my God, Wix, you are so way ahead of the curve. Here's me pigeonholing you as some weepy little princess and you just had the hots for Ford.'

'That's all right, isn't it? I don't know if you've noticed, but he is very attractive.'

Jools wiped her eyes. 'Yeah, I guess so. He's a bit old for me, but I see what you mean. That brooding look he gets in his eyes.'

Hannah nodded, smiling. 'That's what attracted me to him in the first place. And he's obviously very good at what he does, which is interesting to me. I don't like incompetence.'

'I'd not thought of being competent as a turn-on before.'

'Oh, it is! For me, anyway. In the US, I had a very intense sexual relationship with a senior FBI agent. His name was Harris Delaney. We did it almost every day for six months. Harris was very imaginative. In the office and, you know' – Hannah lowered her voice – 'in bed.'

Jools had just taken a mouthful of wine, and sprayed it out over the table.

'Miss Fellowes, you're outrageous!'

She was too busy mopping up the wine to see Hannah staring at Ford, her head cocked on one side.

Ford opened his eyes. The room was too bright – he must have forgotten to pull the curtains – and it worsened the pain lancing back and forth behind his eyes. He groaned. Checked the time: 5.50 a.m. Too late to try for a final dose of sleep to ease his hangover. Too early to get up. He lay there and tried to remember how he'd got home after leaving the pub. He must have walked, though he had no recollection.

The night had been filled with an unending erotic dream about Charlie. He could still feel the weight of her hips as she rose and fell above him, eyes closed and murmuring his name as she ground herself down on to him.

He lifted his head just enough to turn over the pillow before laying his cheek back on the newly cool cotton. Something fluttered on the dented pillow next to his. Raising himself on his right elbow he picked up a small sheet of paper with a torn edge. It had something written across it. For a surreal second he imagined he'd somehow found Rachel's suicide note and brought it to bed with him.

He raised it to his eyes.

Thanks for last night. It was fun.

C xx

He sank back, letting the handwritten note fall from his fingers.

◆ ◆ ◆

Ford arrived at Bourne Hill just after nine. Washing down a couple more paracetamol with coffee, he leaned back and closed his eyes, waiting for the painkillers to kick in. The night with Charlie had been good. He'd enjoyed it. She was bright, sexy, independent, feisty. But how could he let her down gently, tell her he wasn't ready for a relationship? He tried to imagine telling Sam he had a new girlfriend. The thought made his stomach flip.

A knock at the door brought him back to reality.

Mick came in and sat down. 'All right, H?'

'Never better. You?'

'Not counting my bitch of a soon-to-be-ex-wife, tip-top.'

'Did you want something?' Ford asked.

'I heard you were swapping intelligence with our army liaison last night,' Mick answered, grinning. 'Well, that or spit.'

'News travels fast,' Ford said, already resigning himself to being the focus of station gossip.

'I wouldn't know. Anyway,' he said, getting to his feet, 'hope you enjoyed being on manoeuvres again.' He winked, then left.

Mick had to step neatly to one side to avoid colliding with Jools, who came in to take the recently vacated seat.

'Morning,' Ford said.

'Morning, guv. All right?'

'I'm fine, thank you. How are you?'

'Yeah, good.'

'Good, so we're both fine. Was there something you wanted to discuss?'

She frowned. 'You might as well know – you were seen in the Bricklayer's Arms last night.'

'I gathered.'

'Well, it was me and Hannah.'

'Ah.'

'Yeah. But it wasn't me who blabbed.'

'No?'

'Nuh-uh. Not guilty, your honour.'

'Then . . .'

'I thought she was going to be really knocked sideways by it, but she turns out to be even more' – Jools's eyes flicked upwards for a second – '*Hannah* than you could imagine. I think she might have told a couple of people she saw you and Charlie kissing.'

'A couple?' Ford asked, already seeing Hannah's gift for straight talk coming into its own.

'I think she just found it interesting. She said she'd told you she fancied you. But then, when she saw you with Charlie, she sort of parcelled it up as a completed action and, I don't know, moved straight on like there was nothing left to think about.'

'She wasn't upset?'

Jools smiled. 'I think it's safe to say she wasn't upset.'

'Business as usual, then?'

'Probably your best bet, guv.'

'Thanks, Jools.'

After Jools had left, Ford turned his mind to Hannah. How would she *really* be feeling about it? He felt sure he'd find out without the need to ask her.

When he wasn't using her nickname, he thought of Hannah as 'Miss No-Filter'. It was one of the things he liked about her. He could hardly complain if she turned her questing intelligence on his own behaviour, now could he?

Someone knocked at his door. He looked up to see Charlie walking in.

'Morning,' she said with a grin. 'Sleep OK?'

'I think it was more unconsciousness than anything else.' He hesitated, aware of his heartbeat and feeling unclothed before her despite his black suit. 'Look, Charlie, about last night. I'm not sure I'm ready for this. You see, I'm a widower and—'

Charlie held up a hand. 'Relax! I just fancied letting my hair down and the moment presented itself. I'm not looking for a relationship.' She smiled. 'I meant what I wrote, Henry. It was fun, but it didn't mean anything.'

Ford frowned, realising he'd fallen behind the times. 'OK, but we were spotted in the pub so you should at least know you might be the subject of some station gossip.'

'Don't worry,' she said, winking. 'I'm a big girl. I can take it.'

◆ ◆ ◆

'Did you enjoy kissing Charlie last night?' Hannah asked, when she met Ford in the corridor later that day.

Ford realised he didn't need to be coy with Hannah. 'I did enjoy it, thanks, Wix. I'm sorry you had to see us, though.'

'Oh, don't worry, Henry,' Hannah said dismissively. 'Jools thought I'd be upset, too. But I'm not. I like clarity and now I have it. I expect you had sex with Charlie later: you both seemed quite drunk. I hope you'll be happy together.'

'I think it was more of a one-off kind of thing. We're not planning on getting married, if that's what you're thinking.'

'I'm not. Although statistically, widowers almost always remarry, usually within three to five years of their spouse's death.' She coloured and put her hand to her mouth. 'I'm sorry, Henry. That was very direct and extremely insensitive.'

He sighed, and smiled at her. 'It's fine, Wix. I know you didn't mean anything by it. Look, regardless of last night, I like you, OK? A lot. And I hope we can go on being good friends.'

She nodded. 'Oh, yes. This doesn't change anything.'

She turned and walked away, head down, swerving to avoid having to walk between two oncoming people.

CHAPTER TWELVE

George emailed her report on Rachel Padley's post-mortem at 8.45 a.m. on Friday morning: the official report as an attachment plus an informal summary for Ford. Ford had spent most of the previous day fleshing out the investigative approach for the Padley homicide investigation.

He'd asked Olly and Jools to brief him on their research into Rachel's life. On top of their caseloads, both DCs were studying hard for their sergeants' exams and were competing with each other to see who could be the most thorough in their assignments. What they told him underlined the rightness of his original instincts about the case.

Olly had trawled through Rachel's financial records. After tax and the army's own deductions for food and accommodation, Rachel took home just shy of a thousand pounds a month. She was frugal with her spending, and her outgoings amounted to just three-fifty.

Most of that was the monthly payment to a finance company for her car. Her deposit account held over thirteen thousand pounds. Olly had found no unusual patterns of spending, nor any recent changes. That meant ACC Starkey couldn't point to money worries as an indicator for suicide.

Jools told him she'd been unable to find any evidence of a relationship, abusive or otherwise. The people she'd spoken to, though guarded, painted a picture of a well-liked, amiable and outgoing young woman with her eyes fixed firmly on her career. Another cross on Starkey's school report.

He clicked on George's email and before opening the attachment, scanned down to the 'Manner of Death' line George always included in her summaries. He hoped he knew what it would say, but it was important to see it in black and white. And there it was: the first line of official text supporting his conclusion.

> MOD: ambiguous. Suicide very unlikely (staged?); or homicide, probable.

Three strikes against Starkey. Ford felt his mood lifting. He nodded as he read George's next conclusion.

> There is no physical evidence that the injury was caused by collision with the cart. I found no blood on the wood and no damage to it either, which should have occurred during an impact hard enough to fracture the skull at one of its thickest points. The BFT would have rendered Rachel unconscious, possibly comatose, <u>but it did not kill her</u>. I consider it unlikely to the point of being virtually impossible that Rachel dealt the blow herself.

What George *had* found was grit embedded in the wound, which she'd sent to Hannah. She'd concluded that the cause was forceful impact by or against some kind of masonry or brickwork. Not only that, but as there was no matching grit beneath or around the body, the blow must have been delivered elsewhere. *Ante-mortem*. Ford read on.

> The wound to her throat was the fatal injury. She bled out. But from the measurements I took, and the

lack of hesitation cuts, I'm not at all convinced it was self-inflicted.

George's final conclusion was chilling.

Rachel was alive when her throat was cut.

It was 12.30 p.m. and the all-white-painted meeting room they called the 'sugar cube' was full. All the chairs were taken and a few people who'd arrived late were standing at the back. As Ford operated a strictly first-come-first-served policy, that meant a couple of plain clothes people were standing while punctual uniforms including Sergeant Nat Hewitt and PC Lisa Moore were seated.

Sandy had bagged a seat on the side of the square facing Ford. Beside her sat Martin Peterson in a soft brown suit paired with a knitted mustard-coloured tie.

Ford would sooner have avoided the PCC being present, but sadly it wasn't within his power to ban him from meetings. Peterson was holding forth on something or other. Ford caught the single word 'outreach'. Sandy was scrolling through messages on her phone as Peterson talked at her, but it didn't seem to faze him: he just kept on talking.

Ford's inner circle – Jan, Mick, Jools and Olly – occupied one side of the square; the other was taken up with Hannah, two uniformed sergeants and a couple of police staff investigators. Charlie sat to Ford's right. She'd caught his eye as she arrived and offered an unreadable bland smile, but that was it. Had she been teased as he had? He hoped not.

He called the meeting to order by rapping his knuckles on the table. He waited for the hubbub to die down and then counted to three in his head. It was an old trick, but it worked every time. The silence thickened as people looked at him, waiting for him to speak. His stomach was jumping. He wasn't surprised, given the move he was about to pull on Sandy.

He began by asking Charlie to introduce herself. Then he caught the eye of a uniform standing by the door.

'Could you get the lights, please, Ian?'

In the semi-darkness, he turned on the projector hooked up to his laptop.

The screen behind him was filled with Rachel's dead body slumped against the overturned cart.

'For those of you who haven't met her yet, this is Private Rachel Padley of the Black Watch. During the hours of darkness on the night of Saturday the twenty-sixth of September, Rachel was lured out to Imber on Salisbury Plain and,' he said, staring at Peterson, 'murdered.'

He clicked on to the next photo, a close-up of Rachel's right hand.

'This is the knife used to inflict the fatal wound. Nothing special: there are tens of thousands of hunting knives like this all over the country.'

'And you're absolutely, one hundred per cent sure she didn't do it herself?' Peterson asked.

Ford pictured Starkey operating Peterson with a hand up inside his back, working his clacking lower jaw up and down. Then he glanced at Sandy. Wondered for a second whether Peterson's operator wasn't closer than Trowbridge.

'Sure enough to launch this homicide investigation, yes. And sure enough to hold a press conference tomorrow.'

Sandy glared at him but said nothing. He valued her loyalty, and her management skills. She'd have a few choice words for him, but they'd be delivered in private, not in front of his team.

'Can you be more specific?' Peterson asked.

Peterson never failed to waste time in briefings. Usually, Ford just wanted to shut him down, but today the police and crime commissioner had gifted him an opportunity to make peace with Sandy.

'Thank you, Martin. Yes, I can,' he said. 'I received the post-mortem report from Dr Eustace earlier. Here's her official conclusion as to manner of death.'

He clicked the remote for the projector and a line from George's formal report filled the screen.

> While suicide is a *possible* manner of death, it requires a
> set of assumptions and coincidences so improbable that
> <u>I consider homicide to be the only realistic conclusion</u>.

'Based on the evidence, and our differing but equally long experience, the pathologist's judgement and mine are in perfect alignment,' Ford said, staring at Peterson and then offering Sandy a less confrontational look. 'Rachel Padley was murdered. For the benefit of Martin Peterson, and anyone else who hasn't been paying attention to this case since Sunday, I'll go through the evidence.

'Firstly, her hand wasn't gripping the knife as it should have been if she'd been holding it at the moment she died. Now,' he said, holding up a hand as he caught Hannah opening her mouth, 'the phenomenon I'm describing, known as cadaveric spasm, is not one hundred per cent present in all self-inflicted violent deaths, but it's a tick in the column.'

'So there are other ticks?' Jools asked.

Ford nodded, grateful for her helping him sideline Peterson. He clicked the remote. The screen filled with the lurid image of the throat wound. He heard a few hisses of indrawn breath.

'Sorry, folks. Should have warned you. Dr Eustace took a set of measurements of the wound at each extremity. She also measured the direction of drag on the soft tissue along the wound track,' he said. 'Based on her experience, she concluded that it was highly probable that the cut was made from right to left.'

He explained his thinking on what that suggested, illustrating the different anatomical positions required of hand, wrist and arm for a self-inflicted wound contrary to the natural cutting direction.

'Whereas, for a right-handed *attacker*' – he drew an imaginary blade across the throat of an invisible victim – 'the natural stroke and measurements taken by Dr Eustace are in accord.'

'What about if the attacker had been behind her?' a PSI asked. 'Then you'd be looking for a left-hander.'

'It's a good point,' Ford said. 'But before her throat was cut, Rachel was hit from behind with a piece of breeze block. The killer used enough force to fracture her skull. She'd have collapsed. I see the murderer dragging her out to the crossroads, positioning her with her back to the cart and then cutting her throat in the face-to-face position.'

'I don't see any hesitation cuts either, guv,' Jan said.

'No, and that's another tick in the murder column.'

'But ticks aren't evidence, are they?' Mick called out. 'Maybe she just decided to do it and did it, fast and hard. She was a squaddie, after all.'

Ford shook his head and walked them through the statements from the two soldiers they'd interviewed from Rachel's section, Willis and Wren.

He held up the evidence bag with the letter to Rachel. 'Finally, Hannah found this in Rachel's clothing. It's a letter from someone called "J" telling Rachel to meet him out at Imber the night she was killed. My feeling is, whoever J is, he's involved in Rachel's murder, if not her actual killer. Our number one priority is to find J.' He turned to Charlie. 'Don't suppose the army have coughed up a list yet?'

'Sorry,' she said.

Jools and Jan confirmed Mick's assessment of the progress of interviews at Larkhill Barracks. The soldiers Rachel had served with were adept at being unavailable for interview, even at agreed times.

'Did you form the impression anyone was hiding anything?' Ford asked.

'Not really. But something's changed. I think when everyone thought it was suicide, they were OK about talking,' Jools said. 'But now it's a murder investigation, they've got a lot more tight-lipped. I think they're worried about incriminating someone.'

'Any thoughts about the best way to break them down?'

'If I may?' Charlie said.

Ford nodded. 'The floor's yours.'

'I don't know if any of you apart from Jools have investigated crime on an army base before, but it's different to civvy street. The MPs, my lot, we come up against weapons-grade truculence, literally in some cases,' she said with a brief smile. 'I'm afraid that, faced with civilian cops, the average squaddie is going to clam up unless arrested or given a direct order by a superior officer to cooperate.'

'What do you suggest?' Jan asked, pushing her black-framed reading glasses higher up her nose.

'Say we're not really looking at someone in uniform for it,' Charlie said. 'Give them the idea we've got forensic evidence pointing to somebody outside the wire. They might be more willing to open up if they think it's a civilian.'

'Isn't that somewhat misleading?' Martin Peterson piped up.

Ford heard a few sighs and at least one muttered swear word.

But Charlie wasn't fazed by the interruption at all. 'Not at all, Martin,' she said smoothly. 'In SIB, we call it Articulated Response Strategy. Obviously that's a bit of a mouthful, so we shorten it. In fact, you could have a valuable role in the investigation as the ARS executive liaison between the police and the army.'

He nodded eagerly. 'Yes, absolutely. Can't have the brass' – he made air quotes – 'getting their collective knickers in a twist about investigative strategy.'

'Good. That's settled,' she said. 'I've found nothing to indicate that Rachel was having any personal issues. Her record, with one single exception, was that of a soldier at the beginning of their career. Spotless and filled with positive remarks from those who assessed her performance.'

'What was the one exception?' Sandy asked.

'In January of this year, she made a complaint about her section leader.'

'A Corporal Wren,' Ford said.

'Rachel accused him of favouring the men in his squad over her when it came to the more exacting physical tasks on exercises and on deployments,' Charlie said. 'She felt he was being unduly lenient in his treatment of her.'

'What?' Mick said. 'You mean, she was pissed off because he *wasn't* picking on her?'

'Yes. She claimed that his belief that women shouldn't be in combat roles led him to sideline her.'

It made sense to Ford. He'd seen for himself that Wren was at best conflicted and at worst downright hostile to the idea. He'd be worth talking to again. If Rachel had persisted with her complaints, or expressed them to him directly, he could have decided enough was enough. He made a note to reinterview Wren.

Next, Ford showed the wound to the back of Rachel's skull, followed by the letter Hannah had found in her trouser pocket. He concluded by saying they had the murder weapon, but not the object used to knock Rachel out.

'Hannah, any updates from Forensics?'

She nodded and straightened in her chair. Looked quickly around the room before speaking.

'I found a wood fragment in the neck wound, which we're having analysed by an external expert. I also analysed the masonry residue Dr Eustace recovered from the head wound. I examined it under a regular optical microscope, and under a polarised light source,' she said in a clear, carrying voice. 'This revealed a distinctive pattern of shimmering silver and grey flakes.'

Admiring her growing talent for storytelling, Ford nevertheless felt he had to prompt her to reach her conclusion. 'Distinctive to . . .'

'Breeze blocks. Or, as my former colleagues at Quantico would have called them, cinder blocks.'

Ford thanked her, and summarised their progress. They had two promising leads in the wood fragment and the letter. And they had four crime scenes. The crossroads at Imber. Rachel's car. Her room in barracks. And her workplace, which, unfortunately, was the entire barracks, plus Imber itself.

'That's a lot to cover, but somewhere in there we'll find more clues as to the identity of Rachel's killer. I also want a deep dive into her life,' he said, looking at Olly and Jools in turn. Both nodded. 'If she fell out with someone even over a can of Coke, I want to know about it. If she spent anything on clothes, I want to know which shops. Did she go out to pubs or clubs? Which ones? Who with? What did she order? You know the drill. Thanks, everyone.'

The meeting ended as people gathered their files, papers and briefcases and clustered into groups to share out tasks. Ford intended to return to Imber. But that meant another meeting with Colonel Hemmings.

Ford drew Charlie aside. 'Did you just get the Wiltshire police and crime commissioner to agree to being an arse liaison?'

She rolled her eyes. 'I had him pegged from the moment I saw him. That type love appropriating other people's jargon. You get them in the army, too. But he's a prime case.'

'I might have to appoint you our PCC wrangler.'

She shook her head and wagged a finger for good measure.

'Not bloody likely.'

CHAPTER THIRTEEN

In his office, Ford motioned for Charlie to sit in the visitor's chair. He tried to keep his tone professional and made a point of focusing on the bridge of her nose. *No lower, Ford.*

Charlie frowned. 'You all right?'

'Yes,' he said loudly. 'Sorry, yes. Just a bit on edge with the case.'

'OK. Well, there's something that's been bothering me. You need to know that I haven't worked any homicides before. I mean, there've been accidental deaths – shootings, accidents on manoeuvres, that kind of thing. Even GBH that's gone south and turned into manslaughter. But I'm not sure how much help I'm going to be.'

'Don't worry about it. We'll work it together. Even if you just make sure the right doors are opened and don't mind brainstorming ideas with me, that would be great.'

She smiled. 'Have you got any thoughts about the murder in general? I mean,' she added, 'where we should be looking for suspects?'

She'd put her finger on the central question for him in this homicide, as in every other he'd investigated. Even out at Imber on the Sunday, while seeing what everyone else assumed was a suicide, he'd begun constructing alternative scenarios. At the very top of his list had been the big question. Was it someone Rachel knew?

He'd concluded swiftly that if she'd been murdered, she must have known her killer. No way would she agree to meet a stranger in the middle of nowhere, in the depths of night. And there was simply no chance that both Rachel and an assailant unknown to her had met, by chance, in the centre of Imber.

He knew Olly would probably frown at that conclusion and bring up the idea of coincidence. But in the real world, the world Ford had lived in since before Olly had learned to tie his shoelaces, some events really did have a zero probability.

The note Hannah had recovered confirmed it. He saw two possibilities there. Either it was genuinely from the mysterious J, or it was faked to lure Rachel to her death. Time would tell. And some imaginative police work.

'It must have been someone she knew,' he said. 'It's the only way she would have been off her guard. I assume she was trained in close-combat techniques. I don't see how a stranger could get close enough to kill her.'

'Do you want to go back out there? To Imber?'

'We should. As soon as possible. Only thing is, I don't want to get shot while I'm poking around.'

Charlie grinned. 'Don't worry. I've got clearance to access the online schedule for the exercises. Hold on.' She pulled a slim laptop from her bag and put it down on the desk. After a few minutes she nodded, pursing her lips. 'They're breaking at fourteen hundred hours tomorrow. There'll be a walk-through by the MPs to check the place is clear and they'll be gone by fourteen fifteen.'

Ford made a note. 'We'll leave here at ten to two then. That's' – he hesitated, trying to convert the time into army-speak – 'fourteen hundred, no, thirteen—'

She grinned. 'Thirteen fifty. Maybe we should agree to use the civvy clock for the rest of the investigation.'

He nodded. 'It might save time. And you're OK working on a Saturday?'

'It's either this or do my washing, so on balance, yeah, bring it on.'

Ford nodded in agreement. Sam wasn't due back until Sunday, so if he could use the Saturday to get ahead of the case, it would be time well spent.

After Charlie had left, Ford called the media liaison officer and asked him to set up the press conference. Then he made his way to Sandy's office.

As had become his habit, he stopped off to make her a cup of coffee. Having been caught one too many times nicking the ground coffee from General CID, he'd brought a bag of Colombian medium roast from home. He filled a cafetière and took it with two mugs and a carton of milk to his boss's office.

She looked up and scowled when he came in.

'Try that trick again, H, and I'll have your scrotum for a make-up bag,' she said, when he'd closed the door behind him. 'You didn't need to bounce me into the press conference. If Doc Eustace says it's homicide, we've got decent backup to your famous gut to give to the ACC as justification.'

'Sorry, boss,' he said. 'I just needed to get things moving. We're running out of time.'

She sighed deeply and accepted the mug of coffee he poured for her. 'What do you want from the press?'

He outlined his thinking about Rachel's death and finished, 'We need to trace J. There could be hundreds of people at Larkhill whose names begin with J. I don't have the luxury of methodically TIEing them all, that's if the army bureaucrats ever give us the list.'

'You think if J's a helpful witness, he'll come forward?'

'Or if he's the killer, someone who knows him might give him up.'

'What are your thoughts on the family?'

Ford pursed his lips, taking a sip of the coffee to collect his thoughts. 'After his outburst at Imber, the dad's taken the whole idea of the stiff upper lip to its extreme,' he said. 'You know, when I worked up north, I met some really old-school working-class men. You know the type: crying at funerals is a short step away from wearing lacy cuffs. David Padley makes them look like Liberace.'

'What about when you told them it was a murder?'

'He wasn't there, but I'm not convinced he would have reacted any differently if he had been.'

'What about the mum?'

'It's poleaxed Helen. She can hardly even make eye contact.'

'How's Charlie working out? I've seen her around Bourne Hill quite a bit.'

Ford glanced at her, searching for a sign she was taking the piss. Found none. Or none he could see. 'She was honest enough to admit this is her first murder investigation, which I took to be a good sign,' he said. 'If nothing else, she gets me on to MOD property without a whole lot of form-filling. And she's pretty good at running interference with Colonel Hemmings.'

'And how *are* we getting along with the colonel?' she asked, fixing him with the look known station-wide as the Python Death Stare.

'Officially, the police and army are working hand in glove on the investigation into the tragic death of Private Padley.'

'And unofficially?'

'I think Hemmings is a self-important, officious prick who wishes the glove in question was red, padded and laced up at the wrist.'

'So, no bromance just yet, then?'

Ford sighed in exasperation. 'I know you think I've got a chip on my shoulder about people in authority—'

'Me?' she said, laying a fan of fingers across her chest, swathed today in an expensive-looking cream silk blouse. 'Just because you treat Martin like a tumour and dropped an F-bomb in ACC Starkey's office and almost gave him a coronary?'

Ford grinned despite himself. 'Hope you didn't get any flak for that.'

'You need to watch your step with Starkey,' she said, all trace of her earlier good humour erased from both voice and facial expression. 'He's got it in for you.'

'Why? Doesn't he like my clear-up rate? He was good enough to mention it in the meeting.'

She shook her head, setting her sleek ash-blonde hair swinging. 'It's not funny, H. Starkey's a political animal from his handmade Italian shoes up. You might think operational success is what counts' – she held up her hand to forestall his interruption – 'and at your level, and mine to an extent, it does. But Starkey's more interested in' – her mouth twisted – 'the *metrics*. Budget overruns, staffing levels, Home Office targets, diversity quotas, complaints from the public, resource allocation, sickness days as a percentage of overall rostered shifts . . .'

'All the admin crap, you mean.'

'Yes, if you like. All the admin crap. You know why he made ACC, don't you?' she asked. 'When he was a front-line copper, he was always one of those not bad enough to fire but not good enough to keep. He used to be the chief con's bagman, back in the day.'

'So they booted him upstairs?'

'Exactly. From where he likes to lord it over the rest of us.'

'That doesn't explain why he's got it in for me.'

'Don't you get it? You're the thing he never was: a bloody good detective. Call it professional jealousy if you want, but I can just see he'd like nothing better than for you to fail.'

'I'd better not give him the opportunity then.'

At 10.58 a.m. the following day, Ford sat at the table at the front of the meeting room, looking out at the journalists gathered for the press conference.

A large clock on the back wall told Ford he had two minutes to go before the official start time. He saw a couple of unfamiliar faces. The media liaison officer had had the bright idea of inviting the defence correspondent of *The Times*, who lived locally.

Ford made a point of seeking out and smiling at Emily Latimer, the news editor at the *Salisbury Journal*. She nodded back and offered a smile of encouragement. He'd laid a sheet of paper on one of the seats on the front row with RESERVED and her name printed beneath it. His palms were sweaty and, hoping nobody would catch him, he dropped his hands from the table to wipe them on his trousers.

Sandy and Charlie sat flanking Ford. He detected the scent of Sandy's Chanel No5, the perfume she always wore for press conferences, claiming it gave her confidence. Martin Peterson, who had recently taken to attending what he liked to call 'mission-critical media briefings' was sitting to Charlie's right. Anticipating the move, Ford had instructed the media officer not to position a mic behind Peterson's name card.

Ford leaned forward and switched on his table mic. He cleared his throat so that the sudden noise brought the journalists to a respectful silence.

Sandy kicked off by thanking everyone for attending and introducing Ford as the lead investigator. As in his own team meetings, Ford counted to three before introducing himself and the case. He nodded to the media officer, who dimmed the lights and projected Rachel's official army ID photo on to a screen set up in one corner.

Ford read out his prepared statement. It included Rachel's rank and regiment and outlined the details of the murder. In conversation with Sandy beforehand, he'd proposed holding back details of the nature of her injuries to screen out the serial confessors. Anyone unable to provide details of the wounds and the knife would be warned about wasting police time and hung up on or kicked out of the police station.

Then he turned to Charlie, as they'd agreed. She introduced herself and explained her role in the investigation. She stressed that this was a joint investigation in which the civilian police, under Ford's command, were the 'lead agency'.

'We're very keen to identify the person who wrote the note to Rachel,' Ford said. 'They signed themselves as "J". It's clear they were in a relationship of some kind. I'd like to ask the public' – he found the red light of a TV camera and imagined speaking to a single witness – 'if you recognise yourself as J but didn't write the note, or if you think you might know who J is, please come forward. You can call me at Bourne Hill police station in Salisbury, or via Crimestoppers on the number shown on your screen.'

Peterson pulled Charlie's mic close and leaned over to his left to speak into it. 'As DI Ford said, this is a tragic murder and we're working flat out to solve it. I am acting as the ARS executive liaison with the army on this one, so please address any questions relating to police-slash-military protocols to me.'

He leaned back, smoothing his hair into place, a self-satisfied smile on his face. For once, Ford had no urge to punch Peterson. Gratifyingly, he saw *The Times*'s defence correspondent smirking as he bent over his notepad.

Ford set off for Imber with Charlie at 1.50 p.m. On the drive out across the plain, brief flurries of rain spattered the windscreen, triggering the wipers. As Ford turned off past the barn full of farm equipment, the sky darkened dramatically, deepening from a uniform dove grey to a sickly greenish charcoal.

Rain advanced towards them from the direction of Imber: dark smears linking the darkest clouds to the ground.

The wipers jerked in a panicky rhythm until he twisted the control to switch them to a steady beat. They entered the rainstorm. Large drops drummed on the roof and lashed the windscreen until Ford had to speed up the wipers or lose visibility.

He drove up the hill towards the trees, noticing that the cows had disappeared from the field to their right. He turned the headlamps on as the light outside diminished.

A jagged spear of lightning crackled down, bleaching the cabin. Seconds later, thunder exploded overhead, the initial blast followed by a long, rolling boom.

'Hope you've got a hat,' Charlie said.

'Two. And cagoules. And wellies. And a golf umbrella. No coffee though. Sorry.'

She laughed and produced a metallic green flask from the rucksack between her feet. 'I did, though. And chocolate.'

Ford nodded in appreciation. 'Come and work for me,' he said. 'Please.'

He swung off to the left and followed the curving road down into Imber. This time he drove into the centre of the village, only stopping when he reached the crossroads.

The rain was still hammering on the roof. Ford leaned forward and peered up at the sky. 'I don't think this is going to stop any time soon. Happy to go for it?'

'Yup. Can we reach the gear from inside?'

'Hold on.'

Ford clambered into the back and then leaned over the rear seats. He passed a cagoule to Charlie, almost stabbing her in the eye with the point of the umbrella. Another stretch and he grabbed a pair of wellington boots. Normally he kept them for Jools, when she was acting as his bagwoman.

'Not sure if they'll fit, but you're welcome to them,' he said, as he retrieved his own pair.

They struggled into the wet-weather gear in the confined space then climbed out into the storm. The noise as the rain battered the stretched nylon canopy of the umbrella made conversation at normal volume impossible.

'I think Rachel was attacked in the Marriott,' he shouted. 'That's how her killer could get the element of surprise. She was knocked unconscious then dragged out to here, where her killer cut her throat.'

'What are we looking for?' Charlie yelled back.

'Signs of a struggle. If we're lucky, a blood-stained piece of masonry. Just look for anything that shouldn't be there.'

The rain was thrashing down so hard it was bouncing back up off the pitted tarmac. They walked side by side over to the white-washed building, splashing through puddles in which shell casings glinted like gold in a prospector's pan. They were everywhere, hundreds of little brass cylinders that crunched and rolled under Ford's boot heels.

Up close, the bare, white-painted structure resembled nothing more than one of Sam's childhood drawings. A square topped with a triangle, four squares for windows and a taller rectangle for the door. Only, where Sam used to put three smiling figures in front – Mumma, Dadda, Sam – this house was devoid of any human life at all.

Inside, he pushed back his hood and wiped the moisture from his face.

'You go left, I'll go right,' he said.

With Charlie investigating the other side of the building, Ford looked around his half. Whereas Sam the artist would have struggled to draw the interior of *his* house, the military builders had equipped theirs with a rudimentary layout of metre-tall breeze-block walls to indicate the different rooms. Useful for house-clearing exercises, he assumed.

Ford worked his way through each room, using a torch to light the dark corners. He found nothing bar a couple of dozen flattened lead slugs.

He peered out of one of the glassless windows. If anything, the rain had intensified. The sloping road surface was running freely with water, which created V-shaped bow-waves leading downhill from each discarded shell casing.

Ford penetrated further into the interior, negotiating a low grey wall of breeze blocks that dog-legged into a larger back room.

He swept the torch left to right and from the ceiling to the floor, already growing despondent that they wouldn't find anything. After all, how likely was it that a killer cunning enough to lure his victim to a classified military site on MOD-owned private land would then be so careless as to leave clues behind?

One hundred per cent turned out to be the answer.

At the end of one of the low walls, on a corner of the upper-most breeze block, Ford's torch beam picked out a dark-red clot of muck. He looked closer. Blood, a couple of hairs and what appeared to be a shred of skin about the size of a fifty-pence piece.

He took photos on his phone then stood and stared at the blood stain. He breathed deeply, stilling his mind and allowing the drumbeat of the rain to act as white noise, suppressing all thoughts.

He ran a hand slowly down over his nose, mouth and chin before letting it dangle by his side.

What had happened in this grim little room? Ford tried to inhabit Rachel's thoughts. To experience the world the way she would have done in her last few moments on earth . . .

. . . I've got J's note folded and rolled in my trouser pocket. I'm driving out from Larkhill Barracks to Imber. I'm excited but also intrigued. My stomach's fizzing. Why all the cloak-and-dagger stuff?

I arrive under cover of darkness, park the Corsa and walk into the centre of Imber. A cold wind is blowing across Salisbury Plain, chilling me through my uniform tunic. I head for the crossroads.

There's nobody here.

I call out. No worries about being overheard. Not unless the cows are mooching about outside the perimeter with parabolic mics.

Then I roll my eyes. Of course! The Marriott. Like J said. Duh.

I walk up the road until I come to the Baghdad Marriott. Smiling, I enter, using the torch on my phone for some light.

'J?' I call out. 'Where are you, babes?'

'In here,' J answers from the back room.

Stomach fizzing, I hurry through. We greet each other and then, after we've chatted for a bit, J grabs me and shoves me backwards. I'm shocked. Too surprised to do anything. I fall back against the edge of the wall and crack my head hard. The lights go out. The last thing I see is J holding a knife.

CHAPTER FOURTEEN

Swinging the torch left to right at the floor, Ford crossed the room to a walled-off corner that he supposed might have represented a downstairs toilet.

The small windowless space had no lead slugs on the floor or bullet holes in its walls. He assumed a soldier sent in to clear the ground floor would peer in, rifle at the ready, then retreat having given the all-clear.

Ford made a note. The murderer could have hidden here. A fifth crime scene.

'In here!' he yelled.

Charlie appeared in the doorway. She stood back, checking the wall where Ford was pointing.

'Is it OK to come in?' she asked.

'Yeah, the floor's so scuffed up our prints aren't going to matter one way or the other.'

Charlie looked at the gore-spattered wall. 'She was shoved against the wall. She would have collapsed. Then the killer—'

'Or killers.'

'—or killers dragged her out to the crossroads and one of them cut her throat. Is that how it happened?'

'I think so. We need to secure this building. I need Hannah to forensicate it from top to bottom.'

Charlie frowned. 'We'll have to work fast. They're due back at six tonight. Night exercise right through until seven tomorrow morning.'

Ford checked his watch: 3.42 p.m. It would take Hannah at least forty minutes to get out to Imber. As for a full team, that could take hours.

'It's not long enough. We need to shut this whole place down until we've finished.'

Charlie bit her lip. 'I'm really sorry, Ford. I just don't think that's possible. We can try. But these things are planned months, sometimes years in advance.'

'I don't care! This is a murder investigation now. In which I have primacy, remember,' he snapped. 'Who do we have to speak to?'

'You won't like the answer.'

Ford felt anger welling up inside him. 'Colonel Hemmings.'

'Yup.'

He sighed. 'I'm sorry for snapping. I think I already knew I'd be butting heads with Hemmings. I took my frustration out on you.'

She grinned. 'Don't worry. They breed us tough in the army. Come on. We'd better get over to camp right away.'

They sprinted through the rain to the Discovery, threw everything on to the back seats, laughing at the soaking they'd got despite Ford's gear.

'I need to call Hannah,' Ford said, pulling out his phone.

'OK. Let's have some coffee and chocolate before we head off, yes?'

Ford nodded, already holding the phone to his ear. 'Wix, listen, you need to get as many people as you can out to Imber on the double.'

'Yes, sir!' she said in a sharp voice.

'Sorry, I've been hanging around with army types.' He glanced across at Charlie, who grinned and offered him the cup from the top of the Thermos. He shook his head. 'You have it,' he mouthed.

'There's only me here at the moment,' Hannah said. 'It's Saturday. Most people are at home although a few are at other crime scenes.'

'OK, well for now just you, then. I'm just leaving with Charlie to see if we can buy some more time. The fifth crime scene is the building signposted Baghdad Marriott,' he said. 'I found blood spatter and tissue in the big back room.'

'I'll come now. It should take me, hold on' – Ford could hear Hannah's breathing, knew what she'd be doing: checking Google maps – 'thirty-eight minutes.'

'Great. See you later.'

He gratefully accepted the proffered coffee this time and drank it down in a long gulp. Then he clicked his seatbelt, started the engine, turned the heater up full and pulled away. Beside him, Charlie unwrapped a bar of chocolate and snapped off a couple of chunks for him.

'Thanks,' he said. 'What's the protocol with Hemmings? Do we have to phone ahead to make an appointment?'

'Well, as he's the CO, I'd say that would be a courtesy. And the diplomatic thing to do.'

She stopped talking. Ford noticed she wasn't using her phone. 'But?'

'I have authority to investigate crimes involving army personnel any way I see fit. Like you,' she said. 'That goes for conducting interviews with witnesses or asking for help. Let's just rock up and see if we can find him.'

'You don't like him.'

'I wouldn't say that. He's perfectly civil when we meet, which is rarely.'

Ford smiled, relieved to see that, finally, the rain seemed to be easing off. The sky had lightened enough for him to turn off the headlamps.

'You don't warm to him, then.'

'Let me give you some background to Colonel Steve Hemmings,' she said.

As they drove across Salisbury Plain and shafts of bright yellow sunlight beamed down through gaps in the cloud, turning the fields emerald green, Charlie painted an interesting portrait of the Black Watch CO.

Unlike most commanding officers, Hemmings had not gone to Sandhurst, the army's traditional college for producing commissioned officers. Nor had he come from an army family. He'd joined at sixteen and worked his way up to the pinnacle of operational rank.

Hemmings had embraced the traditional military culture like a long-lost friend. He tolerated women in his battalion because he had to. As for those few in combat roles, he'd made it plain in several unguarded moments in the officers' mess that he regarded it as a terrible idea.

The bright spot in her recounting of a one-man obstacle course for Ford's investigation was Charlie's sketch of the colonel's second-in-command.

Major Robinson was the eldest daughter of a landed family with estates in the north of England. A woman who, as a young girl, had been featured on *Country Life* magazine's coveted inside front page, where it liked to display to its readers portraits of 'society girls'. A Sandhurst-trained officer. And a fully committed member of what Charlie dubbed, 'The Queen's Own Progressive Regiment'.

'You're saying she could help us get through to Hemmings,' he said, slowing at the roundabout where tourists were queuing to get into the car park at Stonehenge.

'Not quite. He's the CO and what he says goes, I'm afraid. But she'll do what she can to smooth the rough edges off any of his decisions that get in the way of our investigation.'

'Why does a hard nut like Hemmings have someone like her as his deputy?'

'One word. Politics.'

Ford nodded as he accelerated away from the roundabout. It was good to hear Charlie referring to it as their investigation. He liked to know everyone on his team was pulling in the same direction. Clearly, she had no divided loyalties. And he appreciated her candour about both Hemmings and Robinson.

CHAPTER FIFTEEN

Ford pulled up at the red-and-white-striped barrier pole across the roadway entering Larkhill Barracks. The uniformed guard, carrying a rifle across his chest, came round to the driver's side.

'We're here to see Colonel Hemmings,' Ford said.

Charlie leaned across him and showed the soldier her SIB ID card in its black leather wallet. The guard screwed his face up as if she'd shoved dogshit under his nose.

'He still needs a temporary ID, ma'am,' he said, then looked back at Ford. 'Unless you've got an MOD 90, sir?'

'That's the official army ID form,' Charlie said. 'No, he doesn't, Private, so hurry up and sort him out, would you?'

With a nod, and a muttered, 'Ma'am,' he beckoned Ford into the guard house where he took a photo and printed out a form.

Back inside the Discovery with his new ID, Ford waited for the guard inside the red-brick guardhouse to raise the barrier.

'Friendly type,' he said, driving under the pole.

'You get used to it. They hate the red hats even more. Call them monkeys.'

Ford followed Charlie's directions, winding around the perimeter road to the administration block where the colonel had his office.

Charlie led Ford into the reception area. A civilian behind the low counter raised his eyebrows in enquiry.

'Yes, ma'am? Can I help you?'

'Is the colonel in?' Charlie asked brightly.

He looked momentarily flustered. 'He is, but he left instructions not to be disturbed.'

'We won't take up much of his time. Come on,' she said to Ford before striding off towards a set of double doors with circular reinforced glass windows cut into them.

The passageway reminded Ford strongly of Bourne Hill. In fact, of every police station he'd ever set foot in. Institutional grey-green carpet of some hard-wearing, bristly-looking fibres. Off-white walls. Wood-framed, glassed-in noticeboards inside which were pinned health and safety posters and information about various rules and regulations.

Charlie stopped outside a brown wooden door which bore the words Col. S. Hemmings, CO.

She turned to Ford and smiled brightly. 'Ready?'

He nodded. She seemed on edge. He was not. Hemmings could be difficult but that was all. He held no power over Ford. Charlie knocked twice and pushed the door open. Ford followed her in and stood to one side as she closed the door behind her.

Hemmings was at his desk, scrutinising a map. Beside him, leaning over and stabbing a bony finger at it, was Major Robinson. Both looked up as Charlie and Ford crossed the eight feet of blue carpet between the door and the desk.

Major Robinson straightened and regarded Ford with a look that signalled amusement: a slight upcurve to her mouth that wasn't quite a smile, and eyes that narrowed just a fraction. As if to say, *Well, this should be interesting.*

Hemmings scowled at Ford but then turned the full force of his glare on Charlie. 'What the hell do you mean by barging in here uninvited, Miss Daniels?'

Ford supposed the form of address was appropriate; he could hardly imagine Hemmings being anything other than one hundred per cent correct. But it sounded odd. Diminishing, somehow.

'DI Ford and I were just out at Imber, Colonel. We've found forensic evidence in the Baghdad Marriott that indicates it's where Private Padley was first attacked.'

Hemmings leaned back and folded his arms. 'Yes, word has reached me of your new . . .' He paused. 'Theory. I gather you now believe she didn't kill herself.'

'You gather correctly, Colonel,' Ford said. 'She was murdered. Someone calling themselves J wrote to her, telling her to meet him at the Marriott at midnight on Saturday. We found blood spatter on the wall. I think she was dragged from there to the crossroads where she was killed.'

Hemmings's face darkened, just as the sky had over Imber an hour or so earlier. Perhaps sensing that her boss was about to lose it, Major Robinson stepped in.

'What exactly is it you want?'

'I want you to suspend tonight's exercise while I get a full forensics team out there,' Ford said. 'We need to go through that building in detail and investigate all the other structures.'

Hemmings barked out a short, mirthless laugh. 'Do you really? Well, as I think I may have mentioned at our first meeting, I have my orders, just as you do, Inspector. And mine involve getting a thousand infantrymen' – a beat – 'and women combat-ready before the twenty-first. At which point they, and I, will be leaving this green and pleasant land for the slightly more threatening environs of northern Somalia.'

Ford caught a movement to his left. Charlie had looked down at the carpet. Hemmings took a deep breath, but only to refuel for the second part of his speech.

'And even if I didn't have my orders, I wouldn't throw away the chance at putting my boys through the final stage of their training so a bunch of overgrown chemistry students in white romper suits can spend a week picking up shell casings with tweezers.'

Ford sighed. What was it about brass hats? Starkey and Hemmings ought to shack up together. They'd make the perfect couple. The thought made him smile.

'There's nothing funny about it,' Hemmings said, clearly only partway through his peroration. 'So, no, I won't be postponing anything. You've got until . . .' He looked at Robinson.

'Eighteen hundred hours, sir.'

Hemmings eyeballed Ford. A blue vein was visible beneath the thin white skin at his left temple. 'There you are, then. You've got until six this evening and then I want your people gone,' he said. 'Unless they fancy getting a few live rounds up their arses, in which case tell them they can stay as long as they like.'

Ford regarded the man seated in front of him. Was he hiding something? Hoping that tonight's activity would remove any remaining evidence of the crime? Covering for somebody he knew was implicated in Rachel's murder? Or for himself?

Stranger things had happened. But he could see he wouldn't get anywhere like this. Locking horns with Hemmings would produce what he already had: a stand-off. And by the time he'd negotiated the tortuous corridors of power that connected civilian law enforcement, the courts and the army, the exercise would have finished anyway and the troops would be heading south, way out of his reach.

'Sorry,' Hemmings said, regarding Ford with a quizzical frown. 'Was there something else?'

'No. Thank you, Colonel.'

Hemmings smiled triumphantly. 'Major, would you escort Miss Daniels and DI Ford to their vehicle, please? Then come back and let's knock this bloody plan on the head.'

Outside in the car park, Ford walked back to the Discovery with Charlie and Major Robinson flanking him. He felt like a prisoner being escorted to the cells.

'Inspector Ford,' Major Robinson said as they reached the mud-spattered 4x4.

He turned. 'Yes?'

'He's not as bad as he seems. He just feels the weight of tradition very keenly.'

'As far as I understand, he doesn't *come* from a tradition.'

She offered a tight smile. 'That's what I mean. Steve hasn't had the smooth passage through life some of his brother – and sister – officers have had,' she said. 'He feels he's had to earn the right to climb each rung on the ladder. It's made him, I would say, somewhat conservative in his outlook.'

Ford shrugged. 'His outlook is none of my business, but he's obstructing my investigation and that's a problem.'

'What can I do to help?'

'Won't that rub your CO up the wrong way?'

'Let me deal with that.'

Ford paused for a moment. She'd offered him an olive branch. He wanted to get a good strong grip on it. 'Rachel was murdered on MOD land. Miles from anywhere. The chances of her killer being a civilian are tiny,' he said, looking sideways at Charlie.

'Ford's right,' she said. 'Even those who know about Imber wouldn't have the resources to trick a soldier into going out there in the middle of the night.'

Major Robinson frowned. 'You're saying it was a soldier?'

Ford shrugged. 'Or a civilian member of staff working on-base. That's going to mean we'll need to interview personnel here at Larkhill. Anything you can do to smooth our path would be welcome.'

She nodded. 'Leave it with me. But in future' – she gave Charlie a hard stare – 'probably best to come through me rather than bearding Steve in his office. I mean, for God's sake, what were you thinking?'

'Sorry, Major. It won't happen again.'

Major Robinson nodded then turned on her heel and marched back to the admin building and her meeting with Hemmings.

'What *were* you thinking?' Ford asked when they were out of the camp and driving back to Salisbury.

'He's an arsehole. A very senior arsehole, but an arsehole all the same. Luckily for me my badge means I don't have to take orders from him.' Charlie turned in her seat to look at him. 'This is a murder investigation, Ford. We can't let the brass get in our way.'

He heard it then. The enthusiasm of a detective investigating her first murder. He knew the feeling. And he'd seen it with younger officers in his own team.

'It is, you're right. But speaking as one maverick to another, will you let me give you a word of advice?'

'Go ahead.'

'It pays to keep powerful people onside. If Hemmings does have the power to hinder our investigation, then he also has the power to help it. I'd rather have him working with us, or at least neutral, than against us.'

'Fair enough. Sorry,' she said. 'It's just, like I said earlier, I've never worked on a full-blown murder investigation before.'

He smiled. 'Don't be. I enjoyed the sound of bayonets clashing. And for once neither belonged to me.'

◆ ◆ ◆

Ford left the office at five, taking his policy book and all the documents generated by the investigation so far. He read them all at the kitchen table, breaking at seven for a ham sandwich and a beer.

He'd been checking his phone every few hours while Sam had been away. Apart from the abseiling photo, Sam had maintained radio silence. A good sign. If he was too busy to text that meant he was having fun. And no texts from teachers meant no accidents.

At eight, he closed the final document and leaned back in his chair, rolling his head and massaging the base of his neck. He thought that if he had a dog, now would be the moment he'd take it out for a walk through the darkened streets.

He didn't have a dog, so he went out alone. With the moon rising in the east, casting a silvery light over the quiet suburban road, Ford felt his thoughts settling.

The face of the murdered girl swam into view. Her eyes were closed and her mouth suggested a smile was never far away.

The Victorians believed a murder victim's eyes retained the image of their killer. Debunked shortly after it was proposed, the idea nevertheless retained a hold on the popular imagination well into the twentieth century. What would Rachel's retinas reveal if optography – the pseudoscience of photographing the victim's retinas – actually worked?

I'm looking into the face of someone I know. A soldier from my unit, or the wider battalion. A friend. A family member. A lover. And then the image snaps to black as I am hurled or pushed backwards with enough force to knock me cold, splashing my blood on to the walls of the Baghdad Marriott.

He would find her killer. He would deliver justice for Rachel. And nobody, not Martin Peterson, not ACC Starkey, not Colonel Hemmings would stop him.

CHAPTER SIXTEEN

Ford spent Sunday morning revising his strategy for the investigation. He sketched out new lines of enquiry, additional avenues he might want to explore, permissions and additional resources he'd need. All the details that would ensure the investigation progressed as smoothly and as fast as possible.

Sam's coach was due at 3.00 p.m. Ford's phone had buzzed with a series of texts from about lunchtime, informing him of their progress back from Wales. After a snatched lunch of beans on toast and a mug of strong tea, he wandered round the house, unable to settle.

He'd been trying to ignore a background thrum of anxiety ever since Sam left for the climbing trip, and the case had been keeping him so busy he'd been able to sideline it most of the time. But now, just minutes before he was to be reunited with Sam, the tension bubbled up, leaving him feeling short of breath and on the edge of panic. But this was all wrong, wasn't it? Sam had made it through the trip unscathed. He hadn't fallen from a crag. He hadn't broken a bone. Or worse. Ford's world hadn't ended in a short, awkward text from a teacher. So why the butterflies?

He went upstairs and plugged his guitar into the amp, then switched it off again before the valves had even started glowing. He checked his watch. He still had ninety minutes before he could reasonably set off to collect Sam. On an impulse, he left the house, locked up and drove the two minutes to Hannah's house.

The last remaining roses around the front door had disappeared. The stems ended in fresh diagonal cuts where the blossoms had hung. Ford rang the doorbell.

Hannah's face materialised behind the frosted-glass panels in the upper portion of the door. He watched it move as she peered through the peephole. Then he heard the scrape of a safety chain being slid free. The door opened wide. Hannah smiled out at him. She was simply dressed in a pastel blue sweater of some soft-looking wool over indigo jeans.

'Hello, Henry. What are you doing here?' She frowned and tutted in irritation. 'I'm sorry. What I meant to say was, how lovely. Come in.'

She held the door wide and he stepped over the threshold.

'I'm at a loose end,' he said, following her into the kitchen. 'Sam's due back at three and I can't seem to settle.'

'I'll make us some tea. Or coffee?' she added, eyebrows raised.

'Tea's fine, thanks.'

While Hannah busied herself filling the kettle and spooning leaf tea into a white ceramic pot with a bamboo handle, Ford took the opportunity to look around. He'd not been in her house before and couldn't resist giving in to his natural curiosity, which his profession had sharpened to a fine edge.

As he'd expected, her kitchen was neat, orderly and spotlessly clean. She'd limited the palette to just a couple of shades: a soft cream and a pale duck-egg blue. The effect was restful. He knew she didn't like strong colours and even smells, so the muted effect no doubt helped her stay focused and relaxed. He wished it would have the same effect on him.

Once the tea was poured, Hannah sat opposite him. 'Why are you feeling anxious?' she asked before sipping her tea.

'I don't know. I was hoping you might be able to shed some light for me.'

Hannah pursed her lips. 'Well,' she said, 'Sam wasn't in any real danger before. As I told you, the chances of his having any kind of accident at all, let alone a fatal one, were millions to one against. But now that you perceive the danger to have passed, it would be logical to assume your anxiety levels would have dropped.'

'That's where I'd got to. But clearly nobody told my gut.'

'It wouldn't have been able to hear you anyway. Because it doesn't have ears,' she said, with a perfectly straight face.

It was getting harder and harder to tell when Hannah was joking and when her Asperger's was leading her into stating the obvious. He thought it was a good sign. She'd said a couple of times how she felt she'd discovered a family at Bourne Hill and that had helped her to relax. He'd stopped asking about her background, having sensed early on she'd rather keep that part of her life separate. But he wondered whether her real family hadn't been so accepting of her condition as they might have been.

Then she cracked up, laughing loudly and making the wine-glasses on the dresser ring. 'That was good, wasn't it? My joke? Because, you see, the gut, or to be more specific, the organ comprising the small and large intestine, really doesn't have ears.'

'It was great, Wix. You'll be doing stand-up next.'

She shook her head. 'I don't think I will. My job is far too demanding.'

'That was my attempt at a joke,' he said, smiling to undercut the correction.

'Oh. Well, it was a good one. But here's an interesting fact about the gut, Henry. You'll love this. Well, I hope you will. It's interesting anyway,' she said, frowning slightly. 'Eighty to ninety per cent of the messages between your brain and your gut travel *from* the gut *to* the brain. It's talking to your brain. So even if it can't listen, it can speak.'

'What do you think mine is trying to tell me?'

'I think it's saying' – she adopted a comically deep voice – '"Oh, Henry, I am worried Sam will come back changed. He is growing up and becoming more independent, and soon he will not need me so much. Then what will I do?"'

Ford felt a prickle behind his eyes. He looked at the long back garden beyond the diamond-leaded window and tried to swallow down a lump that had formed in his throat.

'That was very perceptive, Wix,' he said, irritated by the thickening of his voice.

She beamed. 'Thank you!' Then, frowning again, she said, 'You mean it? That was actually a helpful insight? You're not just being kind?'

'Yes, it was,' Ford said, smiling. Hannah was more aware of how other people related to each other than she realised. Maybe her training in psychology had helped. 'He's sixteen, for God's sake. My grandad had been working for two years by that age.'

'What about your father? Did he leave school early, as well?'

'No. He went to university and became a lecturer.'

'I've noticed that you never talk about him. Why is that?'

Ford took a mouthful of tea. He counted Hannah among his friends: she deserved the truth.

He sighed. 'I've never told anyone in Salisbury about this. But you've helped me start to move past Lou's death so I owe you an honest answer. My father was an alcoholic.' Ford swallowed, aware of a painful obstruction in his throat and the threat of tears. 'He was abusive towards my mum. And me, from time to time, though he reserved most of his spite for her,' he said. Unpleasant memories flooded his mind. The relentless criticism of his mother's appearance, cooking, shopping habits, even the way she pruned the shrubs in their back garden. 'Nowadays they call it coercive control, but back then there was no word for it. He was just a total bastard. She left him, in the end, when the control turned violent.'

Hannah's forehead wrinkled and her mouth turned down. 'I am so sorry. Should I not have asked you about him?'

He stretched out a hand and briefly squeezed hers where it was resting on the table. She flinched slightly.

He withdrew his hand. 'It's fine. Of course you should have done. You weren't to know.'

'Do you see him now at all?'

Ford shook his head and finished his tea. 'I can't. He died five years ago.'

The information seemed to satisfy Hannah. These sorts of statements acted like the ends of songs, he'd noticed. A natural point to switch topics. She was as likely to start talking about blood spatter or gunshot residue as keep worrying at the subject that had fascinated her just a few moments earlier. As happened now.

'I managed to investigate the house signposted Baghdad Marriott,' she said. 'I took pictures of the blood spatter but I'm afraid I didn't have time to reconstruct the attack in detail. They literally escorted me off the premises. With guns!'

'What could you tell from the blood stains on the wall?'

'It was medium-velocity impact spatter. Caused when Rachel's head came into contact with the masonry.'

'How fast would that be?'

'Technically, MVIS is when force is applied at 1.5 to 7.62 metres per second. I measured the droplets at an average diameter of 1.5 mm. That's at the upper end of the range, indicating the higher speed. It's characteristic of wounds sustained from stabbings or beatings.'

'She was either kneeling or falling,' Ford said. 'If she was kneeling, her attacker must have grabbed her and slammed her backwards against the wall.'

Hannah nodded. 'Probably by gripping her around the front of the head.'

'But there were no bruises on her face consistent with that grip.'

'No. And I'm sure she would have reacted by grabbing her assailant's arms, leading to a struggle and either defensive injuries or more bruising when he overcame her.'

The scenario simply didn't ring true. Ford had already decided Rachel must have been upright to start with, but it was good to have Hannah confirm it. He saw the murder with another detail filled in, as if in a mental director's cut. Rachel had been standing, facing her attacker.

'Did she fall or was she pushed?' he asked.

'Pushed. I'm ninety-five per cent sure.'

'Because?'

'To stand any chance at all of sustaining that sort of injury from a fall, a person would need to be rigid at the point of impact. But that's not how people fall,' Hannah said. 'They stagger, they stumble, they put their arms out behind them, leading to the classic double broken wrist injury.'

'Right, so the attacker shoves her. With enough force to propel her backwards. She goes over, or trips, and her head accelerates in a downwards arc before meeting the breeze blocks.'

'That's what my measurements would suggest.'

Ford was happy to take Hannah's word for it. She might have used the word 'suggest' in an effort to be diplomatic, but the look in her eyes told him she had no doubts on the matter.

Defence barristers weren't always so accommodating. They enjoyed nothing better than trying to trip up an expert witness on a technical point. Ford wanted to lock every stage of the investigation down tight. He felt he had to push her.

'Just for the sake of argument,' he said, '*could* she have been kneeling?'

Hannah nodded. 'She could. But now you need to make a second assumption. That there were two people there besides Rachel. One to force her to her knees, probably at gunpoint, and the other to propel her backwards hard enough to achieve the required impact velocity. If it was just one person with a gun, I think she'd have tried to take it off them. You're back to defensive injuries.'

'And a third assumption,' Ford said. 'That they'd kept a firearm back from the exercise. I can't see that happening. The army are paranoid about checking them in and out. Can't have a squaddie going AWOL with a machine gun in Salisbury on a Saturday night, can we?'

Hannah smiled. 'That would look bad, I suppose.'

'What's your interpretation of the letter?'

'Rachel trusted J. I would say they enjoyed a sexual relationship,' she said. 'And it was therefore natural that she would agree to the meeting, and the slightly odd conditions.'

Ford nodded. This was far from a straightforward case, and yet they had most of the ingredients they needed to solve it. The body. The murder weapon. The scene of the crime.

As for the motive, it looked like the oldest one in the book to Ford: sex. A partner unable to face the fact they were being dumped. A jealous ex, enraged at being supplanted. Or a thwarted suitor. In all three cases, the murderer's thought process was flashing at him in ten-foot-tall neon letters: *'If I can't have you, nobody can.'*

He sighed. Why couldn't people move on?

CHAPTER SEVENTEEN

Ford's phone buzzed at 2.55 p.m.

just coming into Salisbury

He told Hannah he had to go and arrived at the coach station ten minutes later. Across the wide, empty tarmac apron he saw a few other Chequers parents waiting for their offspring.

He could have walked over to join them, make small talk and stamp his feet in the cold. He chose to stay in the Discovery and the residual warmth from the heater. There he could think through the next set of actions he needed to complete.

He wanted as many bodies as he could lay his hands on conducting interviews on base. And he wanted to reinterview the family, separately if possible.

Then there was the limited forensic evidence. The fragment of wood Hannah had pulled from the neck wound might yield a valuable clue, if it could be traced back to its origins at the killer's home. His hope – forlorn, he knew – was that the murderer might have caught the blade on a piece of domestic furniture before going out to meet Rachel and, on a routine search, they'd match the fresh cut to the sample. Yeah, right. Because that sort of gold-plated luck was *always* falling into DIs' laps.

He also wanted CCTV footage from any cameras on the approach routes to Imber between 10.00 p.m. and 3.00 a.m. the previous Saturday. They might have caught the killer either driving towards the village, or leaving after murdering Rachel. He knew it was a long shot. There were very few villages within five miles of Imber. Even those might not have cameras.

Which meant that by the time they'd widened the circle far enough to encompass CCTV cameras on main roads or the centres of the surrounding towns like Salisbury, Andover or Warminster, the number of vehicles would be huge. Most would be driven by innocent people going about their business. To find out who was who, they'd have to trace, interview and eliminate – TIE – thousands of motorists. And he simply didn't have the time.

Victimology held the key. He was sure of it. If he could unpick the threads of Rachel's life, he would find not only the specifics of the motive, but the identity of her killer.

His thoughts were interrupted by the distant groan of a diesel engine and the hiss of air brakes. He looked up to see a silver and green coach executing a wide circle and then coming to a stop in the centre of the parking area.

He climbed out and locked the doors then wandered over to stand with the other parents, nodding at a couple he knew. He looked at the coach, from which grubby-looking teenagers were spilling, grinning, chatting, checking their own and each other's phones and pointedly ignoring their parents.

Sam was standing in the centre of a group of mostly gangly boys. Ford held up his hand in a half-wave. Sam looked over, nodded, then turned back to his friends.

Was this how it was going to be from now on? Ford reduced to the role of chauffeur: useful for lifts, but unworthy of so much as a smile? He knew the thought wasn't fair on Sam. It wasn't cool to wave to your 'daddy'. Anyone doing so would be teased mercilessly by the others. Best to let him make his way over in his own time. They could talk later.

Sam and his best friend Josh had reached the front of the queue to retrieve their bags from the belly of the coach. The driver was dragging out rucksacks, wheeled suitcases and holdalls and depositing them, none too gently, on the tarmac.

They came staggering over to Ford, heads turned inwards, chatting away more like long-lost friends than boys who'd just spent a week in each other's company.

'All right, lads?' he asked as they arrived.

'Yep,' Sam said.

'Hi, Henry,' Josh said.

'Here,' Ford said, grabbing two of the bags, 'I'll take those. Let's stow these and we can get going.'

Sam and Josh maintained a ceaseless conversation that consisted entirely of anecdotes from the trip. Ford smiled at the way they asked each other, 'What about when . . . ?' And 'Do you remember that time . . . ?' As if somehow they might have missed a clearly hilarious event both had witnessed first-hand.

Outside the Pitts' house, Ford parked and helped Josh up the path to the front door with his luggage.

Josh rang the doorbell.

'Haven't you got a key?' Ford asked.

'Yeah, but I lost it somewhere.'

The door opened. Miles Pitt stood there, dressed down in a baggy forest-green jumper and rust-coloured cords. He smiled at his son, who was virtually the same height, and ruffled his hair.

'Hello, mate. Good trip?'

'Great. What's for tea? I'm starving,' Josh said, squeezing round his father and heading for the kitchen.

'Beef stew,' Miles called before turning back to Ford. 'Coffee? A beer?'

Ford looked over his shoulder at Sam and beckoned to him. 'Coffee, please.'

In the kitchen, large, untidy, smelling deliciously of slow-cooked meat, Josh made himself and Sam huge lopsided sandwiches of ham and cheese and grabbed cans of Coke from the fridge. Then the boys disappeared off to Josh's room, no doubt to watch videos they'd taken on the trip.

Eleanor Pitt arrived in the kitchen from the garden, pulling off a pair of well-worn leather gloves. She pushed her floppy fringe out of her eyes and came forward to kiss Ford on both cheeks.

While Miles made coffee, she sat at the table opposite Ford.

'Thanks for bringing Josh home,' she said.

He smiled. If he drove their son to and from every school trip, prom, speech day and off-site visit, he couldn't repay even a fraction of what he owed the Pitts.

They'd done so much to help him raise Sam, simply by being there and having Sam round or for overnight stays whenever Ford's duties kept him at work. And when his grief had threatened to overwhelm him in the early days, there had been plenty of late-night drinking sessions where he'd ended up sobbing on Eleanor's soft shoulder while Miles sat beside him, saying nothing, just being there.

'He said he's lost his key,' Ford said, bringing himself back to the present.

She smiled, revealing crooked teeth. 'If by "lost" you mean on the floor of his bedroom under a pair of boxers, yes, he did.'

Miles placed three cups of coffee on the table and pushed one towards Ford. Ford took a sip. The coffee was excellent. Strong and richly flavoured. He thought of Sandy's likely response to a cup of Miles's Java. The thought made him smile.

'What?' Miles asked, grinning.

'My boss would probably ask you to marry her if she tasted your coffee.'

Eleanor's eyebrows elevated. 'Really! Bigamy's still a crime in this country, isn't it? Or did I miss something?'

Ford laughed. 'Sandy'd just style it out.'

'I don't know, darling,' Miles said, winking at Ford, 'it could be an advantage being married to a top copper. We'd probably never have to worry about speeding tickets again.'

'Oh, right, we're back to that again, are we?' she asked, feigning outrage. 'Honestly, Henry, I get one speeding ticket . . .'

Miles spread his hands wide. 'Am I being unreasonable? Eleanor was doing ninety on the A36. She was lucky they didn't impound the car and make her walk home.'

Over Eleanor's laughter, Ford shook his head. 'Don't ask me to comment. Traffic's not my department.'

Eleanor laid her hand across Ford's. Her face had turned serious. 'How was Sam? Was he OK?'

Ford nodded. He pulled out his phone and showed her, then Miles, the abseiling photo. 'That was it until the one telling me they were arriving back. I think it's safe to say he had a good time.'

Miles pushed his sandy hair away from his eyes. 'We had a single text from Josh on the first night. One word. *Awesome.*'

'It's all they talked about on the way home,' Ford said. 'You'd think they were reminiscing over something that happened years ago instead of yesterday. No, "Hi, Dad, how was your week, thanks for coming to collect me."'

Eleanor pulled a face. 'I'm afraid you've reached the stage where you're just Dad's Taxi.'

Miles nodded. 'Yep. Shortly to be promoted to CEO of the bank of Mum and Dad.' He coloured instantly, the words hanging in the air between them.

'Oh, Miles,' Eleanor said.

Ford shook his head. 'Come on, it's fine. I can cope. Really. You guys saved my life. And it still is the bank of Mum and Dad in our house. Lou's life insurance is going to see Sam through university and out the other side.'

'Sorry all the same, mate,' Miles said.

Ford smiled at his oldest friend. 'Really, it's fine.'

Half an hour later, Ford called up the stairs to Sam that it was time to go. He'd told Miles and Eleanor that his son had enjoyed the climbing trip, but he wanted – needed – to hear it from Sam in person. Had climbing brought up any painful memories, or half-buried fears?

In the months and years after Lou's death, Sam had woken regularly in the grip of night terrors. Ford would hear sobs, or occasionally screams, and find Sam wandering along the hallway, crying or shouting, eyes staring, arms stretched out in front of him. Held captive in that freakish zone between sleep and wakefulness. Able to control his limbs, navigate the house in the dark, even speak. Yet clearly in the grip of a terrifying vision that owed nothing to reality and everything to the trauma he'd only partially understood or processed.

Ford closed his front door behind him. He'd bought steaks the previous day and now put some chips in the oven.

Twenty minutes later, while Sam laid the table, he grilled the steaks with a little olive oil and sea salt, adding the chips and some fried onions to the two plates he'd just warmed in the oven. As a gesture to the idea of healthy eating, he microwaved a plastic bowl of peas and set it down on the table beside the tomato ketchup, mustard and horseradish sauce.

It never failed to amaze Ford how Sam could eat an eight-ounce steak as if it were no more substantial than a slice of factory white bread. Hardly pausing to speak, Sam wielded his steak knife with a butcher's skill until all that remained was a puddle of pinkish

141

meat juices. He began spearing the chips up, first dipping them in the ketchup on the side of his plate.

Choosing his moment, Ford looked across the table at Sam. 'How was it, then?'

Sam nodded and swallowed his mouthful. 'Yeah, good.'

'Is that it?'

'What do you want me to say?'

'I don't know. You seemed pretty excited when you were chatting with Josh in the car. What was the best bit?'

'It was all good, OK? Jesus! Is this, like, an interrogation or something?'

Ford frowned. This wasn't like Sam at all. Sure, he'd been through stroppy phases, but the last few weeks had been smooth sailing. Ford had even begun to hope, tentatively, that Sam was emerging from the 'teenage tunnel', especially now he was in sixth form. A sixth form, moreover, that had only that year decided to admit that rare, exotic species: girls. He'd seen a couple emerge from the coach, though Sam had studiously ignored them.

'No, it's not an interrogation, or, *like*, anything,' Ford said, regretting mocking Sam's speech patterns as soon as that ironic echo passed his lips. He ploughed on anyway. 'It's just I thought maybe you'd like to talk about it. I was worried about you. You know that.'

'Yeah, I know. But I'm here, OK? I survived. Unlike Mum.'

'What?'

'You heard me. I just can't see how it could have happened. You told me she was a good climber. Yet somehow she just breaks her leg and then drowns. How is that even possible?'

Ford looked at his son. Was this it, then? The moment when he explained what had really happened seven years earlier at the foot of Pen-y-Holt? He tried to weigh up the risks and rewards of being honest. But time was running out, and he had to say something even if it risked ruining everything he'd so painstakingly built between them. Maybe he could tell Sam a cleaned-up version of his role in Lou's death.

He opened his mouth. 'Sam, there's something . . .'

His phone rang. Frowning with irritation he glanced at the screen. Sam folded his arms and rolled his eyes.

The caller was Sandy. He had to take it.

Ford looked up to apologise, but Sam was already on his feet and striding away from him, plugging in his earbuds.

'Evening, boss,' he said.

'I'm sorry to bother you at home, Henry, but you need to hear this. Major Robinson just called me. Apparently there's been some almighty snafu at the Ministry of Defence. The Black Watch aren't leaving for Somalia on the twenty-first after all.'

Ford felt the relief wash through him. He'd have more time to work the case.

'That's fantastic,' he said, then immediately wondered why Sandy had called him on a Sunday evening with something that could surely have waited until the following day.

'No, it's the opposite of fantastic,' she said.

And suddenly Ford knew why she'd called him. 'They're going earlier, aren't they?'

'They're flying out on the sixteenth. You've got five days less.'

Ford ended the call. He wanted to go and talk to Sam, but instead fetched his laptop and opened it at the kitchen table. The living could wait; the dead were calling.

In one of Ford's long periods of wakefulness that night, he got out of bed and walked along the passageway to his music room. He lifted the Stratocaster out of its case and settled it across his knee.

He cradled its curved wooden body in his arms and looked out of the window across the fields. A stiff wind was blowing, throwing shifting stripes of moon shadow across the lawn from the trees at the far end of the garden.

Hannah had been right about his feelings towards Sam. He was on the cusp of adulthood. Soon he'd be gone, to a job or university, or maybe the other side of the world. And then what would Ford do?

But that wasn't all of it, he realised. There was a deeper source of anxiety about Sam's return from the climbing trip. And at supper that evening, he'd hinted at it.

What if Sam wanted to keep climbing? He'd learn more, and then he'd start asking questions. What equipment they'd used. Who'd planned the route. Who'd pulled a bloody great rock out of the stack and broken his wife's femur.

The more questions Sam asked, the more lies he'd force Ford to tell him. *That* was where the fear was coming from. That Sam would discover the truth. Lou had told Ford to leave her. And Ford had done what he was told.

He stayed in the music room until five in the morning, when he crept back to bed and tried for an hour's sleep before he had to get up for work.

CHAPTER EIGHTEEN

Ford left for Bourne Hill at eight the next morning, weighed down with a sense of unease caused by his conversation with Sam the previous evening.

Sam didn't normally surface much before half past on school days, especially now his slimmed-down A level timetable gave him free periods all over the place. Ford sent a text:

Let's talk tonight

Later, at his desk at Bourne Hill, he started working through a backlog of paperwork. Bored after five minutes, he called Hannah's tree expert at Reading University. Hoping Merilyn Goldstein spent her days doing nothing but waiting for police officers to request help, he asked how long she thought it might take her to analyse the specimen. The answer was depressing. The best she could do was to have the results back to him in three weeks' time. He thanked her and ended the call.

He left his office and found Charlie, who was talking to Jools by her desk.

'Briefing in ten minutes,' Ford said. 'Morning Jools, morning, Charlie.'

'Morning, guv,' they chorused.

On his walk through Major Crimes, he stopped at Mick's desk and sat on one corner. 'How's it going?'

Mick nodded. 'We've been interviewing at Larkhill, but it's like pulling teeth, H. Those bloody squaddies just clam up. We get one-word answers to everything,' he said in a complaining tone. 'Even if you ask them an open question about what Rachel was like, you get "OK", "Sound" or "Reliable".' He slapped his forehead theatrically. 'What am I saying? I did get a longer answer. In full, "One of the lads."'

Ford offered a sympathetic smile. Jools and Charlie had both warned him they'd be lucky to get much out of the ordinary soldiers. Mistrust of authority ran as deep as their training to obey it. And Ford and his sergeants weren't even part of the chain of command.

'How about at home?' he asked, dropping his voice, though nobody was within fifteen feet of Mick's desk at that moment.

'We had the financial settlement last Thursday. No big surprises. Kirsty gets the house and the car. I pay child support,' he said. 'All that's left now is the decree absolute, which I should get in a couple of weeks. After that, I'm a free man.'

Mick was clearly putting a brave face on it. He had a reputation as the hard man of Bourne Hill to maintain. But Ford could see the pain behind the DS's close-set brown eyes.

He clapped Mick on the shoulder, the closest to a gesture of friendship both men knew Mick would permit, and told him to be in the sugar cube for 9.30 a.m.

Olly was hunched over his keyboard, pounding away at the keys as if he meant to subdue them by brute force.

'Everything OK, Olly?' Ford asked.

'Morning, guv,' Olly said, leaning back and rolling his head on his shoulders. 'Just working through the CCTV footage. I thought we might get lucky and catch the killer driving out ahead of Rachel.'

'Any joy?'

'Not yet.'

'OK. Well, keep at it.'

Ford returned to his office. Wheels were turning. He had a good team working with him, including Charlie. He was sure he'd be able to pay a visit to the Padley family to tell them they'd arrested someone on suspicion of murdering their daughter. The only question was, when? The answer was straightforward. Before the sixteenth or not at all.

He knew it was murder, but ACC Starkey, Colonel Hemmings and Martin Peterson would still prefer him to abandon his investigation and agree with their suicide narrative. He wanted something more that he could add to the file to rebut their next attack. It was a diversion of precious resources, but one he felt was justified given the pressure he was under.

He jiggled the computer mouse to wake up his PC and called up the crime scene photos. He started going through them one by one, taking his time with each photo.

After looking at them the right way up, he flipped them vertically. Now every element was still present, but the temptation to focus on the familiar or expected vanished. He used the technique to spot unlikely connections and to see anomalies. Like the young soldier had said, *'Presence of the abnormal, absence of the normal.'*

Something about the fifth photo he looked at made him stop and peer closer at the screen.

Hannah had taken the photo from a low angle, from Rachel's right side. The knife in her hand was in the centre of the image, its blood-stained blade glinting in the pale light slanting across the village from east to west.

Suppose Rachel *had* taken the knife out to Imber? How had she carried it? In a pocket? Wrapped in newspaper? Just lying on the Corsa's passenger seat? In the boot? He rubbed the end of his nose. Even a civilian would take care of a hunting knife, especially one with a wicked edge. But a soldier? An infantry soldier? They'd keep it in a sheath, wouldn't they? Leather, or tough nylon. They were trained to look after their kit. It was drummed into them from day one.

So, if it was suicide, there ought to be a sheath.

He got up from his desk, went to the door and looked around for Jan. He saw her just returning from the coffee station. She had two mugs in her hand and a Tupperware box.

She looked up, caught his eye and smiled. 'Don't worry, guv. I was just coming to see you.'

She joined him in his office, setting down in front of him a mug bearing the logo of the local rugby club. He thanked her and took a sip while she unsnapped the four catches on the plastic storage box. She pushed it across to him.

He looked inside. It contained deep-brown chocolate brownies, their cracked tops dusted with icing sugar.

'You trying to fatten me up for Christmas?'

She tutted as she helped herself to a smaller piece. 'Chance would be a fine thing. If you ate a proper lunch now and again, I wouldn't need to, would I?'

He took a bite and groaned with pleasure. The intense hit of chocolate and the squidgy texture flooded his mouth with saliva.

He mumbled his appreciation, drawing a smile from Jan, who'd unfolded her reading glasses and perched them on her nose. She looked at him over the top of the frames, taking out a black notebook.

'What do you need?'

'When you searched Rachel's quarters, did you find a knife sheath at all?'

She shook her head. 'It's all in the log and my report. Just the things we talked about before.'

'What about her car?'

'Clean as a whistle. The jack, basic tools, some change in a little pouch for parking. Service book in a vinyl folder.'

He explained his thinking about the absence of a sheath refuting the suicide narrative.

'Nobody here thinks it was suicide,' she said, 'but I agree it'll help fend off the brass.'

She left him to his coffee and the brownie. He fancied he could feel his arteries hardening as he ate it. He spent the rest of the day pinned to his desk, reading and rereading the steady stream of documents crossing his desk as more interviews were conducted, more reports filed, more enquiries made.

By the end of the afternoon, he felt he was no further forward. He had everything except a suspect. He decided to go back to the beginning.

Why did people commit murder? The most common reasons were soured relationships, disputes over money or drugs, or turf wars where displays of brute force were being used depressingly frequently. Then there were the outliers: the motiveless stranger killings.

Out of all these, the first was the motive that struck Ford as the most probable in Rachel's case. But they'd failed to turn up any relationships at all, much less one that had gone south.

Was he ignoring the family when he should be looking straight at them? Had Rachel been a small child, he'd have interviewed both parents and the brother by now, quite possibly under caution. But the statistics said that parents almost never killed their adult offspring.

To hell with statistics! He realised he'd been ignoring the family, shattered as they were by the death of their daughter. It was time to remedy that oversight.

He called Kate Chisholm. Time for an update from his woman on the inside.

'Hi, guv, what's up?'

'What's happening with the family? How are they?'

'David's either out at work or in the pub. He comes home for his tea then goes out again. Rachel followed him into the Black Watch. He puts up a tough front, but I think secretly he was proud of her for that,' she said.

'What about Helen?'

'The doctor gave her some tablets. Tranquillizers, I assume. She's practically a zombie.' She dropped her voice to a low murmur. 'They're quite religious, did you know that?'

'I saw a religious painting on the wall, and Helen's quite fond of quoting the Bible.'

'Fond? I asked her if she'd read any good books lately. You know, just making conversation. And she said, "Kate, the only good book you need is *the* Good Book".'

Ford nodded. 'Sounds about right.'

'Hold on, guv. I'm at the house now, in the hall. I'll just pop out into the garden.' Ford listened to rustles and the sounds of a door being opened and closed.

Kate came back on the line. 'Sorry about that. I was chatting with Helen last night and she mentioned her church. I don't know whether you'd call it a sect or a cult, but it's a very strict Christian group,' she said.

'I met the pastor.'

'Simeon? Yeah, he's been round a couple of times since. Nice enough bloke, as far as it goes.'

'Which isn't very far.'

'They call themselves the New United Church of the True Holy Doctrine of Christ the Redeemer.'

'Bit of a mouthful.'

'Yeah. From what I understand, there've been a few splits down the years since it was founded in 1925.'

'Anything there relevant to the investigation?'

'Not sure. I tried to talk to David about it and he was very tight-lipped. But to be honest, he's pretty tight-lipped about everything,' she said.

'Keep me posted, OK? And remember what I said.'

'Big I, little s. I remember.'

He heard the humour in her voice.

'Sorry. No need?'

'Not really, guv.'

He ended the call and went to find Jools.

'Grab something warm, we're going out,' he said, shrugging a padded jacket on over his suit.

She stood, grabbing her messenger bag. 'Where are we going?'

'I want to show Rachel's photo around some of the pubs in Salisbury. Squaddies come in for a drink on Friday and Saturday nights.'

'Yeah. A drink, a curry and a punch-up for pudding,' she said, grinning.

'Maybe she got into it with a local who took it personally.'

'But how would they know about J?'

'Maybe we can find out. Come on.'

'There's over a hundred pubs in Salisbury, guv. Shouldn't we put a proper team on it?'

'Yes, and tomorrow I will. Right now, I just need to wear out some shoe leather. We'll start with the city centre pubs and see where we get to.'

Ford divided the city into half, using the east-west axis comprising Fisherton Street, Bridge Street, Silver Street, Butcher Row, Fish Row and Milford Street as the cut-off line. He took the streets themselves and everything to the south, leaving Jools with the north.

The route he'd chosen was known locally as the Yellow Brick Road. Any Friday or Saturday night you'd find the youth of the city, more likely looking for a brief sexual encounter than a wizard, parading from one end to the other. The boys, as groomed as Premiership footballers, showed off gym-built bodies in tight white T-shirts. The girls tried to outdo each other with the heights of their heels, and hemlines.

One cold night the previous year, Ford had realised he was getting old when he nudged Jools and pointed to a girl in a backless turquoise mini-dress that barely skimmed her arse and said, 'Look at her! She'll get a chill on her kidneys.' The memory of the look she had bestowed on him still made him cringe.

In each of the pubs he visited, nobody had seen Rachel drinking there, although a few drinkers and bar staff recognised her photo from the press conference. After trying seven, he called Jools and arranged to meet her back at Bourne Hill.

'Any joy?' he asked her, stirring a spoonful of instant coffee granules into each of two mugs.

She shook her head. 'Everyone knew who she was, and I could see that a couple of people really wanted to convince themselves that they had seen her, but honestly, guv? It was a bust.'

Ford returned to his office. Was it a good use of resources, putting more people on canvassing the pubs? He was already stretched tighter than a top E string with TIEing the military personnel. He decided to let it alone for now.

He got home at nine. Sam had texted to say he was staying over with Josh that night. The words were few and shorn of all emotional content, but Ford couldn't help reading resentment into the brief message.

He poked around in the fridge for something to eat. He made a sandwich of ham a day past its best-before date and some Cheddar from which he had to scrape a thin scrim of white stuff he convinced himself was harmless. He added a bottle of beer to a tray and carried it through to the sitting room where he turned on the TV and looked for a film to watch.

He spent half an hour searching, but he'd seen all the decent ones too recently to want to rewatch them. He moved on to the next level down. Everything from classic black-and-white thrillers to low-budget sci-fi whose casts – Nikki, Rolf, Shayla, Tawnee – sounded like porn stars. He started, rejected and backed out of three, giving up altogether when the first line uttered in the final film was clearly being read from an autocue.

With nothing else to do, and feeling that if he reread the case reports again he'd go mad, he retreated to his music room. He played for an hour, but then, eyelids drooping, realised he'd be better off using the time to sleep and hopefully recharge his batteries.

Sitting up in bed, he wondered if he should read a book for a bit. Something to drown out the demands of the case. The thought immediately sparked another. What had Helen Padley said to Kate Chisholm? *'The only good book you need is the Good Book.'*

They hadn't found a Bible among Rachel's pared-back possessions. She clearly had a different view of what constituted a good book to her mother.

Wondering if Rachel's choice of reading material would reveal something about her that was absent from their real-world research, he went online and downloaded *The Price of Salt* to his Kindle. While he waited for the patchy Wi-Fi in the house to deliver enough bandwidth for the book to download, he fell asleep.

CHAPTER NINETEEN

Ford's working day started in the worst way possible. His phone displayed a brief message:

Missed call: ACC Starkey.

There was also a single voicemail. He checked and when he saw the same name beside it, deleted it without listening and called Starkey back instead. He reached the ACC's secretary and after introducing himself found she was putting him straight through.

'What the bloody hell's all this I hear about you launching a murder investigation?' Starkey demanded.

'I don't know, sir. What have you heard?'

It was a provocative way to answer, Ford knew that. He didn't care.

Clearly ACC Starkey did.

'I'd watch my mouth if I were you, DI Ford,' he growled down the phone. 'Or I might just stuff a direct order down it.'

'Sorry, sir. Out of line.'

'Forget it. You're under pressure, I get it. But I thought I made myself perfectly clear at our little conflab last Tuesday.'

'Yes, you did, sir. And I think I did, too. If it was incontrovertibly a suicide, I'd policy it as such and close my investigation.'

'"Incontrovertibly"? That's a bloody big word for a DI. Keep it simple, Ford, I'm just a working-class lad from Manchester made good. I don't have the benefits of a private education.'

'Nor do I, sir. But, to keep it simple for you, Rachel Padley didn't top herself. She was murdered.'

Ford listened to the clicks and hisses on the line as Starkey paused before responding. Why were the brass hell-bent on closing him down? He had an unpleasant vision: middle-aged men in black or khaki uniforms, or maybe rose-pink cords and their grandfathers' tweed jackets, clinking cut-glass tumblers brimming with expensive cognac in the drawing room of some country house, discussing how best to keep order in the city.

'How can you be sure?' Starkey asked.

What should Ford do? Give Starkey chapter and verse on every piece of evidence, circumstantial and physical? Explain his hunch? Outline the lack of reasons for Rachel to kill herself?

'Evidence plus experience tells me it's murder, sir.'

Starkey adopted a wheedling tone. 'Look, Ford, come on. I get it. You're the star homicide detective. You call them the way you see them. I understand, truly I do,' he said. 'But surely you can see this is in nobody's interests. Why can't you accept things the way they are?'

Ford had to stop himself answering at once. Because yet again he felt that someone inside Bourne Hill was leaking information. Not Mick this time. A traditional copper to his socks, there was no way Mick would voluntarily tell a brass hat like Starkey anything.

But Peterson, on the other hand. He'd spill the beans on his wife's choice of underwear if he thought it would win him Brownie points with the ACC.

'I'm afraid you're going to have to trust my judgement on this one, sir,' he said. 'And as for its serving nobody's interests, respectfully, I have to disagree with you. It serves the family's interests. They've just lost their daughter and sister. And more importantly, it serves Rachel's interests. She's the victim here. And I need to deliver justice for her.'

'Fine. You get on your bloody white charger and round up the bad guys. But let me give you a little bit of friendly advice,' Starkey said. 'You've got a reputation as a good cop. Don't sacrifice it for a case as good as solved already.' He paused. 'I hear the Black Watch are off to Somalia in a couple of weeks.'

'That's right, sir.'

'I want it cleared by then, Ford. Cleared, or shelved. If you've got any fancy ideas about pissing off to Africa to carry on some kind of personal quest for justice, you can forget them. I've a budget to think of and it's like wrestling bloody polar bears, believe me.'

As soon as he got off the call, Ford dragged everyone back into the sugar cube.

He wasted no time. 'Listen up, I know you're all working hard. But I need to remind you that we've only got until dawn on Friday the sixteenth to make an arrest in the Rachel Padley murder,' he said. 'After that, the whole bloody battalion is on transport planes to Somalia. The ACC's putting me under pressure to wind it up by then whether we've found Rachel's killer or not.'

Over the sudden outbreak of chat, Ford raised his voice to be heard.

'Whatever you've got going on in your personal lives, can you put it on hold, please? I'll try to sort out more overtime with Sandy.'

He asked for updates from everyone with a specific responsibility. It made for a bleak twenty minutes. With a little help, Olly had identified 17,000 cars on the CCTV. Jan had returned to Rachel's quarters and literally reduced every item of furniture to its constituent parts without finding a sheath or scabbard of any kind.

Mick reported that of the hundred or so soldiers they'd interviewed so far, none had offered so much as a sniff of bad blood between Rachel and anyone else on base.

Sergeant Nat Hewitt had been coordinating uniforms showing Rachel's picture in the city centre pubs and those in the nearby barracks towns of Larkhill, Tidworth, Bulford and Ludgershall. She, too, had come up with nothing.

After the meeting, Ford headed straight to Sandy's office. The door was open so he went in and closed it behind him.

Sandy looked up from the sheaf of printed-out spreadsheets she was annotating with a red biro and raised an eyebrow. 'No coffee?'

'Sorry, guv, no time.'

'Got any suspects yet?' she asked.

'No. And that's the trouble. Even though we have the murder weapon, the body, the crime scene, the ID, everything, I keep hitting brick walls.'

'Bit like our victim. What about forensics?'

'We've got stuff, but it's all either in limbo with outside experts or only identifies Rachel.'

'I'm assuming you didn't come here just for a moan,' she said, staring at him.

'Of course not. I need more budget. For overtime, mainly.'

'Remind me what the category is?'

'It's a B.' Even as he said it, Ford knew what her likely response would be. As were the high-profile stranger murders. Cs were the straightforward but still tragic ones between spouses, or conducted in the glare of pub lights or outside a nightclub with dozens of witnesses.

'And I gave you how much?'

'Ten grand.'

She shook her head and tapped the report in front of her. 'I've been on this bloody budget all week. I'm sorry, H, there's just no way I can authorise more money,' she said. 'You'll just have to get it done in office hours. You're salaried, so you can spend as long on it as you like, but no more overtime. I'm sorry.'

He pasted a winning smile on his face. 'Is it worth me fetching you an extra-shot latte and an almond croissant from the cafe on the park?'

She smiled. 'Nice try.'

'I could wash your Merc for you?'

She laughed. 'Make those puppy eyes any bigger and I'll call for a dog-handler to take you away.'

Ford hit her with his other question. 'Once they go to Somalia, if Colonel Hemmings refuses to cooperate about returning a suspect, how would you feel about me going out there to bring him back in person?'

'Was that a serious question?'

'Yes, absolutely it was.'

'OK, Henry, let's work through this. One, as far as my limited knowledge of geopolitics goes, Somalia is a pretty dangerous place for Western civilians. Strike that, *any* civilians.' She held up her hand and began counting off more points on her fingers, each folding digit flashing a scarlet nail signalling *no*.

'Two, last time I checked, EasyJet don't fly to Mogadishu, so you'd have to get a military flight sorted, which would be prohibitively expensive. See earlier remarks about overtime. Three, even if you could get yourself out there, I'd have to take out an insurance policy, which *my* boss wouldn't authorise,' she said. 'Four, what if your suspect is up-country, or whatever the military call it? Are you going to jump into a tank and pursue him into a war zone?'

Ford waited for her to catch her breath. Her cheeks had flushed while she'd been talking.

'So you're saying it's a maybe,' he said.

She glared at him, though the corners of her mouth curved upwards. 'Tell you what. You ring up the Foreign Office and ask them what their advice is on travel to Somalia,' she said. 'If they say make sure you pack Factor 50 and a nice pair of Bermudas, come back and we'll discuss it.'

He stood. 'It was a worth a try.'

'Yes, it was. But that's it. I'm sorry. You'll just have to get a shift on. If it turns into a runner' – she ran her fingers through her hair – 'then we'll have to think again.'

CHAPTER TWENTY

Determined to speak to Sam that evening, Ford dragged himself away from his desk at just before six. He'd cook a nice meal and try to find a way to explain what had really happened at Pen-y-Holt.

He parked on the gravel at the front of the house and walked up to the front door. It started to rain, fat drops that slapped his face as he passed the low slate sign reading 'Windgather' by the door. He and Lou had named the house after the place in the Peak District where they'd had so much fun together learning to climb. Now it was a permanent reminder of his failure to save her life when she'd needed him.

Inside, he dumped his bag on the pew in the hall and called out to Sam. No reply. But that meant nothing. Sam listened to his music through earbuds. He went into the kitchen and assembled ingredients for dinner, pausing to text Sam. The reply pinged back in segments, interwoven with Ford's own messages:

u upstairs

ye

tea at 7

ok but not that hungry

it's burgers

we had chips in town

Ford shrugged. It was the occasion to talk, not the food, that concerned him. He and Lou had agreed early on that if and when they had kids they'd never make a big deal out of cleaning the plate, eating up or any of the emotional pressures their own parents had put on them as children.

Lou had never been a dieter as an adult, but she'd told Ford once that she veered uncomfortably close to anorexia as a sixteen-year-old girl. Their rule, devised spontaneously and parroted by Sam as he grew old enough to understand it, was a simple one. *'Eat when you're hungry. Stop when you're full.'*

However, Sam loved Ford's home-made burgers, and Ford was betting on securing at least a minimum willingness to open up if tempted by a fat, juicy half-pounder. He set a heavy skillet, blackened by many years of use, on to the hob.

Fifteen minutes later, he assembled two towering burgers: bun, meat, cheese, onions, lettuce leaf, tomato slices, gherkins. He balanced the top halves of the rolls on the garnish and took the finished burgers to the table.

'Sam!' he yelled up the stairs. 'Dinner's ready!'

For good measure, he texted again.

burgers on table

He put a glass beside Sam's plate, took a swig of his beer and waited. The smell of the food had him salivating like a dog on the wrong side of a fence from its dinner. But he waited just the same.

Three minutes later, he heard the clack as the latch on Sam's warped bedroom door gave, and then Sam's feet appeared at the top of the stairs that led into the kitchen.

He took them at speed, amazing Ford once again that he could perform this feat without falling.

He sat opposite Ford, then jumped up, fetched a carton of orange juice from the fridge, filled his glass and gulped down half of it.

Ford picked up his burger and managed to get his mouth around it. He took a bite and watched Sam. Slowly, Sam lifted his own burger and bit off a small mouthful.

'Is it OK?' Ford asked, mumbling around his own food.

'Mm, hmm. Good.'

Ford put his burger down. 'Look, about the other night—'

'It's fine, Dad. I know you did all you could to save Mum.' Suddenly Sam's lower lip started to tremble. He sniffed loudly and swiped a hand across his eyes. 'Dad, I'm frightened I'm forgetting her,' he moaned in a cracked voice. 'That's why I wanted to talk about the accident. At least it's something.'

Then he was crying, and Ford rushed around the table, knelt on the floor by his hip and hugged him fiercely. Maybe after all now wasn't the best time to explain how his father had left his mother to die.

'You won't forget her, Sam. I'll help. I'll tell you stories about her. And there are our photo albums,' he said. 'I know it's so twentieth century, but there are dozens of them upstairs. We could look at them together if you like. After tea?'

He felt some of the tension leave Sam's shoulders. He heaved a huge, shuddering breath and shook his head so that a couple of longer bits of hair flew out and flicked Ford in the eye.

'Hey! Careful, you'll have my eye out. You need a haircut! Smarten yourself up a bit!'

It was a gamble. Ford held his breath. But he'd made the right call.

Sam laughed. 'In your dreams,' he said. 'I'm growing it out.'

Ford got to his feet, ignoring the pain from his right knee where it had been in contact with the slate floor tiles. He returned to his side of the table.

'You don't have to finish your tea if you're not hungry,' he said.

Sam shook his head. He looked at Ford and smiled. Ford saw Lou again in that uneven tilt to Sam's mouth.

'No, it's great. I lied about the chips. I'm starving.'

Over the next five minutes, Ford watched Sam demolish the burger, pour himself a second glass of orange juice, then grab a tub of ice cream from the freezer and dig himself out a couple of scoops.

Spoon in hand, he raised his eyebrows at Ford. 'Mm? *You?*'

'No thanks, I'm stuffed.'

After clearing away the tea things, Ford led Sam upstairs to his office. Directing Sam to the leather chair, he grabbed a leather-bound photo album. He dragged over a stool upholstered in shiny red vinyl with the Fender logo screen-printed in white, and opened the cover.

'This is you, five minutes after Mum gave birth to you,' he began.

CHAPTER TWENTY-ONE

Ford read through some case documents before turning out his bedside light. He checked the time. Midnight. Not too late. And the evening with Sam had gone much better than he'd expected.

He really felt they'd made a breakthrough, able to talk about Lou in neither sentimental nor accusing tones. Ford had enjoyed it, too, paging through photos of the three of them at play parks, on holidays, larking about in the back garden, washing Izabella. He'd felt a little of his guilt leave him, too.

He closed his eyes and turned on to his side. Maybe things with Sam were going to work out. As he felt his limbs relax and grow heavy, he smiled to himself. He might not have to tell him what had happened at Pen-y-Holt after all.

He found he was looking down at the skull-like houses of Imber from the top of a towering limestone stack. Flashes of gunfire punctuated the shadows in the village like tiny yellow fireworks. He caught the tang of burned gunpowder.

In the high wind, the block he and Lou were standing on swayed back and forth, threatening to pitch them both off, down to the boulder-strewn road a thousand feet below. Gulls wheeled around their heads, screeching obscenities from cruelly curved yellow beaks, each dotted with a carmine drop of blood.

His stomach churned as he turned to Lou. 'We should tell him what happens here, darling. Sam has a right to know.'

'Now isn't the time,' she said. 'You need to protect him.'

Ford looked into those cornflower-blue eyes. 'But we can't just leave him hanging, darling. I mean, look at him.'

He leaned out over the drop and pointed down to where Sam was dangling at the end of a frayed rope, his boots spinning above empty air.

'Tell me,' Sam screamed up at Ford. 'Tell me!'

'He'll be fine,' Lou said. 'You should go.'

Charlie's head and shoulders appeared over the far edge of the rock. She wore camouflage fatigues, though the buttons on her tunic were undone, revealing her cleavage. Ford tried to avoid staring.

'You're wrong, Lou,' Charlie said, getting to her feet. 'Sam has a right to know what kind of man his father is.'

She drew a hunting knife from a sheath at her belt and took a step towards Lou.

'But I'm a good man,' Ford said, feeling his throat closing up until his words came out as a whisper. 'A good man.'

'I know,' Charlie said.

Then she sprang at Lou and swept the knife across her throat from right to left.

Ford turned away and leapt from the stack, screaming all the way down as Lou's blood drenched him and Sam.

He awoke soaked in sweat, heart pounding, barely able to resist the urge to scream. After staggering to the bathroom to splash cold water on his face, he returned to bed, calmer but wide awake. The clock by his bedside read 3.22 a.m. He knew better than to lie there fretting, so he switched on the light and reached over to snag his Kindle from the night stand. He tapped the screen to wake it from its own slumbers and opened *The Price of Salt*. If nothing else, it might help him get back to sleep. He skipped all the prefatory matter and went straight to page one.

The book started slowly but intriguingly. A new employee of a Manhattan department store sat alone, eating her lunch in the staff canteen and reading the employee manual. She wondered whether she'd ever reach the hallowed status of a twenty-five-year veteran.

Gradually, thoughts of going back to sleep faded as despite himself, Ford became engrossed in the story of Therese Belivet and a sophisticated customer, Carol Aird, to whom she impulsively sent a Christmas card.

Slowly, and then, at the turn of a page, with a flash of insight, Ford realised why Therese Belivet was unhappy with her boyfriend. She was gay. The next paragraph confirmed it. He put the book down.

He felt as though he was back at the top of that nightmarish version of Pen-y-Holt again. Alone this time. But in sunlight. Teetering on the brink of something that might explain why they'd made so little progress in the case.

All along, he, and everyone else, had been assuming they were looking for a man. It was back to the statistics again. It was one of the first things they taught fledgling detectives. When a woman was murdered, it was overwhelmingly likely that her killer was a man. Almost always a current or former partner. He thought of his own parents. How, in drink, his father had turned on his mother, hand raised, then stormed out before 'doing something I'll regret'.

But what if they'd been focusing on the wrong half of that perpetrator profile? What if it was indeed a partner, but not a man?

Ford immediately began to question his own thinking. Why? Just because Rachel had a lesbian novel in her room? He was sure lots of women read works of gay fiction. It didn't mean they were gay themselves, did it? The same probably went for men. He thought he had a copy of *Brokeback Mountain* somewhere in his own house.

He went back to the book, hoping to find a passage that would speak directly to what little he knew of Rachel Padley. He finished it at 6.45 a.m. There had been no suicides. Nobody died. And the ending, while not precisely happy to modern eyes, wasn't tragic either. He looked it up on Wikipedia. There he learned that the book had been republished as *Carol*. One line struck him. *Carol* wasn't the first novel about a lesbian romance, but it was the first that portrayed the lovers sympathetically and allowed them a measure of happiness at the end. Could Rachel have found comfort in its pages?

He needed to discuss it with the team, but he felt that here at last was a strong line of enquiry. Because if Rachel had been in a relationship with another woman, she might well have wanted to keep it a secret. Especially in the army. And where there were secrets, there could often be violence.

The army had made great play in recent years of its open and inclusive approach to recruitment, but he wondered just how far down the chain of command the more welcoming attitude had percolated.

To hard-nosed ranking officers like Colonel Hemmings? To squaddies like Corporal Wren and Private Willis? And what about female officers like Charlie Daniels and Major Robinson? What would they think about lesbians serving in the army?

Questions piled up. If Rachel had been gay, had she come out? On the basis of what little evidence he'd been able to amass, he suspected not. Nobody had mentioned it. He'd detected no innuendos or euphemisms. OK, so one of the soldiers had said she was 'one of the lads', but in the world of soldiering he felt that was simply a turn of phrase, nothing more.

He showered, shaved, snatched a quick breakfast of toast and tea and was at the station by 7.45 a.m. He texted Sam on the way up the steps into Bourne Hill.

mornin! at work early

l8rs

His phone buzzed as he took the stairs to Major Crimes.

ye

btw nobody says l8rs anymore

its sad

◆ ◆ ◆

Once everyone had arrived, Ford called a meeting. He jumped straight in with the point he'd been turning over in his head all morning.

'I'm wondering whether we've – I've, I mean – been looking at this all wrong. What if it was Rachel's partner who killed her, but she was a woman, not a man? It would potentially double our suspect pool and bring other motives into play.'

'Any special reason you're asking that, guv?' Jools asked.

'This is going to sound a bit thin, I know, but one of the books Jan found in Rachel's room was a lesbian romance. I started wondering whether I'd been too close-minded.'

'What, *The Price of Salt*, guv?' Jan asked.

'That's the one. I read it last night. Well, this morning, really. You might be more familiar with it as *Carol*.'

Jan nodded, smiling. 'I went to see it with a friend from my book group last year. Cate Blanchett, wasn't it?'

'That's right.'

'Sorry to interrupt your film club discussion.' This was Mick, his face screwed up into an expression of doubt. 'But *I* read George Michael's autobiography a couple of years ago. Doesn't mean I'm gay, does it?'

Ford had to smile. 'No. And I said it looks thin. But shouldn't we at least consider the possibility that we're looking for a female killer? Which most likely fits with what we know about murderers of women if we also accept she was Rachel's partner.'

'Well, I think you're being borderline homophobic. I might report you to HR.' Mick looked round, winking at one of the PSIs.

There was a soft swell of chuckles from the assembled cops. Nobody would be less likely to follow that course of action than Mick Tanner.

Shaking his head and smiling despite himself, Ford tried again. 'Rachel's life is – was – outwardly a totally smooth surface,' he said. 'Apart from a single instance where she made a complaint against her team leader, it's like she just skated through life and life returned the compliment. There has to be a reason why somebody lured her out to Imber and cut her throat.'

'If she *was* gay, then it could be a hate crime, guv,' Olly said.

'It's a possibility, obviously, but let's clear the ground under our feet,' Ford said. 'When a woman is murdered, ninety-nine times out of a hundred it's the spouse-slash-partner. Current or former. Who's the remaining one?'

Olly's eyes flicked up to the ceiling. Ford followed his gaze, seeing an open textbook. 'Member of her circle of close acquaintances followed by work colleagues, followed by stalker, stranger and sex-killer.'

'Something like that, yes. So before we start with the rarer motives, let's look at the most likely ones first.'

'Jealous ex-girlfriend, then,' Olly said.

'Or she was about to dump her girlfriend and the girlfriend didn't take the news well,' Jan said.

Ford turned to Charlie. 'This is all supposition on my part at the moment. Have you found anything on base that would suggest, however indirectly, that Rachel might have been gay?'

She shook her head. 'Honestly? No. Nothing. It's perfectly possible, of course. But if she was, I don't think she was out.'

'What's your take on how people would have reacted if she was?' he asked.

Charlie shrugged. 'These days, there's a lot more talk about diversity, but' – she turned to address the assembled detectives – 'on the ground? Things are slow to catch up with what's happening in Civvy Street. I'd say there's probably more tolerance of gay women than men. Probably because the guys perceive them as butch. Which' – she held up a hand – 'is a completely outdated stereotype, but there you are. The army's the army.'

'These are all potential lines of enquiry, as they were when we were looking for a jealous boyfriend,' Ford said. 'The added pressure is if she was keeping her sexuality a secret, we'll have far less luck finding anyone willing to talk.'

'How do you want to approach it then, guv?' Olly asked.

'I did have one thought. We've been canvassing the pubs roundabout, but maybe we should focus on any that host gay nights or are known within the gay community,' Ford said. 'Anyone got any contacts?'

The room fell silent. Mick leaned forward. Ford half-expected him to crack an off-colour joke, but when he spoke it was to offer a ray of hope.

'I have. My brother-in-law is gay. He drinks in the Knave of Hearts out on the Devizes Road. Says it's popular with the LGBT community. And there's a cafe in Andover. It's called, hold on—' Mick frowned, tapping the table while everyone waited in silence for him to remember. 'Yes! Radclyffe's. It's on Newbury Street. Also has anyone been into the White Horse on Railway Approach?'

One of the uniforms spoke up. 'I was there just yesterday. Nobody recognised Rachel.'

'They might have a specific gay night. Weekly or monthly. Might be worth popping back,' Mick said.

Ford felt it then. The pickup in his pulse that signalled more than just a line of enquiry. This was a door opening. A way into Rachel's life. And maybe that of her killer's, too.

'Nice one, Mick. Thanks. I'm thinking we might get better results if we have female officers on this one,' he said, looking at Jan, Jools and Charlie in turn. They nodded. 'Can you pay a visit to the Knave of Hearts, the White Horse and Radclyffe's today, please?'

'What about us, guv?' Olly asked.

'I want everyone else on the interviews up at Larkhill. I'm convinced we'll find Rachel's killer there. We may have interviewed him – or her – already.'

CHAPTER TWENTY-TWO

While the three female detectives sorted out the pubs between them, Ford left the office. He wanted to talk to the Padley family again, preferably one at a time.

He called Kate Chisholm from the car park. 'Where are you?'

'I'm in Larkhill. Just leaving to come back, actually.'

'Who's at home right now, do you know?'

'Just Helen. David's on duty.'

'All right. Thanks, Kate.'

He arrived at Lightfoot Road twenty minutes later and parked outside the Padleys' house. Helen answered the door. She was dressed simply, in a long denim skirt and a plain cream blouse with long sleeves and a high frilled collar, another bandana tied tightly across her head. The ensemble was disconcertingly old-fashioned, as if she had stepped out of an earlier world, possibly the prairies of America in the nineteenth century.

She led him to the sitting room and offered him an armchair.

'What is this about?' she asked in her usual quiet voice.

Somehow, he had a feeling that asking her straight out if she knew her daughter was a lesbian wouldn't be helpful. *You think?* a sarcastic inner voice asked.

'Helen, I need to ask you something about Rachel. Something quite personal,' he said. 'I think it might help us solve her murder, so I hope you'll accept my reasons for asking.'

She frowned and focused her watery blue eyes on his.

'Sounds ominous,' she said slowly.

He smiled. 'I hope not. But can you tell me whether Rachel ever gave you any inkling that she might be gay?'

He waited, then. Observing the grieving mother closely, looking for anything that might reveal the truth before she spoke. A fluttering eyelid or twitching muscle around the mouth might do it.

'Of course she wasn't,' she said finally, with a half-smile. 'Rachel was a good Christian girl. She might have strayed sometimes from the path God set out for her, but she wasn't like that. And it's forbidden by scripture in any case.'

Ford caught the hard edges of Helen's strict religious beliefs in her answer but forbore from entering into a moral or theological debate with her. For him, whether lesbians or anybody else were good or bad had nothing to do with their sexuality. If they harmed other people, they were bad. End of. And Rachel was the victim here. That was all that mattered.

He pressed a little more. 'She never talked about having a girlfriend, for example? Or ever told you she didn't like boys?'

'No. Nothing like that. Anyway, she wasn't married, so sex didn't enter into it. She loved her work, even if it went against God's will.'

Ford frowned. 'Sorry, could you explain how being a soldier went against God's will? Your husband's a soldier, after all.'

She smiled at him as if he were a simpleton, unaware of the higher planes of existence others inhabited. 'But David is a man, Inspector. Rachel was a girl. The Bible tells us, "Your wives, your little ones, and your livestock shall remain in the land that Moses gave you beyond the Jordan, but all the men of valour among you

shall pass over armed before your brothers and shall help them."
Joshua, one, fourteen and fifteen.'

Seeing he would get no further with Helen, he thanked her for
her time, assured her he and his team were working flat out to solve
the murder, and left.

He drove round the barracks to the main gate. Having completed the tedious business of obtaining another temporary pass,
he asked where he could find David Padley. The soldier on the gate
pointed him in the direction of the sports field.

'He was heading over that way last time I saw him, sir.'

Ford thanked him, parked the Discovery and walked in the
direction the guard had indicated.

He encountered a group of young soldiers in full uniform
carrying enormous rucksacks and rifles with bright-yellow plastic
covers on their muzzles, jogging around a perimeter track. A couple of them nodded a greeting, but most, red-faced and sweating,
appeared to be concentrating on maintaining a steady pace and
presumably not collapsing.

Ford walked on and saw a uniformed figure in the distance
that, from his gait, looked to be David Padley. He broke into a
trot and caught up with him a few minutes later on the far side of
a football pitch.

'David!' he called out.

Padley turned and, seeing Ford, held up a hand in a stiff wave.
He turned and marched over.

'Have you found him, then?' he asked as he arrived in front
of Ford.

'Found who?'

'The bastard that killed our Rachel! Who else?'

'Not yet, but I do have a promising new line of enquiry. That's
why I came out to talk to you.'

'Oh, well, good. D'you mind talking while we walk, only I'm on my rounds.'

'Not at all.'

David set off at a smart pace, and Ford fell into step alongside him.

'What did you want to talk about, then?' David asked, his eyes scanning the front, left and right as he marched.

'Do you think there's any chance at all Rachel might have been gay?'

David pulled up sharply, leaving Ford a pace ahead of him and forcing him to turn round.

'A lesbian, you mean?'

'Yes. Did she ever say anything to you?'

David shook his head, frowning. 'No. I never even thought of it. She didn't seem to have any relationships like that,' he said. 'I mean, there were a couple of lads she were sweet on when she were younger, but not lasses. Have you spoken to Helen about it?'

'I have.'

'What did she say?'

Ford went for the concise version of his conversation with Helen Padley. 'She said that Rachel wasn't gay.'

David shrugged. 'There you are then. She knew Rachel better'n I did. I'm better wi' lads, to be honest. Jason were always hangin' round me when he were a kid. It's only natural, in't it? Fathers and sons. Got any of your own?'

'A son, yes.'

'Well, there you are then. You know what I'm talking about, don't you?'

'Your wife mentioned that Rachel's choice of career was against your religious beliefs,' he prompted, wondering whether it might unlock an aspect of the family dynamics he needed to understand better.

'Oh, she did, did she? Did she start quoting the Bible at you, an' all?'

Ford nodded. 'One or two verses.'

'Yeah, well, as I told you before, she's what you'd call devout, is Helen. I go wi' her on a Sunday if I'm not on duty, but it's more to keep her sweet than anything else.'

Ford left David to his rounds and returned to the Discovery. Two down, one to go. Would Jason have a different take on his sister's private life?

He drove over to Tidworth and Raj's Bodyshop, where he found Jason Padley on his back beneath a silver Mondeo. Squatting down, Ford shouted over pop music blaring from a dusty radio on a shelf.

'Jason! I need to ask you a question.'

Jason heeled his way out on the inspection trolley and got to his feet, wiping greasy hands on his overalls.

'Fire away,' he said.

'Fancy a quick walk? It's about Rachel.'

'Oh. All right. I just need to check wi' Raj.'

He trotted over to where the gaffer was leaning into the open engine bay of a custard-yellow Toyota Supra laden with aftermarket plastic spoilers. Ford saw him gesture in his direction. Raj looked over, held up a hand in greeting then turned back to Jason and nodded.

'Come on, then. Call it me tea break,' Jason said when he returned, motioning for Ford to follow him outside.

Ford felt he could take a more straightforward approach with Jason. He was only a couple of years older than Rachel. 'Do you think Rachel might have been gay?'

Jason shrugged. 'How would I know? Like I told you before, 'er and me, we weren't exactly close, were we?'

'She never mentioned it to you?'

'Is that why she were killed, then? 'Cause she were a lesbian? A hate crime, like?'

'It's too early to say. It's just an angle we're looking at,' Ford said, realising he was questioning a man whose name began with J. 'Tell me, Jason, if Rachel *was* gay, and she told your parents, how do you think they'd react?'

'Are you joking? They'd have had kittens,' he said. 'Probably drag her off to that nutty church of theirs for conversion therapy.'

Ford felt he'd found the insight into the family he'd been looking for. And for the first time, he began wondering whether he should be looking more closely at David and Helen Padley.

'You're not a fan, then?' he asked.

'What? All that waving your arms in the air and gabbling like you swallowed a foreign phrase book? Not bloody likely!'

'Did Rachel have any close female friends, do you know?'

Jason shook his head. 'No.'

'Sorry, is that no she didn't, or no, you don't know?' Ford asked.

'No, I don't know.'

Ford thanked Jason. And he really meant it. This was a proper lead. He added the vicar or pastor of Helen's church to his list of people to interview, as well as making a note to think more about Helen herself.

CHAPTER TWENTY-THREE

Jools pushed through the door into Radclyffe's on Newbury Street in Andover. The owners had painted the place in a soft shade of sage green up to a dado rail of black and white tiles, then cream above. Together with the black and white chequered floor tiles and brass table lamps with green glass shades, it gave the place a thirties feel. Art Deco travel posters – stylised ocean liners, speeding trains, palm trees – reinforced the impression.

A few of the round wooden tables were occupied, and not solely by women. A man and woman in their late sixties were chatting and smiling over lattes and croissants, and a guy in a blue and black plaid shirt and flamboyant red beard was tapping away on a MacBook.

The fiftyish woman behind the counter had glossy black hair threaded with grey. She wore it swept up into an untidy bun with a pencil poked through it. A pair of glasses suspended on a string of red beads rested on her chest.

She smiled at Jools. 'Take a seat, love, I'll be right over.'

Jools was about to go straight into her official routine, flashing Rachel's photo, when she realised she really wanted a coffee. And the cakes under glass domes on crackle-glazed green ceramic stands were tempting her. She'd skipped breakfast that morning and her stomach had been growling ever since. She smiled back and nodded, choosing a table in the far corner where she could observe the cafe's clientele.

Behind the woman's head, Jools noted a row of optics and a small wine rack screwed to the wall beside them. The place was licensed. That meant there was probably an evening scene. Maybe quite different from this unremarkable daytime atmosphere.

The woman came over and handed Jools a menu.

'Actually, I know what I want,' Jools said. 'Could I have a large cappuccino and a slice of the carrot cake, please.'

The woman nodded and smiled. 'Good choice. It's my favourite.'

When she returned with the coffee and cake, Jools was ready with Rachel's photograph and her police ID.

'Have you got a minute to answer a couple of questions?' she asked.

The woman frowned, but sat all the same. 'Of course. But if someone needs me, I'll have to go.'

Jools showed her the photograph. 'Do you recognise her?'

The woman settled the glasses on her nose and took the photo from Jools. 'May I?'

'That's Rachel,' she said, finally. 'She's a lot prettier than that makes her out to be. But I suppose that's the Army for you.'

Jools picked up on her use of the present tense. The conversation would have to take a difficult turn.

'I'm really sorry, but it sounds like you haven't heard the news about Rachel.'

'Well, you're here, love,' the woman said with a wry smile, 'so I assume she's in some kind of trouble. But—' She stopped mid-sentence. She blinked. Twice. Jools could see from her face that she'd made the connection. 'Oh, no. You're going to tell me she's dead, aren't you?'

'I'm afraid so. She was murdered ten days ago. It was on the news,' she couldn't help adding.

The woman slumped. She took her glasses off and rubbed her eyes.

'I've been abroad. I only got back yesterday. I make a point of avoiding the news in any case,' she said. 'Poor Rachel. How was she – no, don't tell me. I don't want to know.'

'We're trying to trace a friend of hers. But we don't have a name. All we know is that their first initial was J,' Jools said. 'We're working on the assumption it's a woman. Did Rachel ever come in with a friend? Of either sex?'

'We don't like to give out details of our customers' private lives. If you're here asking about Rachel, I assume you know we're lesbians, me and Molly?'

'Is she your partner?'

She nodded. 'In life . . . and in the cafe. We've been together for ten years, married for five. My name's Sal, by the way.'

'Hi, Sal. I didn't know about you and your wife specifically. One of my colleagues mentioned Radclyffe's was LGBT-friendly,' Jools said. 'I do understand your reticence, but as I said, this is a murder investigation.' A thought occurred to her: a way of getting Sal to open up. 'And I have to consider the possibility that someone may be targeting gay women.'

Sal's eyes widened. 'Shit! You mean there might be a serial killer out there?'

Jools immediately felt guilty for planting that idea, and resolved to squash it. She didn't think Ford would be best pleased at the thought she'd been raising public anxiety. 'No, nothing like that. And it's probably someone on the base. But my point is, if you do have information, you'd be really helping us catch Rachel's killer.'

Sal sighed. 'I suppose it can't hurt Rachel now. She used to come in with a dark-skinned girl. Well, not super-dark, but, you know, a sort of lovely glowing colour. Honey? Amber? About the same age as Rachel, maybe a little older. Shorter than Rachel, and slim. Dark curly hair.'

'Did you catch her name?'

'No. But they were definitely an item.' Sal's lips parted to say something else, then she closed them again.

'What?' Jools asked.

'I don't know if it's important, but they always arrived separately.'

'Maybe they didn't want to be seen coming in together.'

'Maybe,' Sal agreed. 'Andover isn't Soho: there's still the odd Neanderthal who can't get his head round the idea women might fancy other women rather than him,' she said. 'But a lot of couples do come in with each other. We have poetry nights, a DJ sometimes. There could be all kinds of reasons why two women would come here together.'

'How did they seem with each other?'

Sal shrugged. 'Fine. Just like any other couple, you know?'

'Did you ever see them arguing?'

Sal retrieved the pencil from her bun and fiddled with it. 'There was one time, just before I went on holiday. It was nearly closing time,' she said, looking away from Jools. 'Rachel raised her voice just as there was a gap in the general hubbub. You know when that happens and you're saying something inappropriate?'

'More than once, in my case,' Jools said easily.

'Well, she said something like, "I've got to end it."'

Jools felt her pulse kick up a notch. Had Rachel committed suicide after all?

'And her girlfriend's reaction?'

'Pretty pissed off, to be honest. But then the noise started up again and I couldn't hear anything else.'

'And you're sure she said, *I've* got to end it, not *we've* got to?'

Sal frowned. 'I think so. I couldn't swear to it in court or anything.'

Jools offered a reassuring smile. 'Don't worry, we're a long way from court.'

The bearded guy looked up from his laptop. 'Excuse me, Sal?'

Sal looked round. 'Coming, Ben.' Then she turned back to Jools. 'I have to go.'

'You've been really helpful.' Jools gave Sal a card. 'If you think of anything else, please call me or email me.'

Jools called Ford from her car and relayed the details of her conversation with Sal.

'Great work, Jools. I'll try and get on the evening news with another appeal for J to come forward.'

'I think she didn't come forward before because she's nervous,' Jools said, remembering Sal's caution about revealing anything of her customers' personal lives.

'Or she's the murderer,' Ford added. 'Could you get back out to Radclyffe's with a police sketch artist and see if you can get something I can show on the TV?'

'On it,' she said.

CHAPTER TWENTY-FOUR

Unlike the Larkhill garrison church, St Alban the Martyr, with its square tower and tall narrow windows, the small evangelical church attended by the Padleys seemed almost embarrassed to be a place of worship.

It was a single-storey red-brick building at the start of a road that snaked its way up a hill through a modern housing estate bordering farmland. The developers had named all the roads after nearby historical or archaeological features. Approaching the church, Ford drove up Long Barrow Drive. He saw turnings marked Top Field Way, Drovers Yard and Old Green Lane.

A laminated sign screwed to the wall bore the name of the church in green capitals on a white background:

NEW UNITED CHURCH
OF THE TRUE HOLY DOCTRINE
OF CHRIST THE REDEEMER

Beside the sign, a noticeboard advertised 'Bumps 'n' Babies' classes and coffee mornings for new congregants. 'Bring a friend to meet Jesus!'

Unsure of the protocol, given how different it was from the country church where Lou was buried, Ford knocked on the door. Then, feeling foolish waiting outside, he pushed through.

Inside he caught a mix of smells in which wet wool and furniture polish predominated. The interior maintained the plain, unadorned appearance. He might have been in a community hall of the sort shared by Girl Guide and Scout troops, local history societies and camera clubs, were it not for a rudimentary altar at one end: a simple table draped in a white sheet on which rested an enormous black Bible and a plain wooden cross. Several dozen green plastic chairs with tubular steel legs faced the altar.

Ford walked forward and lifted the leather-bound front cover of the Bible.

'Can I help you, Inspector?' a male voice asked from the shadows, startling him.

Ford turned. Pastor Simeon bore down on him, wearing a faint smile.

'I have a few questions for you, Pastor.'

'Let's talk in my office. It's a little more private.'

Ford glanced round the empty church but followed the pastor to a small office off the main room. It was hardly bigger than a broom cupboard and equipped with a small battered desk and two chairs. Dominating one corner was a large and ancient wooden filing cabinet with brass handles.

'Please, be seated,' the pastor said, inserting himself between the desk and the back wall and sliding his bony frame down into the chair.

'Rachel Padley was murdered,' Ford said.

There, that ought to knock a little of that piousness out of you, he thought, and then instantly regretted it. The guy was only doing what his calling told him to.

Eyebrows raised a little towards that shiny expanse of pink forehead, the pastor stared at Ford. 'Are you sure? From what I've heard it was an open-and-shut case. She killed herself.'

'Perhaps that was what Rachel's murderer wanted us to think,' Ford said. 'What can you tell me about the Padleys?'

The pastor resettled himself in his chair, wincing slightly as if he had a boil on his backside and the seat offered insufficient padding.

'They are a quiet, loving couple. They worship God, of course, as do all our members. And they believe in his teachings,' he said, with a small smile. 'They are generous givers to our mission, both here and in Africa, where we perform outreach activities.'

'Did they ever talk to you about Rachel?'

'No.'

'No? Even though she was their daughter and had followed her father into the Black Watch? Weren't they proud?'

The pastor smiled patronisingly at Ford. '"Pride goeth before destruction, and an haughty spirit before a fall." Proverbs, sixteen, eighteen.'

Ford tried a different tack. 'Tell me a little about your church, Pastor.'

'What would you like to know?'

'The name, for one thing. As one of my team remarked the other day, it's quite a mouthful, isn't it?'

There was that little smile again. 'We are used to sneers, Inspector. We believe in the truth of the Bible as the revealed word of God. If other' – he paused, and his mouth twisted as if he'd bitten on something sour – '*denominations* have chosen to deviate from His wishes, that is a cause of sorrow. But' – he sighed again – 'they shall go their way while we shall follow His true path.'

'Are you saying that for you and your flock, every word of the Bible is literally true?'

'Yes. That is exactly what I'm saying. What else could I possibly mean by it?'

Ford wondered what the pastor and his flock might think about lesbians.

'Tell me about Helen Padley.'

'What about her?'

'She's devout?'

The pastor smiled and nodded enthusiastically. 'Helen is dutiful in her devotion and modest in her outward manner, as befitteth a woman. But often it is from the quietest vessels that we may hear the loudest ringing of faith.'

To Ford it sounded like the pastor was inventing his own Bible quotes. Or at least attempting to capture some of the poetry. Though his last utterance sounded suspiciously like a pious reworking of the old saw about empty vessels making the most noise.

'We believe Rachel was gay. How do you think David and Helen would have reacted to that if they'd known?'

'I have no idea. I'm not a psychologist. You'd have to ask them.'

That was interesting. Three short sentences in decidedly modern English. Not a 'goeth' or 'befitteth' in sight.

'Does the Bible have anything to say on the subject of lesbianism?'

'If you believed, you'd have a Bible of your own to consult, Inspector,' the supercilious young man said, before continuing with his lips curled into a smile once more. 'But to save you the trouble, no, it does not. Various Jewish scholars tried to provide exegetical reasoning that pointed to the practice being prohibited in Leviticus – Maimonides chief among them.'

'The Jews got it wrong, then?'

'I am afraid they are incorrect in their reasoning, as they are in so many other aspects of their beliefs. Although if Rachel *was* a lesbian, I do think that would point to suicide rather than murder,' the young priest said. 'Living in opposition to the life ordained for women by God would naturally have placed Rachel under enormous mental strain.'

'For someone who claims not to be a psychologist, you seem remarkably willing to diagnose Rachel's mental state,' Ford snapped, before he could stop himself.

Shit! He was a DI, not a baby-steps DC like Olly Cable. He wasn't supposed to let witnesses get to him. Even ones as irritating as the man before him.

But the pastor merely offered Ford yet another smile. 'I see I provoke you, Inspector. And I apologise. Faith, and the certainty it brings, can be hard to deal with for non-believers.'

Ford exhaled noisily. 'No, it's me who should say sorry. I came to your church to seek your help. I was out of line.'

The pastor nodded as if accepting what was his by right. 'Was there anything else?'

'Just one more question. Do you offer conversion therapy here?'

The pastor gripped the arms of his chair as if it might buck him off. 'What?'

Finally, Ford had got through to him. 'Trying to *cure* gay people of their sexuality and turn them into heterosexuals.'

Two spots of colour had bloomed high on the pastor's pale cheeks, like blobs of jam on a milk pudding.

'No! Absolutely not! I am aware of such practices, of course, but I can assure you, nothing of that kind happens on these premises.'

'How about *off* these premises. Ever do home visits?'

Ford was pushing it, he knew that. If the pastor complained, Sandy would be well within her rights to give Ford a bollocking.

'I resent your insinuations, Inspector Ford, and I want you to leave my church.'

'You haven't answered my question.'

'No. And I'm not going to. If you have anything else to ask me, I suggest you come back with an arrest warrant,' he said. 'I shall find a solicitor and I shall refuse on the grounds of conscience to answer any more of your, your' – he hesitated, and his lips clamped tight before he opened them again – '*damned* questions.'

Behind the wheel of the Discovery two minutes later, Ford allowed himself to vent some of the steam that had been building inside the stuffy, stale-smelling little office. 'Smug bastard!'

And what sort of name was Simeon, anyway? Probably christened Simon and added the 'e' himself. He knew he'd overstepped the bounds with his final question, but there was something about the young pastor that Ford really, *really* didn't like.

He gunned the engine and pulled away, spraying loose grit from all four wheels. After executing a rough-edged three-point turn into Stonehenge Drive, he pointed the Discovery's nose towards Bourne Hill.

Had he learned anything of value? He wasn't sure. But it sounded as though David Padley was more than merely his wife's bagman during her Sunday devotions. And despite the pastor's blustering, he hadn't denied that his church offered conversion therapy. If the Padleys had suggested Rachel try it, Ford could imagine the sort of reaction their offer, however well-intentioned, would have provoked.

As soon as he got back to his office, he called a journalist he knew on BBC *South Today*. He wanted to get the sketch of J on to the evening news.

◆ ◆ ◆

Later that night, Ford and Sam were sitting together in the cosy little sitting room overlooking the back garden. Ford had some papers spread out beside him on the sofa; Sam was curled up in an armchair with his phone.

'How's the case going?' Sam asked. 'I saw you on the telly. Very professional.'

Ford looked up from the report he was reading. 'Slow. Like I said, it all hinges on the author of the letter the dead woman had on her.'

Sam pulled his mouth to one side. 'It's weird.'

'What is?'

'Well, this is supposed to be her girlfriend, right?'

'Right.'

'And she, Rachel, I mean, was nineteen, yeah?'

'Yes.'

'That makes her Gen Z.'

'Remind me?'

Sam rolled his eyes, then adopted a patient tone that reminded Ford of his own schoolteachers.

'Generation Z is people born after 1995. Some say 1996, but it doesn't really matter.'

'Are you Gen Z?'

Sam nodded. Ford began to see why Sam had picked up on the letter. It wasn't its content, it was its format. Or, to be more specific, its physical form. He decided to let Sam finish the explanation.

'Nobody in my generation would send a letter to arrange a meeting. We'd just message someone,' he said. 'I mean, yes, if we were, like, doing thank-you letters. But even for those, I sometimes do emails or a postcard. Letters are really formal.'

'Who *would* write one?'

Sam grinned. 'Old people.'

'And when you say "old"?'

Ford knew what was coming.

'You know, over forty.' A beat. 'Like you.'

Ford gave it the full eyes-wide, mouth-dropped-open look of horror. 'You cheeky little bleeder! Are you saying I'm old?'

'If the cap fits,' Sam said. Then he shook his head as if resetting the mood. 'But it's true, Dad. If the murderer's a Gen Z, no way they'd send a letter.'

'Why do you think Rachel went then?'

'I don't know. I mean, if I got a letter from a mate, I'd still go,' he said. 'But I'd probably just think they were having a laugh or something.'

'Thanks, Sam, that's really helpful.'

Sam nodded and went back to his phone. Messaging his friends. Not writing to them. Of course. Sometimes Ford wished they could have a teenage DC on the team full-time.

CHAPTER TWENTY-FIVE

Ford spent the whole of the following morning updating his policy book. He also called Kate Chisholm and asked her to get the Padleys' alibis.

'Be subtle,' he added.

A precaution, he told himself. A necessary bit of i-dotting and t-crossing.

At one point he'd spotted Martin Peterson in the main entrance to Major Crimes and hurried out of his office to a door at the far end that led to the stairwell. He wasn't ready for another conversation with the PCC. He wondered whether the pastor had complained after all. It was just the sort of issue Peterson would seize on to score points.

He looked up at a knock on his door. Hannah stood in the doorway. She was biting her lip and fidgeting with something. He looked closer. It was a plastic giraffe.

'Hi, Wix,' he said with a smile. 'Did you want something?'

She came in and closed the door behind her. Then she opened it a little way and closed it again, twisting the knob and pulling on it. She repeated the sequence twice more.

He waited. Seeing her behave like this, he knew something was making her anxious. The best thing to do in these situations was simply to wait. Hannah had by far the best understanding of her condition and the emotional states it produced and would find a way to manage this small crisis.

Eventually she nodded vigorously, three times, turned and came to sit in the visitor's chair.

'Sorry about that,' she said.

Ford waved it away. 'It's nice to see a friendly face,' he said, hoping it would put her at ease. 'I've been avoiding Martin Peterson all bloody morning.'

Hannah smiled. 'Does anybody like him?'

'I expect his wife does.' He paused, aiming to get the timing right. 'A bit.'

Hannah nodded. 'That's funny because she's his wife so she should love him. But you said she only likes him a little.'

Ford gestured at the mound of paperwork in front of him. 'I'm not trying to get rid of you, Wix, but I'm under the cosh this morning. I've got reports coming out of my ears so . . .'

'Did the cosh dislodge them?'

He laughed. 'OK, comedy time's officially over. I really do need to keep going.' He looked at her. She definitely still looked nervous. She was blinking rapidly and seemed unable to hold his gaze. 'What is it, Wix? Is everything all right?'

'Yes!' she said loudly. 'Sorry, Henry. Yes. Everything's fine. I'm re-examining the knife we found in Rachel's hand in the absence of any other work on the Padley case. But that's not the reason I came to see you.'

'Why did you, then?' he asked as gently as he could manage, fighting down the urge to hurry her up. It wouldn't work and would only make her anxiety worse.

Hannah sucked in a quick breath. 'I asked you before but it never happened so would you like to come to dinner at mine because I think it would be nice and it's what friends do and you're my friend so I thought you'd like it because I know I would.'

192

Ford blinked at this rush of words. He sensed how much it had cost Hannah to invite him to her house.

'That would be lovely, case permitting. Just let me know when.'

'Saturday. If you're worried about taking time off from the case, we can call it a working dinner.'

He smiled. Maybe he did need a proper break. And firing ideas off Hannah was always productive. 'What time?'

'Eight,' she said, with a wide smile. 'We'll have something to eat and some nice wine and then there's something I want to show you that I think you'll find interesting.' She clapped a hand over her mouth. 'Oh! No, I didn't mean to say that.'

Hannah sprang up from the chair as if propelled by some sort of hidden mechanism in the seat. Ten seconds later the door had slammed shut behind her and, shaking his head, Ford had peace and quiet again.

◆ ◆ ◆

Hannah marched straight from Major Crimes to the ladies' on the third floor. After checking in all the cubicles, she went to the centre sink, turned on the cold tap and scooped cold water up to her face. Double handfuls that splashed on to the front of her shirt and wetted her hairline.

She gripped the cool porcelain sides of the basin and stared into the mirror. The woman with the blonde hair done up in plaits was very pale. Her lips, to which she'd carefully applied lipstick before going to see Ford, looked thin and pinched. She tried to smile. It looked like a doll's expression. She forced herself to laugh out loud and tried again. Better.

Back in Forensics, she crossed the silent space and slumped in her chair. Everybody was bent over their keyboards or studying the results of various tests on monitors. Nobody came over to her desk, which was good. It was what she wanted right now. To be left alone. She could still feel her shirt sticking to her skin, but that was OK. The shirt would dry.

She opened her eyes. The knife was waiting. That was what she needed to do. Focus on her work. Asking Henry round for dinner had been the single hardest thing she'd done since arriving at Bourne Hill. But what she'd discovered about the accident at Pen-y-Holt couldn't wait any longer.

CHAPTER TWENTY-SIX

Later that morning, Kate Chisholm called Ford to tell him both Padleys had alibis. Helen was helping the pastor at the church and David had been on duty until 10.00 p.m. Neither was watertight but they'd been happy to give the names of witnesses. After that, they'd been at home together watching TV before bed.

As soon as he replaced the handset his phone rang again. It was the front desk.

'There's a young lady here, sir. Says she wants to speak to you.'

Ford sat straighter in his chair. Was it the mysterious 'J'? He could ask some more questions or he could leave his paperwork and go down to reception to meet her himself.

He took the stairs, and was on the ground floor two minutes later.

'Hi, Paula,' he said to the civilian receptionist. 'Where is she?'

Paula pointed towards the main doors. 'She's outside, sir. I did ask her to take a seat, but she said she'd rather wait outside.'

Ford nodded and thanked her, then headed for the little terraced courtyard. He saw his visitor at once. She was in uniform – camouflage fatigues. She fitted Sal's description: light-brown skin and curly hair escaping from beneath a khaki Tam O'Shanter. She was slender and maybe five feet four or five. He assumed she'd met the height requirements for the infantry but she still looked petite to him.

'Hello,' he said, so as not to startle her. 'I'm Inspector Ford.'

She turned to face him, coming to attention. She looked worried but offered a half-smile.

'Thank you for agreeing to see me, sir,' she said.

'Would you like to come up to my office? It's a little more private than chatting out here.'

'Yes, please, sir. Thank you.'

He led her back into reception and, sensing she needed to be moving, suggested they take the stairs rather than wait for the lift. He thought the activity might dispel some of the adrenaline that was clearly bothering her.

He offered her a coffee, which she declined, so he motioned for her to take the visitor's chair and closed the office door before resuming his seat behind the desk.

Ford smiled at her but made no attempt to speak. He wanted to get a read on her. The silence while he waited for her to say something was a good opportunity.

She might be a friendly witness, able to shed some light on Rachel's state of mind in the days leading up to her death. But there was a small but significant chance he might be sitting across his desk from Rachel's killer. Stranger things had happened. And the phenomenon of murderers inserting themselves into investigations was so well known as to be a commonplace of TV dramas.

She was nervous. That much was obvious. Her eyes flitted around the room and she couldn't find a comfortable position, shifting her weight in the chair. He put a tick in the 'friendly witness' column. Psychopaths and cold-blooded killers tended to exude a calm, if not jovial attitude. Wasn't this all terribly exciting? And how lucky were they to be at the heart of a real, live murder investigation!

'I'm J,' she said. 'It stands for Josifini. My surname is Tui.' She spelled it out for him. 'I'm Fijian.'

Ford nodded and made a note. 'OK, Josifini. First of all, I want to thank you for coming forward. But can you tell me why you waited this long? Did you not see our first appeal for you to make yourself known to the police?'

She surprised him by bursting into tears.

He looked around for a box of tissues. Why, he didn't know, as he never kept one handy. He rootled around in his top drawer in the hopes he might find one of the crumpled pocket-sized packets that seemed to breed in there. No deal.

Josifini's sobbing grew louder. Panicking, he jumped up and went to his door. He poked his head out and saw Jan just returning from the kitchen with a steaming mug.

'Jan, you haven't got a clean tissue, have you? I've got a bit of a situation here.'

'Hold on,' she said. A moment or two later she came over with a small box printed with pink roses. 'Everything all right?'

'Not really. I've got J in there. Josifini. She's just burst into tears.'

'May I?'

Jan didn't wait for permission, squeezing past Ford and going into his office. He followed her in and closed the door behind him.

Jan knelt down by Josifini's right side and put an arm around her shoulders.

'Hey, hey,' she crooned, 'what's up, love? You're perfectly safe here. Inspector Ford's not half as fierce as he looks. He's just a big teddy bear, really.'

The girl turned her tear-streaked face to Jan's and smiled. Jan offered her the box of tissues and she yanked a couple free and wiped her eyes and then blew her nose.

'I'm sorry, ma'am. It's just I've been under so much stress.'

Jan motioned for Ford to pull a chair over for her. She got up from her knees and sat beside Josifini.

'I completely understand, love,' she said. 'And there's no need to call me ma'am. Makes me sound like the Queen. And last time I checked, I'm definitely not royal.'

The girl laughed, a broken, cracked sound in the confines of Ford's office, but Jan's gentle humour seemed to have done the trick.

Some of the male detectives often dismissed Jan as unsuited to CID, let alone Major Crimes, mistaking her motherly demeanour for softness. Ford harboured no such doubts. He'd seen hard-bitten criminals spill their guts under her gentle questioning, perhaps relieved to have a sympathetic ear to whom they could pour out their guilt. Only to stare in astonishment as she arrested them and snapped on a pair of Quik-Cuffs.

He nodded to her, a signal that she should stay and start the interview herself. She inclined her head by a couple of millimetres to let Ford know she'd understood.

'Now,' she said, still sitting beside Josifini, 'why don't we start at the beginning. Tell me about Rachel. Is it OK if we record this chat?'

The girl nodded. Ford started the voice recorder app on his phone.

Over the next five minutes, Josifini laid out the story of how she and Rachel had joined up at the same time and found themselves in the same unit within the Black Watch. On the way, she explained how the battalion was especially popular among Britain's tiny Fijian community, just three thousand people. They comprised between one in six and one in seven of the battalion's strength.

Now came the moment when Ford wanted Jan to steer the conversation towards the key to the whole investigation. Her relationship with Rachel. Jan didn't disappoint.

'Can you tell me about you and Rachel?' she asked.

Josifini looked down at her lap, where her fingers were knitted together. She looked up at Ford, then back at Jan. 'This is private? Just for the police?'

Ford knew what was coming, and also that there was very little he could do to keep the girl's sexuality a secret. He personally wished he could, but if she turned out to be a material witness, or the perpetrator, then the media would find out one way or another. As would the local community. Social media would see to that.

'Whatever you tell us in here will be treated in the strictest confidentiality,' he said. 'But what's most important is that if you have anything that might help us identify Rachel's murderer, you tell us now.'

'OK,' she sniffed. 'Well, you probably guessed anyway, but Rachel was gay. Me, too,' she added.

'Look, love,' Jan said. 'Nobody here cares one way or the other whether you're gay, straight or halfway in between. It's nobody's business but your own. What we do care about, passionately, is solving her murder. Do you believe me?'

She held Josifini's gaze and after a few seconds, Josifini nodded with a small smile.

'Thank you. It's just, not everyone's so understanding,' she said. 'Especially in my community. It's why I left Fiji in the first place.'

'Right, well now we've got that out of the way, perhaps you'd better tell us about your letter.'

Josifini's eyes widened. 'That's just it. That's why I came here. I never wrote it. Why would I, anyway? I'd just text her.'

Ford nodded. Just as Sam had said. He made another note and waited for Jan's next question.

'Do you have any idea who did?'

'Not exactly, but there were a couple of the blokes who were always making remarks.'

'What kind of remarks, love?'

'You know. About lesbians. They think any girl who joins the infantry has to be gay. They call us names, they make up jokes. I don't want to repeat them. You can imagine, can't you.'

Jan nodded. 'I'm afraid I can, love. All too easily. Was it any of the men in particular?'

'Corporal Wren. He's a right bastard,' she said, with feeling. 'And just because Rach made a complaint about him, he always took it out on her.'

'What was the complaint about?'

'She said he was discriminating against her, well, me and her, really, on account of we were women.'

'Not because you were gay?'

Josifini shook her head. 'He doesn't know. I'm sure of it. The complaint went right up to Colonel Hemmings, but nothing came of it.'

'How did things change after that?'

'Wren was fairer on us, but you could see he hated it. He got Rach once, at the end of the day, right in front of everyone. He was, like, "OK, Butch, you wanted to be treated like one of the boys. So get your effing Marigolds on and scrub the latrines. I was going to give it to Willis, but you can do it instead as you're so keen on equality."'

Ford leaned forward and cleared his throat softly to catch Josifini's attention. 'Just for the sake of argument, let's pretend there's a lawyer and he's defending Corporal Wren in a murder trial, OK?'

She frowned and looked doubtful. 'OK.'

'He might say to you, "Now, Private Tui, you claim you didn't write this letter. But as it's printed, not handwritten and it seems very intimate, I put it to you that you did indeed write it and you're trying to deflect blame on to my client,"' Ford said in a dry, legalistic tone of voice. 'If a lawyer did say that to you, what would you say to him?'

She nodded, seeming to understand what Ford was getting at. 'I'd say, well, for one thing, I'd never sign myself "J". As simple as that. She always called me Jo-jo.'

'Can you prove that?'

She nodded enthusiastically, smiling properly now. Perhaps she'd realised that even by presenting herself at Bourne Hill she'd be attracting the wrong kind of attention from the police.

'I've got WhatsApp messages. We used it because it's encrypted.'

Ford returned the smile, thinking that here was another youngster who clearly thought he wouldn't know even the basics of internet usage. 'No need for that yet, but if it comes to it, would you be prepared to share them with us?'

She turned to Jan as if for support.

'What is it, love?' Jan asked.

'It's why I didn't come in before. Why he' – she hesitated – 'sorry, sir, I mean Inspector Ford, made me cry. I'm frightened that whoever it was, they killed Rach because of her sexuality. If it gets out I'm gay as well, what if they come for me? Nobody knows, OK? Not my auntie and uncle, nobody.'

Jan frowned. 'You've got family here?'

Josifini shook her head. 'If you're here on your own, like me, then you have a home family,' she said. 'They're, like, from your part of Fiji, or your lineage? It's like being adopted. I take my washing round, have meals with them. They met Rach, too. They wanted her to visit them when they go back to Fiji.'

'Do they know you're gay?' Ford asked.

'No. I introduced Rach as my friend. In Fiji, women can be very close, so we could hug or hold hands and nobody thought anything of it,' she said. 'But we were careful not to kiss or anything. It would have got straight back to my parents in Suva and then the whole world would have known.'

'How about Rachel? Had she come out to her parents?'

Josifini's eyes widened. 'No! She was terrified of what they'd do. They're, like, in this super-strict church, OK? I can't remember the name, it goes on for ever. But she told me one night she was frightened they'd, I don't know, kidnap her or whatever. You know, take her there and try to cure her.'

Ford decided he'd be talking to Pastor Simeon again. He could see how scared Josifini was. He couldn't blame her for hesitating to come forward. He would have felt just the same in her position. He could see no point in suggesting that as a trained infantry soldier she was more than capable of defending herself. It hadn't worked for Rachel, had it?

'Look, Josifini. We're still quite a way from being able to arrest anyone for Rachel's murder,' he said. 'We'll keep this conversation private for now, as you asked. But maybe you can take extra precautions. I don't know how much time you get to yourself, but is there any way you could make sure you're always with other people?'

'Mostly we're all together anyway,' she said. 'It's one of the things everyone complains about, how hard it is to get time on your own.'

'Good. Well, I think as long as you're with other people you're perfectly safe. Whoever killed Rachel did it in the middle of the night in Imber,' he said. 'That tells me he or she is very cautious. A coward. No way would they try anything in broad daylight in front of witnesses.'

'What about in quarters? In my own room, I mean.'

Ford gave her the same advice he'd give anyone living in shared accommodation. 'Lock your door. And on no account agree to meet anyone on your own, even if it seems like a genuine invitation. I know it's not perfect, but it's all I can do. I'm sorry.'

She shook her head. 'No, it's fine. And thanks for hearing me out, sir. People are often quick to judge.'

'Just one more question. Can you tell us where you were on the night Rachel was killed? That was the Saturday before last. The twenty-sixth. Say from 10.00 p.m. to 1.00 a.m. on the Sunday morning.'

'I was watching a netball match on YouTube in my room. Fiji versus Samoa. Lydia Panapasa's my hero. She plays goal shooter like I used to at school.'

'Can anyone else vouch for that?'

'Sorry, sir, "vouch"?'

'Is there any way we can check that you were really in your room?'

'Not really, sir. I mean in theory you can sneak out of camp, but if the Provos caught you, they'd put you on a charge. Lots of trouble,' she added with a small smile. Her eyes popped wide. 'No, wait! I was texting with a friend back in Fiji. You could ping my phone or whatever they do. It'll show where I was, won't it?'

Ford nodded and asked Jan to check it out after the meeting.

'Was there anything else, sir?' Josifini asked. 'Only I'm due back at camp shortly. It's my unit's turn out at Imber tomorrow. We're deploying to Somalia in a couple of weeks.'

Ford felt his guts clench at her mention of the impending deadline. 'Nothing at the moment. Thanks again for coming in. This has been really helpful. You know you can always call me if you want to talk. Any time of the day or night.' He gave her one of his cards then looked at Jan. 'Could you show Josifini to the front door, please?'

She beckoned to Josifini. 'Come on, love. Let's see you safely off the premises. And if you can give me your mobile number, we'll start tracing it for the night of the murder.'

Alone in his office, Ford sifted through the information Josifini had provided, planning the next stage of the investigation. Top of his list of people to speak to again was Corporal Wren. He also felt like having another word with Colonel Hemmings, to find out a little more about Rachel's complaint.

Then his stomach rumbled. Too loudly to ignore. He headed for the canteen, stopping at Mick's desk on the way. 'Fancy some lunch?'

Mick looked up. 'Going soft in your old age, H? Time was, you'd have had a Mars Bar and an extra-strong coffee and worked through.'

'Nah, I fancy something with pastry – and chips. And I want to bounce a few ideas off you. Come on.'

CHAPTER TWENTY-SEVEN

Ford and Mick sat opposite each other at a round white-topped table. Ford cracked the top on his can of Coke and poured it into a glass made cloudy from repeated runs through an old and overworked dishwasher. He cut into his steak pie, releasing a creeping tide of thick deep-brown gravy. He speared a piece of meat and added a fat golden-brown chip.

Once he'd taken the edge off his hunger, he looked at Mick, who was busy working his way through his chips.

'See the girls last night?'

Mick nodded and swallowed a huge mouthful. 'Yeah. Evie had a wobbly tooth. Daddy had to pull it out. She made a fuss but I think she enjoyed it.'

'It's always the dad's job. Did you give her the old, "I'm just going to look at it" line?'

Mick grinned. 'Yeah. Works every time, doesn't it? You'd think they'd twig after the first couple.' Then he frowned and stabbed a chip so hard the tines of the fork screeched against the plate.

'What is it?' Ford asked.

'Caitlin waited till Evie had gone to the toilet then she told me Kirsty's got some bloke in tow. His name's Darius, if you can believe it,' Mick said with a curl of his lip. 'Apparently he's in property. That's how they met, 'cause Kirsty's in the council's planning department.'

Ford nodded. In a way he wasn't surprised. When police marriages ended, often the aggrieved partner, at a loose end for one too many weekends, or missing one too many planned nights out, simply found more attentive company elsewhere. However, now wasn't the time for reasonable analysis. Solidarity was called for.

'Sounds like Caitlin has the makings of a detective,' he said instead. 'Name, occupation *and* details of first meeting. And Darius, yeah, I agree. What was his previous job, king of Persia?'

Mick's brows drew together. 'What?'

'You know, like in the Battle of Thermopylae. The three hundred Spartans,' Ford said, wishing he'd not bothered cracking such a lame joke in the first place.

Mick shook his head. 'Totally wrong, H. Leonidas was king of Sparta and he was fighting King Xerxes of Persia. Plus, it wasn't really just the Spartans. They reckon there were also seven hundred Thespians.'

Ford looked at his sergeant with renewed respect. 'Bloody hell, Mick, are you taking an Open University course in ancient history?'

'Caitlin's obsessed by the ancient Greeks. She's got all these books of myths and what have you,' he said with a smile. 'We watched *300* last weekend and she kept up a running commentary on all the things the writers got wrong.'

'Sounds like you guys are still having a lot of fun together.'

'Yeah. I guess it's because when I see them now, time's so precious, you know? When I was living at home, I wasn't so bothered,' he said. 'I worked in the evenings, sometimes I didn't sit with them for their tea, even if I was there in time.'

Ford shrugged. 'You were doing your best, Mick, I'm sure. And you still are. Listen, just be there as much as you can for them, because they won't be at home forever. How old's Caitlin now?'

'Almost sixteen. She's going into the sixth form next year. Pendle Court.'

Ford nodded. 'Sam's got one more year of school then he's off.' *And I'm still not sure we're good about his mum's death.*

'Any idea what he's going to do?'

'Not really. Sometimes he talks about university, but he's not totally sold on it. He's worried about the loans.'

'Why wouldn't he be? It's a hell of a lot of money to start off owing before you've even got a job.' Mick put his cutlery down, having wiped up the last of the gravy with a final fat chip. 'Did you drag me away from my thrilling report-writing just to talk about our kids, or was there some actual police work involved?'

'I just interviewed a young female soldier in the Black Watch. Josifini Tui. She said she was Rachel's girlfriend but she didn't kill her.' Ford laid out what he'd learned from Josifini. When he'd finished, he asked Mick, 'What do you think?'

'The letter's the problem.'

'What about it?'

'Well, she says she didn't write it, but she can't prove that, can she? I mean, it's printed on generic paper in a generic font.'

'She says Rachel always called her Jo-jo, not J.'

Mick snorted. 'In happier days, Kirsty called me "Tans" but I'd sign off texts or whatever as M. It's just quicker, isn't it?'

Ford had to concede the point. It had been bothering him, too. But even if Josifini's reasoning had been flimsy, he hadn't read her as a perpetrator enjoying pulling the wool over the police's eyes.

'What about your interviews at Larkhill?' Ford asked.

Mick shook his head. 'Same old, same old. Good soldier. Hard-working. Reliable. That word comes up a lot.'

'Well, it would do, wouldn't it? I guess if you're shoulder to shoulder with someone in a battle, knowing you can trust them has to be top of your concerns,' Ford said. 'Anyone make any remarks about her being a girl in a man's world?'

'Nope. I even tried pushing the idea, making out I was sexist. And' – he held up a hand – 'please keep your next hilarious comeback to yourself. Funnily enough, they really pushed back. The basic view was, if she passed selection she was as good as the lads and if she wasn't, she'd have washed out by now.'

'What about being gay?'

'I don't think anyone knew, to be honest. Nobody mentioned it.'

Ford thought back to his conversations with David and Helen Padley. And with their pastor. David had clearly not been entirely honest when he'd said he was just his wife's bag-carrier at church. If they'd discovered Rachel was gay, would they have put pressure on her? Had the stress of resisting them made her careless for her own safety?

'Tell me something, Mick. How do you think Kirsty would react if she found out one of your girls was gay?'

Mick blew out his cheeks. Then he leaned back in his chair and cradled the back of his head as he stared at the ceiling. Finally, he rocked forward to look at Ford.

'I'm going to try to be totally honest, but I don't want you to think this is the divorce speaking. I think she'd be put out,' he said. 'She's always talked about how she'd make a great mother of the bride.'

'But she must know lesbians can get married. Jools interviewed the woman who co-owns Radclyffe's. She's married. Very happily, it sounds like.'

'*I* know that, H. But for Kirsty, I think it'd be, you know, like second best.'

'How about you?'

'Me? I couldn't care one way or the other. As long as the girls are happy, it's fine by me. Look, I know I've got a reputation round here,' he said. 'The way Olly looks at me, you'd think I'd been frozen in about 1975 and only just thawed out, like a cross between Benny Hill and Rip Van Winkle. But that's just because I don't subscribe to all the politically correct bullshit about villains just seeking attention or having fucked-up childhoods. Maybe they have. But when you kill someone, or rape them, or bash them over the head and steal all their personal possessions, that's a choice you're making,' Mick said, jabbing a finger at Ford, as if the DI was the one in trouble. 'And if it was as simple as the bleeding hearts make out, then everyone who came from that sort of background would be a rapist or a serial killer, wouldn't they?'

It was the longest speech Mick had made for some months, and Ford had to admit he had a point. He'd think twice about sending Mick into a local secondary school to talk about the criminal justice system, but deep down he agreed with him. After all, Ford's own childhood hadn't exactly been bathed in sunlight, but he'd joined the police, not a gang.

'Who do *you* think we should be looking at?' he asked.

'Got to be the girlfriend, hasn't it?'

'Because?'

'One, the statistics. Two, she's just inserted herself into the investigation.'

'But I went on TV and more or less pleaded with her to come forward.'

'Yes, but why didn't she straight away?'

'She said she was frightened of reprisals, or of being next on the killer's list.'

'Very convenient. Maybe she only turned up because she realised you'd find her soon enough,' Mick said. 'The sketch wasn't great, but I bet someone from the Black Watch would have made the connection.'

'Anything else?'

'Yes. Three, look at the MO. Rachel was a highly trained soldier, yes?'

'Yes.'

'In an infantry regiment, yes?'

'Yes.'

'In a combat role *within* that regiment, yes?'

'Yes.'

'Yet, despite all that, somebody managed to smack her into the wall so hard she was practically comatose, then dragged her bodily out to the crossroads and, in a single confident stroke, slit her throat open down to the bone. Who does that sound like?'

'Anyone with enough adrenaline and sufficient motivation.'

Mick rolled his eyes. 'Come on, H. Answer properly.'

Ford spread his hands wide. 'It sounds like another soldier.'

'Like Josifini Tui.'

'Yes.'

'Listen, I get that the famous Ford gut is telling you something different,' Mick said, 'and it's been right plenty of times in the past. But I still say you've got to start with the most obvious motives. Look at sexual jealousy or revenge before you start building some fantasy castle in the air full of, I don't know, weird anti-lesbian army cults or whatever.'

Mick's choice of language made Ford smile. But he couldn't shake the idea that all the statistics in the world wouldn't help him find Rachel Padley's murderer. He conceded that they needed to do more to eliminate Josifini Tui as a person of interest before treating her as a friendly witness. Although her reference to Rachel's fear of her parents' church was still echoing in his head.

Five minutes later, they entered Major Crimes together. Ford saw Charlie at her borrowed desk. She looked up as he and Mick came in and immediately got to her feet, clutching some stapled pages.

'Henry, I've finally got the list of all the Js from Battalion HQ,' she said when she reached him. 'I practically had to threaten them with a court order. They weren't so much keeping their cards close to their chest as sewing them up inside it.'

He held out his hand for the document. 'Thanks. I'll have a read through. Anyone stand out for you?'

She nodded. Ford thought he caught the glimmer of a smile. 'Come and find me once you've been through it,' she said.

He closed his office door and scanned the first page. There must have been forty names. Three pages equalled 120 names. He flipped over to the next sheet. Halfway down, one name hit him with the force of a bullet.

Hemmings, Julian Steven, Lt. Col.

He wrote it out on a separate sheet of paper and started again at the beginning. Five minutes later, he'd added two further names beneath the colonel's.

Hemmings, Julian Steven, Lt. Col.

Tui, Josifini, Pte

Wren, James, Cpl

Everyone on the list would need interviewing, but these three were his inner circle of persons of interest.

CHAPTER TWENTY-EIGHT

Hemmings, Wren and Tui: all had first names beginning with J. But only one of them was over forty. The colonel was the likeliest letter-writer.

Ford called Charlie and asked her to print out the list of Js again, this time grouped into cohorts by age: 18–30, 31–40 and 40+.

His phone rang.

'It's the front desk, sir. There's a man on the phone says he has information about the Padley case.'

'Put him through.'

'I'd like to speak to Detective Inspector Ford, please.'

Ford assessed the caller. Working-class London accent. Youngish. Under thirty. Probably another member of the Black Watch.

'Speaking.'

'Sir, it's Private Forrest. I'm RMP. I was out at Imber when you came out to see the body. It was me and Private Kennedy found her.'

'What did you want to tell me, Private?'

'We've had a tip-off, sir. And I didn't want to do nothing till I'd spoken to you,' he said. 'This bloke called me and said we should search Private Tui's quarters. Said he'd seen her going off-base the night Rachel Padley was killed.'

Ford got to his feet. 'Has anyone been into her room?'

'No, sir.'

'Right. I think she's out at Imber on exercises. Secure the room. Don't let anyone in. I'll be there in fifteen minutes. Oh, and Private Forrest?'

'Yes, sir?'

'What did he sound like, this bloke? Any accent?'

Ford heard the shrug in the young soldier's voice. 'Average, sir. Local, maybe? Sorry.'

Ford stopped in at Forensics on the way out. 'Wix!' he called.

'Yes, Henry?'

'Grab your stuff. We're going to Larkhill Barracks.'

◆ ◆ ◆

Ford found Private Forrest waiting for him outside Josifini's room. He nodded at the young MP who unlocked the door. Ford put on a pair of purple nitrile gloves and, with Hannah behind him, went inside. She shut the door behind her.

Here was another version of the room Ford had already observed at the barracks. And just like Rachel's, this one was immaculate. Every item was squared off, stacked neatly or positioned parallel to some external line. He stood next to Hannah just inside the door.

The room was small. He didn't think it would take long to search. But the thought that had been plaguing him since taking the call from Forrest wouldn't leave him alone.

Who had phoned the MPs with the tip-off? And why?

It could wait. Right now, he wanted to see if they could find a piece of evidence linking Josifini Tui with Rachel Padley's murder. Given the room's dimensions, he suggested they simply take half each.

Ford looked around, seeing books, a couple of magazines and a laptop. He checked out the books, but none of the titles matched those in Rachel's room. He opened the laptop and once it had woken up, prodded a key. It asked him for a password. He'd been expecting it and closed the lid again. Somehow, he didn't think that whatever they'd find would be digital.

He followed the charger cable from the side of the laptop beneath the desk to a four-socket extension lead. Even here, where in his own home office he'd have found dust bunnies, paper clips, plectrums and random bits of debris that had fallen off his desk, there was nothing.

Still on his knees, he swivelled round to face the bed. He prodded the blanket experimentally. It was so taut he could have bounced a ball on it. He got down on to his elbows and peered underneath. No detritus here either. Just a single wadded-up tissue.

Apart from a single white edge, it was stained a deep red.

He stretched out his hand and retrieved it then sat on the bed. He opened it out. The blood stain was maroon. Dark and dried-in. Josifini's? Or Rachel's?

'Wix?'

She turned. 'What is it?'

He held up the tissue.

Hannah held out an opened evidence bag. Ford dropped the tissue inside and watched as she sealed it and wrote out a label.

Ford looked under the bed again. Something wasn't right.

'Can you shine some alternative light sources under here?'

Hannah nodded, then closed the curtains. He stood back and watched as she mounted a series of coloured gels over her torch and shone the beam under the bed.

'Anything?'

'No. Why?'

'Let's assume for now the blood is Rachel's,' he said. 'How do you think it got under there?'

'I don't know. Josifini must have cleaned blood off herself and then dropped it,' Hannah said. 'Maybe she kicked it under there and didn't realise. In the hours after the murder she definitely would not have been thinking straight.'

'Wouldn't you expect some of the blood to have transferred to the floor, though?'

Hannah peered at the blood-soaked tissue.

'There is certainly a lot of it. If it was wet after she used it to clean herself, then yes, I would have expected at least a smear on the floor.'

Ford rubbed his chin. It was odd. Then he heard Sandy's voice between his ears.

'Yes, Henry, but what about the evidence? *What is* that *telling you?'*

That was simpler. The dead woman's girlfriend had a blood-soaked tissue under her bed. Her initial was on a letter the killer had used to lure Rachel out to Imber. And, following a televised appeal, she had finally identified herself to the police.

Now, he could be charitable and accept her story about fearing reprisals. Or less charitable, and agree with Mick. With the sketch out there, someone would have recognised her sooner or later and she was just getting her version of events into the record before anyone else's.

First things first. He needed to know whose blood was on the tissue.

Ford called Charlie as they drove back to Bourne Hill. 'I need you to interview Corporal Wren. See if he has an alibi.'

Two hours later, he and Hannah were comparing the results of the blood group test she'd conducted in Forensics with the army's medical records for Rachel and Josifini.

The blood on the tissue was AB-negative. Rachel was AB-negative. Josifini was O-positive. The problem was, it all felt a little too convenient. The RMP get an anonymous tip that they should search Josifini's quarters. Where – lo and behold! – the perfect piece of forensic evidence is duly found.

Hannah had sent the tissue off to the external DNA lab. She'd asked whether he wanted a twenty-four-hour turnaround. Ford had thought hard about paying the extra, given Sandy's strictures on overspending. In the end he settled for Monday.

He went to see Sandy to update her on this latest step in the investigation. He didn't trust the evidence. But that was the trouble. What else *could* he trust? His gut? The brass would laugh him out of court. And that damned deployment date kept moving closer, one day a time.

◆ ◆ ◆

Ford knocked and entered Sandy's office and then immediately wished he hadn't.

Martin Peterson swivelled round and, on seeing Ford, jacked an insincere smile on to his face. Today his suit was of a shimmering, silvery-grey fabric that Ford thought might be called sharkskin.

'Ah, if it isn't the hardest-working DI at Bourne Hill,' Martin said. 'What news from the battlefront, Henry?'

Over Peterson's shoulder, Sandy gave Ford a level stare and a subtle shrug of her shoulders, today draped in an expensive-looking mustard sweater with a soft, floppy polo neck. Eyes widened fractionally, she was telling him it wasn't her fault.

'We've found a blood-stained tissue in Josifini Tui's quarters at Larkhill Barracks,' Ford said to Sandy, as he took the second visitor's chair. 'The blood group matches Rachel Padley's.'

Peterson clapped his hands together. 'Excellent news! So even though suicide is out, you've managed to wrap it up inside a fortnight. Well done, that man. Ya nailed da perp!' he added, in what he clearly thought was an authentic *Noo Yawk* cop accent.

'I'm not so sure we have,' Ford said, still addressing himself to Sandy.

'Go on,' she said.

Ford outlined his doubts about the timing, the positioning and the condition of the tissue. 'Her room was spotless. I can't see how she'd miss a tissue under her bed,' he concluded.

Before Sandy could open her mouth, Peterson was already speaking. 'Now listen, Henry, you know I'm only here in an overwatch role. But even someone as lowly as I' – he laid his right palm over the breast pocket of his suit – 'a mere elected official, can see that finding the victim's blood in the suspect's room is *prima facie* evidence of murder.'

Grinding his teeth at Peterson's repeated use of his nickname, Ford gave serious consideration to slapping the self-satisfied smile off his face. He'd be busted back into uniform, if not kicked out of the service altogether, but he thought it might be worth it. Somehow, he restrained himself. From a physical assault, anyway.

'Right!' he said, rounding on Peterson, making him lean backwards. 'One, we don't know that it *is* the victim's blood. Two, Josifini Tui isn't a suspect. Not yet. And three, please don't use Latin. This is a nick, not a courtroom. Do you even know what *prima facie* means?'

Peterson had flushed as Ford was talking. His face was now only a couple of shades lighter than the silk tie carefully knotted at his throat.

'Well, yes, of course I do,' he blustered. 'It means, the initial, that is, if at first, you—'

'It means at first sight,' Ford snapped. 'And the tissue is *prima facie* evidence of the square root of fuck all. To me, the whole thing stinks like last week's fish. Now, if you'll excuse me, I'll leave you to whatever you were discussing with Sandy before I barged in.'

Breathing heavily, he caught Sandy's eye. She was glaring at him.

'Sorry, boss,' he muttered.

He got out as fast as he could. He'd have to return to patch things up with Sandy later.

CHAPTER TWENTY-NINE

Ignoring all distractions, Ford slogged through a mountain of paperwork so he could try to enjoy dinner with Hannah. Sam was out with mates. It was happening more and more these days. He'd disappear in the morning and not come home until early evening, or sometimes later.

Charlie called him mid-morning to say she'd managed to speak to Wren. He had a solid enough alibi. He'd been playing pool with a group of friends until 1.15 a.m. Then he'd returned to his quarters and at 2.05 a.m. he'd gone next door to complain about someone's loud music. Charlie had followed it up and the neighbour had confirmed the story.

Standing on Hannah's doorstep that evening, he checked his watch: 7.59 p.m. For a moment, he thought about waiting for sixty seconds. Smiling, he shook out his shoulders, then rang the doorbell.

Hannah opened the door immediately and he had the sense she'd been hovering there, waiting.

'Hi, Wix.'

'Henry! You're a minute early. Come in.'

She smiled, but it looked forced to Ford.

As he stepped across the threshold she hugged him tightly then released him with a decisive push. Holding him by his shoulders, she stretched up and planted a kiss full on his mouth.

'I hope that was all right,' she said. 'Wine?'

'It was. And yes, wine would be lovely. I brought you this,' he added, handing over a cold bottle of Sancerre.

Hannah accepted the wine with a jerky movement. She was obviously tense. Ford realised with a sinking heart that Jools had read Hannah wrong. He'd have to deal with her jealousy of Charlie at some point in the evening.

With the business of accepting and refrigerating the wine out of the way, she clinked glasses with him. 'Cheers!'

'Cheers! You look nice. Actually, no, you look great!' he said.

She nodded. 'Thank you for telling me. You also look nice. That must be your favourite jacket. It hangs perfectly and its wear pattern suggests you've worn it a lot.'

'I have. Well observed.'

The conversation switched, naturally, to the case.

While they talked, a large cat stalked across the kitchen and sat before Ford, wrapping its tail around its legs and looking up at him with amber eyes.

'This must be the famous Uta Frith,' Ford said.

'Yes. Although as I only have the one cat, it couldn't be anyone else.'

'True.' He looked down into the cat's unblinking gaze. 'Does she like me?'

Hannah frowned and looked from the cat to Ford and back again. 'She's not sure yet.'

Trying to ignore the cat's scrutiny, Ford drank some more wine. He found it easy to talk to Hannah on her home turf. Over olives and crisps, they finished the bottle of wine while ranging back and forth over the details of the case.

'Sushi time!' Hannah announced at 8.45 p.m., rising to her feet and shooing Uta Frith out of the way. 'You do like sushi, don't you?'

'I don't get to eat it very much, but I love it.'

'I made this myself. Apparently, you should ask dinner guests whether they have any dietary issues, but I forgot.'

Ford sat and marvelled at the platter of slivers, rolls and cones of rice and fish. 'Wow!'

'Try it, otherwise you can't tell whether it's any good. Although it is.'

He selected a salmon nigiri, tweezed a sliver of the delicate pink ginger free with his chopsticks, then dipped the whole thing in soy before popping the rectangle of sticky rice and translucent fish into his mouth.

The aroma of the sea filled his head and as he chewed, the sinus-clearing heat of the wasabi and the sweet-sourness of the ginger cut through the oiliness of the fish. He swallowed, inadvertently closing his eyes.

He opened them again to see Hannah watching him anxiously.

'Do you like it?' she asked.

He was about to go with, 'No, I don't like it . . . I *love* it!', then realised the ironic pause would distress her. 'It's amazing! Honestly, that's the best sushi I have ever eaten. Where did you learn to make it like that?'

'Tokyo Japanese Restaurant at Quantico. They ran classes for base personnel. I signed up for a course and I passed with flying colours.'

Steadily, over the next hour, they finished the platter of sushi and a second bottle of wine.

With the dinner things cleared away, Hannah led Ford to the sitting-room end of the through-lounge. She sat on a sofa, legs curled beneath her, and patted her lap. Uta Frith, obviously waiting for the signal, levitated silently on to her mistress's lap and began to purr loudly as Hannah scratched behind her ears.

'Henry?'

'Yes?'

'There's something I want to discuss with you.'

Ford readied himself. Without hurting Hannah's feelings, he'd have to explain to her how the kiss she'd witnessed in the pub – and its consequences – had been a moment of impulsiveness. How Charlie had let him down gently afterwards. That there was nothing between them.

'I'd like to talk about Lou,' Hannah said. 'And how she died. Would that be all right?'

Ford's carefully assembled reply crumbled into a pile of discarded Scrabble letters. Despite the wine, he felt a surge of anxiety squirming in his gut. Pinned to the sofa, he could only nod.

'I've been thinking a lot about what happened since you told me,' Hannah said. 'And I remembered the way you reacted when Lord Baverstock told us he'd taken his wife to Libertas.' She was talking about the culprit in a case the previous year, whose first wife had had motor neurone disease. 'I think you found it impossible to reconcile in your mind the idea of a man taking his wife somewhere to die when you'd struggled to achieve the opposite. Even though the circumstances were quite different.'

Hostility towards the earnest young woman in front of him flared in Ford's chest. Whether the wine had dissolved some level of restraint – or denial – he had no time to consider before he opened his mouth. 'Am I supposed to be impressed?'

She frowned. 'Impressed?'

'With your masterly grasp of my inner world? How you can read me like one of your bloody textbooks and come to just the right conclusion?'

'But I *am* right, Henry, can't you see? Even though you weren't doing one of the established routes – Ship to Shore, or House of Cards – the climb was well within your capabilities,' she said. 'And after you dislodged the block and fell, you did all you could to save Lou from drowning. Even roping her on to the platform. The coroner's inquest went through the whole event. Her verdict was clear and unambiguous. Death by misadventure. That means—'

'I know what it means! I have, actually, attended one or two inquests in my time.' Something snagged in his brain. 'Wait a minute. Have you been researching it?'

Hannah nodded. 'Yes, I have. And I concluded that you're stuck there, Henry. You're stuck with Lou on that rock slab with the tide coming in. That's why you can't move past it. Why you're still living with the early stages of grief. You have to let go of her, like Lord Baverstock did with Sasha. You're not to blame. You didn't kill her.'

Something cracked in Ford's mind. His carefully constructed story was coming apart. And he couldn't find the energy he needed to keep it in one piece. And it seemed Hannah had discovered the truth anyway. The tension flooding his system receded like a wave running back over the sand towards the sea.

He sighed. 'I'm sorry for shouting at you. You're right: I didn't kill her. But she told me to leave her and I did, Hannah. I left my wife to die!'

'I know. It was in the police report. But they said it was the only course of action left to you. It must have been awful, her telling you to go. No wonder you've never told Sam.'

Feeling the years of deception pushing him close to tears, Ford closed his eyes and gave into the alcohol. He felt the room tilt on its axis, then fade. He heard surf crashing against ancient rock. Gulls crying. Moans of agony.

CHAPTER THIRTY

I'm kneeling by your side at the base of Pen-y-Holt. The rock I pulled out fell and smashed your right femur. Now the tide's coming in, soaking us both. My ears are roaring with the noise of the surf and sheer blind terror.

There's no way you can make it to shore. You're begging me to go. For Sam's sake. Let him grow up with at least one parent to care for him.

I see your lips move and I hear two words through the monstrous hiss between my ears. 'Please . . . go!' you scream.

At least that's what I have always believed I heard. Now I'm not so sure. 'Please . . . go!' What happened in that tiny gap?

I rewind the memory like a video. I spin it back a few seconds and replay it. And now the static has gone. The sound is perfectly clear. I'm the one speaking.

'I have to go for help. If I can make it to the shore, I'll climb the cliff and call the coastguard from the top.'

And you, wide-eyed, say, 'What? No! I'll drown.'

You clutch my arm and dig your fingers into the flesh above my elbow. Firmly, weeping as I do it, I detach your fingers and step back into the freezing water.

'I have to. I'm sorry. I'm so sorry.'

As I turn away and plunge into the icy water, you scream again. And in the eerie silence I hear your final words clearly for the first time since the moment you uttered them.

Not two words. Three.

'Please, don't go!' you scream into the teeth of a wave.

CHAPTER THIRTY-ONE

Ford broke out in a cold sweat. He opened his eyes to see Hannah staring at him, her forehead creased.

He tried to speak, but his voice caught. He cleared his throat and tried again. Saw Lou's bright-blue eyes, filled with pain and something else. Disbelief. Dismay. Horror.

How had it happened? How had he got this far – almost seven years – and lied to himself the whole time? Through the therapy, the nightmares, the waking dreams?

He felt a lump in his throat, hard and unforgiving, not something he could swallow. He spoke round it.

'I lied,' he said quietly. 'She didn't tell me to leave her at all. She wanted me to stay, Hannah. She begged me to stay! I've been lying to everyone. For seven years. The police, the coastguard, Sam, my in-laws, my mum, Sandy, you. Everyone. Even myself.'

'What do you mean?'

'*I* told her I had to go for help. It was *me*, not her,' he said. 'She pleaded with me to stay with her. Said I might get a signal if I climbed higher. But I panicked, Wix. I fucking panicked! I abandoned my wife and left her to die.'

Ford felt his guts turn over and he barely made it upstairs before the dinner and a fair portion of the wine rushed out in a scalding stream into the toilet.

Dry-heaving, he staggered to his feet and leaned on the sink to splash handfuls of cold water over his face.

He gripped the edges of the basin. Who was staring back at him, red-eyed, from the mirror? A murderer? A killer? A man careless enough of his wife's memory to sleep with a casual acquaintance just because he was pissed?

He swiped a hand across his eyes. Or was it just a bereaved husband? Victim of a tragic accident and a bad decision taken in a moment of extreme fear?

He heard a tentative knock on the door.

'Henry, are you all right? Can I come in, please?'

Sniffing, and then drying his face on the towel, he turned and opened the door. Hannah stood there, hands clasped in front of her. Her eyes were damp, her make-up smeared, grey smudges leading away from her eyes.

'Have you been crying?' he asked.

She nodded. 'I am so sorry, Henry. I should never have pushed you like that. Please forgive me.'

As Ford took in the expression of unbearable compassion etched onto her features, something gave way inside him. He sank to his knees and let his head drop into his chest, leaning forward until his head rested against Hannah's legs.

Then, as if the tide at Pen-y-Holt was coming in all over again, he cried. Great, racking sobs that shook him. He felt her fingers on the top of his head, tentative at first, stroking there as she'd done with the cat earlier in the evening. She said nothing. No calming words or pleas to stop. She just let him cry.

Eventually, with a shuddering breath and a sigh, a final sob shook itself free of his throat.

He realised he'd wrapped his arms around Hannah's knees and jammed his head against her thighs, soaking the pale denim with his tears. He let her go and pulled himself up using the edge of the bath.

Hannah was crying, too. He pulled off a length of loo paper from the chrome spindle behind him and dabbed at her cheeks. She took it from him and finished the job.

'Do you want to go home?' she asked with a sniff.

He shook his head. 'No. I'd like to make you a cup of tea, or pour you another drink, and tell you about Pen-y-Holt.'

'I think tea would be best at this point,' she said with a half-smile.

Sitting at the kitchen table ten minutes later with Uta Frith winding herself around his ankles, Ford began. 'First of all, I'm sorry again for raising my voice. I know you were trying to help me. I was being unreasonable.'

She shook her head. 'That's OK. I knew I'd put you under enormous psychological stress. I would have been worried if you hadn't shouted.' She reached across the table, hesitated, then took Ford's hand in hers. 'Henry, please listen very carefully to what I am about to say, and please, *please* don't be angry with me.'

Ford felt his heart thudding in his chest. Because he thought he knew what she was about to say.

'Go on,' he said in a low, quiet voice.

'Say you did as Lou asked and stayed. Climbed the stack again. You might have found a signal at the top, but you might not. And Lou could have drowned anyway.'

'We'll never know that.'

'No. We never will. But, Henry, can't you see that it wasn't your fault?'

He shook his head. 'I pushed her into attempting the climb. I asked if she was chicken. She was so competitive, I knew it would work,' he said. 'If I hadn't, she'd still be alive today and Sam wouldn't have grown up without his mum.'

Hannah's head was shaking vigorously. 'No. You wanted to climb the route. *But so did Lou.* You didn't force her into it, or even bully her into it,' she said. 'You just used your insights into your wife's personality to find her motivation. It's like with hypnotists. They can't make their subjects do anything they don't secretly want to do.'

Ford looked at Hannah. Her eyes were the blue of old china, not the cornflower shade of Lou's. Hannah's were darker, more weathered somehow.

Had Lou been as much the architect of her own death as he had? That's what 'death by misadventure' meant, after all. She'd known the risks, and she'd accepted them willingly. And even if he had stayed, as Hannah said, there was no way of knowing the outcome.

He'd left because he couldn't bear the thought of Sam growing up an orphan. Maybe that was the right decision. Even if Lou didn't want him to make it.

The revelation that swept over him was as powerful and all-conquering as the waves that had drowned Lou. Hannah was *right*. Not ninety-eight per cent right. Or ninety-nine. One hundred per cent.

He *could* have stayed. But the outcome could have been just the same. Or worse. And there was no way on earth anybody would ever know for sure.

He looked at Hannah. 'So, who *was* to blame if it wasn't me? You're not saying it was Lou, are you?'

Hannah shook her head again. 'No. Lou was just following her own instinct. To survive. It's the strongest drive humans possess,' she said. 'But you weren't to blame, either, Henry. Because protecting your child is the second strongest. It was an accident. That's all. A tragic accident.'

He searched inside himself for the guilt he'd been carrying around for seven years. But it had gone. He doubted even Jan could have found it. The talisman he'd moulded from his own grief and baked in the heat of denial had vanished. In its place sat a weary acceptance that he'd suffered a great hurt and needed to heal.

He looked at Hannah and nodded. 'I need to go.'

'Will you be all right?'

'Yes. I will. But, Hannah, before I go, there's something I need to ask you. No, not ask, tell.'

'Anything.'

'I know you and Sam have grown close, and that's great. I'm completely fine about it. But you absolutely must not tell him how it happened,' he said. 'What I told you tonight must stay between us. Do you understand?'

'I understand.'

Without waiting, he hugged her, and although initially she froze, he felt her relax inside his arms.

He held her for a few seconds longer. Then he let her go.

Ford didn't even bother going to bed that night. He knew sleep would elude him. Instead, he showered and changed and sat in his music room. He picked up the Strat, and as he cradled the curved body against his own, he let his thoughts wander.

How had he managed to convince himself for all those years afterwards that Lou had told him to leave her? He'd had counselling, both mandated by Occie Health and on his own account. In session after session, he'd told the therapists the same – false – story. And he'd believed it.

Now it seemed obvious why none of it had worked. How could you move past something you hadn't even faced up to? No doubt Hannah could give him chapter and verse on the psychological and possibly neurological reasons for it. But it didn't matter. For the first time he could see the past clearly.

But what about Sam? Ford had narrowly avoided confessing the false version to him. Should he now offer him the truth? No. They were doing OK, especially since they'd looked at the old photos together. The truth would have to stay buried.

Little by little, thoughts of the past receded, and thoughts of the present loomed. He had a murderer to catch. Just a few days to do it in. And support cut to the bone thanks to the combined opposition of ACC Starkey, Martin Peterson, Colonel Hemmings and now, it seemed, Sandy.

What was he missing? Josifini was no more a murderer than he was. And though he suspected Wren was telling only part-truths about Rachel, he didn't believe he was the killer either.

The family, then. It had to be the family, aided and abetted, possibly, by that creep Pastor Simeon. Had he been ignoring the obvious conclusion because he couldn't face his responsibility for his own broken family? Or waiting for his gut to tell him what to do?

And that was another thing. '*The famous Ford gut.*' That was how people referred to it. He'd assumed they were offering grudging respect. Now he wondered. Was it that? Or were they taking the piss?

It didn't matter any more. He had a killer to catch.

CHAPTER THIRTY-TWO

On Monday morning, Hannah presented the DNA results at the team meeting in the sugar cube.

'There is a ninety-five per cent chance that the blood on the tissue we found in Josifini Tui's room belongs to Rachel Padley,' she said.

This news caused an immediate buzz of conversation as the gathered detectives reached the same conclusion. Case closed. Josifini Tui was the killer.

Ford looked round the room at the grins and nods. Was he the only one who could see a different narrative? That the bloody tissue had been planted, and rather obviously?

Hannah held her hand up for quiet. Ford was impressed once again by how her confidence had grown during the time she'd been working at Bourne Hill. He remembered the first time she'd had to address a team briefing. Her face had flushed and she'd barely made eye contact with anyone.

'I know that you'll all be thinking, well, that's it solved. But I'd like to draw your attention back to the statistic the lab supplied,' she said. 'A ninety-five per cent chance that it came from Rachel still means there is a five per cent chance that it didn't. It could even have come from Josifini.'

Ford thanked Hannah and turned to the assembled investigators. 'I want a DNA sample from Josifini. Something tells me she'll happily provide one. Let's start with the obvious and eliminate her.'

'Why, guv, given the DNA clearly points to Rachel?' Olly asked.

'Because it's not enough, Olly. Juries love DNA but a skilful defence brief can make that five per cent doubt look like fifty. They could even suggest the entire prosecution case has been built on Josifini cutting her leg shaving.'

Olly was blushing furiously. But today Ford had no time to massage his bruised ego. Fast-track kids were all the same. Book-learning coming out of the ears and zero real-world experience. Ford visualised Olly in the stand with a defence QC interrogating him. Didn't like what he saw.

He turned back to the room. 'Listen. The brass are putting the screws on me to close this case quickly. They'll jump at this like dogs at a bone, but I don't believe Josifini Tui's the murderer. I'll bring her in anyway, and we'll get the DNA as a matter of course. The rest of you, get out there and start talking to people.'

After the meeting, Ford retreated to his office. He leaned back in his chair and stared at the ceiling. Questions crowded his thoughts until he couldn't focus on a single one of them. He grabbed his suit jacket.

Crossing Major Crimes, he called out to Jools. 'I'm going for a walk. I need to think. Call me if you need me.'

◆ ◆ ◆

Ford approached the cathedral from the west. The horse chestnut trees were losing their foliage. The tawny, acid-yellow and burned-orange leaves carpeted the close. Under a low, threatening sky whose colour shaded from the grey of a peregrine's back to wet slate, few people had braved the elements to come and goggle.

At the main entrance, Ford turned right, entering the cloisters. Hardly anyone chose this austere stone passageway when the wonders of the cathedral were so close at hand. That was why Ford liked it.

As he walked, Ford tried to imagine Josifini luring Rachel out to Imber, smashing her head backwards against the wall, dragging her out to the crossroads, cutting her throat and then staging the suicide. He shook his head. It was ludicrous.

As for the bloody tissue, he was sure in his bones that it had been planted in Josifini's room.

But if not Josifini, then who? Colonel Julian Hemmings, who preferred the more blokeish 'Steve'? Had he been trying it on with Rachel? Maybe he was one of those men who thought he could 'turn' a lesbian with his own machismo. She'd have rejected him, surely? Or would she have consented to a date out of fear?

Ford could picture a scenario very easily that would put Hemmings in the frame. He'd tried it on with Rachel one too many times and she'd finally told him to leave her alone. That she was gay and it was against all the rules. Threatened to tell his wife, maybe. He'd written the letter and killed her to silence her. Then he'd whispered in Starkey's ear, calling in a favour, which would explain the pressure the ACC had been exerting on Ford to call it suicide.

He had to be realistic. For now. Follow procedure. No more gut feel. The evidence pointed to Josifini. The victim's blood had been found under her bed. She could have got it on her hands or face and wiped it off and somehow dropped the tissue and kicked it under there. Forgotten it in her panicked state.

She was in a sexual relationship with Rachel, so if it had gone south she'd have motive. She had no alibi. It could be her. In all likelihood, it *was* her.

He made a decision. He'd arrest Josifini. Hold her for a few hours. Then let her out on police bail. He put the chances of her being a flight risk at zero. Or not until she shipped out to Somalia with the rest of the Black Watch. In the meantime, he thought it was time to speak to Hemmings again.

◆ ◆ ◆

Ford had made the diplomatically sensible move of asking Charlie to arrange a meeting with Colonel Hemmings. On being shown into the colonel's office, he saw he'd elected to bring in Major Robinson. She sat in a corner, notebook balanced on her knee, pen poised.

Hemmings stared at Ford. He could detect no animosity in the colonel's flinty expression, but not a lot of sympathy either. Ford thought he could manage without.

'Thank you for seeing me again, Colonel,' he said.

Hemmings shrugged. 'Why wouldn't I? It's not as if I have anything else to occupy my time, now is it?'

Ford ignored the sarcasm. He had a question designed expressly to unsettle this man who held so much power within the base and the battalion. Yes: so much within, and none without.

'Were you in a sexual relationship with Private Padley?'

Major Robinson, writing intently a moment earlier, snapped her head up to look at Ford.

'I beg your pardon?' Hemmings spluttered.

'Did you instigate a sexual relationship with Rachel Padley?'

'No, of course I didn't! She was a bloody squaddie, for Christ's sake.'

'Exactly. If you'd come on to her, she'd have found it hard to say no. The power imbalance between you would have made any notional consent she offered worthless. A lawyer would say you'd coerced her.'

'I'm going to ignore that insinuation, Inspector,' Hemmings said, breathing heavily. 'Unless you've got any sensible questions, I'll ask you to leave. I have a deployment to prepare for. As I think you know,' he added.

'Private Padley was gay. Did you know that?' Ford asked.

'Yes. From your investigation.'

'Do you think that's why she was killed?'

Hemmings sighed and passed a hand over his brow. 'It's possible, although I'd be very disappointed if that's what eventually comes out. The army has made great strides in recent years. Diversity is the big buzzword.'

'Maybe for the top brass. But what about at ground level? She made a complaint against her corporal, didn't she? Wren?'

Hemmings inclined his head. 'It was groundless. Listen, Ford, Padley was ambitious. There are very few women tough enough to qualify for front-line combat roles,' he said, looking at Major Robinson, who nodded in confirmation. 'We're talking handfuls, not hundreds. She wanted to push herself and she thought anyone standing in her way was biased because she was a woman. But it wasn't like that. Wren was well within his rights to act as he did.'

'I'd like to talk to him.'

Hemmings spread his hands. 'Be my guest. I don't know where he is. He could be out at Imber.'

Ford got up to go, then turned. 'One last thing. Can you confirm your whereabouts on the night Rachel Padley was murdered?'

'I'm sure I can. If you'll just hold on.' He pulled out a mobile phone, tapped and swiped. 'Yes, here we are. At a meeting with Major Robinson until dinner, which was in the officers' mess among dozens of colleagues. I was there until about eleven, then I went home to my wife.'

'And your wife will confirm that.'

'Unless she has a malicious streak, yes.'

'Thank you.'

Outside again, Charlie touched Ford on the elbow. 'What did you think?'

'Of Hemmings? The alibi's great until eleven, then it breaks down. He could have driven home, kissed his wife goodnight then gone out again. If she's a heavy sleeper she'd never have known.'

'But do you really think it was him?'

Ford drew cold, crisp autumn air into his lungs. 'No. Now, let's go and find Corporal James Wren.'

It turned out they would have to wait for Wren. As Colonel Hemmings had suggested, he was in the middle of a live-firing exercise.

Pleading paperwork on other cases, Charlie left Ford to find his own way out of the base. He drove, not back to Bourne Hill, but to the Padleys' house.

Helen Padley opened the door. Seeing Ford, her face closed in on itself, curtains being drawn behind windows to keep the outside world at bay.

'May I come in?' he asked. 'I have a few more questions about Rachel.'

She nodded silently and turned to lead him into the sitting room. Grateful not to find the pastor occupying one of the chairs, he looked at the family photos. Where was Rachel? Was it normal to omit your adult daughter from every single photograph on display in your house? And then, in a flash of insight, he understood.

This was *all* about disapproval and shame, wasn't it? Rachel had come out to her parents after all. It hadn't gone well. Once she'd left, maybe in tears, David or Helen had stormed through the little house gathering up every single photo, from school days to the Black Watch, and binned or burned them.

Helen gestured with a bony hand to an armchair and then sat at one end of the sofa, her hands folded primly in her lap.

'What did you want to ask?'

'Last time we spoke, I asked you if you knew Rachel was gay, and you told me she wasn't,' he said, watching for a fleeting expression that might reveal Helen's true opinion. 'Can you cast your mind back and think if Rachel ever said someone had taken against her because *they* thought she was gay? Maybe someone from your church?'

Helen shook her head. 'We didn't speak much. But in any case, nobody from church would commit murder. The Bible says thou shalt not kill.'

'Why didn't you speak much? Had you fallen out?'

Helen shrugged her thin shoulders. 'Children grow up, Inspector. And sometimes they grow away, too.'

Not liking the personal implications of that last sentence, he changed tack. 'What was Rachel like as a little girl?'

She smiled then, turning her face to his for the first time since he'd arrived. It was as if she'd accessed some secret power source; her eyes brightened.

'She was such a lovely little thing. A good baby, right from the day I had her. She slept through, took her feeds, played quietly. No trouble.'

Ford looked at her and nodded. No, because the trouble had all come later, hadn't it?

'Did she have many friends?'

'Some. You move around a lot, but the army is like a family.'

'Boys? Girls?'

Her eyes narrowed. He could see her trying to evaluate the question. For a woman like Helen Padley, suggesting her daughter was friendly with boys might carry a whiff of impropriety. On the other hand, answering 'girls' led straight back to the aspect of her daughter's identity she seemed so keen on denying.

'She had no special friends,' she finally said. 'Mostly she liked to read or play by herself.'

Ford nodded. It was a clever answer. 'How did your husband get on with Rachel? Did they see each other at work much?'

She shook her head. 'He's a Provost Sergeant. They make sure the young ones stick to the rules. Rachel was a good girl. Never in any trouble. Why would she see him?'

Ford smiled. 'I don't know. I'm just trying to get a feel for her life, Helen. And I'm sorry if my questions are upsetting to you.'

She plucked a tissue from the sleeve of her dress and blew her nose. 'It's OK, Inspector. You're just doing your job, I know that,' she said, sniffing.

He'd avoided mentioning the impending arrest of Josifini Tui, but it would be wrong to hold the information back any longer.

'I expect to be making an arrest this afternoon,' he said. 'A young woman who claims she was in a relationship with Rachel.'

She surprised him, then, by grabbing the sleeve of his suit jacket so hard he felt her fingers through the thin fabric, digging into his arm.

'Then you must make sure she is punished for what she did,' she hissed. 'And don't believe her lies, either. "Their throat is an open grave; they deceive with their tongues. Vipers' venom is under their lips." Romans, three, thirteen.'

After this outburst, she released her grip on his arm and seemed to lapse back into the semi-catatonic state she'd been in when she'd opened the door. He thanked her for her time and let himself out.

He climbed back into his car and went to pick up Charlie. In his heart he knew he was about to arrest an innocent woman. But with the brass on his back and the looming deployment date, he felt he'd run out of options.

CHAPTER THIRTY-THREE

At 4.00 p.m., Ford and Charlie were waiting on the edge of the concrete apron fronting the motor pool. Camouflaged armoured personnel carriers bristling with aerials, grenade launchers and machine guns surrounded them. Mechanics were working under one, scuttling back and forth beneath its massive bulk on wheeled trolleys like the one Jason Padley had been using at the bodyshop.

Soldiers were not allowed to carry loaded weapons on base. So the arrest plan was fairly simple: wait for Josifini to return from the exercise and pick her up as soon as she dismounted from the troop transport. No flight risk. No fight risk. Plus, Ford had a strong feeling she wouldn't be any trouble.

There. That phrase again. Helen Padley had talked about Rachel being no trouble as a baby and a young girl. But if Helen had ended contact with Rachel after she'd come out, she'd have been cut adrift. The army would be a form of surrogate family, but Ford could imagine very easily how disorientating it would be for a young girl to lose the support of her parents.

If they'd disowned her – '*You're no daughter of ours! The Lord have pity on you!*' – she'd have been emotionally vulnerable. Add in the fact of her sexuality in the hyper-masculine world of a front-line infantry battalion and she'd have been an easy mark for a predator.

Was that it? Had she been killed by one of the young men taught to suppress their adherence to that most basic of laws – the prohibition against killing another human being? Was it Wren after all? His interest kindled rather than extinguished by her complaint against him? Obsessed by a girl he knew he couldn't have? Or determined, perhaps, to pay her back? There'd been no sign of sexual assault at the post-mortem, so it hadn't got as far as attempted rape.

But if she'd fought off his advances, he might have switched from predator to killer. The bruises that George had put down to the everyday knocks of soldiering could have been sustained in a scuffle. He resolved to go back over the report, talk to George as well, if necessary.

The loud roar of a powerful but unrefined diesel engine brought him back to the business at hand.

He turned to Charlie. 'Ready?'

Soldiers in full combat gear, their faces smeared with camouflage greasepaint, spilled out of the back of the truck, laughing and bantering. No rifles to be seen. Ford assumed they'd been collected at the end of the exercise and taken straight back to the armoury.

Wren had them fall in and, after a brief pep talk, dismissed them. Ford strode towards the edge of the group, where he could see Josifini talking to a couple of other Fijian soldiers. She had her back to him, but then one of the men she was talking to caught Ford's eye. He leaned towards her and muttered something. Ford lip-read the word 'cops'.

Josifini turned, a smile sliding off her face. She met Ford and Charlie halfway. Arriving, she stood to attention, looked from Ford to Charlie and back again.

'Sir, ma'am,' she said, chin up, eyes level.

Ford recited the arrest script, feeling as he did so that he was so far off the trail he might as well not bother. But there were protocols, rules, ways of doing things. In the police service as in the army.

241

'Come with us, please,' he finished.

'No handcuffs?'

'Are you going to run?'

'No, sir. I haven't done anything to run *from*.'

'Well, then. I think we can manage it like this, don't you?'

'Yes, sir.'

Half an hour later, Josifini had been booked in by the custody sergeant. She stopped at the cell door, as if realising for the first time exactly what was happening to her, and turned to Ford.

'You'll have writing materials and a copy of the rules governing your detention here,' he said, in as reassuring a tone as he could muster. 'And you're entitled to a solicitor. Is there someone you want us to call?'

'I don't want one, sir. I've got nothing to hide.'

He heard a hint of defiance in her voice and liked her for it. But if it went as far as a trial, he wanted to make sure there'd be no chink in their case because of a lack of legal representation.

'You've been arrested for murder, Josifini. That's a heinous crime,' he added, trying to impress on her the gravity of her situation. 'I really think you'd be better off with a lawyer. I can have one of the duty solicitors here within the hour.'

She shrugged. 'Your call, sir. But it won't make any difference. I'm happy to answer all your questions. I *want* to.'

Her forthrightness impressed him. So many of the toerags he arrested started giving their best gangster impressions as soon as the cuffs were on. They'd be effing and blinding in the car, issuing threats they had no way of implementing, making themselves look ridiculous. In contrast, Josifini Tui maintained a quiet dignity.

'Are you hungry? I can get you something to eat and a drink if you like,' he said.

She'd been silent in the Discovery all the way from Larkhill to the station. Maintaining a stoic distance from her plight. Which was severe. Being arrested for murder, even if you hadn't done it, was apt to leave a body feeling anxious. But now the first sign of doubt stole across her features. The muscles around her eyes were tight as she nodded to Ford.

'Yes, please, sir. I haven't eaten since breakfast.'

'What would you like? A sandwich? Chocolate? A coffee? Coke?'

'Yes, please, sir.'

'Cheese and ham, OK? Or are you veggie?'

'No, sir. That would be great. Thank you.'

The custody sergeant ushered her inside and pushed the door closed, making sure it was latched before turning his key in the lock.

Ford returned ten minutes later with a paper bag containing the food, plus a can of Coke and a plastic-lidded takeaway cup of coffee. He had the sergeant unlock the door. As he handed her the bag, he dropped it. Josifini shot out a hand and caught it before it hit the floor.

'Nice catch,' he said. 'I wasn't sure if you took milk. There're a couple of little pots in there if you do.'

She nodded. 'Thank you, sir,' she said in a quiet voice. 'When will you be interrogating me?'

He smiled. 'Never. But I will be interviewing you as soon as your solicitor gets here.'

With that he turned and left. Sandy would need to be updated and he still hadn't got round to apologising for the scene with Peterson in her office.

This time, he called ahead. 'You alone, boss?'

'Why? Were you hoping Martin-bloody-Peterson would be here so you could start a fight?'

'I'll take that as a yes, then. Coffee?'

'With cream. And a chocolate biscuit.'

Ford headed upstairs. Sandy had sounded pissed off, but not terminally so. He thought he could pull this one back.

After a stop-off to brew what he hoped was the best-tasting cup of coffee he'd made all year and to buy a KitKat from the vending machine, he walked along the corridor to Sandy's office.

Sandy held her hand out for the white china mug and took an exploratory sip before setting it down on her desk.

'Not bad,' she said.

Ford handed over the KitKat before taking the visitor's chair and gulping some of his own coffee. Sandy tore off the red and white wrapper and broke the chocolate bar into two before handing half back across the desk to Ford.

'Thanks,' he said. 'I take it that means you're not going to fire me?'

'Not a chance, sunshine. I need my best detective to close this bloody case and restore me to the ACC's good graces.'

'Did Peterson complain, then?'

She favoured him with a level stare. 'What do you think?'

'I'm really sorry,' he said, meaning it. 'I shouldn't have lost it like that.'

'No, you bloody well shouldn't have!' Sandy said. 'I need Martin onside, even if he is about as welcome in my station as a pubic hair on a bar of soap.'

Ford grinned. 'I mean it. I am sorry.'

Sandy puffed out her cheeks. 'Can't be helped.' Then her lips quirked upwards. 'When you said, "The tissue is *prima facie* evidence of the square root of fuck all", his jaw practically hit the floor. I don't think anyone's ever spoken to him like that. It was almost worth it just to see that expression.'

'Does that mean I'm forgiven?'

'It means you're on probation. Now, apart from coming here to grovel, what else have you got?'

Ford told her he had Josifini in custody. He also outlined his doubts about her guilt. And as he explained his thinking, he realised this was more than a hunch. He knew Josifini hadn't done it.

'Josifini's not the killer,' he said.

'And you're saying this because?'

Should he tell Sandy he just knew? That it was so bloody obvious, it didn't need saying? No. He'd worked for Sandy long enough to know that she'd not let him get away with that. Not for a second.

He thought back to Josifini's reaction-catch when he'd deliberately dropped the bag containing her sandwich.

'Because, apart from the tissue being an obvious plant, she's left-handed,' he said. 'And the killer's right-handed.'

Sandy pursed her lips. 'How do you know the killer's not a leftie?'

'Unless they were going to do something really unnatural, which in the heat of the moment I don't think they would, a left-hander could only cut right to left if they were standing behind Rachel. Once she was down, the cart was in the way.'

Sandy frowned. 'Keep talking.'

It was the sign Ford had been waiting for. Sandy was coming round to his way of thinking.

'Josifini Tui is barely five feet five and slim-built. Rachel weighed over ten stone and stood five ten in her bare feet,' he said. 'I'm sure Josifini passed all the fitness tests, but managing Rachel's deadweight with one hand, keeping her upright *and* using a knife? I just can't see it.'

Sandy nodded. He kept going.

'The killer dragged Rachel out from the Marriott and positioned her with her back to the cart, OK? Her head's lolling forward. There was no way they could have got behind her. And, as I said, why bother? They'd just lean forward or possibly straddle her thighs and do it facing her. A backhand stroke from a right-hander, from Rachel's right to her left. Nothing else makes any sense.'

Sandy put a finger to the point of her chin. She closed her eyes. Ford waited. He'd played out the scenario at Imber in his head many times since that first Sunday. Now Sandy was doing it, he hoped she'd come to the same conclusion he had.

'I'm sorry, H, I just don't see it. On the one hand, you've got a hypothetical bit of physical theatre,' she said. 'On the other, an actual tissue stained with the victim's blood in the suspect's bedroom. You have to go with the evidence.'

Ford left Sandy's office feeling he was heading the wrong way down a one-way street jammed with onrushing traffic. Everything Sandy had said was true. Against which he had Josifini's left-handedness, her genuine distress at what had happened to Rachel, and her refusal of a lawyer until Ford had insisted. And there were too many other oddities about the case that pointed away from her – Helen Padley's pious denials that her daughter could have been gay. The lack of photos of her in the Padleys' house. David Padley's closed-down emotional response. The run-in with Corporal Wren.

His phone buzzed. A text from Jools to say Josifini's lawyer had arrived.

CHAPTER THIRTY-FOUR

When interviewing murder suspects, Ford preferred to use Interview Room 4. It stank. Fear-sweat, stale coffee and body odour. The light bulb often flickered. And some bright spark, not him, had sawn half an inch off one of the legs of the chair used by the suspect.

He'd had Josifini placed in Interview Room 2. It still smelled, and the light from the bare incandescent bulb was harsh. But in the hierarchy of fear-inducing spaces at Bourne Hill, it was a few rungs down from 4. It was the best he could do for the frightened young woman sitting before him.

He'd also asked Hannah to sit in the observation room beyond the one-way glass. Her experience with the FBI made her an invaluable asset.

Ford sat down opposite Josifini. Jools took the seat to his left, facing the duty solicitor, Gillian Kenney. Gillian often looked tired, her suits crumpled. Today the auburn-haired woman in her forties looked fresher than he'd seen her for weeks. Her lips glistened beneath a sheen of soft pink lipstick and her brown eyes were bright and alert. Ford wondered idly whether she was getting more sleep than him.

With the tape recorder's spools hissing and the formal introductions and caution out of the way, Ford began. 'Josifini, did you kill Rachel Padley?'

Gillian leaned sideways and whispered in Josifini's ear behind the back of her hand.

Josifini shook her head. 'No,' she said to Gillian. 'I want to tell him everything. I've got nothing to hide. I'm innocent.' She turned to face Ford again. 'No, I didn't. I loved Rach. I would never do anything to hurt her.'

'Can you explain the tissue soaked in her blood we found under your bed in your room at Larkhill Barracks?'

Josifini sat straight in the hard chair. The look was confident without being aggressive. He didn't detect the blank eyes and emotionless gaze of a psychopath either. Her body language was controlled, but relaxed. He saw zero indications of a woman about to tell lies.

'Someone must have put it there, sir,' she said. 'To make it look like I killed Rach. But I didn't do it. Like I said, I loved her.'

'Why would the killer pick you to frame out of all the people at Larkhill? And there's no need to call me sir, by the way.'

She nodded, offered a tiny smile. 'They must have found out about us. We were always careful, but someone must have, I don't know, followed us or something.'

'Did you meet outside the base anywhere apart from Radclyffe's?'

She nodded. 'Sometimes we went into Salisbury for a drink or a meal, or maybe to do a bit of shopping. But we'd never've done anything to draw attention to ourselves. No holding hands, or kissing. Nothing like that.'

Ford smiled. He felt he was in the presence of someone telling the truth. It was interesting because there was none of the usual *'I swear to God, Inspector Ford, I never done it'* nonsense.

He didn't need Hannah on the other side of the mirror to tell him that people who swore their innocence on their dear old muvver's life or that of their kids, or the Supreme Being, were guilty often as not.

'Did anyone in your unit or the wider community at Larkhill ever make any remarks that led you to believe they knew you and Rachel were gay?'

She shook her head.

Ford flipped through his notebook to the notes he'd taken during Jan's chat with Josifini the day she'd presented herself at Bourne Hill.

'When you came in to see me that first time, do you remember?'

'Yes, sir. I mean yes.'

'You told me and Sergeant Derwent how the men think any girl who joins the infantry must be gay,' he said. 'And then you said, and forgive me for quoting your words back at you, "They call us names, they make up jokes." Now, when you said, "us", that sounds to me like you meant they called you and Rach names. Like they *did* know.'

Josifini shook her head again. 'I'm sorry, that's not what I meant.'

'What did you mean?'

'Just that they called people *like* me and Rach names.'

Ford looked at Jools, a signal for her to take over the questioning. They'd agreed beforehand that she'd be more direct in her approach than Ford. Not the tired old cliché of the good cop/bad cop routine. Just a different approach that might work on Josifini if Ford's avuncular style failed to produce results.

'Josifini, I used to be an MP, OK? I know my way around an army base. Now, I read the account you gave for your movements on the night Rachel was murdered,' she said. 'You said you were in your room and it was hard to sneak out because of the Provos.'

'Yes, ma'am.'

'But that's not really true, is it? I mean, people go AWOL all the time. It's why you have MPs and Provos in the first place, isn't it?'

'Maybe it is, but I didn't leave barracks. Anyway, I thought you lot were checking my phone. I told the nice one, Sergeant Derwent, that I was texting a friend in Fiji. She lives in Suva. Haven't you tracked my phone yet?'

'Oh, we've tracked your phone. And it was on base all night. The trouble is, Josifini, that's all it proves. It doesn't mean *you* were on base, does it? Do you see my problem?'

Gillian spoke for the first time. 'Do you have a question for my client, DC Harper?'

'We've got a tissue soaked in Rachel's blood in your room,' Jools said without breaking eye contact with Josifini. 'We've got no proof you were on base except for a phone you could have asked someone else to use. You were in a sexual relationship with the victim. You're trained to kill. Why should we believe you?'

Gillian placed her hand on Josifini's arm and leaned in to offer more whispered advice, but Josifini shook her off fiercely, displaying the first sign of agitation in the interview so far.

'I didn't, OK? I – did – not – kill – Rach,' she said, poking the tabletop with a little thump to punctuate this declaration. 'Why won't you believe me? Someone is making it look like it was me, but it wasn't!' Josifini's deep-brown eyes were wide and she looked close to tears. It didn't necessarily mean anything: she could be faking. But it was a small tick in the right column.

Jools carried on. 'I spoke to the lady who runs Radclyffe's. Sal. You know her?'

Josifini nodded.

'For the tape, the suspect nodded, indicating agreement,' Jools said in a calm voice. 'Well, Josifini, Sal told me that you and Rachel had words one night when you were in together.'

'No! We never argued. Not when we were out, anyway.'

Jools made a show of referring to her notes though Ford knew she'd have planned out her questions in advance.

'She told me Rachel said' – she flicked over a couple more pages – 'yes, here we are, "I've got to end it." We thought at the time it might have meant she was talking to you about killing herself. But now we've discounted that theory – it sounds like she was breaking up with you. Was that it?'

'It wasn't about that.'

'No? Sal said you looked pissed off. Maybe Rachel told you she was dumping you and you couldn't bear it, so you killed her?'

Josifini's chin was trembling. Ford hoped Jools hadn't pushed too hard.

She shook her head and straightened in her chair. 'I remember it because just as she said it, everyone stopped talking at once. It went dead silent and she blurted it out. Everyone sort of looked embarrassed, then the chat all started up again. She wasn't breaking up with me.'

'So what was she talking about?' Jools asked. 'What was it she had to end?'

'She was going to tell her mum and dad.'

'About being gay?'

'Yes. She couldn't stand it any longer. All the lying. Making up stories about why she didn't have a boyfriend,' she said. 'That's what she meant. She told me she had to end all the secrecy. That's why we were arguing in Radclyffe's that time. I was worried her dad would figure out I was her partner.'

'But you told me last time we spoke that she was terrified of what her parents would do,' Ford said. 'Why the change of heart?'

Josifini slumped in her chair. 'I told you a lie before. Someone did know we were gay.'

'Who?'

'Corporal Wren.'

'Go on.'

'I don't know how he found out, but he got her alone one day and said he was going to tell her parents unless she gave him a . . .' Josifini blushed. 'You know, a . . .'

'Are you saying Corporal Wren sexually blackmailed Rachel by threatening to out her to her parents?' he asked.

Josifini nodded. Then she glanced at the hissing tape recorder. 'Yes,' she said. 'That's exactly what I'm saying. Rachel told him to fuck off. Sorry, sir, but she did. Then she told me she was going to tell her parents first. Pre-emptive strike, you know?'

Ford nodded. More and more pieces of the puzzle were slotting into place. Although he could have Wren charged with attempted blackmail, it would be hard to make it stick. He let it go. He still had a murderer to catch.

'Why didn't you tell me this before, Josifini?'

'I was frightened. We're going to be on patrol in Somalia in a few days. What if him and me are out together? I need to know he's got my back,' she said. 'I couldn't risk dropping him in it. He could shoot me and say it was an insurgent. Or just send me down an alley on my own and let them do it for him.'

'Why did you look pissed off in Radclyffe's when she said she was going to come out to them?'

'Because her parents hate gay people. I thought they might make her leave the army or something,' she said.

'Something?'

'Put her in some sort of conversion camp. They have them, you do know that, right? Back home it would be worse. They'd proba-bly kill us. That's why I came to England.' Josifini leaned forward, clasping her hands on the tabletop as if in prayer. 'Make me do a lie-detector test. Give me the truth drug. Anything. I don't care,' she said, her voice loud in the poky little interview room. 'You'll never get me to say I did it. I loved her and I wish she was still alive.' She burst into tears.

Gillian fished a packet of tissues from her handbag and passed it to Josifini.

Ford had swallowed down a lump in his throat as the last few words left Josifini's lips. He knew genuine grief when he encountered it, and he was encountering it now.

'We don't do lie-detector tests, Josifini,' he said. 'And we don't administer truth serums or any of that other crazy shit you see on the telly, OK?' The use of the swear word was deliberate, to startle her into realising he was on her side.

She looked at him, eyes reddened, and sniffed. 'So you believe me?'

At that moment he realised how young she was. Barely older than Sam, and yet training to kill for her country.

He knew that wasn't the way the army framed service. But at the end of the training, and the discipline, and the cleaning, polishing, squaring-off and saluting – when peace-keeping and nation-building and handing out sweets to local kids were done – there was an infantry soldier, an advancing enemy intent on killing her, and a rifle between them. She pulled the trigger. Or she died.

'I believe that you loved Rachel,' he said gently. 'But sometimes even people in love do things they wish they hadn't.'

He felt terrible for pushing an obviously innocent young woman like this, but the heat on his back from the brass was burning right through his suit jacket and scorching his skin. He suspended the interview and led Jools outside to meet Hannah in the observation room next door.

'What do you think, Wix?' Ford asked as soon as they were all seated. 'Is she telling the truth?'

'I'm eighty per cent certain she is, yes.'

'That's on the low side for you.'

'The thing is, she's a front-line infantry soldier. Do you remember once before I told you about SERE training?'

'Vaguely. Remind me what it stands for again?'

'Survival, Evasion, Resistance, Escape,' Jools interrupted, making Hannah frown.

'Yes, so it's possible she's been through a programme,' Hannah said. 'In which case she might be adept at adopting neutral behaviours, both verbal and physical, to disguise her true intentions and confound her interrogators.'

'I can check that,' Jools said, making a note.

'Don't bother. I'm sure she didn't do it,' Ford said, feeling as he did so that he was one hundred per cent convinced by Josifini's denials. 'What about you, Jools?'

Jools rubbed her nose. 'I mean, she *could* have done it. But I don't see it. The tissue is just too obvious,' she said. 'Even the thickest murderer, and we've met a few, guv, has the basic common sense to clear up their own bedroom.'

Ford nodded. In the stress of the moment after committing murder, people often fled the scene leaving all kinds of incriminating evidence behind. But once they were home safe, they were able to think more clearly. The tissue had been planted.

What were his options? He could let Josifini go now, send her back to Larkhill in an unmarked car to give her the minimum amount of explaining to do. Or hold her for a while. Under PACE he had plenty of time left. And there was one thing she'd said that had jarred with the rest of it. *'You'll never get me to say I did it.'*

It could have been an assertion from an innocent person that she wouldn't be coerced into a false confession. But it could just as easily be a slip from a guilty one. He needed to decide.

'Right, we'll let her go,' he said. 'I can't see her as a cold-blooded murderer. I believe her. Can you organise a car to take her back to Larkhill, please, Jools?'

'On it, guv.'

She left with Hannah.

Alone again, his decision made him uncomfortably aware of an impending deadline. He had three days to arrest the real murderer before the Black Watch deployed to Somalia. And with them, what little chance he had of finding Rachel Padley's killer.

CHAPTER THIRTY-FIVE

Ford got home at 7.55 p.m., having stopped off at the petrol station to buy ice cream. He called out to Sam. Heard nothing. Realised he'd have to resort to texting. That or risk popping his head round Sam's bedroom door and finding who knew what?

A year or two earlier he'd wondered if Sam viewed porn on his laptop. Then he'd chided himself. *If?* Get real, Ford. The more pertinent question was, what kind? And he'd discovered he didn't want to know.

He hoped Sam was just a normal adolescent boy. He didn't have a girlfriend, or not one he'd admitted to. But there were girls in the sixth form for the first time in the school's history, and Sam had mentioned one or two names more than once.

Ford had been careful not to risk bruising their delicate relationship with clumsy questions. He figured Sam would tell him when he was good and ready.

u in? I got Ben & Jerry's

A ten-second gap.

what flavour

Ford smiled.

cookie dough

He put the tub on the table, grabbed spoons and bowls out of the dishwasher and sat down to wait. Lately Sam had developed a style of coming downstairs even louder than his trademark 'box of encyclopaedias falling off a wardrobe'. It suggested to the unwary listener that he might have hurled himself bodily from the top step.

He appeared in the kitchen with an insouciant look, still in his burgundy suit trousers and school tie, yet with one half of his shirt untucked.

'Where is it, then?' he asked, sitting down opposite Ford.

'In here,' Ford said with a smile, tapping the lid with the spoon.

'Can't eat it in there, can we?'

Ford scooped out two enormous helpings of the softening ice cream. Sam popped a spoonful into his mouth.

'How was school today?' Ford asked.

'All right,' Sam mumbled. 'Beth and I had to do our presentation on democracy today.'

'How did it go?'

'Fine. Miss MacKenzie said it was the best one in the class.'

Ford thought back to his earlier musing about Sam and girls. 'You talk about Beth quite a lot.' He went for a jokey tone, praying it wouldn't earn him a look of Sam's most withering scorn. 'Anything going on there I should know about?'

Sam shrugged. 'She's not my girlfriend, if that's what you mean.'

Ford shook his head. 'I was just asking.'

'She is fun to hang out with, though, and I do like her.'

'I understand, really. I just—'

'But, Dad, if I did want to ask her out, I mean, what do I say? I can't just go, like, "Oh, hey, Beth, do you want to be my girlfriend", can I?' He pushed his hair out of his eyes. 'Or can I? Is that what I should do, do you think?'

Ford frowned. He really wanted to get this right. Sam rarely asked for his advice and here was something really important.

'Well, I suppose you could. But maybe it would be easier if you just asked her out for a coffee in town in one of your free periods.'

'Yeah, I thought of that. But the trouble is, everybody does that now anyway,' he said. 'And I don't want other people to be there.'

'Do you think she likes you, too?'

Sam shrugged. 'I don't know. I think so.'

'Then, why don't you say something like, "Beth, I really like you. Do you want to come for a coffee with me?" And then say, "just us two". She'll get the message.'

'But what if she says no?'

'Then you'll know, won't you? And you'll have discovered two things.'

'What?'

'One, asking girls out is easier than you think. Two' – he broke into a high, keening wail – 'you can lo-o-o-ve a woman, but ain't it a shame, ba-ba-bah, when the dame, ba-ba-bah, don't love you back?'

By way of a response, Sam cupped his hand to his ear. 'Shh! Can you hear that? It's the day job calling.'

Sam retreated back upstairs leaving Ford at the kitchen table. He leaned back and closed his eyes. Rachel Padley had been murdered because she was gay. He was sure of it. No knowledge meant no motive. So who knew? It was a surprisingly long list.

Josifini, obviously, but Ford had already discounted her. The colonel, possibly. Or Corporal Wren. Though he doubted it was either of them. Major Robinson. Jason Padley.

The women who ran Radclyffe's, Sal and Molly, knew. So, presumably, did the other customers, but would they have known who Rachel and Josifini were? Probably not. He didn't imagine they'd gone out for a quiet drink together in their Black Watch uniform.

If Josifini was telling the truth, then it looked increasingly likely that Helen and David Padley knew, despite their denials. They might have told members of their church.

He checked his watch. It was just before 8.30 p.m. He texted Sam.

got to go out for work

back later

The reply came as he was climbing behind the wheel of the Discovery.

ok

thanks for girl advice

Smiling to himself, he drove off the gravel and on to Rainhill Road.

Ford pushed through the door into Radclyffe's. Inside, the place was cosy. A log fire was burning in a grate and some inoffensive jazz was playing on the cafe's sound system.

As the door closed behind him, he felt like a character in a Western: the greenhorn from 'back east' who'd chosen the wrong saloon for a glass of milk. The clientele, all women, had turned to see who'd walked in and were now bestowing upon him looks that varied from concern through irritation to outright hostility.

He ignored them all and made his way through the tightly packed tables to the bar. The woman serving had platinum-blonde hair in an elaborate curled style. A wide mouth accentuated with a bright-red shade of lipstick. A beauty spot on the right side of her top lip. She looked like a 1950s movie star.

'Girls only tonight,' she said, not smiling. 'Sorry.'

Now he did produce his ID. 'Are you Sal?'

She shook her head and jerked her chin in the direction of a woman in a black and white polka dot dress swerving gracefully between the tables with a tray of drinks. 'That's Sal. I'm Molly. Co-owner. What do you want?'

'To ask you both a few questions.'

She frowned. 'Can't it wait?'

He'd taken an instant dislike to her as soon as she'd opened her mouth. Didn't have time for polite persuasion. 'No, it can't. I'm investigating a murder. One of your former customers had her throat sliced open a couple of weeks ago.'

Her face fell. 'You mean Rachel. Fine, hold on. Gina!'

Her shout caused a woman with blonde beaded dreadlocks seated towards the front of the cafe to turn round.

'What is it, Mols?'

'Can you take over behind the bar for a bit?' She tipped her head sideways to indicate Ford. 'Business.'

She led him out of the buzzing main room, collecting Sal on the way. Ford followed her up a flight of stairs and into an office. It must once have been a bedroom, complete with a dainty cast-iron fireplace flanked by two long, thin rectangular panels of floral tiles.

The two women sat next to each other on a worn but comfortable-looking green velvet sofa. Ford made do with the visitor's chair, which he pulled out from the desk.

'Look, I'm sorry to drag you away from your customers, but this is really important,' he said. 'My sergeant Julie Harper spoke to you, Sal, last Wednesday.'

'Yes, I remember,' Sal said, glancing at Molly. 'I told her everything I could remember about Rachel and her girlfriend.'

'I know, and I'm not doubting you. But there's something else I want to ask you,' he said. 'Did Rachel ever confide in you? I get the feeling you two are kind of like big sisters to the women here.'

It was a calculated risk. They could laugh in his face, accuse him of all sorts of biases. And nothing in Jools's interview notes exactly pointed to that conclusion. But Josifini and Rachel were young girls, anxious about keeping their relationship a secret. He thought there was a reasonable chance Rachel might have opened up to Sal or Molly.

Molly laughed, a proper throaty guffaw. 'Nice try. Do they teach you flattery at police college or wherever you lot learn to poke your noses into other people's business?'

He couldn't tell whether she was genuinely hostile to the police or just utterly uncowed by having one of them invading her realm and asking questions. He prepared to try again but Sal intervened.

She touched Molly on the arm. 'Come on, Mols, he's only doing his job. And he is trying to find out who killed Rachel.' She turned to Ford. 'I'm afraid Molly doesn't have a very high opinion of the police, Inspector.'

'I can't think why,' Molly said. 'I mean, yes, two of our girls were beaten up on a night bus by a gang of squaddies and the cops did fuck all, but why should I hold that against them?'

A fast-flowing river of mistrust separated Ford from the woman opposite. If he was going to build a bridge it needed to be a strong one. With handrails. And non-slip mesh on the planking.

'I'm sorry if the local police weren't helpful, and I know violence against members of the LGBT community is a problem,' he said. 'But that's why I really hope you'll help me. You see, I'm sure Rachel was killed because she was gay. If someone's attacking lesbians, or gay people in general, I have to stop them before they kill again.'

Molly narrowed her eyes. 'Is that a possibility? You're not just saying that to win me round?'

'Oh, come on, Mols, of course he isn't,' Sal said. 'DC Harper said it, too. In any case, whoever it is has killed one of us. Isn't that reason enough to be helpful?' She turned to Ford. 'Ask away.'

'I'm trying to put together a list of people who might have known Rachel was gay and who might have had a reason to kill her because of it,' he said. 'Do either of you know whether she'd come out to her parents?'

Molly nodded. She'd obviously been won over, whether by Sal or Ford, he couldn't tell. Didn't care. 'She spoke to me about it. Twice, as a matter of fact. She asked my opinion about how she should handle it.'

'What advice did you give her?'

'I told her that it was her right to be whoever she wanted to be. She was an adult, a professional woman. And a fighter,' she added. 'I told her she should just tell them nice and simply, "Mum, Dad, I'm gay. I have a girlfriend and I'm really happy. I hope you can be happy for me, too."'

'What happened the second time you spoke to her?'

Molly shook her head. 'It went about as bad as you can imagine. They basically accused her of being in league with Satan, as far as I could tell. Called her every name under the sun. Loads of that Bible shit that type like spouting off to intimidate people.'

Ford nodded as he made notes. *Talk to the family again* had just become *Talk to the family again urgently*.

He thanked them and left.

◆ ◆ ◆

At home, he sat up in bed for a couple of hours, reading interview transcripts and hunting through the case documents for references to the Bible. Finally, he went downstairs and fished out a battered black leather-bound copy of the King James Version that Lou had insisted they have.

He took it back to bed with him and began combing through it. Google would have been quicker, but he thought poring over its dense but beautiful language might help him sleep. He found what he was looking for just before 2.00 a.m.

CHAPTER THIRTY-SIX

The following morning, Ford sat inside the Discovery outside the Padleys' house. Rain was drumming on the roof. He had the big golf umbrella in the boot, but why get soaked retrieving it? He'd still turn up at the front door looking like a drowned rat.

He'd earned a wry smile and a nod of acknowledgement from an off-duty gate guard he'd passed on the main road. He assumed the word had got out that he was investigating those closest to Rachel in connection with her murder. People talked; it's what they did. Cops, CSIs, civilian staff, the family, interviewees.

When children were murdered, everyone wanted to believe in bogeymen: strangers with the scent of blood in their nostrils and perverse sexual desires that led them to kidnap, rape and murder children. For the public, the media, even sometimes the cops, it was just easier.

Out of those three groups, the last knew the reality. If Rachel had been a child, the odds were that one of her parents had murdered her. Cops saw it every day: a baby wouldn't stop screaming with colic, and its sleep-deprived, barely functioning single mother shook it once too often, just too hard. Or a father, off his face on meth or mush-brained with booze, battered his teenage offspring to death because their looks of concern drove him into a lethal combination of guilt and rage.

But Rachel wasn't a child. She was a grown woman. Strong, fit, combat-ready. David Padley was powerfully built for his size, and no doubt handy with his fists, but Ford couldn't see him overwhelming Rachel in a fair fight.

As for Helen, the woman was bird-boned and a head shorter than Rachel. Her faith might have burned hot but Ford didn't see her engaging physically with what she saw as 'sin'.

There was another option, however. It wasn't such a stretch of the imagination to think that they could have discussed Rachel with their fellow church-goers.

Had a fire-and-brimstone congregant taken it upon themselves to do the Padleys' dirty work for them? He decided to call in on the pastor later.

The rain was still battering the Discovery's thin metal roof. Ford made a run for the front door. He sheltered under the mean little porch and rang the doorbell. While he waited, he flattened his hair with a palm, flicking the drops of water off his fingers.

Helen Padley opened the door. She wore another of her curiously dated long dresses, this one in a thick grey fabric dotted with little bobbles that looked as though the material had kept snagging on something.

'Inspector,' she said. 'I thought you'd be calling. Come in.'

He followed her into the sitting room, aware that he was leaving wet footprints on the pale beige carpet and, when he sat, was dripping on to the upholstery.

She smiled at him. 'You're soaked. Wait here, I'll fetch you a towel from the bathroom.'

With Helen gone, Ford got up and crossed the crowded room to the shelving unit. He looked not at the framed photos but at the spaces around and behind them. Saw what he was looking for. Long, thin rectangles gleaming through the dust.

'Here we are,' Helen said brightly.

He turned. She was holding out a fluffy pink bath sheet, comically oversized for the job required of it.

'Thank you.'

He scrubbed at his hair, then dried his face and hands. She held out her hand and, after he'd returned the towel, folded it into four then laid it across the arm of the sofa.

'Why's she been released?' Helen asked.

He wasn't surprised. Josifini's arrest and subsequent release were hardly the stuff of covert ops.

'We arrested someone in connection with Rachel's murder, but we had insufficient evidence to keep her in custody,' he said cautiously.

Helen frowned. '"Someone"? You mean the murderer, surely? You found Rachel's blood in her room.'

How had Helen learned about that? Only his team and the CSIs knew about it.

'How did you know about the blood, Helen?'

She appeared flustered for a second. Pulled a tissue from the sleeve of her dress and made a fuss of unfolding it and blowing her nose. 'David told me. He has friends in the RMP. It's common knowledge around the base.'

Ford nodded. Yes, of course it bloody was. You could draw a line from Major Crimes through the SIB to the RMP and then the Provos. Maybe not a solid line, but one where the gaps between the dots were narrow enough for information to jump across. Because what good were secrets unless you shared them?

'Well, that's one strand of the investigation, but we have to be sure.'

'But Kate confirmed it. I asked her. She's been so kind to us,' Helen said.

Rather than getting sucked further into a discussion he didn't want to have, Ford asked the question he'd been phrasing in his mind since setting out from home. 'Helen, I need to ask you again about Rachel's being gay. Are you sure she never discussed it with you?'

He watched her. This was the killer question.

Helen clamped her lips together, expelling all colour. It was almost as if she wanted to prevent words escaping of their own volition.

'Helen?' he prompted.

She stood up, so suddenly that Ford jerked back in his chair, convinced for a split second that she meant to attack him physically.

'I want you to leave,' she said. She stuck her arm out and pointed at the door. The pose could have looked heroic in a bigger setting, Salisbury Plain for example, or a real battlefield. The artist would probably title their work, 'Britannia Urging Her Troops to Victory'.

Ford remained seated. It meant he had to look up at her as he spoke. 'Please, Helen. You're upset about Rachel's death. I'm a parent, too. I can't imagine how I'd feel if my son had been killed. But I'd want to catch the person responsible.'

'Then go and force that harlot to confess,' she hissed, all trace of her earlier calm gone now. 'She lured my beautiful daughter into sin of the worst kind and then murdered her when she tried to free herself from her clutches.'

Ford didn't believe this for a moment, but he decided to play along, to see where it took them. 'Are you saying Rachel was trying to break it off with Josifini?'

Helen looked down at him, eyes blazing. 'Of course she was! We spoke to her. Told her what she was doing was wrong. She saw the truth of it.'

'Then she *did* tell you she was gay,' he said.

Helen's eyes widened. 'What?'

'You said you spoke to her about it. So she must have told you.'

'No. No, that's not what I meant.'

'What did you mean?' She was lying now. He was sure of it.

'They were seen,' she blurted.

'Who were?'

'My Rachel and that girl. The dark one.'

Ford was getting a crick in his neck from looking up at Helen, who stood rooted to the spot in the centre of the carpet.

'Helen, sit down, please. Now,' he continued after she'd folded like a wooden puppet, back down into the sofa, 'where were they seen? And who saw them?'

'Andover. This awful place. Full of them.'

'Radclyffe's?'

'Yes. Run by two disgusting women who lure young girls there and draw them into sin. Someone from church saw them. She lives in Newbury Street.' Helen's face had reddened. 'That place is a nest of vipers. They'll burn in the next life for what they do in this.'

As her agitation increased, Helen's language grew more florid. He thought he could use it. He'd memorised a verse from Genesis the previous night. He recited it now, recalling as he did so boring mornings at Sunday School where his mum had sent him to get him away from his father. '"Behold now, I have two daughters which have not known man; let me, I pray you, bring them out unto you, and do ye to them as is good in your eyes."'

Helen nodded and smiled, apparently pleased to be in the presence of another believer. 'Genesis, nineteen, eight,' she said approvingly. 'I hadn't taken you for a follower of Jesus, Inspector.'

He ignored the implicit invitation to side with her. 'Did you talk about Rachel at church? Did someone show an interest in having Rachel *brought out* to them?'

'I did not. It was a private matter.'

Ford doubted that. He could imagine all too easily Helen Padley baring her soul and bemoaning the evil that had befallen her daughter. If not to the congregation at large, then to the pastor. His next call.

CHAPTER THIRTY-SEVEN

Ford pulled up outside the brick-built church and went inside. As before, the pastor was nowhere to be seen. A couple of young men were engaged in an earnest-sounding discussion, seated in the front row of chairs. Neither looked round and he sat quietly at the back, head bowed. Listening in.

They were discussing some point of church doctrine. As they quoted various theological authorities to each other, Ford realised he was unlikely to overhear any juicy gossip that might help him. He stood, wincing as the steel legs of the chair scraped on the hard wooden floor. The debaters turned in their seats to look at him.

He smiled. 'Don't mind me, chaps. Please carry on.'

Frowning, they went back to their discussion. Ford had made sure to phrase his request politely, but there was no mistaking the tone of authority he'd used.

He looked around, wondering whether there might be a leaflet about conversion therapy or a poster condemning immorality. Anything that might suggest the church's stance on aspects of its members' lives that it felt needed 'correcting'.

In a shadowy corner, a folding table of the sort stacked in Scout huts and community halls all over the country was pushed against a wall. It bore a plain wooden box, its hinged lid fastened with a padlock. It resembled a ballot box, twelve inches to a side, with a six-inch slot carved into the top.

Behind it, pinned to a cork-covered wall panel, was an A4 poster.

WE PRAY,
HE LISTENS!

To its left sat a pad of paper. A stub of pencil on a string taped to the tabletop lay beside it. He heard soft footsteps behind him and turned, a smile ready on his face.

'Pastor Simeon, I hope you don't mind my return visit. I have a couple more questions for you,' Ford said.

The pastor looked as if he'd rather entertain a bout of diarrhoea. His face twisted into a scowl. 'I told you last time that I would not be answering any further questions without a solicitor present.'

Ford nodded. 'If I remember correctly, you also told me to come back with an arrest warrant.'

He reached for his inside jacket pocket, moving his hand nice and slowly so the pastor could focus on the movement. He closed his fingers around his mobile and looked the pastor in the eye.

The young man's eyes widened and he took a half-step backwards. 'I didn't really mean that, Inspector. Perhaps, in the heat of the moment, I spoke hastily.'

Ford knew when he was in the presence of a bully. He felt the cowardice coming off the younger man in waves. He wasn't so cocky now, was he, when the threat of personal discomfort was happening in *this* world, rather than the next? He released his grip on his phone and let his hand drift back into plain sight.

'Perhaps we both did, eh?' Ford said in a conciliatory manner.

The pastor smiled nervously. He licked his lips. 'Shall we talk in my office?'

'Here's fine,' Ford said easily, deciding not to cede the advantage of territory to the young priest.

'Very well.' He raised his eyebrows in enquiry. 'What did you want to ask me?'

'Last time we spoke, you told me you had no idea whether Helen and David Padley knew Rachel was gay. Is that right?'

'I did say that, certainly.'

Ford nodded, as if ticking off a point on some mental checklist. But the pastor's evasive answer, though calculated, was amateurish.

'I know you *said* it, but was it *true*? Please think very carefully before you answer,' he added. 'If I need to, I'll get a full list of your members and I will interview them all. Under caution, if necessary. You, too.'

Ford left the threat hanging in the air between them. It didn't dangle there long. The priest looked up. Back at Ford. He swallowed and licked his lips again as though he needed a drink of water. He stroked the hairless skin on top his head.

'It may have come up,' he said finally. 'I'm sorry about before. You surprised me and it totally slipped my mind.'

'No problem. Sometimes I can't remember what day of the week it is.'

'"The memory of the righteous is a blessing,"' the pastor said. 'Proverbs, ten, seven.'

'Who did they talk to about it?' Ford said.

The pastor looked surprised, as if he'd imagined they'd spend the rest of their chat swapping Bible verses. 'Oh. Well, me.'

'Anyone else?'

'Not that I know of.'

'How did the conversation go?'

'Well, they were disappointed, naturally.' The pastor paused, looking to Ford for what – agreement? Sympathy? Ford simply stared back and waited. 'Yes, well, they asked my advice.'

'And what did you tell them?'

'I told them to pray for her. To ask the Lord to guide them.'

'And at any point, did they ask you to help them persuade Rachel she was wrong or sinful? Anything like that?'

The pastor looked sideways towards the two young men, who were still fiercely debating with each other, albeit in hushed tones. 'No. Absolutely not.'

Ford looked the pastor in the eye. Trying to see a glimmering of evil there. A willingness to commit the ultimate crime in the name of a higher power to which he owed his allegiance.

Physically he would have had the strength to at least wrestle Rachel Padley back against a low breeze-block wall and bash her head against a corner. And with enough determination and a healthy dose of adrenaline surging through his veins, well able to drag her unresisting form out to the crossroads at Imber.

He cast a glance at the young men in the front seats. They, too, looked to be physically fit. He saw a new series of TIE interviews looming: the last thing he wanted, but almost inevitable.

'How many people attend the church here?' Ford asked, switching his gaze back to the pastor.

'In total we have sixty-two members. Most attend every Sunday and for Wednesday night services, unless they're ill, obviously.'

'Or on holiday,' Ford added, wondering as he did whether people this apparently devout could countenance a fortnight worshipping the sun somewhere hot and frivolous.

'Of course, yes. Or on holiday.'

'I'd like a list, please. Names and addresses.'

From somewhere, the pastor accessed a new reserve of courage. 'That would be a breach of their privacy, Inspector. I'm sorry, I can't give you that.'

'I could compel you. Get a warrant.'

This was a stretch.

Simeon had gone red in the face. 'Then you'll have to. This is a church. A place of God,' he said, raising his voice. 'You can't simply come barging in here, making insinuations and then demanding people's personal details.'

He was almost shouting now. Ford heard a scrape of chairs and footsteps approaching. The two young men came over. They comfortably overtopped Ford by a couple of inches, and one – dark-haired, heavy jaw – had bunched his fists. The other wore his hair shaved close to his skull – Skinheads for Jesus, Ford thought irreverently – and had the doughy sort of physique no good for endurance but quite capable of brief bursts of energy.

'Everythin' all right, Simeon?' the first man asked in a strong local accent, so that 'right' came out as 'roight'.

Ford turned and squared his shoulders. He pushed his ID into the young bruiser's face and gave him a look that said, *I've put bigger men than you on the ground so don't push your luck.*

'Police,' he said. 'We're just having a chat about the Padleys. Do you know them?'

'What?'

Enunciating his words as if speaking to someone with a failing hearing aid or underpowered brain, Ford repeated the question. 'Do *you* – pause – '*know*' – pause – 'the *Padleys*? It's a simple enough question.'

'Yes, I know them. Of course I do.'

'Friendly with them, are you?'

'We are all friends here. In Jesus' name.'

'I know that. But what about outside?'

'I saw them around sometimes, in town.'

'How about you?' Ford asked the skinhead – Dough Boy, as he'd mentally christened him.

'I've had the odd drink with David down the pub. No law against being friendly, is there?'

'Friendly enough to do him a favour?'

'What kind of favour?'

'I don't know. Lend him a set of jump leads? Or a hand in the garden. A trip to the dump? Help him out if he was in a tight spot?'

'No. Not really. Like I said, just the odd drink.'

'Alcohol's permitted for church members?' Ford asked the pastor, involving him in the conversation to stop any thoughts he might have of slipping away.

'In moderation. There is no Biblical prohibition on alcohol.'

Ford turned back to the two younger men. 'Did David or Helen Padley ever talk to you about their daughter being gay?'

They looked at each other before answering. It was so transparent a gesture, Ford wondered why they didn't just ask aloud, *'What shall we tell him?'*

'No,' Dough Boy said, finally.

'How about you?' Ford asked his companion.

He shook his head. 'Sorry.'

'Then I'll let you lads get back to your argument,' Ford said, turning back to the pastor and making clear he'd finished with them.

Simeon's eyes slid past Ford and he nodded, dismissing his would-be minders. Ford caught movement in the corner of his eye as the two men resumed their seats.

'Where were you on the night of Saturday September the twenty-sixth, Pastor?'

'Here. Helen Padley was helping me stuff envelopes until about ten-thirty. Then I would have been praying until midnight.'

'Any witnesses after Helen left?'

'Only God.'

'Not much of an alibi.'

'Do I need one?'

'You do unless you want me to think you might have been involved in Rachel Padley's murder.'

'Well, I wasn't,' the pastor said, folding his arms. 'Was there anything else?'

'What's in there?' Ford asked, pointing at the wooden box.

'We call it the Casket of Wishes.' Simeon pointed to the tray of stationery. 'You write a prayer and pop it through the slot.'

'What kind of things do people pray for?'

The pastor shrugged. 'That depends on their personal circumstances. If they're from a military family, they might pray for the safe return of a loved one from the field of battle,' he said. 'Or it might be a prayer of thanks for an illness survived.'

Or for someone to murder a daughter who'd *disappointed* them? Ford wondered.

He lifted the padlock with the tip of his index finger and let it fall back against the box with a rattle. 'Could I have a look inside? It might be important.'

The pastor gave Ford a look of incredulity, eyes wide, deep furrows grooved into his forehead all the way to his pink scalp. 'Absolutely not! Those prayers are between us and God.'

'Does he read them personally?'

'Sarcasm, Inspector? Really? No, of course not.'

'What happens to them, then?'

'When the box is full, I unlock it, take the prayers out to the back and burn them in the incinerator.'

'When was the last time you did that?'

The pastor pursed his lips. 'The beginning of last month. Why?'

Ford ignored the question. An idea was forming in his mind.

'Do you take up a collection at your services?' he asked.

The abrupt change of direction drew a puzzled frown from the pastor. 'Yes. We believe in tithing.'

'That's ten per cent of someone's earnings, isn't it?'

'Yes. Although actually I encourage people to give as much as they can afford.'

'What do you do with the money?'

'I take it to the bank the next day, Thursdays and Mondays.'

'Good, good,' Ford said, nodding. 'Only I was worried there might be a security risk. People get to hear of money lying around and they see it as an easy mark. Have you had the local crime prevention officer round to check out your locks?'

'No. Do you think I should?'

'It might not be a bad idea. I can have a word with the local uniformed branch if you like? Their CPO is a very experienced officer. Bob Summerbee.'

'That would be kind, thank you. And I'm sorry if I spoke harshly earlier. This whole situation with poor Rachel has been so shocking.'

Ford waved the apology aside. 'How many entrances to the church are there? So I can tell Bob.'

The pastor looked over his shoulder. 'Just the front door and one at the back.'

'Can you show me the back door?'

The pastor nodded and led Ford through the church and a short hallway. Ford knelt down to inspect the single lock: a very basic Yale.

He straightened up. 'OK, I'll talk to Bob for you. I'm sure he'll be delighted to pop over and talk to you about enhanced security. I know you're a busy man, so I won't take up any more of your time.'

Ford left the pastor staring through the glass to the car park beyond. He could feel the case moving into its final stages. And the identity of Rachel's murderer coming into view.

As he descended the short flight of concrete steps from the front door, his phone vibrated. He glanced down and swore internally. The caller ID said ACC Starkey.

'Hello, sir. What can I do for you?'

'I've just been on the phone to Superintendent Monroe, Ford,' Starkey spluttered. 'And she's just told me you've let this bloody Tui girl go.'

'That's right, sir. I no longer consider her a suspect. I released her under investigation.'

'"No longer consider . . ."' Starkey repeated. 'Now look here, Ford, I don't know what sort of game of silly buggers you're playing here, but as I understand it, you had a bloody great piece of forensic evidence found in this girl's quarters. She was in a sexual relationship with the victim. *And* she's a trained killer. For Christ's sake, man! Even a trainee traffic cop could put that lot together and get a case before the CPS. Have you lost your fucking mind?'

Ford took a deep breath. 'No, sir. But things are more complex than the way you've just painted them. If you'll let me explain—'

'Oh, I'll let you explain. Get your arse over to Trowbridge right now,' he barked. 'It's what, ten to twelve? Salisbury to here's an hour's drive, near as dammit. Be in my office by one o'clock.'

The line went dead.

'Shit!' Ford muttered. That was the rest of his afternoon wasted arguing the toss about procedure, clear-up rates and all the other bullshit that the ACC obsessed over. Time he could be spending nailing Rachel's Padley's killer. Time when the whole bloody garrison was preparing to fly to Somalia.

CHAPTER THIRTY-EIGHT

Starkey's uniform could have been bought that morning, so sharp were the creases, so brilliant the silver braid, shoulder insignia and buttons. His hands, furred on their knuckles with thick ginger hair, rested on a burgundy leather folder, open to a typed sheet with a Wiltshire Police logo. For show, Ford thought.

A large wall clock ticked off the seconds. He looked at Starkey. Waiting for him to speak first.

'Well, Ford,' Starkey said with a sigh, 'what have you got to say for yourself?'

'About what, sir?'

'Don't give me that,' Starkey snapped. 'You know bloody well what. Why have you let Josifini Tui walk?'

'As I said, sir, I don't think she did it.'

'Oh, really? Because from where I'm sitting, it looks like an open-and-shut case.'

Ford rejected his first answer. *Yes, with your fat arse cushioned in a nicely padded leather 'executive' chair, I'm sure it does look like that.*

'The tissue was planted,' he said instead.

Starkey's eyebrows, ginger and bushy like the hair on his knuckles, shot up. 'Planted? We're not in some bloody B-movie, Ford. This is Wiltshire, not Chicago,' he said. 'People don't go around planting evidence. What did she tell you, "Ah, gee, Inspector, I was framed"?'

'No, sir. But she gave us her phone without being asked. The messages between her and Rachel Padley were loving, excitable, maybe; just what you'd expect from two young women in a relationship. No sign of any tension. There's zero motive. Zero evidence apart from the tissue. And she has an alibi.'

Starkey puffed out his cheeks. He pointed across the desk at Ford. Adopted a different tone. Matey, confiding. 'Now look, Ford. We all know you're a good detective,' he said with a smile that stopped just short of his eyes. 'You wouldn't have been promoted otherwise. But I have to tell you, there are people in the force just waiting to see you take a fall. I'd hate for this case to be the one that dents your reputation.'

That was bullshit. Ford knew. Working coppers might banter with each other, even throw playful accusations around about each other's competence. But they were all on the same side.

'What people, sir?'

Starkey's face screwed up in a twitch of irritation. 'Never mind what people. Professional rivalries – let's just leave it at that.'

'That doesn't really bother me either way, sir. I'm close to identifying the real killer and I'm not going to hold a young woman without a good reason.'

'Really? Then allow me to give you one. As you know, the Black Watch are off to Somalia on Friday. I've been in touch with Colonel Hemmings. There'll be no possibility of getting an arrest out there: they'll be up-country. Out of contact.'

'I've said I'd be willing to go, sir. If that's what it takes.'

'No. Absolutely not. The Foreign Office advice is crystal clear. No travel. I mean, do you have any idea how much insurance premiums are for trips like that?'

And there it was. Starkey's true focus. Not bringing murderers to justice. Making the columns on his spreadsheet add up.

'No, sir. I'm a detective, not an accountant.'

It was an insult. Ford couldn't help it.

Starkey's reaction was more controlled than Ford had expected. 'Which is why you are sitting there and I' – he poked a stubby monkey-finger against his chest – 'am sitting here. Leaving aside your snide remark, which I have noted, by the way, I'm going to make life simple for you. I want you to rearrest Tui. Work with the CPS on building the case against her. Understood?'

Ford took a breath. His pulse was bumping uncomfortably in his throat. Starkey was raising the stakes. Ford knew what was coming next but simply couldn't bow to the senior officer's demands.

'I'm sorry, sir, but that's a mistake. If we focus on Josifini, we're going to let the real killer get away with it,' he said.

Starkey's skin flashed with red blotches. He drew those hairy eyebrows together and leaned across the desk.

'Don't push your luck, son,' he growled. '*Rearrest* Josifini Tui. *Charge* her with murder. *Close* the investigation.' He emphasised the first word of each sentence by stabbing a finger at the folder on his desk. 'You get a nice little tick on your record. I get to save the rest of the budget and bump up our performance metrics. And Colonel Hemmings gets to take his men to Somalia without the stain of a murder investigation hanging over his battalion.'

'I'm sorry, sir, I can't do that.'

'This isn't optional, Ford,' Starkey spluttered. 'Did you just hear what I said?'

'Yes, sir, I heard you. It's the wrong course of action.'

Starkey's colour had heightened. The rivers of pallid flesh between the blotches on his cheeks and neck had closed up so that his entire head was a boiled ham colour.

'You see these,' he said, once again pointing to the tipstaffs on his shoulder boards. 'I'm an assistant chief constable. You're an inspector. I outrank you. You have to do what I tell you.'

Ford shook his head. 'You do outrank me, sir. But you're still a constable, just like me. We both made the same declaration. To faithfully discharge the duties of our office,' he said. 'You know that I can't be *instructed* to arrest anyone. It's my personal decision. I serve the Crown and am not to be subjected to undue influence.' He paused. 'Even by you. Sir.'

Breathing heavily, Starkey ran a finger around his collar. Was he on heart medication? His colour was still high and sweat had broken out on his forehead. Or was the colonel exerting his own form of undue influence?

In a trembling voice, Starkey said, 'Detective Inspector Ford, I am giving you a *direct order* to rearrest Josifini Tui.'

'I'd be breaching my oath to follow that order, sir. I believe it's unlawful.'

In his fury, Starkey had clenched his fists on the folder before him. He looked as if he were strangling an invisible opponent. He'd actually bared his teeth. All semblance of protocol had gone AWOL. This was a naked power struggle.

'How dare you lecture me on the fucking law!' he said.

'Maybe if you knew it better I wouldn't have to.'

Starkey's eyes bulged. He opened his mouth, but Ford cut him off. 'I'll policy that you ordered me to arrest Josifini Tui. And I'll policy that I refused because I believed your order to be unlawful. If you want to take it further, that's your call, but I'm willing to pursue this case – and any disciplinary ramifications – wherever it takes me.'

Breathing heavily, Starkey thrust himself back from his desk and stood up. Ford followed suit, not willing to let the ACC get a physical advantage over him.

For a wild moment he imagined Starkey was about to come round the desk and thump him. It didn't happen. Instead, Starkey stood toe to toe with him, so close Ford could smell his cologne.

'I know what you think of me. You think I'm a second-rate cop but a first-rate arse-kisser,' he said in a low tone, all the more threatening for being so quiet. 'Well, guess what? Maybe I am. But I've kissed enough arses to have real power in this organisation. Catch the killer and you might, just, get away with your insolence, insubordination and downright disrespect. But if you let Tui go and it turns out she did it all along and she's playing soldiers in fucking Somalia, then I will have you transferred somewhere so shitty, so mundane, so utterly lacking in any kind of professional or personal fulfilment, that directing traffic will seem like a fucking lottery win. Do I make myself clear?'

Fighting back the urge to push Starkey physically out of his personal space, Ford simply said, 'Yes, sir. Thank you.'

Starkey smiled evilly: a great white shark nose to nose with a seal. 'Don't thank me just yet, Ford. This is on you alone now. Nobody else. No resources. No support. I'll speak to Sandy Monroe. I'll have your team redeployed. Now get out.'

◆ ◆ ◆

Back at Bourne Hill, Ford called his inner circle into his office: Jan, Mick, Olly and Jools. He gave them the gist of his confrontation with Starkey.

'Before any other version of what happened reaches you, I just declined to obey a direct order from ACC Starkey. He's going to shut us down. Now' – he held up a hand for silence as the other four all started speaking at once – 'you've all got plenty of other cases you're working, so I want you to focus on those for now. I think we're close to solving Rachel's murder. I just need to follow up a couple of leads and then, if I need you, well, we can talk about it then.'

'What are they, guv?' Jools asked.

'I'm convinced it's either a member of the family, most likely David, or somebody in their congregation. I need to get a look at some' – he hesitated – 'church records.'

'You're applying for a search warrant, right, guv?' Jools asked.

Ford saw her concern reflected in the tight skin around her eyes. Rule-bending made Jools nervous. God knew what she'd have been like if he'd taken her with him to see Starkey.

'I'll take care of the paperwork, don't you worry.'

It wasn't a lie. He just intended to find out whether there was anything he could uncover before retrospectively applying for a warrant to 'find' it.

'Where have we got to with the TIE interviews on the base personnel?' he asked Jan.

'Mick and I are still working through the J's, Henry,' she said. 'We've got everyone else handling the others.'

'Guv?' It was Olly. Almost holding up his hand. 'I've finished reviewing CCTV from the towns around Imber. But there's nothing. It all stops too far out to be useful.'

'No sign of David or Helen Padley?' Ford asked.

'Sorry, guv.'

'It's fine, Olly. Good work.'

He ended the meeting with a promise to keep briefing them after hours. The team might be officially stood down but they all wanted to keep working with him, even if it risked crossing a line with the brass.

He went to find Hannah. He needed more ammunition to build the case.

CHAPTER THIRTY-NINE

On his way to Forensics, Ford stopped off to see Sandy. He wondered whether Starkey had got to her first. She looked up as he entered her office. He tried to read her expression. She looked calm enough, but maybe she was just biding her time before exploding at him. In all conscience he wouldn't have blamed her.

While he'd been in the ACC's office, every word he'd said had seemed the only thing he *could* say. Now, separated by a couple of hours and thirty-five miles, he thought he hadn't so much tightrope-walked along the line as backed up ten feet and taken a running jump right over it. So far into enemy territory that he doubted even a detachment of the Black Watch could rescue him if it all went tits up.

'I see they're looking for trainee baristas in that coffee shop on the High Street,' she said.

'You heard from ACC Starkey, then?'

Sandy groaned. 'Why, Henry?'

'You know why, boss. I have to. Rachel Padley deserves justice and I intend to deliver it.'

'That sounds more like Judge Dredd than Inspector Ford.'

He smiled, relieved he wasn't going to get a carpeting. 'You know what I mean.'

'Yes, I do. And in case you think I'm cut from the same cloth as the ACC, I'm not, OK? I come from the same place you do. It's all about catching the bad guys and putting them away,' she said. 'I'll do what I can to protect you from the fallout, but you'd better come up with the goods. Or this is going to get very messy, very fast. He's out for blood.'

'I'm close. I think Rachel came out to her parents and they went mental, to use a technical term,' he said. 'I think either they, or someone at their church, lured her out to Imber and murdered her before staging a suicide.'

'What about the forensic evidence you recovered from Josifini Tui's quarters?'

Ford ran through the same arguments he'd put before Starkey. The difference was, Sandy nodded steadily throughout as he enumerated the reasons for his doubts. The convenience. The lack of blood transfer to the floor beneath the tissue. The lack of obvious motive. The fact her phone had been tracked to the barracks throughout the period when Rachel was out at Imber.

Sandy pushed back on the last point. 'But she was texting, not talking. You can't prove it was her sending the messages.'

'No, but I've seen them. There's dozens of them and they're really personal and in, well, not exactly teen-speak, but Sam's always telling me how real teenagers text and this was it. If it was her parents, they wouldn't have got it right, I'm sure of it.'

Sandy shrugged. 'You're the lead investigator. If that's your read on it, I'll back you.'

'Thanks, boss.'

'Hold on,' she said, raising a hand. 'I haven't finished. I'll back you to the limits of what's lawful, to use your current word of the week. But I'm sorry, H, I'm not going to yoke my career to yours. Geoff Starkey was almost incoherent when he called me.'

Ford nodded. 'I appreciate it. Look, give me another couple of days. If it hasn't happened by then, I don't think it will.'

'Fine. Go and catch a murderer.'

◆ ◆ ◆

Ford found Hannah sitting at her desk eating a sandwich. Egg mayonnaise and cress. He could tell because she'd meticulously pulled out the strands of vegetation and lined them up like a little pale-green ladder on the sheet of greaseproof paper.

'Not a fan?' he asked, pointing at the cress.

She looked up and smiled, curving dimples into her cheeks. 'Actually, I am a fan of cress. I just eat it afterwards. Did you want something?' She paused. 'Or did you just come down to discuss sandwich fillings?'

'I need to know what was in Rachel's neck wound. Things have picked up and I can't wait until next week.'

Hannah put down the triangle of sandwich. 'I can call Professor Goldstein now, if you like.'

Without waiting for an answer, she picked up the phone on her desk and punched the buttons in a rapid-fire flurry. Ford wasn't surprised Hannah knew the professor's number by heart. He suspected she rarely used anything as ordinary as an address book or directory. She probably thought the contacts list on her mobile was a clumsy way of doing things.

He sat and listened to Hannah's side of the conversation.

After making her request, Hannah fell silent, head cocked on one side, pulling at the plait on the right side of her head. She frowned. 'No, no, I understand, it's just that this is very important.'

Sensing the academic was explaining the pressure she herself was under, Ford signalled to Hannah for her to pass him the phone.

She nodded. 'Merilyn, I'm going to pass you over to Detective Inspector Ford. He's the lead investigator on this murder case.'

Ford mouthed 'Thanks,' noting the way Hannah had stressed the word 'murder', hoping it had primed Professor Goldstein.

He took the handset. 'Hello, Professor Goldstein, DI Ford here. I know you're very busy but is there any way you can give us even a preliminary analysis? There's a very real risk that unless we have this information the murderer could escape justice,' he said. 'I just need the headline finding. What kind of wood is it? Where did it come from? Can you tell me that?'

'Well, yes. I can. I only delayed because I thought you'd prefer a full dendrological analysis,' she said, sounding relieved. 'First of all, it was cut with a fine edge.'

'A knife rather than a chainsaw, you mean?'

'Exactly. Without wishing to stray too far into detective territory, the person who cut it was most likely a woodworker of some kind rather than, say, a forester or tree surgeon.'

'That's fantastic. Thank you.' Ford meant it. 'What about the type of wood?'

'*Dalbergia maritima*,' she said with a detectable note of pride. 'In layman's terms, Madagascan rosewood.'

'Thank you, that's wonderful. I'll let you go.'

'No, wait! There's one more thing. I don't know if it's relevant or not – it isn't anything to do with the wood, after all.'

'What is it?'

'Our equipment picked up a trace of a chemical. It's naturally occurring, but not in rosewood.'

As she outlined what the chemical was used for, Ford nodded. He was sure that to Hannah he looked perfectly calm, but inside he was fizzing with energy. It tied in with something he'd noticed at the Padleys' house. Something that would help close the case.

He ended the call but continued to muse on what Dr Goldstein had told him.

'Henry?' Hannah looked puzzled. 'You tuned out. I wondered what you were thinking about?'

'How would a killer get a sliver of rosewood on his knife, Wix?'

'All I can think of is those initials you see carved into trees sometimes. You know, W plus H forever.' Then she blushed and looked away. 'Or Jack loves Jill.'

He shook his head, still thinking. Hannah wasn't right about initial-carving. You used the point. The wood chips dropped to the ground. He knew: he'd done it himself, with Lou keeping lookout, acting like giddy teenagers. E+L. Carved with love and great care into the bark of a tree in the Lake District in their first year of marriage.

Hannah wasn't right. But she was close.

He gave her a quick smile, feeling a surge of optimism. 'I have to go. I'll be back later.'

'Where are you going?'

'Larkhill.'

CHAPTER FORTY

Ford realised he'd had a wasted trip. David Padley was out at Imber taking part in that day's exercise and Helen, according to a neighbour, had gone shopping in Andover.

With no way to get round to the back of the house, he reluctantly returned to Bourne Hill and spent the rest of the afternoon catching up on paperwork. He asked Olly to get in touch with the recipient of Josifini's texts from the night Rachel was murdered.

'See if they can confirm that the messages sounded like Josifini had written them,' he said.

He left at seven and ate a quick pasta supper with Sam.

As they were eating, and keeping his voice light, Ford asked, 'Did you talk to Beth today? About going for coffee?'

'Yes.'

'And?'

'She said yes.'

'Great!'

Sam scowled. 'No, Dad, it's crap. Because then she asked, like, a whole load of people to come with us.'

Ford smiled. 'It doesn't mean she doesn't like you, though, does it?'

'You'd know, would you, being such an expert on relationships?'

'What? Where is this coming from?'

Sam shrugged, stuffed another forkful of penne into his mouth. 'Nowhere.'

'Come on, mate. I know when something's bugging you.'

'Do you? You're never here so I don't see how you can say that.'

'I'm here lots. We've spent loads of time together recently.'

'No. We haven't. You just think we have because you're home for tea, like, twice a week. That or bribing me with ice cream like I'm a kid.'

'I have been trying. But this latest case is a bastard. I'm losing sleep over it. Literally. Let me clear it and then things'll be easier.'

Sam slammed his fork down, sending penne flying on to the floor. 'Do you actually *believe* that? Can you even *hear* yourself?' Sam adopted a mock-sad voice. 'This case is really important, mate. I just need to clear it up.' He got up from the table. 'You say that every time. It never changes. You're just stuck on repeat.'

Sam stormed out. The sound of his heavy tread on the stairs was dwarfed by the seismic bang as he slammed his bedroom door. In his own day, Ford would have put a record on and turned the volume up specifically to annoy his father. These days, the kids all used earbuds. Anger was silent.

Ford finished his bowl of pasta and cleared the table. He stacked the dishwasher and set it going.

Four hours later, he went upstairs to change. Black Harrington jacket over a hooded fleece. Black jeans and all-black trainers with air-cushioned soles.

He didn't bother texting Sam. Couldn't bear to think of the sarcastic response. Instead, he fetched a pair of purple nitrile gloves and a small black vinyl roll from his murder bag and went out to the Discovery.

As Ford drove towards the pastor's church, he reflected that if he was caught, the phrase 'you've got a lot for explaining to do' would be insufficient to describe his plight. But then, he wasn't intending to get caught, was he?

'Said every burglar, ever,' he said aloud in the barely warm cab.

The Discovery's dark-blue paint job was a distinct advantage. Anyone out late walking their dog would see, under the depressingly weak orange street lamps, a generic SUV in anything from black to about five dark colours.

He turned off the roundabout and into Long Barrow Drive. Instead of parking outside the church as he had done the previous time, he carried on then took a right into Top Field Way.

The road continued past a row of houses. Each was subtly different from its neighbour, though clearly built by the same developer. Some had decorative flint panels, others small round windows. The houses petered out and a bend led to a view over open fields. He parked, pulled his hood up and began the short walk back to the church.

Outside of one or two streets in the town centre, Larkhill was quiet at night. Quieter even than Salisbury, where it was often possible to drive round the ring road and see no traffic either in front or behind from nine o'clock onwards. Sam used to call it the zombie apocalypse, that sense that every single human being had simply vanished.

The apocalypse helped Ford now because he didn't encounter a single soul in the five minutes it took him to arrive at the small tarmac courtyard behind the church.

He saw two plastic dustbins provided by the council: one for general waste, one for recycling. And a galvanised zinc incinerator with a chimney in its lid. Where the pastor claimed he burned his members' sealed prayers. Did he read them first, though? Did Simeon sit in his office late at night with a glass of whisky at his elbow, eyes glistening with prurient interest, and open the prayer box? Did he swill the fiery spirit as he read the prayers, gaining privileged knowledge of the supplicants' innermost hopes and fears?

Donning gloves, Ford lifted the lid, delicately, to ensure the rim didn't clang against the bin beneath. The smell of charred paper coiled out. He peered in. A layer of fine white ash covered the bottom. He pushed his hand in. The air inside was cold, as was the metal.

Ford looked over his shoulder. A block of flats backed on to the church's courtyard but the windows were dark, occasional slivers of light showing around the edges of curtains. He took the nylon roll from the pocket of his Harrington and peeled it open, muffling the scratch of the Velcro with his body.

Ford reckoned most of his team had a set of lock picks, though nobody would admit to it. There were times when it was simply easier than going through the laborious and often frustrating process of applying for a warrant. An application that might be refused. As he knew this one would have been.

If the search turned out to be a bust, he hadn't gained anything, but he hadn't wasted too much time, either. But if he *did* find something useful, then he'd get a warrant and 'discover' the crucial piece of evidence.

The method belonged to a wider set of behaviours encompassed by a technical legal phrase Ford hated. *Noble-cause corruption*. Juries only heard the second half and forgot the first.

But this wasn't about framing people for crimes they hadn't committed. As was the case with Josifini Tui. This was about delivering justice and not letting scumbags get away with raping and murdering, mugging and burgling, terrorising old ladies in their homes or molesting children at will and smirking at the cops from the dock.

If he needed a warrant, he'd tell the magistrate he noticed a stray prayer under the table during his first conversation with the pastor, and realised the box itself might contain a confession of sorts.

Ford was inside in fifteen seconds. He pulled out a small torch from the other pocket of his jacket and, after satisfying himself the church was empty, switched it on. He cupped his free hand around the lens to restrict the beam to a dull glow. Just bright enough to light his way to the Casket of Wishes. He almost laughed aloud. It sounded like something from an Indiana Jones movie.

He crouched in front of the wooden box and went to work a second time with the picks. Some padlocks were designed to be resistant to the efforts of amateur – and even professional – thieves. But not this one. With a muted click, the shackle sprang out from the lock body.

Ford placed the padlock beside the box and opened the lid. He pointed the torch at the interior where a couple of dozen folded sheets of paper lay in a pile.

He gathered them up and, lacking anywhere to put them, sat cross-legged on the floor with the prayers in front of him. He opened the first one. The petitioner asked God to 'keep Pastor Simeon in your Grace'. The next entreated the Almighty to 'show Catholics, Jews, Muslims and all other Heathens to see the error of their ways and turn to the one true religion'.

So far, so fanatical.

In the silence of the church, he read on. Prayer after prayer pleading with God to smite, punish or variously inconvenience people the writers felt were beyond the pale. Asking for intercession in neighbourly disputes, or guidance in dealing with Wiltshire Council over planning applications. Help with illnesses or, oddly, Ford thought, pleas for worldly riches. Not so pious after all.

Absorbed by the prayers, his perception of the outside world dimmed. Sights, sounds and smells all faded. He opened a tightly folded square of paper, wondering whether he'd miscalculated. Perhaps the murderer hadn't committed their guilt to paper. After all, it was a big jump from suspecting them of murder to imagining they'd plead for absolution in print.

And then his doubts vanished. He'd been right all along. Here it was. The evidence he needed.

Lord, Hear my prayer. My daughter has strayed from the path set out for her by your infinite Wisdom and Grace. She has lowered herself to the state of Lilith, of Salome, of Jezebel, of every sinful woman who ever rejected your Love. She must be brought to Righteousness or suffer the Concequences. Pray for Rachel, Lord. And for me, your True servant: I shall cleanse your world of Sin. Amen.

He took a picture with his phone, then refolded the bile-filled scrap of paper. If David Padley, the archetypal plain-speaking Yorkshireman, had written something that flowery, in such a curving, neat, feminine hand, Ford would take his vintage Stratocaster out to the back garden and burn it, Hendrix-like, with a can of lighter fluid.

The misspelled 'consequences' convinced him that he was reading the work of the same letter-writer who'd lured Rachel to her death. Her mother.

Scooping up the papers with a soft rustle, he tipped them back into the box and locked it. As he unfolded himself from his cross-legged position, his knees popped and he hissed a swear word in the darkness.

'Hello? Who's there?' came an answering voice. Ford recognised it. Simeon.

Ford's heart rate doubled. He killed the torch, and silently replaced the box on the table.

He looked around, fighting panic, trying to assess his options. Trained for it, Rachel would have done a far better job. Should he hide, or run? In reality, there was only one choice. The church, a big, bare, rectangular room with only the pastor's office and a tiny toilet off it, offered no hiding places worth spit.

Long neon tubes on the ceiling flickered and plinked into life. Turning away from the front door and bending low to disguise his height, Ford bolted, hitting the back door at a run and bursting through, slamming it behind him.

Glancing around, he took off, stooping and affecting a drag on his left leg. Hopefully if anyone did see him, the mime act would be enough to portray a completely different man. And people associated hoodies with youngsters: they always did. Ford blamed a previous prime minister and his 'hug a hoodie' campaign.

At the corner of Long Barrow Drive and Drovers Yard, fifty yards distant from the church, he dropped into a walk, straightening and losing the limp. Two minutes later and he was sauntering down Top Field Way, having neither met nor seen a soul on his flight.

Inside the Discovery, he pulled his hood down, started the engine and pulled away, heading out of the estate and back towards Salisbury.

Was he proud of what he'd done? No. Was he glad he'd done it? Yes. Pastor Simeon would suspect a burglar, on the lookout for cash. Ford had planted the idea and now it might bear fruit. He made a mental note to talk to Bob Summerbee at Andover nick about a crime prevention visit.

At home, he headed upstairs to his office, then opened the photo on his phone. It was properly lit, and in focus. No good whatsoever for forensics, but the handwriting might help if he could get a sample of Helen's for comparison. But it was the mention of Rachel that clinched it; that and the spelling error. As a photo, it was of zero evidential value. But as the key to unlocking a murderer's guilt, it was as precise and useful a tool as one of his lock picks.

He transferred it to his laptop, printed out two colour copies, then went next door and got ready for bed, convinced he was very close to making an arrest. He corrected himself: *another* arrest. Tried a third time. The *right* arrest. In two days, the Black Watch would disappear en masse, but Ford didn't think he needed that long.

CHAPTER FORTY-ONE

The following morning, Olly handed Ford another bullet to shoot down Starkey. The DC had managed to contact Josifini's friend in Suva. She'd confirmed that the texts were undoubtedly Josifini's.

Ford left for the car park, nodding at Jools on his way out of Major Crimes.

'Where are you off to, guv? Anywhere exciting?'

'To see the Padleys.' An idea occurred to him. 'Actually, you can come, too.'

'What about Starkey's orders?' she asked with a frown.

'Let me worry about the ACC.'

'In that case, count me in,' she said. 'I don't want you getting *all* the glory.'

As they walked up the Padleys' front garden path together, Ford turned to Jools. 'I need to have a look in the back garden. If the opportunity comes up, just help me out, OK?'

She nodded.

David opened the door. He was dressed for work in his uniform, khaki Tam sitting dead level on his head.

He checked his watch. 'I've got to leave in ten minutes. Can't it wait?'

'I'm afraid not, David. It won't take long.'

Sighing, David led them into the kitchen. 'Coffee?' he asked.

'That would be great, thanks.'

'Yes, please,' Jools said.

While David filled the kettle and spooned instant coffee into three mugs, Ford wandered up to the kitchen counter to stand beside him. He looked out through the window behind the sink at the garden.

'How are things here?' Ford asked. 'I suppose the coroner is still holding on to Rachel's body for now.'

'Aye. Apparently it's twenty-eight days before we can have her back. I told him the whole bloody lot of us are deploying to Somalia day after tomorrow, but he said, "The law is the law, Mister Padley." Told me I should ask the CO for compassionate leave.'

'You could. I'm sure he'd let you join the battalion later.'

'Not how it's done, Inspector. My lads need me.'

'I'm sorry we've not been able to solve Rachel's murder yet. But we're very close.'

Padley turned to him. 'I should bloody well hope so! Especially after letting Private Tui out of custody.'

The kettle came to the boil and clicked off. Padley busied himself stirring in the water, offering milk and pushing a mug at Ford before handing one to Jools.

'Thanks,' she said, before taking a cautious sip.

'Was there something you wanted, or is this just a social call?' David asked, hands on hips.

'DC Harper wanted to ask you a couple of questions about how live-fire exercises work,' Ford said.

David turned to face Jools and as he did so, Ford mouthed 'sitting room' to her over David's shoulder.

'What did you want to know?' David asked, checking his watch again.

Jools stood and walked towards the kitchen door. 'Just a couple of details. Let's talk in the sitting room, shall we?'

Without waiting for his agreement, she left the kitchen, giving Padley no option but to follow her.

'David, I just need to make a call,' Ford said. 'Can I use your back garden?'

'Suit yourself. Door's unlocked,' Padley said over his shoulder.

'Thanks,' Ford called out as Padley's bulky form disappeared into the dark hallway.

He opened the back door and went out into the small neat suburban garden. Six-foot-tall fence panels slotted into concrete posts marked off this rectangle of army property from its neighbours. Ford wandered down to the end of the garden and pulled out his phone. He switched it to silent then held it to his ear.

As he play-acted the call, he walked over to the small wooden shed. He peered in through a window tinged a dirty green by algae.

Small garden tools lay in neat rows on wooden shelves. A long thin canvas bag designed to store pairs of shoes had been repurposed to hold gardening gloves, rolls of twine and black rubber plant ties.

A wooden carver chair occupied the back half of the shed. Old, paint-spattered and well past its days as a piece of indoor furniture. Beside it stood a small table on which lay a few lengths of dark reddish-brown wood. *Dalbergia maritima.*

He turned away and walked up to the house. Jools and David were chatting in the sitting room. He sniffed the air, felt something tickle his nose and fought down an urge to sneeze. Nodded to himself.

'That's a fine piece of wood carving you did for Helen,' he said. 'The key rack, I mean. Hobby of yours, is it?'

David looked surprised. 'Aye. Me life's not all drill and shouting at the lads.'

'It's rosewood, isn't it?'

'Madagascan, aye. Know about wood, do you?'

Ford sat and smiled at David. 'I have an old guitar. The fret-board's made of exactly the same wood. It's pretty rare to find these days, isn't it?'

'Aye, and we've bloody CITES to thank for that. There's been none available over here for donkeys' years. Bloody banned exports, didn't they?'

Ford nodded in sympathy. 'Out of interest, how did you get it, then?'

'I was part of a team sent to Madagascar to help after they got floods. Picked a few bits and pieces up when I were out there. Brought them home in my kit bag.'

'What kind of knife do you use, David? When you're carving?'

Padley looked away for a split second before answering, but it was enough to signal the lie Ford knew would come from his lips.

'I've got an old Stanley knife in me tool box.'

Ford smiled and nodded. 'Is it strong enough? I'd have thought you'd want something a bit sturdier. A Stanley's more of a woman's knife, wouldn't you say?' He'd pushed Padley's button. Calling his masculinity into question. Would it work?

Padley shrugged. 'It's sharp enough for the job.'

A key scraped in the front door. All three turned at the sound.

Helen Padley appeared in the doorway carrying a plastic carrier bag branded with a local convenience store's logo. She looked in at the frozen tableau.

'What's going on, David? I thought you'd be at work by now.'

'Hello, Helen,' Ford said. 'Come and take a seat.'

Frowning, she perched beside her husband and took his hand. 'What's this all about?'

Ford looked from Helen to David, mother to father, and back again. Then at Jools. She offered him a tiny nod. He didn't think this would get physical, but he knew he could count on Jools if it did.

'I think Rachel told you and David she was gay, Helen,' he said, getting to his feet, 'and the two of you conspired to murder her.'

He glanced down at David Padley, who was sitting as rigid as a length of the rosewood in his shed.

'No!' Helen exclaimed. 'We prayed for her. That's all. It was immoral. Wrong. But we didn't kill her. How could we? She was our own flesh and blood.'

Ford shook his head. 'Let me finish, please. I think she told you she was gay *before* your friend saw her at Radclyffe's, if she ever did,' he said. 'I think Rachel expected love, support and understanding, and instead, you told her she was a vile sinner or some such language. She left in tears and you decided something had to be done.'

He turned to David. 'Helen wrote a letter, and you delivered it to Rachel,' Ford said. 'You were waiting out there at the Baghdad Marriott. When she turned up, you knocked her out against a wall, dragged to the crossroads and cut her throat.'

David was shaking his head, a repetitive movement that seemed to be occurring automatically.

'No,' he muttered. 'No, no, no. It weren't like that. It were *never* supposed to be like that.'

'What *was* it supposed to be like, David?'

Helen cleared her throat. 'Inspector?'

Ford turned.

'David had nothing to do with it,' she said. 'It was me. I killed her.'

Ford had been expecting this. He saw Helen for what she was: a controlling, overly religious woman who saw the world in all its shades of grey simply as black and white. Them. Us. Good. Evil. Family bonds meant nothing compared to the bands of iron fastening her to her faith.

He stood. And he arrested her. Then he turned to her husband.

'David Padley, I am arresting you on suspicion of being an accessory to the murder of your—'

'Wait!' Helen screeched. 'No, you can't! It was me. I just confessed. You've no right to arrest him.'

'I have every right, Helen.'

He finished arresting David and then he and Jools led them both outside to a waiting police van that he'd arranged to follow him out to Larkhill.

CHAPTER FORTY-TWO

Ford booked the Padleys into the custody suite. Unlike her husband, or Josifini before him, Helen refused point-blank the offer of a solicitor.

He entered Major Crimes to a round of applause from the assembled detectives. He looked for the rest of his inner circle but all were out of the office. He felt a pang of regret that although they were doing what they ought to, wearing out shoe leather chasing criminals, there was nobody here he could share this bittersweet triumph with. Apart from Jools, of course.

'Coffee?' he asked her.

'Blimey, guv. You should arrest murderers more often. Yes, please.'

Sitting together in his office, he went over the next phase with her. 'Now we have the killer, you're back on the case officially. Starkey'll back down,' he said. 'I want you to interview David. I'll take Helen.'

'On it.'

He left her to make her own preparations and went downstairs to see Helen. After the custody sergeant had let him into her cell, he stood with his back against the door.

'Are you still sure you want to do without legal representation?'

'I've no need of lawyers, Inspector,' she said in an oddly calm voice. 'God will be my witness.'

He shrugged. 'Let's go then. I'll need you to confirm your decision on tape.'

Five minutes later, he sat facing her in the poky interview room, the tape recorder spooling in the silence.

'Helen Diane Padley, you have been arrested on suspicion of murder and been read the official caution,' he said. 'You have also been repeatedly offered legal representation and you have refused every time. Do you still wish to proceed without a lawyer?'

Staring straight at him, her face calm and untroubled, she spoke a single word. 'Yes.'

Ford repeated the official caution. 'Tell me what happened,' he said finally.

He had a feeling she was waiting for a chance to tell the story her way. No need for a sly verbal dance getting her to trip over a piece of evidence.

'I wrote the letter on our home computer. I went to the single soldiers' quarters and I slid it under her door.'

Ford leaned forward and clasped his hands on the table between them. 'Really? How did you get inside the base? Do you have an MOD 90?'

'A what?'

'It's the official ID. They won't let you past the barrier without one.'

'I . . . I told the guard I had an urgent message for Rachel. He let me through,' she gabbled. 'Then I took David's knife out of the shed and drove out to Imber to wait for her.'

'Whereabouts did you wait?'

'At the back of the house with that silly sign on it. Baghdad Marriott.'

'And then what?'

'Rachel came in. She shouted out "Hello?" Then, "Are you there, Jo-jo?"'

Ford nodded. 'Did you worry she was suspicious because you signed the letter with just a J?'

'Yes. But it didn't matter in the end, because there she was. I called out. I said I was in the back.'

'Weren't you worried she'd just leave?'

'She wouldn't leave. I'm her mother. She came to the back room and I told her she had to change. Forswear the sinful path she'd chosen or she'd spend eternity in hell.'

'What did she say?'

'She used profanities I'd never heard before. Must be all those men she mixes with. Or the women,' she added, shuddering theatrically. 'I tried to reason with her. I took her by the shoulders, but she was always a strong one, our Rachel. She pushed me away and then she just stumbled, or tripped, on a brick. Anyway, she went over backwards and her head hit the wall and that was that.'

'What do you mean? "That was that"?'

'What do you think I mean? She was dead! I dragged her out to the middle of the crossroads – it took me a while, she weren't a little thing – and that's where I did it.'

'Did what?'

'I cut her throat. I had to. To make it look like suicide. She *had* just killed herself, after all,' she said. 'Then I drove home. I had blood on me, which I cleaned off while David was out.'

Ford wasn't about to let her get away with suggesting on tape that killing her daughter with a knife was an afterthought following an accident. 'You've already said you went to the meeting carrying an offensive weapon. Why, if not to murder your daughter?'

Helen hesitated, and the trace of a smile glimmered on those pale lips.

'You're trying to trick me, Inspector,' she said. '"Now granted, I have not burdened you; yet sly as I am, I took you in by deceit!" Two Corinthians, twelve, sixteen. All I wanted to do was talk to her.'

'I'm not trying to trick you at all, Helen,' he said. 'I just want to know, if all you wanted was a nice mum-and-daughter chat, why you took a wickedly sharp hunting knife with you?'

'Imber's in the middle of nowhere. I was frightened I'd be attacked.'

It was a flimsy excuse. Ford realised something about Helen Padley. She was overconfident. She'd prepared for everything except what to do if she were ever arrested for it. Now she was freewheeling, mixing lies and Bible verses in the hopes of getting off. He could just picture her in court.

'Attacked by whom? I assume David got you the schedule so you knew there was no exercise that night.'

'A wild animal.'

He sighed. 'She was alive when you cut her throat, Helen, did you know that?'

She shook her head. Ford saw no sign of horror or even regret. She accepted the news as if he'd told her a taxi had arrived to take her home.

'No, but it makes no difference, does it?'

He took a moment to compose himself, looking down at his notes and turning over a page. Just to prevent himself from screaming at her.

'Let's move on. Who planted the bloody tissue in Josifini Tui's room?'

Her eyes flicked to the vacant seat beside her. Ford imagined she'd be wishing she'd asked for a lawyer after all.

'I did.'

'I don't think so, Helen,' he said. 'Maybe you charmed your way past the guard once, but twice? No. David planted it, didn't he?'

'No. *I* did it. The guard *did* let me through. He . . . He knows me.'

Ford looked into her eyes. They jittered in their sockets, unable to settle on his. She was lying. But this wasn't the most important question. It could wait.

'Helen, help me out here. Because I'm struggling to understand how you could kill your own daughter for being gay at all,' he said. 'But given your faith, isn't that going to damn you as surely as you thought her sexuality was going to damn her? Didn't you tell me, "Thou shalt not kill"?'

'The Lord moves in mysterious ways, Inspector,' she said. 'Aside from her sin, Rachel would have brought shame not just upon her own head, but mine and her father's, too. David is a respected man in the Black Watch. He has a position of authority. The young ones look up to him. He keeps them on the straight and narrow path. He would have lost their respect. I couldn't allow that to happen.'

'Why cover it up, though? Why stage a suicide? If you thought you were doing the Lord's work, why not simply confess as soon was Rachel was discovered?'

'I have important work, too. Our African mission needs funds. I raise them. I could hardly do that from inside a prison cell, could I?'

Ford wanted to grab this implacable woman sitting opposite him. To take her by the throat and yell into her face that a prison cell was exactly where she was going to be spending a great many of her remaining years on Earth.

But he didn't. What good would it do? None. And it would probably compromise the interview. If Helen changed her mind about a lawyer, they'd make great play of his irrational outburst, claiming he'd terrified Helen into confessing.

'What was David's role in all this?'

'David knew nothing about it. He is blameless.'

Ford very much doubted that. But with a full confession from Helen, if David went 'no comment', getting him on accessory to murder would take all Jools's interviewing skills.

'Did he dispose of Rachel's phone?'

'No. I did that. I dropped it down a drain.'

'Did he suggest you used his woodwork knife?'

She smiled at him then, as if she'd been waiting for him to throw the final piece of evidence at her. 'No. I took his knife while he was on duty. I threw the sheath in the rubbish just before the dustmen came.'

He ran a hand over his head, scrubbing at the back of his neck as if to dislodge something snagged in the short hair there. 'Helen Padley, do you admit that you murdered your daughter, Rachel Padley? That you lured her out to Imber and you killed her? In cold blood,' he couldn't stop himself from adding.

'Yes.'

'And you've made this confession freely, without any undue influence and despite my repeated offers of a lawyer, all of which you refused?'

'I do.'

That was it. Signed, sealed and delivered with a big black ribbon tied in a bow round it. The CPS lawyers would smile delightedly at him. But he felt no such sense of triumph.

'Why did you do it, Helen?' he asked on a sighing out-breath.

'Don't you see, Inspector? I had to. I had no choice.'

He announced that he was ending the interview and reached out to switch off the tape. He nodded to the uniform standing silently against the back wall. A simple signal, easily understood. Take her down. Then he left.

CHAPTER FORTY-THREE

In contrast to his wife, David Padley had requested a solicitor. The wait had taken until late in the afternoon. Sitting in his office, Ford texted Sam.

going to be a late one tonight

sorry

He felt the need to sort things out with his son. To be there for him, pulling him in to the safe shore of family life, like the waves that he'd swum in on after leaving Lou at Pen-y-Holt.

The trouble was, a second force was always acting on him. The pull of duty. The visceral need to put murderers behind bars. It was a rip tide, dragging him away from the beach and out into a black sea filled with wickedness.

He caught himself thinking in the sort of Biblical language Helen Padley and her enabling pastor used, and despised himself for becoming infected by their piety.

How could she have written a prayer asking God to help her murder her own daughter? How could Simeon run a church that held such people in its embrace?

Jools knocked on the door.

Ford looked up and smiled. 'How's it going with David?'

She dropped into the visitor's chair. 'He's denying everything. Says it was all Helen. Says he had no idea what she was planning.'

Ford scratched his neck. They were stuck, weren't they? Helen had made a full and detailed confession. The only evidence linking David to the crime was the chip of rosewood transferred from his knife to Rachel's throat. Ford made a note to have forensics sweep Josifini's room again, this time looking for David's DNA.

Jools broke into his thoughts. 'How did you know it was the Padleys?'

'One, the rosewood. The chip in Rachel's neck wound is from the same rare species as the wood I saw in David's shed. It's been banned for export since 2013. We'll get Dr Goldstein to do a comparison of the samples, but I'm sure they'll be an exact match.'

'What else?'

'Dr Goldstein told me she found limonene molecules on the rosewood chip,' he said. 'It's a common ingredient in lemon-scented cleaning products. I noticed when we did the death knock; their sitting room reeked of it. I'm allergic – it made me sneeze.'

Jools frowned. 'Lots of people use those, though.'

'They don't also carve pieces of prohibited wood with a knife contaminated with it, though, do they? Nor do they misspell the word "consequences" in their prayers mentioning their own daughter.'

She narrowed her eyes. 'How would you know Helen Padley makes spelling mistakes in her prayers?'

Ford ignored the question. Best if Jools didn't know about his spot of B&E at the church. 'How did you approach the issue of Rachel's sexuality?'

'In about ten different ways. I even tried winding him up about it,' she said, spreading her hands wide. 'I suggested there must be something wrong with his sperm to have fathered a gay girl. Nothing. He just stared me out and kept denying it.'

◆ ◆ ◆

Ford had told Jools to use Interview Room 2 for her first interview with David. He'd thought David would recognise 4's oppressive atmosphere for what it was, an artificial attempt to discomfit cocky or reluctant suspects. Now, he thought they might as well use it.

After the formalities were out of the way, Ford opened the folder in front of him.

'This is the pathologist's report on Rachel,' he said, looking at David.

The man seemed to have sunk in on himself. Outside the precincts of a police station, Ford would have interpreted the grey cast to his skin and lacklustre posture as a sign of fatigue. In here, though, it looked like guilt.

'If you think showing me gory pictures will get me to confess, you're wrong,' David said in a flat tone. 'Anything in there, I've seen a hundred times worse.'

Ford shook his head. 'I wasn't going to show you anything, David. I just want you to listen to a short paragraph from the pathologist's official report. How Rachel died.'

'Inspector, you should be asking my client a question,' the solicitor said. He was young, fresh-faced, the box creases on his shirt visible inside his suit jacket.

'And I will. Listen, David. "1a Exsanguination." That means—'

David scowled. 'Save your breath. I've done the battlefield trauma medicine course.'

Ford nodded and carried on reading aloud from the report. '"1b Large incised wound to throat. The BFT to the back of the head (parietal bone sustained depressed fracture) appears to have been caused by contact with a piece of masonry. It would have rendered her unconscious, *but it did not kill her.*"' He paused to look at David. 'She underlined that bit. Then she says, "Rachel would have been alive but in all likelihood unconscious when her throat was cut".'

He didn't explain straight away. He waited, allowing David time to digest the meaning of George's words and the implications behind them.

David's eyebrows drew together, then relaxed. He raised them in mute enquiry, so that his forehead took on the appearance of a ploughed field. He rubbed his scalp furiously.

Finally, he spoke. 'You're saying she were alive when Helen—'

'Cut her own daughter's throat? Yes. That's exactly what I'm saying. She could have saved her. Even after she'd bashed her head against the wall, there was still time to offer help instead of hatred. Tell me, David,' he said, glancing at the solicitor to say, *yes, now I'm going to ask my question, so get your pen ready*, 'how did you help Helen kill Rachel? What was your part in all this?'

Beside him, he could hear Jools breathing. The clock on the wall ticked away the seconds while they waited for David to make his decision. Ford inhaled and could almost taste the stale atmosphere of sweat and stale cigarette smoke from prisoners' clothes at the back of his throat.

'I did nothing,' David said, finally. 'First I knew of it were when I saw you at Imber.'

It had been worth a shot. But Ford didn't think David would break no matter how much he leaned on him. And there was always the chance, the outside chance, that he was telling the truth.

He turned to Jools. 'Would you take David down to custody and have him released under investigation, please?'

He left the room as Jools explained to David what would happen next.

Ford went to find Sandy, but she'd left the office. He looked in on Major Crimes. It was empty, too. A cleaner in a flowered apron was emptying the rubbish bins. She turned when she heard Ford's footsteps.

Smiling, she offered the usual sing-song Salisbury greeting. 'Hiya, y'all right?'

He gave the standard reply. 'Yeah, good, thanks. You?'

But he wasn't good. Not at all. He felt depressed. No sense of elation that normally accompanied the end of a case.

You'd meet the Padleys in the street and not give them a second glance. Nothing off about them. No mumbling or talking to themselves. No look of sly cunning or the vacant, unemotional stare of a psychopath. Mr and Mrs Average out to do a bit of shopping. Yet Helen had murdered her daughter. For the simple crime of not being the woman her mother thought she should be.

Ford drove home enveloped in sadness, which deepened when Sam texted him at nine to say he was staying over with Josh.

Halfway down his second beer, he must have dozed off. He awoke sitting at the kitchen table and checked the time. Midnight. While he still had the phone in his hand, it rang. No caller ID.

'Ford.'

'It's me, Inspector. I'm at Imber. I need to see you.'

He sat up straight, the bleariness of a moment ago utterly gone. 'David? Is that you?'

'Aye, it's me. Can you come, then? There's something I need to get off me chest.'

'Why Imber, David? Why can't you come and talk to me at the station?'

'Do you want to hear what I've got to say or not, man?' David sounded exasperated, verging on angry. But there was something else. A note of despair. Fear, maybe.

'Give me an hour.'

'Don't be late.'

Ford grabbed a coat, pulled it over the baggy jumper he was wearing and was in the Discovery a minute later. He called in at Bourne Hill before heading out towards the plain.

CHAPTER FORTY-FOUR

In the moonlight, the houses in the centre of the ghost village looked as though they'd been cut from flat sheets of wood, their solid black shadows stretching across the gritty tarmac in distorted rectangles.

Glancing up at the sky, Ford saw the pale swirl of the Milky Way. An icy wind sliced across the village from east to west, nipping the tips of his ears. He drew his coat tighter around him.

He'd wondered on the drive whether David had armed himself and intended to take Ford hostage until they released his wife. Strictly speaking, he should have consulted Sandy. Maybe even got a couple of authorised firearms officers in support. But she'd have stood him down, ordered him to wait until morning. Starkey was leaning on her, Ford knew that.

It was him alone. That was how it had to be.

After his row with Starkey and his illicit operation at the church, he felt he'd already crossed so many lines that one more wouldn't matter. And when he asked himself whether he was in danger, he'd felt sure the answer was no. What purpose would it serve for David to take a detective hostage?

Nevertheless, as he strode on, he felt a pang of doubt. All those years ago, he'd left Lou to die – despite her pleas – to save Sam from growing up an orphan. Had he gone through all that pain, so much at the time, and since, to throw his life away now in some wild fit of ego that allowed him to play the gung-ho cop?

He didn't have time to find out. David Padley marched out from cover behind one of the nearer houses. The moonlight had rendered his uniform a mixture of greys, except for the cockade on his Tam: a dull red splotch.

They met at the centre of the crossroads. The overturned cart was gone, and Ford realised that so were the thousands of spent cartridges. Nothing but grit crunched beneath the soles of his boots.

His eyes slid to David's waist. A khaki holster was clipped to his belt. Ford thought he could see the black grip of a pistol beneath the retaining strap. He'd been sure soldiers couldn't get a firearm off-base except for specific purposes such as the live-firing exercises that had just concluded. His pulse jolted in his chest and he felt a worm of fear uncoil in his belly.

'Well, then, David,' he said, steadying his voice. 'What was so urgent you dragged me all the way out here in the middle of the night?' He smiled, but the effort, and the cold wind, hurt his cheeks.

'Helen lied to you, Inspector.'

'How?'

In that moment, Ford realised he knew. Knew how Helen had lied, and knew the extent to which the Padleys' guilt was intertwined.

'She wrote the letter. Because I asked her to. It weren't her that delivered it. It were me. I wanted Rachel to change her ways,' he said. 'It's not natural, is it? It's not right. Not in nature. Not in th'army. Not in the Black Watch.'

He put his right hand on his hip, unsnapped the strap holding the pistol down.

Ford couldn't take his eyes off the firearm. 'David, leave the gun alone. You don't need to do this,' he said in as calm a voice as he could muster.

But the cold was making his jaw tremble and his words came out in a stammer. He sounded scared. He *was* scared.

'I argued wi' her,' David said, clutching then releasing the pistol grip in a spasming movement. 'I begged her. I said why couldn't she just go wi' a fella? Or nobody at all? Just get on with the job. It's why she joined up, weren't it?

'But she weren't having none of it. Said it were none of my fucking business. Her exact words. To me! Her own father. I'm a Provost Sergeant in the Black Watch, Ford. They look up to me. Or most of 'em do.' His voice took on a whining tone. 'She pushed me, tried to hit me. Well, I couldn't stand there and take that, could I? Not from a lass.'

'What did you do, David?' Ford asked. He saw a glimmer of hope. Could he keep David talking long enough to wear him down? Persuade him to leave the gunplay for the firing range?

'I pushed her. Hard. She fell and hit her head on the wall. I thought I'd killed her. There were a lot of blood.'

'Didn't you feel for a pulse? You must have known she was still alive.'

'Of course I bloody did! I couldn't find one, could I? I weren't thinking straight. Panicking, like.'

'Are you saying it wasn't Helen who dragged her out to the crossroads? Was it you?'

David shook his head. He took the pistol from its holster and pointed it at Ford. 'Don't think about running. I'm not done yet. That's not what I'm saying at all. It were Helen all right,' he said. 'I never meant to kill Rachel. I drove home and told Helen what 'ad happened. She told me I'd been a fool. Called me a bloody barmpot. Said summat about sending a man to do a woman's work. Then she asked for me knife and she went.

'She came back much later. She 'ad blood on her. Said she'd laid out Rachel like she'd killed herself and she 'ad a plan in case that didn't work. I was to do nothing. Say nothing.'

316

He was crying now, the tears glistening on his cheeks as he turned and the moonlight caught them. The pistol wavered, but its black muzzle still pointed at Ford.

'On your knees,' David said, his gun arm extended.

Ford stayed standing.

'Down!' David roared.

The muscles in Ford's legs twitched, as if preparing to obey despite his own determination not to. He stared into David's eyes, searching for a way to connect with him.

'David, please. You don't have to do this.'

'Yes, I do!' David shouted, waving the pistol. 'Don't you get it, man? Rachel were *alive* when I left her. You *told* me. I could have brought her home. I could've saved me little girl.'

'I thought you wanted her dead. Isn't that why you got her out here?'

'No, you fool! I didn't like her being gay, but I never wanted her dead for it. But Helen were different. When she found out, she went mad,' he said. 'She were up at that church every spare moment, praying with that idiot, Pastor Simeon. Said to me she wished Rachel'd be killed in a car accident rather than carry on living like that. I thought she might do summat stupid. Or get one of them at the church to do it for her. I thought if I could persuade Rachel to, I don't know, give it up for a bit, I could've got Helen to calm down. But now she's dead and I'll never see her again. Never hold her again. My baby's dead, Ford, and it's all my fault!'

Ford heard a voice inside his head, somewhere far off: Lou's voice. *Just like me.* And he understood what he could say, the only thing he could say that might work.

'It *wasn't* your fault, David. You didn't mean to kill her,' he said. 'I understand. You have to believe me. Sometimes, we think we're doing the right thing, and even if it goes wrong and we lose the one we were trying to save, it's still not our fault. You loved her.

You were trying to protect her. But this' – he extended his arm out wide – 'this won't help. It won't bring her back.'

'I know. That's why it all ends here. You've cost me everything, Ford. My position. My honour. The respect of my comrades. Every-bloody-thing. It should have been suicide and I could have gone out to Somalia with my lads. Now it's all gone to shit because you wouldn't stop bloody digging.'

Ford spread his hands. 'It's my job, David.'

'Good for you! But if I've lost everything, you're going to lose everything, too. Who knows, maybe I'll carve you a nice new guitar out of *fookin'* rosewood while we're kickin' our heels up there,' he said, jerking the pistol heavenwards before pointing it back at Ford. 'You first. Then me.'

'David, let's go back to the cars and I'll come home with you,' Ford said, trying to ignore the trembling in his muscles. 'Make you a nice cup of tea. Strong enough to stand a spoon up in, isn't that what you Yorkies like?' He pointed at the pistol. 'But there's no need for the gun, OK? Just put it back in its holster.'

'You're wrong, Ford. There's every need.'

He raised his right arm and pointed the gun directly at Ford's face. Ford felt a weird sensation of pressure between his eyes.

Ford heard running footsteps. Hannah appeared from behind the Baghdad Marriott, sprinting towards the crossroads. She was fifty feet away.

'Don't shoot!' she screamed.

Ford snatched a glance at her then looked back at David, whose eyes narrowed. Then the gun went off.

Ford felt the bullet slam into his chest. There was no pain at first, though the force of the impact knocked the wind out of him. He sank to his knees then keeled over sideways.

Like the incoming tide, the agony arrived in a rush of heat, spreading out through his chest from the region of his heart. He could barely breathe. His vision clouded.

Hannah crouched by his side and cradled his head in her arms, pulling him close.

'Oh, Henry, I'm sorry. You'll be OK,' she moaned.

Ford could barely hear her over the roaring in his ears. But he could see clearly enough. David Padley looked down at him then lifted his gun arm, pushed the barrel deep into his open mouth, and pulled the trigger.

The report in the empty village sounded huge. A loud, flat bang that snapped back off the white-painted walls of the houses, turning one shot into two. Hannah screamed and released Ford's head so it smacked against the tarmac.

David toppled backwards, blood fountaining from his skull and splashing the road: scarlet arcs and spatters across the grey tarmac.

Breathing easier now despite the pain, Ford pushed himself up on his elbows and levered himself into a seated position.

Hannah's eyes widened. 'No! Stay still. I'll call for an ambulance.'

He shook his head and heaved in another breath, wincing as he felt a sharp pain from his ribs on the left side.

'It's OK. Help me out of my coat,' he said. Frowning, Hannah did as he asked. 'Now the jumper.'

He grunted with the pain as she pulled the baggy sleeves up and dragged the heavy sweater off him.

Shivering, he unsnapped the plastic catches on the Kevlar vest he'd collected from the armoury at Bourne Hill and dropped it beside him.

Hannah was crying. 'I thought he'd killed you,' she whispered.

'No chance,' he said with a wry smile. 'I may be a maverick, but I'm not stupid. I knew Sandy would never authorise this so I had to go it alone, but I thought there was a good chance David had something planned: a final confession. He was unstable. I knew I needed to protect myself.'

'What if he'd shot you in the head?'

Ford grinned. 'I was ninety per cent confident he'd go for a body shot. And I was planning to run, anyway.'

She shook her head. 'No. Those were terrible odds. It was stupid. *You* were stupid,' she said. 'Henry, you could have *died*. Then who would have looked after Sam?'

'I made the wrong decision once before trying to protect him. I was trying to do the right thing this time.'

He inhaled sharply as a bolt of pain hit him. 'I think I've cracked a rib.'

'I hope you have!' she said. 'Now lie still. I need to call an ambulance and get some people out here.'

He reached out and laid a hand on her arm. 'Get our lot but forget about the paramedics,' he said. 'There's nothing they can do apart from give me painkillers and I've got plenty of them at home. By the way, how did you know I was out here?'

'Sam called me. He told me you'd shared your location with him on Find My Phone before he went on the climbing trip. He couldn't find you at home and he checked the app and it said you were out here. He was worried about you. I was, too, so I drove out here.'

Ford lay back on the cold tarmac and allowed Hannah to cover him with his coat. She made a pillow out of his jumper and wedged it under his head. He listened as in a few short, detail-filled sentences, she called it in and explained what had happened and who she needed.

There would be phone calls and visits to pay the next day. To Josifini, letting her know what had happened to her girlfriend.

To the colonel, informing him the investigation was closed. And to ACC Starkey, a call he would enjoy, even though he knew he'd made a dangerous enemy.

But they were for the new day. For now, he would lie silently and mourn the dead. Keeping his breathing shallow, he closed his eyes. In the distance, across the plain, he thought he could hear the cathedral bells chiming the hour.

◆ ◆ ◆

With the Paracodol fighting a losing battle against the pain in his chest, Ford sat opposite Sam at the kitchen table. It was 3.00 a.m.

'You saved my life tonight, mate,' he said.

Sam had done his best to fight down tears when Ford had explained what had happened out on the plain. But his eyes were still reddened. He rubbed them again.

'I was worried about you, Dad. I thought . . . I don't know what I thought. It's just . . .'

'You thought you were going to lose me, like you lost Mum?'

'Yeah,' Sam said with a small smile that reminded Ford of the little boy he'd once been.

Ford sighed. He realised he'd arrived at the moment he'd been dreading since Lou had died. The moment when he came clean to Sam. He had to risk shattering the fragile calm in which they'd existed ever since that sunny day on the Pembrokeshire coast.

Ford closed his eyes. His own memories of that time were burned into his brain by a caustic mixture of fear and love. Fear that he would die with Lou. And love, both for her and for Sam. He breathed in, wincing at the sharp stab from his ribcage.

'I need to tell you the truth about what happened to Mum.'

ACKNOWLEDGMENTS

I want to thank you for buying this book. I hope you enjoyed it. As an author is only one of the people who make a book the best it can be, this is my chance to thank the people on my team.

For being my first readers, Sarah Hunt and Jo Maslen.

For so generously sharing her story and experiences of Fijian life, culture and community, both in Fiji and in the UK, and especially attitudes to women and gay people, NoaPaulini Tuima-Kautoga.

For sharing their knowledge and experience of The Job, former and current police officers Andy Booth, Ross Coombs, Jen Gibbons, Neil Lancaster, Sean Memory, Trevor Morgan, Olly Royston, Chris Saunby, Ty Tapper, Sarah Warner and Sam Yeo.

For sharing their insights into autistic spectrum disorder, Amanda J. Harrington and Dr Hazel Harrison.

For her advice on strategies for detecting lies, Professor Dawn Archer, Research and Knowledge Exchange Coordinator for Languages, Information and Communications, Manchester Metropolitan University.

For lending Hannah's cat her name, Uta Frith, Emeritus Professor of Cognitive Development at UCL Institute of Cognitive Neuroscience.

For helping me stay reasonably close to medical reality as I devise gruesome ways of killing people, Martin Cook, Melissa Davies, Arvind Nagra and Katie Peace.

For their advice on climbing, Coel Hellier and Norrie Tate.

For their patience, professionalism and friendship, the fabulous publishing team at Thomas & Mercer: my old editor, Jack Butler; my new editor, Victoria Haslam; development editor Russel McLean; copyeditor Gill Harvey; and proofreader Jill Sawyer. Plus the wonderful marketing team including Davide Radice and Nicole Wagner.

And for being a daily inspiration and source of love and laughter, and making it all worthwhile, my family, Jo, Rory and Jacob.

The responsibility for any and all mistakes in this book remains mine. I assure you, they were unintentional.

Andy Maslen, Salisbury, 2021

ABOUT THE AUTHOR

Photo © 2021, Kin Ho

Andy Maslen was born in Nottingham, England. After leaving university with a degree in psychology, he worked in business for thirty years as a copywriter. In his spare time, he plays blues guitar. He lives in Wiltshire.